SHE REACHED OUT WITH HER MIND. . . .

This far past human-charted space there should have been nothing for Hanna to touch. She brushed against something and jerked away, chilled. It thought of the treasure in her ship's guts.

Telepathy could not tell her exactly where this unknown enemy was. She went to Rubee's room and pounded on his door. He answered at once.

Talking quickly, Hanna tried to explain the danger they faced.

"How long will it take a human spacecraft to find us if all you say is correct?" Rubee finally asked.

"Hours."

"Hours have gone by already."

"Then we had better think of evasion instead of escape," Hanna said.

They went quickly to the bridge and Rubee ordered the ship to begin a search pattern, stopping when the scanning display showed the arrowhead-shape of an atmosphere-efficient spacecraft.

At last Rubee spoke, confirming Hanna's fears. "They are moving with great speed. This vessel could not match the speed of theirs even at full power; not in a hunt. It was not made for chase or pursuit. There is no hope of escape. . . ."

TERRY A. ADAMS HAS ALSO WRITTEN

SENTIENCE

THE MASTER OF CHAOS

TERRY A. ADAMS

DAW BOOKS, INC.

DONALD A. WOLLHEIM, PUBLISHER

DAW Book Collectors No. 777.

First Printing, April, 1989

2 3 4 5 6 7 8 9

Printed in Canada
Cover Printed in U.S.A.

THIS BOOK IS FOR MAURINE K. KELLY

I.

Rubee of Ell of the world Uskos said to Hanna ril-Koroth of D'neera, "You are the possessor of a wonderful house. It is fair as the Wonderful House of Piore."

Rubee lied, with utmost courtesy. Hanna accepted the courtesy and disregarded the lie.

"It is your house as well," she answered with equal politeness, and lay back on a pale blue couch that glimmered cool pastel in the dusk, like everything in her house at twilight; wonderful to her, at least, as the Wonderful House of Piore could ever have been to him. Or to her? Or it? Uskosians all were called "he," because they had to be called something. But no human word was really right.

Rubee and his selfing Awnlee wandered about and touched things in the growing gloom. Their fingers at full extension resembled thin tentacles; flexed, they were like roots. An Uskosian had not truly seen a thing until he had touched it, and here on the world D'neera, where nothing that could be embellished was left plain, the lively fingers of Rubee and Awnlee were busy.

There was not much to touch in this house, however. Though it was the home of a D'neeran, the place was austere, the character of its rooms a matter of color and form. The sunward wall of Hanna's sitting room was transparent; the house was built into a hillside, so that this upper level looked down on a lawn and water garden (the pool frozen now), and past that a line of trees, and beyond that a distant fringe of light marking the edge of the city D'vornan. That was decoration enough for Hanna, and the view was fresh after her long absence.

Hanna had been gone from home for six Standard months. Since the Uskosian envoys' announcement of their presence in human space, she had spent all her time on the powerful Polity worlds, Earth mostly, studying Rubee and Awnlee—and often feeling more like a tour guide than a scholar. Neighbors had tended her home, made sure the servomechanism kept working, cleared away the debris of autumn storms. She thought, smiling, that when she came home for good, she would owe a great arrears of community service.

But that would not be for a long time. There was yet a longer journey to make first.

Rubee formulated a question. Hanna was a telepath, but she knew Rubee so well that she saw it coming with her eyes. The alien said, "You live in this house alone?"

"When I can. When I can live on my homeworld at all, I mean; when I am not on other worlds doing its business. I lived here alone for some months before you came. Before that I lived in City Koroth, in the House of its governing women, which we visited yesterday. I lived there with many others. I came here to D'vornan to teach at the University, which we visit tomorrow. I like it better here."

"But I thought," Rubee said, "D'neera is a—" (*something,* said the translator tucked into Hanna's ear) "—society, because it is a society of telepaths."

"Think that again," Hanna said wearily, and dipped into Rubee's thought, unclipped the memory bank at her waist, and gave the translator a new word.

Communal.

She said, "On the whole D'neerans live communally. I am an exception. Exceptions are freely tolerated."

"Ah," said Rubee, understanding, or thinking that he understood, and Hanna watched Rubee and Awnlee and wondered how long it would be before she saw her home again.

She was so glad to be there that for all her liking for these strange guests, and in spite of the importance of her work with them, she dreaded going away with them again. She was only at home because the envoys were making courtesy visits everywhere, and Hanna's own planet was a stop on the itinerary the Polity's officials had made up for them. The portion of her duty that would start in a few months more—to accompany the envoys when they returned to Uskos—meant it would be at least two Standard years before she saw her home again.

The six months she had been gone were already too long. *No one else can befriend and guide these beings as well as you can,* Polity Alien Relations and Contact had said to her when the Uskosians arrived; *no one has your experience, there is no one like you.* The director of Contact had given her other reasons for accepting the task, not including personal ones. If he had included personal reasons she would have listened, even though that was another story, an old love story, a finished one; for Hanna it was not as finished as it ought to be, and perhaps memories had helped make her decision. Yet in the end it was no one's good reasons, no flattery, no sense of duty that had captured her. It was curiosity. She was heir to the governing House of Province Koroth and would one day be its Magistrate, but first she was an exopsychologist. She knew the aliens of F'thal and Girritt, she had walked among the Primitives, and she was humankind's authority on the People of Zeig-Daru, but she could not resist a new thing.

Awnlee was too young to be anything but honest. He said, "This home cannot really be like the Wonderful House of Piore."

Rubee turned and looked at his selfing. The Uskosian face was rigid except for the ciliated mouth, the eyespots were shifting patches of gray sparked with iridescence, and the gaze was a new experience for humans. Body language said everything the face did not, and Hanna saw (from the position of the whiplike fingers, the carriage of the lumpy body, even the angle of the stubby feet) that Awnlee meant to return to the plane of realistic assessment.

Rubee conceded, "It is not. But it has its own beauty."

"It belongs to you as well as me," Hanna said correctly. Then—because she was working, because she was always working—she said, "What was the Wonderful House of Piore?"

"Do you wish a formal presentation?" Rubee asked.

"Informal," Hanna said promptly, because she was less interested in ritual presentation of the elaborate myths of Uskos—though that was an important art form—than in their function in everyday life.

"In a year," Rubee said, and his unmelodic voice was richer, deeper, "Piore sought to build a house. 'I will shelter me from the elements,' Piore said, and he builded a house of importance, and admired it, and widely admired it was. The earth quaked, and it foundered. Piore stood in the ruins lamenting, and the Master of Chaos came to him and signified amusement. 'Why do you signify amusement?' said Piore, and the Master of Chaos answered, 'High was your house and imposing; yet the foundation was not strong.'

"And Piore said, 'I will build me a house of great strength,' and he did. Yes, strong it was, well-founded and impenetrable, so that all his selfings came there saying, 'Now we shall be safe.' And safe they were and earthquake did not move it. Yet it was forbidding, and save for Piore's selfings no one came to it, and Piore was lonely; and the Master of Chaos came to him and signified amusement. And Piore said, 'Why do you signify amusement?' 'I signify amusement,' said the Master of Chaos, 'because you have forgotten the Tale of Taree.' "

(The— *Oh, God,* Hanna thought. *Myths within myths within myths!*)

"Then Piore remembered the Tale of Taree, and he pulled down the house and rebuilded it, and now it was both strong and fair; but Piore was jealous of it, and let no one in, and sent away his selfings. But Authority came and said, 'It is not permitted to make such a thing just here,' and tore it down. Piore stood in the ruins lamenting, and the Master of Chaos came and signified amusement. Piore said, 'Why do you signify amusement?' 'I signify amusement,' said the Master of Chaos, 'because you can't win.' 'I know that,' said Piore, 'as who does not?'

"The Master of Chaos disappeared, and Piore builded again. He chose a place by a beautiful river, but consulted Authority first. He made a fine foundation and the beauty of his home was remarkable, and it endured through quake and windstorm, and all came there and were happy.

"Yet finally Piore died; and the Master of Chaos came, and signified amusement. So it is until this minute!"

Rubee made a quick motion of the feet that meant he was finished. Hanna mentally assigned the tale to the category she had begun to think of as "the dark stories" and did not ask for interpretation. She was not in a mood to hear how Chaos always got the last word. She only said politely, "Thank you for your fine telling."

"It is now ours," Rubee said graciously.

"Yes. Well." Hanna pulled herself to her feet. "Now there are friends I promised to call. Later we will feed, and later sleep. We have a busy morrow."

"I wish," Awnlee said wistfully, "we had not to address your colleagues. I am weary of speeches."

"Me too . . ." Hanna reached for a light and was shocked when her fingers did not at once remember where the control was. Then they did, and the room was bright. For a second the outer wall reflected all of them, before the house damped the image to transparency: the aliens with their changing hands, bundled against the cool air, so like in appearance that one might have been a reflection of the other, except that age had altered one; and the slight human being, dark and blue-eyed, looking about as if she were the stranger here.

"I would like to see the waterfall you love so much, and the sea you love to walk beside. And your sib-selfings, no, your 'family,'" Awnlee said with increasing enthusiasm. "And, oh, the beasts on whose backs you learned to ride nearby, which are beautiful through your eyes. Must we have speeches?"

Hanna was very fond of Awnlee. She looked at him

with affection and said, "My dear friend, I'm afraid we must. The university program here is me, or I am it, at least sometimes I think so. Anyway it's here and important because of me. They would never forgive me if we didn't go."

"But I will show you all of my world when we go there !"

"Well, I will show you as much of this one as I can. But I think it cannot be as beautiful to you as your own."

"Perhaps," Rubee said. "But remember the Journey of Nlatee," he added, and looked at her sharply.

Hanna knew that one, and signified amusement properly.

The order had all the frills and flourishes at the beginning that the administrators of the Interworld Polity could wish. Underneath the frills there was a line specifying that the order had been issued by the Director of the Department of Alien Relations and Contact. The document looked official, but it was only a draft. It said: "The following personnel will report on the schedule shown to Level 14, Conference Room A." That was innocuous; it gave nothing away. The schedule that followed was a long one. It stretched over three weeks, and assigned dates and times for one hundred and fifty names.

Commissioner Edward Vickery scrolled through the list. His mouth was screwed up with distaste. He said, "You can't do this, Starr."

"Why not?" said the Contact director, who had written the order.

"Probes of this many people? With no legitimate reason? They've all got clearance for the Uskosian project, they've all been investigated—you have to have evidence to justify a probe, Starr. *Each* probe, on an individual basis. And what have you got for justification?—one unconfirmed rumor. No. I don't know why you even brought me this."

The Contact director said, "Your authority might

carry sufficient weight. And think of the consequences if the rumor, as you call it, is true.''

"It isn't. It can't be.''

"What if it is?''

Vickery looked up from the moving script, exasperated. He preferred to be tactful with Starr Jameson, but it was not easy. Vickery was Heartworld's representative to the Coordinating Commission of the Interworld Polity. Seven years ago the man on the other side of his desk had held that high positon, and left it, if not quite in disgrace, at least under duress, to accept the directorship of the then-new Contact department. The Commissioner from Heartworld also was chairman of the Commission's Committee on Alien Relations, so Vickery had inherited that from Jameson, too, and with it hegemony over Contact and Jameson himself. Jameson had never said to Vickery: *I ought to be still in your place.* But maybe he thought it.

Vickery said, ''When I say you can't do this, I mean literally that you can't get away with it. Mass probes are a rights violation on the face of it, not to mention a gross breach of protocol. There would be an appeal to the Commission and you wouldn't have a hope. Don't try it.''

Jameson did not answer at once. He was a master of the uses of silence; Vickery knew that, and resolved not to speak first. The list of times and names finished its passage and went dark. It was summer in southeastern Namerica on Earth, and the morning sun shone placidly on the river that ran by Vickery's office; this room also had once been Jameson's. The water came to the very edge of the room, its whisper the only sound.

Jameson said finally, ''There is something you should see. Tap into my office files.''

"I don't have much time, Starr.''

"It isn't long.'' Jameson began to recite a string of codes. *Humor him*, Vickery thought, and entered the sequence in his desktop. ''Holo,'' Jameson added. Vickery made an adjustment and there were flickers of darkness in the center of the room: moving shadows of roughly human shape. Jameson swiveled to watch them.

Vickery said, "What's wrong? I can't make it out."

"The figure on the left is an Intelligence and Security undercover operative on Valentine. The one on the right is an informant. The visual and vocal patterns have been scrambled to protect their identities. Listen."

"—satisfactory?" the shadow on the left said. The voice was metallic.

"All right. I guess. Not exactly getting rich."

"Come up with something good."

"That was good, wasn't it? The . . . connection?"

Vickery said, "What?"

"A name," Jameson said. "Censored."

The agent said, "We had it from another source. Give me something new."

"All right, here's something, you'll like this. Somebody knows where the bird will fly."

The agent said after a minute, "Well?"

"Well, what?"

"What's that mean?"

"The *Bird. Far-Flying Bird*, the aliens' ship. Somebody's interested in how it gets home. It's carrying value, isn't it? I think: hijack."

"You're spaced."

"All I know is what I hear."

"You must've heard wrong. Can't intercept a ship in Inspace flight, not even in the realspace interludes. Too many variables. Ship's computers can't predict on the mark where a Jump brings it out. Much less an outsider. Takes time to home in, gives a target time to get away."

"What I hear. Anyway it's been done. Man right here on Valentine did it."

"That was different," said the agent. "That was a trick. Nobody's going to fall for that again."

"So you won't pay me?"

"No bonus. Not for that. Get me more."

Jameson's deep voice cut into the conversation. "The rest is just haggling. Turn it off."

Vickery touched a switch and the figures were gone. Jameson said, "Suppose it is true. Suppose the Uskosian vessel's course program for the return flight has been, or can be, tapped in detail, so that interception is possible. Would you care to explain to the Uskosians how their envoys died on the way home?''

Vickery said, ''What if somebody just wants to get to Uskos before a diplomatic party does? One of the non-Polity worlds. An alien alliance is the kind of thing they'd think of on Nestor.''

Jameson said, ''The risk is negligible. Uskos is a sophisticated society. The difficulties for Nestor would be insurmountable, with or without the presence of the envoys and Hanna ril-Koroth. I am concerned with the cargo, the gift, the treasure the *Bird* will carry. It is enormously valuable. The rumor that has come to the attention of I&S came from criminal circles. I think the issue is the material value of the *Bird's* cargo. I&S even has a likely name—the name of the man the informant referred to. Do you want to know what it is?''

A red light began to blink on Vickery's desk. He was overdue for an appointment. ''Later, Starr.''

''Do you remember the piracy of the *Pavonis Queen* twenty Standard years ago?''

Vickery shook his head impatiently. Jameson said, ''It carried a fortune in negotiable currencies of all sorts under the terms of the Colonial Credit Standardization Agreement of ST 2822. Its course was known, or was supposed to have been known, only to a few of the highest-ranking officials of the Polity. Nonetheless the *Queen* was intercepted, and all the monies stolen. The perpetrators were never formally identified. The man believed to be responsible was never charged. I&S has mentioned him in connection with the supposed accessibility of the *Bird's* course.''

''I have to go.''

''His name is Michael Kristofik. He lives on Valentine, and he has been a very rich man since the *Pavonis Queen* incident. The *Bird's* cargo would appeal to him.''

''Is I&S in favor of this mass probe?''

''Of course.''

''They would be. But I tell you anyway—you can't do it. Think of something else. Alter the program.''

''The Uskosians will not alter it.''

''Have you asked them?''

"I have not. But I have read all Hanna's reports. I do not think they will alter it."

"Ask them!"

"Naturally," Jameson said. He got up without warning and went to the door. When he got to it he turned around and said, "All the same, they won't."

Vickery supposed Jameson was right. Usually, infuriatingly, he was.

Coming down through the great sky the planet looked like any other world where humans could breathe the air. It might have been Valentine, it might have been Earth—but Michael Kristofik, looking out the nose of the sporting yacht *Golden Girl*, automatically corrected the thought. He didn't go to Earth any more. He could never go there again.

The name of this world was Carrollis, and it was not safe for offworlders. That was not because of natural hazards, but because of the colonists. The name of the planet's only town was Town. Carrollis produced furs, brilliant blue, poisonous green, flaming gold; the fauna were colorful there. The skins of hard-hunted amphibians, splotched with color, dazzling, decorated the richest women in human space.

There was no government. Governments meant taxes, and the colonists did not tolerate taxes.

If you went to Town on the night of Market Day you went armed, and everybody went; tonight Michael Kristofik did, too. He did not worry about danger. He was tall and broad-shouldered and visibly armed, and he was not alone. He went through Town asking questions with two people at his back. The fair young man with the uncertain face might not be much protection, but the woman was something else. Like Michael she carried a stunner, but her hand kept going to the butt and she caressed it sensuously. There was a glitter in her eyes that made men look away.

Michael was looking for a man called Prissy. He wasn't hard to find.

Prissy ran the only sensory all-around in Town. On Market Day the shows were continuous and Prissy packed them in, the hunters and the trappers and the offworld buyers, so the whole-sense bubble a man occupied might overlap his neighbor's and the edges of the scene and the sound were blurred, the smells and the tastes and the pressures on the skin got mixed up. The shows in the morning were not so bad, sex and skin in tired old patterns, old as video. They got rougher as the day went on. By nightfall on Market Day every trader and trapper in Town was spaced and flying, there were no more restraints, and some of them liked to watch recorded death.

Prissy took hard money or barter for payment, either way. He kept the skins locked away in the most sophisticated vault Polity technology could provide. He liked to count the cash, though, especially on Market Day, when it poured in. He counted it in a locked room behind the all-around, where a window that from the other side looked like a wall let him monitor the sensory generators running the show.

On the night of this Market Day he counted his money while the show went on. He did not look at the video monitor, but he heard the sounds: screeches and moans and sometimes a shout, rattles, screams. It was a new show. Not all the performers in it had survived it, neither the women nor the men, and they had died in peculiar ways. While the taped agonies played out, Prissy counted his money and a girl sat at his side and watched. She was a child on the edge of adolescence, very fair and pretty. Her face was bruised and she was sulking. Her name was Lise.

Something hit the door from outside and then it fell in without much noise, not enough for the crowd behind the other wall to notice. Prissy had a disruptor in his hand before it finished falling, but there were three of them running in, two men and a women, and he didn't decide fast enough who to aim for first. He fell over his money, stunned. The girl was out a second later.

They laid Prissy out like a dead man. The fair man unstrapped a case from his waist and took out instruments. He began to feed a yellow liquid through a tube into Prissy's right arm. The woman glanced at a monitor, where numbers were superimposed on the action. She looked at the convulsed bodies without expression and focused on the numbers. "Twenty minutes," she said, and set herself to face the broken doorway, stunner at full power. Dark hair licked with bronze, taut body cased in black: her face might have been carved in stone.

Michael Kristofik looked down at the pair on the floor and waited. He also wore black. Theo the medic had known him six years, but looked up now and was struck as if by a stranger's face, the tension and the concentration. Theo thought: *Portrait of a Man Waiting*.

Theo said, "He ought to be ready, Mike," and backed away in a crouch. Michael knelt and took hold of Prissy's flabby chin and turned it. The woman moved a little, still watching the door, to shield Michael's back.

The eyes of the unconscious man opened, focused on nothing. Michael said, "Prissy. That's what they call you, isn't it? Prissy?"

"Yeah . . ." Barely a word.

"You had a meeting," Michael said, "two weeks ago, here, with a man who called himself Chrome. Remember?"

"Remember," Prissy said obligingly, slurring it.

"Where was he going from here?"

"Val'ntime."

"Valentine?"

"What I said."

"Christ . . ."

The woman with the stunner made a hissing sound. Michael looked up and met Theo's eyes. He made a wry face. "Might as well have stayed home," he said.

"Shit."

"Prissy. This Chrome. What's he calling himself on Valentine?"

"Maz'well."

"Mazwell?"

"Max. Well."

"What Maxwell? Where?"

"Shor'ground."

"Shoreground. Maxwell of Shoreground. They're

having a festival in Shoreground. It's packed. How long was he going to be there?''

Prissy heaved. It was a whole-body shrug.

''You have any way to get in touch with him?''

''Gran' Square Inn. Just ask. Maxwell.''

''What about after that? What if he's left the inn?''

''Won't. Be there awhile.''

''How long is awhile?''

''Just said awhile.''

Theo said, ''We have to get back to Valentine.''

''Yeah. Now. Six days home, Christ! Our timing's bad. He's up to something and on the move. If we lose him now, we start all over. All right. Knock him out.''

They grouped at the door a little later. The sounds still went on from the all-around. The screams were steady now, and terrible, and the crowd roared.

''Mike . . .'' The woman touched his sleeve. She pointed at the girl whose bruised face in sleep was that of an angelic child. The woman said, ''You hear in there? Around here today, I heard this Prissy'll do a new show, the fatal kind, like that. She's in it. Doesn't know it. Kill her slow, she doesn't know.''

Michael's arm twitched. His face, alive and expressive the moment before, went dead. He said, ''Where'd he get her?''

''Don't know. Some mother some father some poor sick colony place sold her. Thought, better life for her, maybe. Innocent, maybe. Maybe not so innocent. Maybe they knew.''

Michael went to the girl and picked her up. He slung her over his shoulder without difficulty. He touched one thin arm; there was an old scar on the back of it. He said, ''Come on, Theo. He's yours, Shen. I don't care what you do.''

Theo said in a strangled voice, ''What's wrong with you?''

''Look,'' Michael Kristofik said. He jerked his head at the monitor but did not look at it himself. Theo did. He turned away quickly; a second later, as if squeezed by a violent hand, he vomited.

''Somebody else just pick up what he leaves,'' Shen said.

''I know. I hate this place.''

Theo whispered, ''He wouldn't have remembered a thing.''

''I know.''

Michael and Theo slipped out. Shen followed a minute later, flexing her fingers. She said, ''Anyway this Prissy might have warned *him*. Nobody's looking at us. Gotta keep it that way.''

They melted into the night, the girl still unconscious and so light she was little burden.

* * *

Now they were on Willow. The five worlds of the Interworld Polity had among them most of humanity's people and nearly all its wealth. Willow was the only one Hanna found tolerable.

Earth, oldest and first, was too crowded. Flying above its knots of light at night she longed for darkness, caught in the cities' ceaseless noise she wanted silence, met at every turn by servos she was conscious as nowhere else of the power in her own slim strong body, the talents of her hands. The planet also was too ancient, groaning with the weight of its past. Hanna was a child of the colonies, none of whose histories went back more than seven hundred years. (Yet she thought of seven hundred years because that was how long it was in Standard years, and Standard was synonymous with Earthly.) Earth furthermore was the seat of Polity Administration, and Hanna's whole experience of humankind's first home was colored by her work for and with and sometimes against that triumph of committees and bureaucracy. Earth was where she had learned to navigate the currents of power, more dangerous and deceptive than the tides between the stars.

On Co-op the air changed erratically and sometimes was hard to breathe. Some years the wind scraped the best lands clean of growth. Coopers taught their children early how to shoot; they had good reasons; a boy

of eight had once saved Hanna's life there, shooting by
reflex before she turned and saw the toothed shape behind her. Coopers did not like D'neerans. Their ancestors had not wanted to go to Co-op in the first place.
The Founders of D'neera also had been outcast from
Earth, but more justly, Coopers thought. It is one thing
to engineer a populace to telepathy, another to live with
the results. Why had true-humans gotten Co-op, and
the telepaths lush D'neera? It was not fair. It ought to
have been the other way around.

Hanna didn't like Coopers any better than they liked her.

Toward Colony One she was indifferent. It sought to
be another Earth and disregarded what Earth should
have taught it. There were towns without beauty, one
much like another, forests falling, air dark with grit,
machines carving the land, a maddening buzz of change.
Colony One, Hanna thought, lacked character.

Heartworld had character, but she did not like what
it had. That was Starr Jameson's home, and while she
lived with him—though she had lived with him only on
Earth—she had learned all she needed to know about
Heartworld's character.

*(I could not take you home with me. Not permanently.
As a visitor, of course—"*

*"As mistress you mean, then. Never the partner of
your life."*

*"Impossible for many reasons. We should not even
talk of this."*

*"I know there are other reasons. But this is the only
one to cause me bitterness. I am not good enough for
the aristocracy. That is what you mean."*

*"You are good enough for anyone. But appear-
ances."*

"Are more important than the love I bear for you."

*"Yes. You cannot reproach me with dishonesty, at
least. Yes.")*

So when she went to Heartworld (because she had to
go; as unofficial ambassador to true-humans she went
everywhere), she stayed in the cities and never saw the
lands where a family estate might take up an appreciable
part of a continent, and Starrbright not the least; never

saw the silent wilderness or the harvests that fed much of the human race. And he was right, of course. H'ana ril-Koroth of D'neera was an important person everywhere—except on Heartworld. They made her feel it, too, and they did not even mean to.

Willow, though: all its meanings to Hanna were good. She was in love with the sky-capped trees that gave the world its name. They did not grow in a wide range, so that many citizens of Willow had never seen them close up, but they grew where the first settlers had proclaimed a capital city. The sinuous branches came to the ground in cascades of delicate green, and to stand within the hollow space they made when the sun shone was to feel that you rested inside the peace of a single leaf, so sweet a green was the light.

Unlike Heartworld or Earth or Colony One or Co-op, Willow had a single government and one capital, the city of Ducelle. It was named after one of the explorers who had come upon this jewel in the night of space, and its buildings were fair and commodious. Many were built of a pink-tinged stone quarried nearby, and the rosy facades were impudent against the willows' green.

Hanna had spent some weeks in one of them, before she was famous. She remembered Ducelle's good wines and its strong young men with pleasure. When she went to Willow she did not feel thirty-one and official. On Willow, sometimes, she could forget what she had gone through to get that way.

Now that Hanna was famous, when she came to Willow she lived comfortably in private homes. She and Rubee and Awnlee were lodged in the home of Willow's Commissioner, bright-eyed Andrella Murphy.

On the party's last night in Ducelle, which was not supposed to be its last night, Hanna and Rubee and Awnlee dined in Murphy's home. There were no visitors, Murphy's husband had gone out, the meal was informal, and Rubee and Awnlee were relaxed. They had taken many meals among humans now, but they had not learned to like being stared at while they ate. Hanna was too used to the pair and their foods and their habits to stare, and Murphy was too polite. The four shared the evening companionably, Awnlee doing most of the talking and bubbling about the willows, which were so famous that many persons had forgotten they were named after an Earthly tree instead of the other way around. The wines of the region were as good as Hanna remembered. She became a little light-headed. She wished to learn to speak and understand the major language of Uskos without a translator and so she had switched it off; but she was not yet proficient in the tongue, and resorted automatically to telepathic receptivity, so that Awnlee's excitement, imperfectly understood, entered her blood with the wine and aroused her.

She stopped listening to Awnlee and drifted with the lavender evening and the blushing stone, thinking of Uskos. Hers would be the first human eyes to see it, as they had been the first to see Zeig-Daru. This time the privilege would cost much less. Rubee's folk were not like the People of Zeig-Daru. Probably nothing was, anywhere. The People were almost a good enough reason to give up space. But this time there would be no horror to face. "I promise you," Starr Jameson had said when he first told her of the envoys, "that this time there is no threat, no hostility; you will be guarded and protected until you are satisfied; if you find the slightest cause to fear them, you can stop at once. No pain this time. No torture or danger or fear."

Only excitement. Only the work she loved best. And the long voyage, longer than any human had yet taken, to a civilization that next to those of Zeig-Daru and F'thal seemed blessedly comprehensible.

Into Hanna's reflections, and the gentle lights that twinkled in her head and kissed every part of the room, there came from somewhere in the business part of Murphy's home an aide. He bent low and spoke in Murphy's ear. She excused herself and left with a look of surprise. Awnlee rambled on: "—and the horses possessed by D'neera, but they came from Earth, you said. But we saw none there. You ride as one with them, but I fell off. Did it take you long to own that skill—?" He did not wait for an answer, but went on. He liked humans' wine, if not their food; his ready speech was stimulated.

Murphy returned. She sat down and said to Hanna, "I have just talked with Starr. I have news for you."

Everything seemed agreeable to Hanna. She anticipated no anxiety. "What news?" she said.

"Your visit is to be curtailed. You are to return to Earth, all of you."

"Why?"

"I don't know. He wouldn't say. He said he will speak of it when he sees you."

"Should I call him?"

"No, no, it won't do any good. He means: when he sees you. Not before."

"Is something wrong?"

After rather a long pause Murphy said, "Perhaps."

Hanna looked at her silently in the candlelight. It was clear that Murphy had some knowledge connected with this matter, yet had not expected the call. She felt Murphy waiting suspiciously, waiting for Hanna to search out the current of thought withheld. Ordinary humans, true-humans, nontelepathic, thought such currents were crystal to D'neerans, and easily accessible. In the usual way of things, though, they were murky as the mudpits of Nestor. It took effort to bring them to light.

Hanna let it go. *How like Starr to summon us so; a trip of days through space without explanation, and worry at the end.*

She smiled at Murphy, poise unflawed. And changed the subject.

Rubee and Awnlee had understood the words they heard, but the nuances of human communication were beyond the translator. They could not hear what happened between the words. Hanna talked of something else, and that was enough for them. The night passed quietly to its end. Next day they were traveling again.

* * *

Her mouth was soft and delicious. Oh, blessed desire. He did not wake all at once. Body first: *yes yes yes.*

Skin painfully smooth, hair drifting on his hot cheeks like cool tangled cloud. Mind was slower. There was no one here to do this, no one who should be doing this. Trapped between alarm and lust he called for light. Lise smiled down at him. The smile faded when she saw his face.

"There she is . . ." Shen stood in the doorway. She leaned against it with folded arms. "Interrupting?"

"No. Not. Take her," he said with regret, "out of here."

His bed was on a platform, not very high. The wall at his head was cut away to show the stars. He turned and they spun; he buried his head in thick cushions.

"C'mon," Shen said from close by. "He doesn't want you that way."

Michael muttered, "Don't bet on it."

A hand slipped under the single cover and trailed down his back. His skin quivered and the fine hairs stood up. Lise said to Shen, an edge in her soft voice, "Are you his woman?"

"I'm nobody's woman. Come on. Mike? Some help."

He came out of the cushions long enough to say, "Go with her, Lise. That's not what I brought you along for."

"You like boys?" she said dubiously.

"Not especially. Tomorrow I'll try to explain. Again. Go on, now."

She let Shen take her away. When they were gone Michael got a time readout. Still early, Shen's watch, but he wanted no more sleep. He got up and discovered that the burst of longing so painfully ended had left him feeling physically sick. Self-congratulation on morality was no consolation. He had gotten little Lise mixed up with the women who came to him in dreams, perfect, elusive. While he dressed the room sang to him sorrowfully.

Dear, when I from thee am gone
Gone are all my joys at once.
I loved thee, and thee alone;
In whole love I joyed once . . .

The sweet harmonies belonged to an age a millennium gone. A lute kept them company. Michael sang along with the voices, fluent in the archaic language. His voice was an excellent baritone, not untrained but unself-conscious. He stopped singing when Shen came back.

"Put her to bed," Shen said. "Maybe stay there this time. Thought you told her yesterday."

"I did. And the day before that and the day before that. I thought she understood."

"Doesn't understand much. Thought about what she'll do?"

"Not much. I don't have any idea what to do with her, to tell you the truth."

Shen waved at the bed. "All she knows. Since eight, nine, maybe sooner."

"Don't tell me about it. I'll get sick. How old do you think she is now?"

"Eleven Standard, maybe? Tried talking to her. School, home, like that. Blank. Like I said—all she knows."

"So we keep her a few years and when she's old enough she can be a Registered Friend. If that's what she wants. We couldn't leave her there."

Shen did not answer. Perhaps she was thinking they might very well have left her there. Michael said finally, "All right. What?"

Shen said, "Bad time, Mike. No room for a kid."

"Wasn't room for you, Shen Lo-Yang."

The green eyes snapped. "Not fair."

"You talk fair to me? Never mind fair. Listen, when we get home I'll talk to Flora. She'll come up with something."

"She want a baby girl? Dump her back in your lap. Be gone a long time, Mike. If we catch up this time."

It was a long speech for Shen. When Michael did not answer she added, "Long time maybe before a start. 'Maxwell of Shoreground.' Say he's not at the inn. Then?"

"Find a lead and keep moving."

"He started 'bout when we did. Moving. Running?"

"No. Not away from something, anyway, certainly not from us. He doesn't even know we're after him. Look at the pattern of his contacts. On Nestor he bought a corvette. With its teeth pulled; but there was the arms operation at home, the one I thought shut down a year ago. He made that buy. Look at what he bought. Heavy stuff. He's arming that 'vette for big game. Then Carrollis—that Prissy brokered more than blood. He's moving in on something."

She sat down on the edge of his bed and said unhappily, "New. Don't like new."

"Not so new. He's had armed craft before. And used the arms," Michael said, and there was another wrench in his stomach.

"Not here." Her eyes slanted up and she waited for the effect.

But the answer was calm. "Not here. Nobody knows him here—at least, the Polity doesn't, not Fleet, not I&S. He can go anywhere. Nobody looks twice. He wants to keep it that way. Why guns? What's he going after? So maybe he's getting ready to head out."

"Better catch up quick."

"Right."

" 'Cause if he goes we lose him. Couple years at least."

"Yeah."

"Got this kid."

"I know. It's a day yet to Valentine. We'll think of something."

"Strays," Shen said on her way out.

"What?"

"You got another stray."

Michael smiled. When Shen was gone he stopped smiling, not because of anything she had said but because the aftermath of desire had left him hollow. *The trouble with a dream*. He sat down and thought about it carefully. The trouble with a dream was that it had everything you wanted, promise and fulfillment at the same time. When you were awake there was the promise, or you thought it was there; then fulfillment was elusive. Not the women's fault. They thought you promised something, too. *Do you know what you want? What is the promise you think you hear?*

* * *

The *Far-Flying Bird* orbited Luna. Hanna had been aboard her many times, but she never approached the *Bird* without feeling the pleasure first sight had given her.

An Interworld Fleet harbor jockey took her from Earth to the *Bird*, so she had nothing to do but watch the glorious silver sight come closer. The *Bird* was long and slender and carried what appeared to be folded-back wings like those of a diving water bird. The "wings" harbored the *Bird's* mechanical and Inspace-analog systems, and they had an arrogant curve to them, a daring arch that challenged space. They were in no sense functional wings. The *Bird* had never entered atmosphere, and her designers might have housed her guts in a thousand different ways. But the Uskosians, so far as Hanna had been able to ascertain, made nothing without making it beautiful; not consciously or deliberately, but carelessly, easily, without thinking much about it.

Presently the shuttle she rode docked at the junction of wing and body. When she stepped off the shuttle, she walked into a world where it was a little hot and she weighed just a little more than on worlds the human race had claimed. The walls were curved and colored so that the self-contained environment of the *Bird* offered an infinite selection of vistas. That was intentional. Rubee and Awnlee had been in space for three Standard years.

Starr Jameson waited for her by appointment in a room designed (she had been told) to lift the spirits. It was an eruption of color and had many odd angles she liked. She heard voices far away, filtering through the air with a distant sound, as if they came from another star.

They were human voices piped through the *Far-Flying Bird's* internal communications system.

"What is that?" she said. "What are they saying?"

"It's a check of the navigational computer seals," Jameson said.

She frowned at him. "Why?"

"It's a long story," he said.

She tried to pick out a comfortable-looking seat, but none looked better than another. The *Bird* was supposed to get some human-contoured furnishings before it departed with Hanna on board. She gave up and fitted herself as well as she could into a boxlike affair that had bumps in the wrong places. Jameson was standing. Hanna said, "Does Rubee know about this?"

"Not yet . . ." He looked around and chose a seat for himself, easing into it gingerly. The apprehension that had grown on Hanna all the way from Willow bit at her.

"Something has gone wrong," she said, and it was not a question but the words for what she felt in him.

"Maybe."

"What is it?" But he did not answer at once, and she said, "We came very quickly, and disrupted the official schedule dreadfully. Rubee and Awnlee don't like to do anything quickly—at least, Rubee doesn't. While we were coming here, they learned from my thought that I was worried. They're puzzled and unhappy and I couldn't explain. Because I didn't even know what I have to worry about."

"You will be able to explain when we have finished talking. I think you will like it even less than they will."

He told her in a few words what he had told Edward Vickery. She listened in bewilderment to the strange story: an informant, some suspicions, a name. "It is clear," Jameson said at the end of his recital, "that if the *Bird's* course program has been or will be pirated, someone within the project, someone who has been bribed, must be responsible. I tried to obtain authorization for probing all project personnel; of course I could not get it, but I thought that if I followed that with a request for probes of half a dozen key persons, the lesser demand might be met. It was not. There are political complications . . . So we must think of another way to protect the *Bird*. Changing the program is a logical solution. Rubee and Awnlee are highly skilled in trailblazing, in navigating unknown space. You are trained in the equivalent human techniques. It seems to me that the three of you could develop an alternate if less direct course. I want you to explain the situation to Rubee and Awnlee, and persuade them to do this.''

Hanna looked at him in silence. What he said meant—and he knew it—the difference between a journey of weeks and one of years. Each Jump of an interstellar voyage required days of calculation, sometimes weeks—if it were the first-ever leap between one point and another. Charting a new course was a different matter from following, in reverse, an established path. And Rubee was determined to come home on a date already fixed in his mind.

''They will not change it,'' Hanna said.

''Oh, but they must,'' he said.

''They know the difficulties of making contact in deep space, when one vessel does not want to make it, as well as you and I do. It's a hard thing to take seriously.''

''I have a feeling about it,'' Jameson said, and Hanna blinked. She had never heard him say anything of the kind before.

''That's my specialty,'' she said. ''Premonitions, hunches—what's got into you?''

He took the question literally. ''I don't know,'' he said.

''Well—start from the beginning. What's the beginning?''

He leaned back in the awkward chair cautiously, folding his hands and looking past Hanna as if he picked a pattern from obscure details and saw it clearly regardless of where his eyes rested. The ability was part of his genius. He also was exceedingly clever in the manipulation of human beings, and his will was potent. He did not respond to the anti-senescence procedures in universal use, and age had come upon him prematurely. The dark hair had grayed since Hanna's firs⁺

meeting with him, and a network of lines encroached on the hooded gray-green eyes; but they emphasized the strength locked in the bones of his face. The big body was strong and desirable as ever, the presence as self-contained. Even now a well-remembered movement could take Hanna by surprise, so that she would look at the powerful hands, their touch once intimately familiar, and feel her knees weaken. She had seen him so often as he was now that her heart tore a little though five years had passed since the day he told her they were not suitable for one another.

She gave no sign of the movement in her chest. She had learned from him how to conceal what she felt. She had learned a great deal from him.

"An Intelligence and Security undercover agent on Valentine was the beginning," he said. "This man or woman—I don't know which, I don't have a name, I don't want one—has an informant— You've been to Valentine. How much do you know about it?"

"What everybody knows. You can get anything you want there. About all you can't do is kill somebody, because that discourages the vacationers."

"True, as far as it goes. But the salient point is that Valentine is concerned only with wealth. If you wish to transfer cash or credit to Valentine, no one will ask how you got it. If you get an illegal fortune elsewhere and can get it away, you can safely take it to Valentine. Occasionally—rarely—the authorities of Valentine will turn over an individual to the law enforcement agencies of another world; almost always a person known to be violent, with no appreciable wealth. But in general it is a safe place for men and women who would not be tolerated in a decent society. Consequently all the law enforcement agencies of the Polity are interested in Valentine, and so is I&S, which shares information with the domestic agencies. This is no secret, although you might not have known it."

"I didn't . . ." She had been very young when she visited Valentine. Every amusement known to human-kind was there, wholesome or not. Not all her pleasures had been those "tolerated in a decent society."

"That's where the informant comes in. He, or she, told the agent, for a price, that—I quote—'somebody knows where the *Bird* will fly.' This seemed to be the extent of the informant's knowledge. He confirmed—I say 'he' for convenience—that he was indeed talking about the Uskosian vessel, and specifically about its detailed course program. So," Jameson said, coming back abruptly to the present, "the course must be changed."

"Couldn't he find out more?"

"Could not or would not. He was encouraged to do so. He has not been heard of since, although he was promised a rich reward. Or perhaps he tried, and asked too many questions. More murder is done on Valentine than comes to light."

"You said I&S suspects someone—what about him?"

"Michael Kristofik? He disappeared from Valentine three weeks ago; another cause for concern. And he is protected, Hanna. He is very wealthy, and has become respected on Valentine, as such things go. He has been politely, adamantly sheltered. He is quite safe on Valentine—though he has not dared to set foot on a Polity world for fifteen years—not since his connection with the *Pavonis Queen* affair was discovered."

"What was that?—I never heard of it."

"It began the same way," he said. "With a pirated program . . ."

He was silent for a moment. She saw him gather and pattern the threads of the story. Then he said, "The course was taken by a man named Ivo Tonson. He was a high official of the Polity, a member of the Exchange Committee. He had arranged all the details of the *Queen's* mission. That was to pick up from many worlds an enormous quantity of currencies of all sorts given up by governments, banking organizations, merchants based everywhere, in trade for equal value in the credit networks of the Polity. Nothing wrong with the money, though. No, it was spendable. No doubt some of it circulates still . . . I must talk with the inspection team."

There was a reader near his hand. He picked it up and scrolled through the index. When he had found what he wanted he held it out to her. She got up, moving

carefully because she was suddenly aware of the extra
weight the *Bird* seemed to have piled on her shoulders.
When she took the reader it was unexpectedly heavy,
too, and she nearly dropped it.

"What is this?" she said.

"An eyewitness account of what happened. It is the
report of the chief of security on the *Pavonis Queen*."

"He survived it, then?"

"She did. All of them did, except one of the attackers. Study it carefully."

He got up, too. She did not look up at him; she looked
at the reader in her hand. She said, "What am I supposed to learn from it?"

"Whatever you can," he said.

The first page the reader showed was an unintelligible
mix of file codes. When Hanna tried to go on to the
next, nothing happened; then the reader began talking.
A woman's voice came out of it, cold, methodical, untouched by the twenty years that had passed since the
statement was recorded. Hanna put the reader on a chair
and settled on the floor in front of it. The voice said:

"My name is Honoria Hood. I have the rank of commander in the Interworld Fleet, and I am a specialist in
the transport of sensitive materials. On ST July 21,
2822, I was assigned chief of the Interworld Fleet security team ordered to accompany the merchant *Pavonis
Queen*, a civilian vessel which was under contract to
the Coordinating Commission of the Interworld Polity
for a one-time mission involving the transfer of negotiable currency.

"The mission schedule called for the *Pavonis Queen*
to leave the Terrestrial stellar system on September 20,
2822, and to return to her point of departure on or about
January 27, 2823. All security arrangements were approved and in place before the *Pavonis Queen* departed
Earth. The vessel carried a civilian crew of twenty-six
and a security force of ten. The *Pavonis Queen* was
unarmed, but warships of the Interworld Fleet were to
meet her at each berth and remain in sentry position for
the duration of each stop on the itinerary. Precautionary

measures were concentrated at all times on the *Pavonis Queen's* ports of call.

"The itinerary of the *Queen* included Nestor, Lancaster, and D'neera, along with twelve lesser settlements. The last port before the *Pavonis Queen* returned to Earth was Alta. We left Alta on January 4, slightly ahead of schedule. The final leg of the journey was Common Route Gamma between Alta and Earth. This route uses one hundred twenty Jumps, and for a ship of the *Pavonis Queen's* class the usual time in transit is five-point-five to six-point-five days.

"The *Pavonis Queen* completed Jump Number Fifty-five at oh-two-hundred hours on January 6. At approximately oh-three-hundred hours I was awakened by First Officer Philip Seal, who told me that upon completing Jump Number Fifty-five the *Pavonis Queen* had picked up a mayday from a vessel identifying itself as the freighter *Pastorale* out of Colony One. I met on the bridge with Mr. Seal and Captain Karsh. At that time we were in position near Relay Number 18.09.232, through which the mayday was being transmitted. The *Pastorale's* reported position was also in the vicinity of the relay. According to the mayday, a reactor malfunction had rendered the *Pastorale* unfit for habitation, and the crew had abandoned ship in lifeboats. Of the crew of fifteen, five men were said to be suffering acute radiation poisoning, and rescue was urgently needed.

"After discussions with Captain Karsh and Mr. Seal, I approved their request to proceed to the aid of the *Pastorale*. I made the decision at oh-four-thirty hours after discussions with Colony One, Intelligence and Security, and my Fleet superiors. My opinion of the authenticity of the mayday and the minimal security risk involved was based on the following facts as they were reported to me. One, the owners of the *Pastorale* had reported her out of contact twenty-two hours previously. Two, search efforts already were underway—not at Jump Number Fifty-five, however, but at Jump Number Sixty-one, her last reported position. Three, the *Pavonis Queen* was three hours away from the point of contact, whereas all other vessels were no less than ten hours away. Four, the reported condition of the ill crewmen made early rendezvous essential. These are the reasons I agreed to Captain Karsh's request to undertake the rescue, with the approval of my superiors.

"We made audio contact with the *Pastorale* at once. A transcript of Captain Karsh's and Mr. Seal's communications with the presumed captain of the *Pastorale* is available. They were marked by the highest degree of tension on the part of the presumed Captain Weng. We were told that the sickest of the crewmen was aboard Captain Weng's lifeboat, and background sounds bore this out. Crewman Durand was said to be—well, never mind. They had invented a history for this imaginary man. It's still hard to believe there isn't a Crewman Durand with a sick mother and a very young wife. It was impossible not to be concerned about him. This was meant to keep our attention engaged, and it worked.

"Visual contact with the supposed *Pastorale* followed at oh-eight-hundred hours. It was definitely radioactive. There were three lifeboats, each said to have one or more toxic patients aboard, and Captain Karsh ordered all three to be onloaded at once. The men in them did not come out immediately, even when the docking bay was fully pressurized and all the *Pavonis Queen's* people were waiting, with the medics at the front. I believe they had a scanner and were studying the dispersal of the persons aboard the *Pavonis Queen*. Everyone was in the docking area except myself, Captain Karsh, and Communications Officer Alves on the bridge; two persons in the engineering section; and two members of the security team, who were standing their regular watch at the internal entry to the cargo hold. Three members of the security team were on standby in the docking bay staging area, with a clear view of the bay itself. The others were inside with the *Pavonis Queen's* crew, having reported to offer assistance.

"After approximately two minutes, the men inside the supposed lifeboats attacked without warning. A large quantity of sleepygas was released from all three vessels. None of the persons in the docking bay escaped; all were unconscious in less than half a minute.

Simultaneously with the release of the gas, the personnel in the vessel nearest the hull fired on the inner pressure seal of the *Pavonis Queen's* docking bay, damaging but not disabling it. The attackers threatened to vaporize the inner and outer seals, which would have resulted in the deaths of all the sleepygas victims, if the guards in the staging area did not lay down their arms. I ordered them to comply. Immediately upon entering the bay, they also were overcome by gas. At that time the attackers finally emerged from the lifeboats. There were four of them; I do not know if others remained inside the vessels. They were dressed in utility spacesuits, so no physical description of them is available, and by sight they were indistinguishable. There were now only seven able-bodied persons free to defend the cargo—myself, Captain Karsh, Mr. Alves, the guards by the cargo hold, and two members of the engineering staff. I advised the civilians to remain where they were, although I am told that Captain Karsh later disregarded my order and was stunned for his trouble. Note that the attackers did not at any time use lethal weapons, only sleepygas and, later, stunners.

"I left Captain Karsh to call for assistance and ran to the docking bay after obtaining a gas filter and a hand-held colloidal disruptor. I could not enter the bay because Captain Karsh had sealed off the area to trap the attackers in the bay. However, the main cargo hold on the *Pavonis Queen* backs onto the docking bay. For this mission the connecting entryway had been sealed with a security wall. But the attackers removed a heavy-duty laser cannon from one of the lifeboats and brought it to bear on the interface between the bay and the cargo hold.

"I therefore proceeded through the interior of the ship to the alternate entrance to the cargo hold. I had the combinations for the locking mechanisms of all three of the intervening doors, but the sequence was so long, and included so many halts for identification, that several minutes were required to effect an entrance. We found that the attackers had entered the hold and were using the *Pavonis Queen's* own equipment to move the cargo. My personnel were armed with disruptors, and all of us began firing as soon as the last door was opened. One of the attackers fell at once. I believe a clean hit was scored in the chest and that he was killed immediately.

"We continued to direct heavy fire at the attackers. At one point more sleepygas was dispersed, but Mulready and Serlio also had filters, and none of us were affected. The attackers were unable to proceed with the transfer of cargo to the lifeboats as long as they were under fire, and it was my intention to harass them until, one, all were dead or disabled, or, two, help arrived. However, they took cover behind the largest of the cargo pallets. These were antigravity pallets, and the one they chose was solidly packed to a height of four meters and was opaque to the disruptor beams. They activated the pallet and began to move it into position in front of the entryway, making it necessary for us to enter the hold to avoid being trapped outside. We therefore came into the hold, at which time Ms. Serlio was stunned. Mr. Mulready and I reached the barrier. I waved him to the left of the pallet, intending to rush the attackers from the right myself. That is the last thing I remember. Mr. Mulready told me later that just as I fell he was conscious of a movement overhead, and was then stunned also. I believe one of the attackers had scaled the barrier from the other side, and fired on us from above.

"I was unconscious for six hours. When I awoke, the *Joyeuse* out of Willow was on the scene, and I was in its sickbay. The cargo of the *Pavonis Queen* was gone."

The voice ended, impersonal and didactic as it had been at the start. The reader did not make another sound. Hanna's cheek was pressed against the smooth covering of the chair, and her eyes were closed. At the beginning and the end the voice had belonged to the quintessential bureaucrat, but in between there had been pictures in its hesitations, its stilted formality and the lapses from that, its confidence in the recitation of numbers and dates, the omissions on less sure ground. Everything had been so neat out there. Everything had been planned. Even the urgency of an emergency in space could be handled, there were procedures; then the unexpected entered, the men and women falling in heaps, a man dead with his heart turned to jelly . . .

Jameson said close by, startling her, "What do you think of it?"

"I'm sorry for Honoria Hood . . ."

"Oh, it didn't ruin her. It was a long time between promotions, but she's still with Fleet. What else?"

Hanna opened her eyes finally, and straightened. "How could they do it?" she said. "How could anybody know ahead of time that the real *Pastorale* would be out of contact?"

He smiled at her. It was a particular smile which she recognized; it meant she had said something naive.

"They arranged it," he said.

"Arranged it?"

"The *Pastorale's* communications system was sabotaged. The damage was repairable, but it took a day or two. The man responsible had been hired to do only that, he knew nothing of the plot, and he was not punished very severely."

"All right. Still. The *Pavonis Queen* was ahead of schedule, isn't that what Hood said? The timing—"

"It was not as close as you think," he said. "Remember the accomplice at Admin; he knew the *Queen's* precise location at all times."

"Who was he? What happened to him?"

"I told you: Ivo Tonson. He left Earth and vanished a few hours before the robbery. One supposes he went to a new identity and a comfortable life."

Hanna tried to fit it together. The more she thought about it the more improbable it seemed. The restrictions, the safeguards, the controls, the agencies, the Interworld Fleet, the hounds of I&S—! In the last few years she had become well acquainted with them. She herself was ordered and official, pigeonholed and tamed. Someone had looked on all the regulations as simple problems to be solved, one by one. She could not imagine it.

She said, "They must have known every detail of the mission."

"They got the information from Tonson, undoubtedly."

"What happened to the one Hood killed?"

"The body was taken away, along with the lifeboats, the money, and the *Pastorale* replica, the decoy—which must have been safe in essential areas."

"And all those people in the docking bay—"

"They had Alves and the two engineers move them all to safety before they cut their way out of the bay and escaped."

"They thought of everything."

"Everything."

"Then how did I&S hear of that one? Kristofik?"

"The name was brought to their attention by a man whose grievance—there must have been a grievance—is unknown. The information produced by the initial investigation was promising. Kristofik's activities at the time of the incident bore out the theory of his involvement. But when the investigators sought to question the informer further, he had disappeared. No trace of him was found. Probably he was dead."

"And you think that now the same people, or Kristofik at least . . ."

Her voice trailed off. It seemed impossible to bridge the space of twenty years; when the *Pavonis Queen* was attacked, she had been a child, running barefoot in the bright morning of Province Koroth.

Jameson said, "That's what the I&S computers think. They were asked to generate a list of known felons who might be capable of planning and carrying out a theft on the scale this would be. There were four possibilities. One is in prison on Nestor; one was Adjusted, and is now tending cattle on Lancaster; one is dead, ID certain. The fourth is Kristofik."

"Who is he?"

For answer Jameson took the reader from its place. The long fingers moved delicately, searching the index. She could not ask a question the file could not answer. It was all there, neatly cataloged. She wondered if the robbers had been patient with files, kept them tidy, known where to look for everything. When Jameson handed the reader over, a face showed on its screen. He watched Hanna's eyes and saw the pupils of her eyes dilate. He said, amused, "A typical woman's reaction, I'm told."

"What?" She did not know what he meant at first; then she did, but she did not take her eyes from the image. The man was beautiful—there was no other word for it. There was just enough sharpness in the lines of brow and jaw, nose and cheekbones, to save them from effeminacy. She said doubtfully, "Is that his real face? Or did he have it constructed?"

"From all accounts it is his own. No one really knows."

"Why not? Valentine has good records."

"He has not always lived on Valentine. He turned up on Alta as a child of twelve or thirteen. The monks of St. Kristofik have a school for homeless children there, and they took him in. That's where he got the name he uses. Before Alta there is nothing. Certainly his face was not changed afterward. But his origin is unknown."

"Unusual. But possible. So many little settlements, half forgotten, or more than half . . ."

She bent over the reader, studying Michael Kristofik's eyes. They were amber-brown in color, long-lashed, oddly flecked with gold. He looked out of the picture with half a smile, as if someone had just said something pleasing.

She said, "He doesn't look dangerous."

"It's true no one was hurt on the *Pavonis Queen*. But there were incidents of violence on Alta and Valentine both before and after that, and later everywhere. And don't forget the man who accused him. Do you think he disappeared naturally just then, by coincidence? Kristofik was dangerous. He is still dangerous."

Hanna turned off the image and got up. The faraway voices sang around her and she felt misplaced in time.

"I will try to persuade Rubee to change the plan," she said.

"You don't have much hope," he said.
"No."

When Rubee and Awnlee left the Far-Flying Bird for good to sojourn among humans, it had been necessary for the three of them—the aliens and Hanna—to establish semipermanent lodgings near Admin. Starr Jameson had offered his own home for their use. Hanna refused it. She had lived in that house, and had not entered it since the day she left without farewell; she would not enter it now. She was obliged to explain her refusal to Rubee and Awnlee. At that time—when human beings were new to them—they knew in an abstract way that humans came in two sexes. The principle was not new, it was commonplace on life-bearing planets, but Uskos had not met it in a sentient species. Linguistic analysis then had laid in only a foundation for the translator, and much of Hanna's communication with Rubee and Awnlee was telepathic. Her explanation therefore was three parts emotion, and it shocked them. It was their first glimpse of the complications human sexual arrangements made. They got them mixed up for a while with the permanent bonding of the People of Zeig-Daru, of which Hanna had recently informed them.

"Does obtaining such loss mean that like those beings you will die?" they said.

"Humans don't die when they lose a love," Hanna said. "It only makes them want to."

Such discrimination was beyond Rubee and Awnlee at the time, but they were pleased to acquiesce in whatever Hanna might suggest. Therefore when they were on Earth they rattled around in a pile of a house that occasionally slipped its moorings and floated above the hills and meadows around it, high enough for the inhabitants to see Admin and its city sixty kilometers to the east. When the house had taken flight four or five times, Hanna found that it did not do so of its own accord; Awnlee had found the key to the place's programming, and had something to do with the phenomenon.

Even at rest the house made them giddy. It was fili-

agreed, frescoed, fretted and gilded. The ceilings
crawled with molding, the exterior with mosaic and bas-
relief. The first time Hanna stood in a jet of perfumed
air after bathing, she saw that even the airstream nozzles
were engraved with detailed scenes so tiny that they
were almost indecipherable; she deciphered them, and
discovered their theme was scatalogical. Rubee, at about
the same time, tried to revise gravity in the area of his
bed, and spent a night on the ceiling. He could not get
down until Hanna and Awnlee missed him in the morning and went in search of him. The house or the estate
or both for some reason were called Puddin'. Hanna
could not remember the names of the people who owned
it, nor where they had gone while they left their property at the disposal of aliens.

Here Hanna told Rubee and Awnlee what she had
heard about the *Far-Flying Bird.* They sat in a grove of
maples whose shade at noon did little to cut the muggy
heat. Rubee and Awnlee were thoroughly comfortable;
Hanna, wearing nothing, tolerated the heat. D'neerans
as a rule were not particular about clothes, and with
only the indifferent aliens for company, it did not matter
if she were clothed or not.

They took the news well. Uskosians understood
crime. They were even pleased, Hanna thought, that the
gifts to be made to them by the peoples of human worlds
should be great enough to inspire it.

But they would do nothing to avert it.

"Tell me why," Hanna said. She lay on her back,
arms clasped behind her head; wiggled a toe, closed
one eye, and took aim at the toe with the other. The
heat soaked into her bones. Should she, before going to
Uskos, have her long hair cut and its growth inhibited?
She would spend much of her time in hot climates, so
it would be wise, but she did not want to.

Such a question seemed ordinary. Nor did it seem
odd to lie under a tree with beings from another star,
talking of a crime to which all three of them might fall
victim. She had done stranger things.

"To alter the course is to alter the design and end of

our voyage," Rubee said. "I have fixed the day of return."

"Yes, I know, but why?"

"Why not?" said Awnlee, and shook all over, fingers flexing rapidly. This was laughter. He had once heard Hanna respond thus to an absurd question, and lost no chance of using the phrase.

"We are expected on the fourteenth day of Strrrl," Rubee said. "That is the appointed time."

"Yes, I know that, Rubee, but I do not understand. I am sorry. We have had fixed dates for our travels together here and changed them. We ought to be on Co-op now, in fact. The changes have annoyed you because they are a nuisance, just as they have annoyed me, for the same reason. But if we are on Earth instead of Co-op on the eighteenth day of an Earthly August, how is that different from being in space instead of at home, on the fourteenth day of—what you said?"

"Details change," Rubee said gravely. "Grand designs must not, except by the hand of the Master."

She thought she felt her ears prick, a physical movement. She said casually, "You mean the Master is the only permissible agent of change in a grand design?"

"Not at all. Yet if the design is beneficent, who would wish to change it? And this that we wish to recreate is a design of peace and amity between peoples divided by distance."

"But what if the Master does intervene?"

"Then it is a new design, and the meaning may remain obscure forever."

Hanna concentrated on her toe. They were within a step of granting the Master of Chaos the status of a physical agent, it seemed; she had formerly gotten no hint that he might be so regarded.

"By whom are designs made?" she said.

"By persons."

"And persons can alter them?"

"They may; but each alteration may be a place for the Master to enter, and the persons who make them his tools. Therefore, in such a case as ours, the old," said Rubee simply, "is better than the new."

"So this journey of yours . . ." She looked up into the shadows of leaves. "You set out to seek—something. Intelligent life, anyway. Not specifically us. You didn't know we were here. You didn't know you would find us. Or if you would find intelligent life at all. And yet you mean this is not something new, but something old?"

"Very old."

"It was once new, wasn't it?"

"In part. But only in part."

"What is it, then? What is the old thing?"

"It is best illustrated," said Rubee, "by The Travels of Erell."

"Will you tell me of the Travels of Erell?"

"Gladly. Do you wish a formal presentation?"

Hanna almost said no, but hesitated. The Travels of Erell might illuminate an attitude that to humans seemed entirely irrational. She did not want to summarize a summary to Jameson in a matter so important, nor make him further summarize it for Vickery.

"I would like that," she said.

"We are honored."

"I think I would like for Starr to see it, too. If he can come tonight, would you do it then? Is that too soon?"

The restless cilia around Rubee's mouth moved in a way that meant he agreed with grace and pleasure.

"Then it will be his, too," Rubee said.

There was no taboo against watching preparations. The aliens prepared in Rubee's room, and Hanna stood by with Starr Jameson and watched them get ready.

First each put on a garment of white cloth, plain but fine in texture, so soft that it fell about his chunky body in a hundred delicate folds. Round the neck went another piece of cloth, this woven in a seamless circle and falling in equal lengths over chest and back. A pattern was woven into it: an endless spiral.

The outer gown was brilliant in color and made of such heavy stuff that it kept its shape by itself. It was floor-length and hooded, and covered everything except the face and the elusive fingers. Rubee wore a blue so bright it was shocking to human eyes; Awnlee wore scarlet. They also had masks colored like their gowns. These were simply constructed of some artificial substance, and were pierced so that the eyespots and tendrilled mouths were visible.

They were not doing the thing the way it ought to be done. At home the vast costumeries held accessories for every conceivable performance. "The Travels of Erell" rightly called for more than two hundred participants, each with his own individually painted mask, special jewelry, and symbolic garments. Rubee and Awnlee had apologized before for the poverty of their resources; they apologized again now.

"Thank you, the loss is unimportant in your company," Hanna answered properly in their tongue.

Jameson was using a translator; he did not know a word of Ellsian, the principal language of Uskos. He said, "You're picking it up very well."

"It's not difficult. The grammatical structure isn't nearly as mad as Pan-F'thalian."

"Does knowing the language help? We saw that recording of a 'formal' together, you remember, shortly after they came. I got nothing out of it."

She thought for a minute, remembering "The Journey of Nlatee." She and Jameson had gone to the *Far-Flying Bird* to see what Rubee had to show them, hardly anyone knowing about it; information about the aliens was jealously guarded then. Jameson had managed to look as if he were not hot. Hanna's hair was damp. The translator did its best, an adequate job in fact, since the tales used a simple, straightforward vocabulary while the drama was acted out. Jameson watched the play courteously but without much comprehension; so did Hanna, until—guessing already the importance of the tales—she began "listening" to the Uskosians' emotional reactions to the show.

She said slowly, "I can understand it as they do—sometimes. It's not only because of the language, though. It takes practice, saturation. Even with the translator you might not understand this very well, and it's only a sort of outline anyway. Rubee is going to be both narrator and principal actor for this, and Awnlee will be all the others . . . Narration doesn't seem to be really important in a true formal presentation, but it will be almost all you have.''

"But you don't rely entirely on narration.''

"Oh, no.'' She glanced up at him. The comment was not idle; he was getting to something. He was right. Since that first recorded presentation, Rubee and Awnlee had allowed her to enter their minds while they performed, as thoroughly as her considerable ability allowed. Her perception was multifaceted and enriched in ways words could scarcely explain, and sometimes in her reports she did not even try, and made audacious statements of fact and prayed no one would ask for an explanation.

"Could you share it with me?'' he asked, and she started.

She looked at Rubee and Awnlee for want of somewhere to fix her eyes; they were making final adjustments to each other's gowns with darting fingers. She said, "I thought you didn't like it when I thought to you.''

"It's tolerable, within reason,'' he said. "And knowledge is my job, too.''

"Then I must do some preparation, too,'' Hanna said, and walked out on all of them.

She went out to the terrace where the little party would assemble. Lights were sunk into the stone, making sharp constellations in near-night. The sky was blue-black and stars were coming out, and the evening air smelled of grass and earth. There was a balustrade set at intervals with glass-clear flowers from Co-op. She leaned over it, seeking the scented breeze. She was angry. Jameson asked for an intimacy denied her when it might have counted. Her abilities were cheap now, they might have been tools wielded by a computer. The computer had a name and reputation: Lady Hanna ril-Koroth of D'neera, the human race's leading authority on aliens. She knew her official biography by heart, having heard herself introduced to too many expectant audiences.

". . . member of the Goodhaven Academy for the Study of Alien Species since the remarkable age of twenty-five . . ." *Twenty-one,* god damn it, screw Standard chronology, what's wrong with D'neera's years?

"Consultant to Polity Alien Relations and Contact, chief architect of the Zeigan Contact Project, she also organized the nucleus of D'neera's program in alien studies at the University of D'vornan . . ." It's called The University, idiot; just happens to be at D'vornan.

". . . and many other honors."

And. And. And.

(And when they get to me after the speech, late at night when they've had a few drinks, they want to know what the People *did* to me . . .)

That's your job, woman. "Alien relations."

Her hands were too tight on the railing. She relaxed them, with an effort.

True-humans never liked it when she touched their thoughts. It taught them more about her than they wanted to know, and exposed them uncomfortably to her. Jameson was no different from the others. But she had learned a thing or two since their time together.

She went to the shelter of the wall of the house, sat cross-legged on the stone, and cleared her mind.

Four years ago she had thrown herself into the study of D'neera's Adept disciplines with a passion whose source was not precisely as disinterested as its teachers advised. She had said: *I must master my body so pain cannot master me; for now that I know my own weakness I live in fear.* The teachers had not sent her away. Motives more reprehensible than fear had led some of them on the same quest, but the studies themselves had a way of shaping the student. Her progress had been rapid, and now she had some skill in the art of consciousness clarified and disciplined to pure purpose.

She had also learned not to regret her ignorance at the time of her first contact with the People of Zeig-Daru. If she had known more, even if they had done the same terrible things to her, she would not have felt any of it. But history would have been different.

Presently the soft summer air and the dark and the

stars drew far away. Her body lost its weight and vanished.

Jameson came outdoors to something that seemed a statue, so still was Hanna. If he watched her closely, he saw at long intervals an eyeblink or a slow breath. Otherwise she did not move until he sat down nearby and spoke her name. She turned her head without haste. Her face was remote: alien as Rubee's. He waited warily for the first stab at his consciousness, the sense of an intrusive presence in one's own inviolable mind. What came was barely perceptible, a cold thread like nothing he had felt before, devoid of personality as the eyes that a little while ago had been Hanna's.

He was relieved.

The aliens came in their rich vestments like gliding stones, figures of geometry with substance and bulk. The lights at their feet cast shadows behind them which bent over the balustrade and flowed into the night. Shadow seemed to thicken round them and slowly, like the swirl of black cloud in black sky, the darkness shaped other forms. Their masks were of all colors. Jameson did not see them with his eyes. He saw Rubee's knowledge and memory: what ought to be. So now he had two kinds of sight, one of them directed by that force he could not identify with Hanna; also he heard the rasp of Rubee's voice, and laid over it, impersonal, mechanical, the Standard translation.

"And this is the story of the Travels of Erell," Rubee said; and at a distance a gong sounded, or seemed to.

"In a year on the second day of Urrt, Erell set forth. At his side was his selfing Awtell, and they sailed a fair ship; for Erell was of Ell by the ocean."

The night wind blew from an Uskosian sea. At parting the people played the Path of Stoell; no, the shadows played the people's play; no, it was only Awnlee playing a multitude of players.

Awnlee sang in a voice like rough metal and was the wind that bore the ship away.

"They crossed the eyeless ocean steering by the moons. There were storms and the Master appeared in the towering waves but neither sank nor aided them.

They sailed on without hesitation until they came to an empty land. They rested and went on."

Rubee faced the terrible waves and Awnlee, compressing fifty roles in one, was the sea. The storm keened with a furious voice. No one ever played the Master's part; but in the patterns of the movements of the play, a space was left for him. Then they were still, resting, though sea and wind murmured on. In rest the cowled shapes bent toward one another with great dignity, selfing sheltered by sire.

"Days passed and the moons dipped and danced. A great bird of a kind unknown appeared and sought to seize Awtell, but Erell drove it away. Then he knew this voyage was not discouraged."

Awnlee danced like the icy moons, and his fingers wove strange figures about one another. He and Rubee clashed with formal violence: Erell and the bird.

"On they went and came to empty lands and the seas were long. They they came to the land of Sa. And they could not understand those of Sa, but then they learned. And they feasted and were welcome."

Some distant part of Jameson's consciousness told him he was in trance; but all the rest of it saw the emptiness of the water and land, and later the welcoming.

"At length they departed; and when they left the land of Sa they bore rich gifts, and with them traveled Porsa of Sa. They knew fair winds as they went; and on the fourteenth day of Strrrl they came again to Ell. And when they told those of Ell what they had learned there was rejoicing, and welcoming and feasting of Porsa of Sa, and in after years many went from each land to the other, and Awtell was a leader of all. So did the beings of sundered lands come first to know one another in the ages of the world. And the bond of the lands of Ell and Sa to this minute is not torn by war nor broken by any thing.

"Precious is this minute!"

Rubee and Awnlee withdrew. The shadows went with them. Some time passed, but Jameson did not know how much; time might have stopped until suddenly the presence he had forgotten withdrew from his thought, and he came awake. When he looked at Hanna, she also had returned to normal consciousness, though a trace of remoteness lingered in her eyes. She got up slowly, as if it took a minute to get used to her body again.

She said, "Do you understand now?"

He shook his head. "I thought I did while it was going on," he said.

"Yes, that's right. I can't keep it up all the time either."

"I guess you have to be a little inhuman," he said, meaning no insult.

"That's right," Hanna said impassively.

"It's got some kind of symbolic meaning, then? This schedule they're tied to?"

"Symbols come in differing degrees of abstraction," Hanna said. Her voice was cool, pitched in the lecturer's mode. "They stand for living forces that shape the way we think and live. Humans often dissociate visible symbol from its sources. Your sun and crossed spears, the seal of your world—your people think what they feel for it is pride. What it is, is the comfort of the tribe. The Uskosians are fully conscious of all that underlies their symbols—but those foundations are just as powerful for them as ours are for us."

He said frankly, "I can accept what you say as an intellectual proposition, and I take it on faith that you're right. But I will not be able to convince Vickery and the others that Rubee will not change his mind if only the situation is explained to him clearly enough and logically enough."

"Well, I promise you that I will keep explaining it, clearly and logically. But what is the logic of the gifts we take to Uskos?—jewels, art, a treasure to tempt a thief. What is the logic of that?"

"Everyone knows that," he said.

"Yes," Hanna said, "and everyone on Uskos will understand Rubee's logic."

"Then we'll have to think of something else," he said.

* * *

It was hot in Shoreground that year. Outside the central dome the air had a rank ocean smell, and the wind blowing inland carried sand and grit that clung to damp skin and stuck in eyes and hair.

Inside the dome it was different.

Inside the dome at midnight the streets were cool and full of light. Michael Kristofik walked through them invisible, hidden in patterns of shadow that tricked an observer's eye. There were other figures like him in the streets, anonymous clouds that looked half-real, transdimensional. Many who came to the dome did not wish to be recognized there, and there were vendors to supply the generators that broke up the light around them.

Shoreground-under-glass was called Carnivaltown. Michael stood at the center of the cauldron and looked up. At intervals shapes lit up the sky: flowers, beasts, abstractions some of which were salacious. The names of establishments flashed in the air, and images of their attractions. Near the top of the dome, perched precariously on the curved surface, habitats clung to the inner skin, their windows dots from the ground. The masters of Carnivaltown ran the dome from there. Michael had been there often, the last time not long ago: a rich man among his peers, looking down on the lights, removed from the activity below.

This was the third consecutive night he had spent walking the streets of Carnivaltown. Before that, he had not come to them for a long time.

He turned through an entrance wreathed with arabesques. Synthetic happiness jolted him. It ended when he stepped into the room beyond, leaving a residue of good feeling. A woman with polished silver skin greeted him. The happi-bar lobby was nearly dark and she glittered, a creature of quicksilver eyes, the top of her head a gleaming bald dome. She wore only a golden anklet, but she looked too made of metal to be tempting. She was used to apparitions like Michael. He was used to apparitions like her.

She took him to the kind of cubicle he wanted: a watcher's station, half of one wall a telescreen. From here a customer could overlook the private ecstasies in all the cubicles of the other kind, occupied by people who liked to be watched. The watchers paid heavily, but the others paid just as much, and complained about it; did they not provide the entertainment?

Another silver woman brought the dram of Fantasee Michael ordered. He left it untouched and used the telescreen methodically, ignoring what he saw except to search for a face. This was the third night he had looked for it, and he was prepared to keep going a long time. But in the happi-bar he found it almost at once: the face of a boy perhaps twenty years old with black eyes, fresh white skin, mouth curved in a professional smile. He was alone. Waiting.

Michael looked at the young face for a long time.

Good thing to do when you've been earning well and don't feel like working hard. Display in a voyeur's haven, the quiet kind, like this. Relax, have a drink, let the peepers peep, let them make the moves. Just make sure they know what you are so there won't be an argument later.

Tricks of the trade. Who had told him about that one?

You couldn't miss Gian Filarete's trade. The medallion round his neck showed, prominently, the clasped-hands symbol of the Registered Friend.

Michael touched the Talk switch and then the credit plate. Making contact cost extra. He left with Gian a little later.

He took the boy home with him, an hour from Shoreground by groundcar. The car could have found the way, but Michael piloted it to cover a rare, bad case of nerves. He put away the distortion device when they got in the car and when he looked into Gian's speculative eyes, he could almost hear the boy thinking. *Good-looking. I like that. Strong, though. Mean? Or the soppy kind? All night. Weird?* There was music in the car, but it was not helpful.

As the spur is to the jade,
As the scabbard for the blade,
As for digging is the spade,

As for liquor is the can,
Man is for the woman made
and woman for the man . . .

The song was in a dialect fourteen hundred years old, and the voices wove a dance around one another. Gian did not like it. He was not impressed with the car, either, which was not new. Michael's stock did not go up until he offered wine and Gian saw the goblets. Gian held his carefully, stroked the crystal, became friendly. He got even more friendly when he saw where Michael lived.

They ate on a terrace overlooking a night-black lawn, and past that the heavy shapes of full-foliaged trees. The lighter darkness farther out was the sky. Beyond the trees a cliff dropped away to the sea. There was just enough light at table to show the food they ate and, dimly, their faces. Theo served the meal, and Gian took him to be a personal servant. The boy ate well, drank sparingly, and tried too hard to charm. His head was full of possibilities: standing appointments, bonuses, gifts, the mansion behind them. He had come to Valentine from Co-op less than a year before. Michael knew that, but he did not know why Gian had come. He would not have the stability that came with belonging to one of the old Valentine families for whom prostitution was an honorable business; he was not attached to a combine like Flora's, where he might have learned to move in the best society anywhere in human space. He was only pretty and cunning and young, and the shell that had begun to grow around him sooner or later would be impenetrable.

When they finished eating, he followed Michael indoors without suspicion. By day, big as it was, the house was bright and airy. Tonight the darkness weighed on it. Few interior lights were on, and they went through the shadows to a central room with no openings except the door through which they entered. A single light floated unsupported near a chair. There was a table nearby with an odd assortment of objects on it, part of the casual litter that accompanied Michael wherever he went. The weightless globe made one sharp-edged pool of light, and shrank the universe to the man and boy within it. Gian sat in the chair and looked up at Michael expectantly. Michael stood half in shadow and studied the boy.

If there were problems, Theo would come with his kit of chemicals. But simple bribery would be better.

Michael said, "All I want from you is information."

The practiced smile stayed in place for a minute, lost its gloss all of a sudden when the words penetrated. For Gian the expected stood on its head. Michael's manner was subtly changed. There was no threat in it, but there was sureness. The common meaning of what had gone before vanished; none of it was what Gian had thought it was.

"There was a man at the Grand Square Inn last week. Red hair. Blue eyes, very light. About my height, heavier build. I don't know what name he used with you. Whatever it was wasn't his real name."

Gian's smile disappeared altogether. He was a long way from Carnivaltown, and this had not happened to him before. He looked around once, quickly. Michael had chosen this spot by instinct, and chosen well; Gian could not remember where the entrance lay, and the little space of light trapped him.

He said, 'I don't know what you mean."

"Sure you do. You're thinking of the Guild rule, right? Don't jaw the customers. Not to each other."

"I'm registered," Gian said. "I don't want whines."

"Save the ethics for the slops. In the Guild it goes, 'unless the price is right.' "

He had the inflection right. Gian looked at him in surprise. Michael said, "Don't get righteous. I was in the Guild five years."

"*You?*"

Gian looked around again, this time speculatively, as if he saw through the dark. He had seen enough to know how Michael lived. He said, "Five years for this?"

Michael grinned in spite of himself. "I didn't get it that way. I was good. But not that good."

The boy's face was transparent; Michael watched him

reevaluate the situation. Haggling over an indiscretion that could get your registration canceled was one thing. Professional gossip was something else.

Gian said, "What's it worth?"

"You tell me."

"I can't till I know what you want."

"He left Valentine the day after you had him. Private ship, private business, no flight plan. I want to know if he said anything, did anything, if you noticed anything, that'd tell me where he was going next."

"Why?" The boy was curious; almost impudent, now.

"He owes me money," Michael lied.

"How much?"

"None of yours. You're not in for shares. Give me a flat."

"I'll think about it," said the boy. "Throw me in?"

"In already, infant. Can't hook me this way."

The patois came easily. Gian was visibly relaxing. He said, "How'd you target me?"

"Security. A favor."

Gian nodded. Shoreground security officers were almost incorruptible—because very little was considered corrupt. The woman who had found Gian was near retiring. Not much provision was made for security personnel after they retired. As a rule not much was necessary; with a little initiative, an enterprising officer could provide well for the future. Gian understood, and took it as a matter of course.

Michael came all the way into the circle of light. He picked up an object from the table and held it out. Slender vase with graceful lines, a little darker than turquoise; it looked like glass, but it was not. The material was thin, and opaline sparks danced in its fragile skin. There was considerable value in the medium, but Michael held it so that Gian saw the bottom and the finely etched mark that referred to an embedded electronic pattern worth a great deal more.

Gian looked at it appreciatively. "One of a kind. You got more?"

"Sure. Some better than others. But ones, yes."

"I got a couple."

"What you got?"

"Sisty Whitemore from Earth, you heard of her? She does ones for walls. Programs a robo, that's what you get, the robo does it all. Got a big bonus once, flashed it all on that. You got a Whitemore?"

"Downstairs. Show you later."

"The robo self-destructs."

"Yeah. You have to jet it out fast."

Gian took the vase and held it lovingly. A work like this, like Sisty Whitemore's multidimensional walls, like anybody's work of art, could be reproduced down to the last molecule. Most were. Those that were not, that were certified as one-of-a-kinds, were prized.

"You want it?" Michael said.

"Sure. Sure I do."

"You know how to get it."

Gian made up his mind. "He was going by the name of Pallin."

"Just that night. Just with you."

"So it doesn't mate. All right. Didn't say much. Just told me what he wanted. You know how some are? Better than the talky kind, though. But no repeat for this one. Too rough. Don't mind if I flap him. He made a call."

"Who to?"

"Don't know. Didn't hear a name, couldn't see the face. He thought I was asleep. I didn't hear much," Gian said apologetically.

"Anything about where he's headed?"

"Yeah. He said—" Gian thought about it, caressing the blue vase. "He said, 'When we get to the Rose we'll start the countdown.' "

"The what?"

"The Rose. Like the flower."

"Sure?"

"As tomorrow."

"What else?"

"That's all."

Gian got anxious. It wasn't much. He held the vase harder, wondering if Michael would take it away from him. But Michael was only thoughtful. "Have to do," he said.

He showed Gian around and called an autocab for him. At the last a streak of conscience pricked Gian. He said, "I could stay. You paid for the night."

"Never mind. Go on back. Take that pretty home."

"You don't like boys?"

"Not especially."

"Is it good being rich?"

"Very good."

"I guess you get anything you want." Gian said with greed. *Nothing like*, Michael thought, but he did not say so to Gian.

* * *

I&S patiently turned over pebbles. All the project personnel had been investigated before; now they were screened again. Toward the end Vickery said to Jameson. "It's just what you'd expect if there was nothing to it. We're talking about an impossibility to begin with, you know."

Gil Figueiredo, who had been in charge of security for the aliens since Rubee's first incomprehensible call touched the edge of human space, sat in front of Vickery's desk. Jameson stood at the outer edge of the room and looked at the river going on its peaceful way. Vickery's office was on the lowest level of the fifty-story administration complex. The other forty-nine were heavy as a mountain overhead. You could walk through their passages for days and never find the place where you had started.

"We're missing something." Jameson said. "Is there, anywhere, another source for the program?"

"No," Vickery and Figueiredo said together.

"There's the *Bird* herself. She's been studied."

"Only the Inspace engineering," Figueiredo said.

"Could anyone have gotten into the navigation computers that way, without breaking the seals?"

"No," Figueiredo said positively.

Jameson stared across the water, where trees dreamed

in the summer heat. The nights had gotten cooler, and the mass of green was softened by hints of gold. He said, "What I'd really like to do is get Kristofik under probe."

Vickery said, "You've got him on the brain," but Figueiredo laughed out loud and said, "That's been the dearest wish of some people at I&S for fifteen years."

Jameson's tenure on the Coordinating Commission had given him a certain disregard for law. He said, "There ought to be a way to do it."

"Oh, it could be *done*. He doesn't bother with personal security on Valentine. But we've never tried it because even if we probed him there, we couldn't get him back to the Polity without creating a hell of an incident. If we couldn't transport him for trial, there's no point starting it. You remember his name didn't surface for something like five years after the *Pavonis Queen* robbery, when he was already established on Valentine. There were talks then, and Valentine shut us down. And that was fifteen years ago. He's an important citizen now."

"He is also back on Valentine where he belongs," Jameson said. "Perhaps we've gone wrong there instead. Perhaps he's not the man we should be looking at."

Figueiredo said impatiently, "You saw the reports on the other names. He's the only one left."

"It's too neat."

"All we have to deal with is known factors. That's what the known factors give us."

Jameson almost heard Hanna's laughter. Figueiredo could not know what it was like to specialize in the unknown. Figueiredo added, "Don't forget the *Golden Girl*. It fits."

"What is that?" Vickery said a little wearily.

"Kristofik bought a yacht a few months ago. Dru class, beautiful thing. Six staterooms, two lounges, gymnasium, staff quarters. He refitted it and named it the *Golden Girl*. The color's not really gold, though— more like brass."

"Appropriate," Jameson murmured, but Figueiredo

went on, "He provisioned it for a long, long voyage. He hasn't taken one yet. But there are indications he's planning to leave Valentine again and be away some time. He's turned over his business interests almost entirely to his head manager, Kareem Mar-Kize, for one thing."

"The *Golden Girl* is not armed," Jameson said quietly, but Vickery was more interested now.

"Is he in financial trouble?"

"No. And that's where it doesn't fit," Figueiredo admitted. "He just keeps getting richer. He might be crazy enough to want the cargo for himself, though. From what we know of him, he'd appreciate it."

Vickery's interest waned. He shook his head. "Chances are he's just like everybody else in human space. One, all he knows about the *Bird's* course is what direction she's going and what star she's headed for. And two, he doesn't care."

"Maybe," Figueiredo said. "All the same, if Director Jameson could get them to agree to an armed escort, it would solve everything."

Jameson said, "I will push Hanna as hard as I can. She will, in turn, push Rubee and Awnlee as far as possible. I doubt very greatly that she could under any conceivable circumstance get that result."

Vickery said, "She's under your direct supervision."

"The aliens are not."

Figueiredo said, "There's another option. If we didn't send any gifts, there wouldn't be a target."

Jameson said, "If the gifts go, Hanna goes. It's a package. And the Commssion strongly favors her preceding a diplomatic party by some months, since that's what Rubee wants."

"Very advantageous for her. Her professional reputation, I mean. The gifts—is that how she persuaded them to take her along?"

Jameson turned around at last. His eyes were so cold that Figueiredo shut up abruptly. He said, "Perhaps it's time I&S officers charged with protecting aliens spent some time at D'vornan under Hanna's tutelage. The arrangement was Rubee's suggestion. It has to do with the

Travels of Erell. If you don't know what that means, you had better find out. Check out the navigational systems once more, if you please. I will see to it that Hanna knows as much as possible about this man Kristofik. She may have to negotiate with him.''

Figueiredo was not happy, but he nodded.

Now there were no more places to go. The aliens and Hanna stayed on Earth. For their protection—and to their bewilderment—they were placed under the surveillance of bugs, spyeyes, airspace monitors; the aliens could ignore them and forget that they were there, but Hanna could not. She thought of them as everything that was worst about Earth, about Polity Admin for that matter. They gave you no privacy, if they thought they had a good reason to take it away. What if she needed real aloneness? What if she were to take a lover?—an academic question, because she had had no lover since Jameson. She had discovered in herself, with him, an unsuspected capacity for exclusive love. Passion had no power to touch her now, and after five years celibacy had become a habit, so that she had nothing to be private about. There was a principle involved, though, and she had good-byes to say. She would have liked having privacy for that.

"I found I liked teaching better than running things, but you will listen to one more suggestion, won't you? Institute the program in F'thalian mathematical thought, and get Tai-Tai Ling out from Earth to teach it. You will? Good, oh, good. And, oh, if you should hear from my mother, tell her I tried to find her . . ."

Communications that ducked through Inspace—that disappeared at one point in realspace and appeared in another—never reappeared at all if they were sent too far, and over long distances had to be transmitted from one automatic relay to another, just as a spacecraft could not go from star to star with a single Jump and so made each journey piecemeal. Rubee and Awnlee had left no relays behind them. They had not been able to speak to Uskos for nearly four years. As the day for departure came close, Hanna thought of her own voyage on the exploratory vessel *Endeavor*, the one that had led to contact with Zeig-Daru. She had never examined her dependence on the relays that marked *Endeavor's* path. The controllers of *Endeavor's* voyage—among them Jameson, a commissioner then—had always know what was going on. *Endeavor* had always been able to shout for help. Its crewmen had remained in contact with their homeworlds, though the contacts had been censored. It had not occurred to Hanna that space exploration could proceed in any other way.

The gulf Rubee and Awnlee had crossed—silent, beyond help, incredibly vast—was a gulf indeed. The way they had done it marked them alien more clearly than anything else Hanna had learned about them. They did not even know how courageous they were. They did not think about it. They followed in the footsteps of Erell, and Erell had not said, "Good-bye until I think of calling home." He had only said: "Good-bye."

"I noticed the stoneveins were fading in the snow. They need to be cut back. You will? Oh, thank you, thank you. You can keep the fish. And, oh, if my mother comes by, give her my love . . . Good-bye, good-bye, good-bye . . ."

Jameson wanted her to come to his office. He wanted her to study a file which could not be transmitted out of Admin. She did not want to spend any more time in offices. Her days in human space were going away quickly. She would be isolated for the last seven of them, having her immunities (as she thought of it) fine-tuned. She had paid no more attention than she had to the army of biotechs who at the start had tampered first with her, then with Rubee and Awnlee, then with all of them, then with the *Bird* itself; now they were going to do it all over again, in reverse. So she would spend a week in a sealed environment and go straight from that to the *Bird*, and she did not want to waste time at Admin.

"I will have plenty of time to study whatever you want when I can't go anywhere," she told Jameson.

"You have to see it *here*," he said stubbornly.

"Nothing I have to do with now is *that* highly classified."

"When it comes from I&S it is."

"You weren't always so careful about regulations!"

"I wasn't always accountable to Vickery," he said.

Hanna had had an inadvertent hand in Jameson's fall from power. She took his last remark as a reproach, though perhaps it was not meant to be one.

Dear Samuel, I didn't know you felt that way for me. You didn't when I left, did you? It's just missing me? I'm sorry, I'm sorry, I never thought of you that way. Don't wait for me. Go on to someone else. But please say you'll still be my friend. Good-bye, good-bye.

"How can you negotiate with a man you know nothing about?" Jameson asked another day.

"The same way," Hanna nearly snarled—she had been saying good-byes all the morning—"I negotiated with the People on Zeig-Daru. And with Rubee and Awnlee. Do you think I can't assess a human being?"

"It's never been your strong point in the past!" Jameson's temper was frayed, too.

"From what I remember about the *Pavonis Queen,* there won't be *time* to negotiate. You can't negotiate when you're full of sleepygas!"

"He has left Valentine again. His offices there say he may be away some time. He filed no flight plan; Valentine does not require the filing of flight plans by private pilots. You have never met anyone like him before."

"There are not that many varieties of true-humans."

"He was a Registered Friend at seventeen. He must have known every worst thing there is to know about men, yes, both men and women, before he was twenty-one. He put much of his earnings into education, and saved the rest: an aberration in a Friend. He also cultivated extralegal contacts from the day he came to Valentine. When he met Tonson—who made several trips to Valentine in those years, and was Kristofik's client—he was ready. I&S believes he had been searching for such an opportunity from the start. You need to know about him, Hanna."

"I do not." She smiled; not a pretty smile; savage.

"I'd like to meet him, though. He'd be a refreshing change, don't you think? I have some calls to make. If I come see you it will be from curiosity."

Jameson's smile was not pleasant either. "I don't care about your motives. Just do it."

"I hope that when relations are established and I can come home, I can come back to the House and do my work for Koroth. I have worked so much for the Polity that I have been useless at home. If I cannot end it, perhaps I should leave the House altogether. If you find out where my mother is, would you please tell her I love her? And say good-bye. Good-bye. Good-bye."

* * *

Something tickled the far reaches of Michael's memory from time to time. *The Rose.* He could almost remember something it meant. When he repeated the phrase it had an edge to it, as if there were connotations buried in his mind that distorted the common flower name.

He might have started a search program for The Rose as soon as Gian left, but the general access information networks would have a billion references to roses. He did not even know what category to start with.

In the night he woke to a thought that stopped his breath: might The Rose be one of the things he could not remember, the whole reason for the search for the many-named man?

But then he started breathing again. He was certain that wherever he had heard of The Rose, it had been recently; part of his adulthood, at least.

The next day he searched a few classes at random. Planets?—he had never heard of one so named, but it might be a variant or the local name for a world known officially as something else. It might be a star or a satellite or an asteroid. But it was not, or so the networks told him.

"Spaceships?" said Theo, and got a quick response, and tied up data retrieval the rest of the day tracking down forty-two vessels named *Rose*, none of which were likely to have anything to do with the man Michael wanted.

"People," Shen suggested the morning after that.

"Bars," said Theo wistfully.

"I don't think we're getting anywhere," Michael said.

He got them back to work, with some difficulty—it was this week's day for an army of housekeepers and groundskeepers to descend on the estate and impose order on it—and tried to work himself. He had investments to look after. It was hard to keep his mind on them, though, and anyway he was not necessary to their success.

"In fact," said the man who managed most of them, "I was looking forward to that long trip you were talking about."

Michael smiled at the dark face on the telescreen. "I just couldn't stay away, Kareem. I'll leave again; any day now."

"The sooner the better!"

Shen was nearby, taking a break from haranguing gardeners. When Kareem Mar-Kize's face disappeared, she said, "Not so."

"What's not so?"

"Better. Not so." She glided closer, stood over him, leaned over and poked a rigid finger into his belly. The flesh did not yield, but she said, "Soft."

"I am not."

"Lived good too long. Baby girls, stray cats—"

"Like you."

"Like me. Listen, that Gian, say he knew more. Call that an answer? You want answers? Ways to get 'em. One way or another."

"I know Valentine. I know how he thinks. Go away and let *me* think."

The thing he was trying to remember twitched at intervals through the day. Theo and Shen stayed away. The animals of the house came one by one to doze in the warm afternoon. None were native to Valentine; humanity's bonds with its pets stretched back beyond recorded history, and humans had not been on Valentine long enough to breed anything native into something that could be loved. But dogs lay at Michael's feet, cats stalked through the shade, a kitten slept on his knee; presently a F'thalian tourmaline, an exotic abandoned by some human visitor to Valentine, inched up his arm and perched on his shoulder. Later Lise, too, came to the open-air study where he watched the sun and shadows. She stayed some distance from him, curled in a chair with a reader in her lap that showed pictures of pretty clothes. She did not say a word and it was impossible to guess what she thought. He supposed she was occupied with new plans for ravaging his credit, to which he had given her access; the string of deliveries, having driven Shen nearly mad, had tapered off, but probably not for long. Lise had not wanted to live with Flora, she refused with lamentations to be parted from Michael, and was on her way to becoming a permanent member of the household.

The sun finished its morning arc and the shadows grew long. The blossoms of the trees Gian had seen only in darkness blazed brighter in the slanting light. They were hardly more colorful than the flowers mounded at their feet: D'neeran millefleurs, difficult to grow most places, but here showing their native bent for taking over everything around them. They were so much a fixture that most days Michael scarcely saw them. But it was the millefleurs—little known outside their home, obscure symbols of a place off traveled paths—that gave him the idea.

In the evening he went back to the computer and specified a search. He wrote: "Subject—human settlements, associated features, geographical or social, Standard or colloquial terminology. Exclude Earth. Exclude all cities above population 100,000. Exclude all official place names. Mark: Rose. Search."

He left the program running and went for a walk outdoors. He had bought the house and grounds two Standard years before from the heirs of a gambling magnate who had finally died in spite of all that artificial organs could do. There was no satisfactory replacement for the whole of a deteriorating brain. The place was not a home, but it was the closest he had ever had to one.

When he was tired of walking, he sat on a wooden bench and listened to the sea. He was high above it, but it was audible from here, a steady thump-and-rumble, the pulsebeat of a planet.

After a while Shen came to find him, unerring in the dark. She carried a light and a long printout. She sat beside him and gave the things to him without comment. He looked at the printout and saw that the computer had finished its search.

"The Rose: Colloq. Mt. Greene, near Thule, Montana, Heartworld.

"The Rose: ST. Biennial underwater race limited to modified human organisms. Town of Eiger, Nestor.

"The Rose(s): Colloq. Metatree forest near Hai, Coop."

There were more entries like that. He scanned them impatiently. Near the bottom of the list he saw: The Rose: ST (1) Stone venerated by The People of the Rose, Riordan's Revenge. (2) The People of the Rose."

Shen saw his attention. "That it?"

"I don't know. I've been there. A long time ago, ten years maybe. I forgot about the 'Riordan' part, I only heard it called Revenge. Come on, let's look it up."

They went back to the house and got what they wanted immediately. Riordan's Revenge was obscure, but properly cataloged. Michael read:

"Riordan's Revenge is one of thirty planets visited and reported as habitable by Miles Riordan in the years 2463 through 2481, only two of which—Riordan's Revenge and Isle—are actually classifiable as such.

" 'Revenge' is little known and is seldom visited except by representatives of the Colonial Oversight and Protection Service once each Standard year, and by merchantmen on no fixed schedule. Though terrestrial in composition and atmosphere, the planet is locked in an ice age which may be permanent. (See Subfile 1.) Revenge is considered marginally habitable, under the guidelines of the Colonial Oversight and Protection Service, only in the following regions: (a) The so-called Long Archipelago, approximately 8N-12S, 60E-75E; (b) the southernmost portion of the planet's largest continent, the habitable portion lying 6N-4S, 94W-113W. Even in these areas the growing season is short, and the population of Riordan's Revenge relies exclusively on accelerated-growth crop strains for agricultural sustenance.''

There was more, but Michael quit reading. His memory had gotten the jog it needed. The City of the Rose was not a city but a scanty town, ugly under a cold sun. Stone ranging rust to scarlet in brutal outcroppings of rock; rose-shapes everywhere and a temple whose interior no unbeliever could see; pathological rejection of outsiders, so that Revenge did not have Inspace communications, not even a single transmitter; veiled women he had hardly glimpsed, because they feared defilement if an infidel's gaze fell on them—

A man could hide on Revenge.

''Mike?'' said Theo, reading over Shen's shoulder

''Yeah?''

''Why would he go there?''

''Stay out of sight. Stay hidden. Maintain a base? Where'd he dock that 'vette he got? Where'd he go to install the guns? You want to be hidden for something like that. Cheaper to do it in atmosphere.''

He spoke with authority; from experience.

''Think this might be it?'' Shen said.

''Worth a try, maybe. It's his kind of place.'' His breath caught. Shen looked at him narrowly. ''God, yes, it's his kind of place,'' Michael said with feeling. ''Isolated, primitive, helpless—that's why I went there. But it wasn't the place.''

Theo had punched up a subfile. He said practically, ''It's a long way out. That Riordan, he must have been right out on the edge when exploration slowed down. That was just before it did, wasn't it?''

''It was at the very end of the Explosion,'' Michael said. He did not have to search his memory for details of the great age of exploration; he had made himself an expert on the topic. ''I know about Miles Riordan. He was one of the reasons they put the freelancers out of business. Then the big colonies started breaking away,

Heartworld first and then Willow and Co-op, and nobody had time for exploring.''

Shen folded her arms and stared at him without expression. She said, ''Catch up this time, maybe. Lousy place. No people. No people, no cover. You get spotted first. GeeGee's got no guns. Shields'll stop a meteorite. No more. Stupid.''

''Yes,'' he said.

''Crazy man.''

''I want him alive. I want his records intact. The guns come later.''

Shen said to Theo, ''Crazy man wins all the arguments. You noticed? Start packing.''

Michael nodded. They would be in space by morning.

* * *

There was a full moon the night before Hanna entered quarantine, the night she finally went to see Jameson. She rode under it in an Admin aircar, and the moon-frosted land below slipped past like water. The aircar made no sound. It homed in on Admin and guided itself. Hanna, with nothing to do but be carried through the silver night, thought she stood still over the turning Earth. She thought perversely that she could change course, fly away at random, look down on the busy towns and quiet countryside contemplative and unseen. Why not?—all her good-byes were said. Admin could not possess her much longer; her ties with Earth, with all of human space, attenuated. It was the same for Rubee and Awnlee. Of late they seemed more alien, not less; as if the days running past already brought them nearer to their home, and they could begin to take off a conforming skin they had worn politely through the months with humankind. The vast gulf waited for all of them.

The guards at Admin's rooftop hardly bothered to check Hanna's identity. *Not bad for a spacer from D'neera.* The tubes that wound through Admin shot her down, south, east, and spat her out at Jameson's door.

With luck I will not come here again, she thought, saw in his puzzled face that some of the thought had escaped her, and to forestall a question said good evening hurriedly.

"What is it you want me to see?" she asked.

"Oh—" Her abruptness startled him. He drew her into Contact's deserted rooms and said, "It is an historical piece. In a manner of speaking."

"It is about this man? This ghost who haunts I&S?"

"Yes, of course. Also this is farewell, or nearly," he added, and when they came to his inner chamber she was prepared to accept with courtesy a glass of wine, a stirrup cup—courteously, because Rubee and Awnlee had taught her more about manners than all her life before.

"You can regard the file as the evening's entertainment," he said.

He had forgotten or chose to ignore the past days' strain. Hanna was glad to let it pass. She settled onto a couch that tested the contours of her body, shuddered and reshaped itself to her measure. Jameson sat beside her and the couch shuddered again. *Universal minor earthquakes,* she thought.

"Is it a pageant?" she said. "Like Rubee's tales?"

"How odd that you should say that." He smiled; the parting near at hand might be a relief to him, too. "I haven't been immersed in the tales as you have," he said, "but I must confess I find myself at times reinterpreting events as an Uskosian might, or as I imagine he might. What you'll see is interesting enough without adding an alien perspective, however. It's neither text nor pageant; it's a holo recording of an interview between an I&S investigator and the former head of the Abbey of St. Kristofik on Alta. The abbot is dead now; the monks believe an extended lifespan pleases the Deity less than a natural one. I'm told that shortly after he died an anonymous donor made a generous gift to the school in his memory. The source was Valentine; you can make what you want of that. The interview took place fifteen years ago, five years after the *Pavonis Queen* incident. It concerns events that happened even earlier, between the time Kristofik appeared on Alta and the time he left—ran away, the abbot said, to Valentine.''

Hanna started to say: *It seems irrelevant.* But Jameson spoke an order and the room went dark, and before she could say anything there was a new burst of light, the light of a holographic projection that took up most of the room. In its center, stone-still but three-dimensional, stood two men. One, cloaked and booted in black, had the look of assured competence that marked the men and women of Admin. The morning light left no shadows on his ebony skin. Surely he looked just the same today, performed the duties of the present with confidence. Fog lay on the fields behind him, as on a damp morning in autumn. Also he stood on gray-white stone, so that Hanna's eye fell automatically on his darkness and solidity, drawn to the only thing of substance in that land of mist.

The other man was old and pale. His cropped hair was snowy, and the top of his head was bald. He wore a long white robe loosely belted with rope. He was frail beside the investigator, an aged wraith, part mist, part old white stone. More than age twisted his face, but Hanna did not know what it was until the figures moved; then she saw that it was sorrow.

"I am still trying to assimilate what you have told me . . . Accept it? No, not yet. I cannot accept it yet. I must forgive, but my charity falls short. In time. Time and prayer . . ."

The investigator listened, but the old man spoke to himself. They walked together on stone pathways, past twisted trees or treelike shrubs, stone walls, stone statues, white and ghostly.

The old man said, "To think the boy I knew could do that deed! And then you say he turned to evil long before!"

The other man said quietly, "There is evidence to support the theory that he was involved in the matter I spoke of. There is no doubt about the rest of it."

"Oh dear, oh dear, how distressing this is! Please

forgive me. You have questions, don't you? I'm not helping much.''

"I'm sorry to have such news to bring. Believe me, I am sorry. You were fond of him?''

"Yes. Yes, I was. It was a blow when he ran away. I always hoped to hear of him someday. To have news at last, and such news!''

There was a stone bench by the path. The old man sat down on it, gathering his robe with a wrinkled hand. His face was unabashedly grieved. "Oh,'' he said, "his immortal soul! How I pity him!''

"I'm very sorry.'' The investigator remained standing.

"Yes, yes, I know. Pray for him. I will, all of us will. That's all that's left to do. We failed, you know, failed at everything else we should have done. That's plain enough!''

The I&S man waited a moment. Then he said, "You understand that I must get as much information about him as I can. I hoped you could tell me how he came here, what he was like, what he thought about, why he left.''

"Oh dear, oh dear. What he thought about? Who knows? Things I never guessed. There must have been things I never saw. His confessor, maybe—but that is out of the question,'' he said, the old voice suddenly stone, and he looked at the investigator with eyes of iron.

"Of course,'' said the I&S man mildly. "I don't think we need to worry about that. Just tell me where he came from.''

"I don't know where he came from.'' The old man stirred; there was a new glint in his eye. "Do you want to hear a mystery?'' he said.

"By all means.''

"Well, then, I will tell you a mystery. You can confirm it with the secular authorities. I won't say you can find out more about it; you won't find out any more. Eleven years ago—pardon, me, fifteen in Standard time—I came out of the rear gate one morning—have you seen all our grounds? No? The rear gate opens on

an alley behind the sheds where we keep our tools.
Sometimes we put food scraps in the alley. It doesn't
happen often. We waste very little here. That morning
Brother Cook burnt the bread. Some of it was past saving, and so it was put out for the dogs. Later I went
out, I forget why I went, I forgot it then and never could
remember. I found him in the alley. He was too busy
eating to hear me. He was so starved there was no room
in his belly for caution; there was only the hunger. When
I spoke to him, he would have run away, but he would
not leave the bread. I think he would have killed me if
I had tried to take it from him. A wild animal. Nothing
but bones, and at the time when a boy can hardly keep
up with his bones, they grow so fast. His eyes were
yellow, a strange sick color. Later it went away. Do you
know how I finally got him to trust me? With food. Like
an animal. And so we took him in."

"Was he from Alta?"

"Oh, no. I don't know where he came from, but it
wasn't anywhere on Alta. Listen to this. He did not
understand Standard speech, and we could make nothing of what he said. We recorded it and sent it, oh,
everywhere. To Earth; even to Earth. The report would
be still in his file. It said the language he spoke came
from Earth, originally, I mean. As long ago as the
twenty-fourth century, they said, his people must have
been isolated; just before Standard was mandated, or
maybe just after, so they hadn't got into the habit of
using it. I don't remember what language it was. He
learned Standard fast. He always learned fast."

"So he came from a colony? Which one?"

"That's the mystery, you see. I said there was a mystery. No one knows. The dialect didn't match anything."

"Who did this report?"

"Oh, famous people. Experts." The old man looked
up, bright-eyed. "You know, during the Explosion, in
the early days, the colonists went out so fast, so many
from all parts of Earth, the records broke down. Ships
vanished, too. Hundreds of them. Hundreds of thou-
sands of people, I think it was millions, they fell into
space and disappeared. I think about that sometimes. I

thought about it when he was here. You've heard of the Lost Worlds?''

"Yes," said the other man, "but I don't believe in them. I'd like to see that report, if I may.''

"Of course you can. But you'll find it says just what I've said.''

"All right. How did he get to Alta from wherever it was?''

"I don't know. We guessed. A month before I found him a merchant put in at the port here. There were others, merchants and freighters come here all the time, but the others had nothing to hide. They were tracked and questioned. They'd never seen him. One of them couldn't be tracked. The port here isn't as careful as the ones in the Polity. That's what I'm told; I wouldn't know. When they looked into it they said the registration was false. There was no ship with that number and name.''

"He could have told you something, surely. When he learned Standard.''

"Could have, but didn't.'' The old man's grief had eased as he told the story. It caught up with him now. He bowed his head and took hold of the coarse rope that gathered his robe. There were knots in it; he fingered them as if for comfort. The investigator waited patiently. Presently the abbot began to speak, slowly.

"We asked him. He said he didn't know. I think he told the truth. That was at the beginning. When he said it, his eyes had that lost look, the look you see on children's faces when they've lost everything, parents, homes, and don't know why, don't understand why they've been hurt. We had sixty boys here then, homeless children from everywhere. It's near eighty now. Their faces run together now that I'm old. But he stands out. He was a beautiful child when we got some meat on him. He had beautiful hands, too, except, you know, they'd been broken. Broken on purpose, the doctors said, and set too late and badly. They weren't good for much. So I took him to Willow myself to have them fixed. There were signs of—of other kinds of violence. I don't need to tell you about that. It's in his file.''

The I&S man hesitated, let it pass. "All right. He

was injured, starving, came out of nowhere, as far as he and you knew. What about later? There should have been evidence of his origin.''

''He said he didn't remember anything. He always said that.'' The old man lifted his head. His face was dreamy with remembering. The investigator let him run on unchecked. ''He meant he didn't want to talk about it. At first we told him if he helped us find the place, maybe he could go home. I think he didn't want to. I think it was the worst thing we could have ever said. 'I remember nothing,' he said, he was frightened, and he stuck to that always, though I taxed him with lying, scolded him, taught him the evil of falsehood as well as I could. Yet for the most part he was a good boy. He was lively and intelligent, a leader. The boys of his time looked up to him. Did his lessons, did his chores, worked hard, played hard, the way a boy should. I don't know what he said to God. He went through the forms. I don't know what they meant to him, I don't know what the memories meant that he wouldn't tell us. I used to worry about it. It was deceptive because he seemed—''

The old man stopped suddenly. A minute went by. The investigator stirred and seemed about to speak. But the other man went on, slowly now. ''When he had been here awhile, he seemed so open. Sunny. When I think of him, I see him smiling. It makes me forget—it made me forget. The first year wasn't smooth. He fought with other boys, bigger boys. When he did, he was like an animal again, the wild animal I saw at the start. We told him finally we couldn't keep him if he kept doing that. After that he mastered it, we thought, the demon in him—''

The pause was longer this time. At last the investigator said neutrally, ''Perhaps he did.''

''Oh, I know, you don't believe in demons, do you?'' There was irony in the old eyes now. ''They come in many forms, you know. They gnaw at human weakness. They fatten on pain. Our exorcisms are sophisticated, these days. We tried. We tried all that love could do. We tried to help him trust us. But he never talked about where he came from, never told us what he'd been through, not even a hint. Brother Healer tried every trick he knew, too. Said he knew pain when he saw it, said it wasn't good to let it fester in a child, said it could make monsters. But he never got anywhere.''

The old man fell silent, eyes on the stone at his feet. After a while the investigator said, ''Did he say anything to you when he left?''

''Nothing. One morning he wasn't here.''

''Had he given you reason to think he might go?''

''No. I don't know why he did it. I must not have known him at all. I must have been blind.'' The old man had been staring at the paving stones. He lifted his head and looked outward, straight at Hanna. ''The seeds must have grown all the time he was here. I never saw it. I know *how* he left. A freighter from Willow signed him on. He was not well educated, not by your standards, but he was strong and quick to learn. We learned the freighter took him to Valentine. I was afraid when I heard that, but I thought . . . He had a strong will. He wasn't docile; when I say a boy is good, I don't mean that. I prayed. I did not think he would be bent to vice against his will.''

''I've heard nothing to indicate it was against his will.''

''No. No, of course it wasn't. Corruption doesn't work that way. The sinner collaborates with the sin. He knew about Valentine. He knew enough to choose. We don't try to keep the children from the knowledge of evil. They need to know the enemy to guard against him. We teach them to shun the tempter. Sometimes we fail.''

The old man looked as if he might weep. The investigator said, ''I won't trouble you any more now, sir. Except that I'd like to get a record of his file, especially the linguistic report.''

''Certainly. Certainly.''

The old man got to his feet. He was even paler now, the color of the stone, and bent.

''Where did you get his name?'' the investigator asked. ''Did you name him Michael?''

''We did. What he said when we asked him his name sounded something like that.''

They walked in silence; thinned to mist; disappeared. Hanna found she had been holding her breath. She

said, as if she had been listening to a good story ended
too soon, "Isn't there more?"

"Hmm?" Jameson looked at her curiously when normal light returned. The light was warm, but not bright;
after the pearly radiance of a fog-washed morning on
Alta, it was stuffy and confining.

"Nothing . . ." She held herself still. The gaze she
turned on Jameson was cool. She said, "Why have you
shown me this?"

"It's interesting, don't you think?"

"You did not have me watch it for its intrinsic interest."

"Granted." He got up and moved across the room. She
regarded the broad back coldly, knowing that in the silence
he examined a range of words and picked among them. At
last he said, "If the worst should happen you will need to
know how to deal with him. I believe the key to this man
lies in his earliest days. Which are dark. Dark to him because they are shadowed by hunger and violence; dark to
everyone else because they are hidden."

"Perhaps I can take a thorn from his paw and make
him my friend," Hanna said a little wearily.

He swung around and gave her a look that was not as
friendly as before. "A classical reference? From you?"

"Me? The over-specialized H'ana? No, don't worry,
I won't disillusion you. I only know about it because
there is a similar tale among the Uskosians, and someone told me about the parallel. Starr, you take this man
too seriously—all because the I&S computers bumped
out his name."

"I take their judgment seriously enough to be glad
the person going with Rubee is capable of quick defen-
sive action."

She said immediately, "No. I'm done with that."

"I hope so," he said, and now he was deliberately
mild. "I know how you feel about it; about, especially,
the Zeigans you killed. I understand your reluctance to
consider doing anything of the kind again. Yet the fact
remains that you were trained for war, and you fought
in an interhuman war; and later, in a desperate situation
with the People of Zeig-Daru, you were capable of do-

ing what you had to do. I hope you are never again put to that test. But consider, Hanna, what this man is. Consider: after the monks had saved him and sheltered him for years, he left them without a word and went straight to a life they despised. Then there was the leap to piracy and, most likely, murder. Will you smile at him and wait for him to kiss your hand?''

Hanna's mouth twisted. Put that way it was horrible. She said, ''There was a Lost World. Nobody knew about it fifteen years ago. But the Zeigans destroyed it long before our time, before his time. He couldn't have come from there.''

''If he got to Alta from a Lost World, it couldn't be considered lost,'' Jameson said sensibly. ''There are enough backward pocket settlements even within the Polity to keep a linguist occupied for eternity. I don't put much stock in the abbot's speculations. I should think their healer was right, though, when he spoke of monsters being made.''

''I would be interested in seeing his psyche profile,'' Hanna said, and then, because he gave her an odd look, ''what's wrong with that?''

''I don't have it,'' Jameson said.

She might have let it go, except that she sensed a rare uncertainty in him. ''Did you try to get it?'' she said.

''Yes. Figueiredo said it was not to be disseminated outside I&S. He said it was anomalous and contradictory. He ascribed this,'' James said—with a straight face, but Hanna saw the amusement behind it—''to the fact that an I&S operative who got close to him, and ought to have been a definitive source of information, was female.''

''Oh, nonsense!''

''I think so, too. Still, for whatever reason, there is no consistent and therefore no valid profile.''

''Well, if you start with the presumption that your subject is a monster, and then he doesn't act like one, I suppose you have trouble putting the pieces together.''

Hanna gave up. She wanted to go home, or to what passed for it here. This would be her last night planet-bound for some weeks; the quarantine facility orbited

Luna. After that her course would take her outward; past Heartworld, which she had visited, and Carrollis, which she had never seen; past a settlement named Revenge, which she had never even heard of until the *Bird's* course became important; and after that on and out and out. She said before she left, though: "All this is a waste of time, isn't it? There's no sign of tampering with the program; not if you've told me everything."

"I've told you everything. I'm uneasy, all the same."

She gave the last words little thought when he said them. She did not mean to think about Michael Kristofik any more at all. But she yielded to her wish to ride the wind in the Earthly night, high above silver and black; and as she sailed through the moonlight the reason came to her for Kristofik's irrational effect on I&S and Admin, Jameson and Figueiredo and all of them. They were the keepers of order and rules, and the stranger from nowhere cared nothing for any of it, and ignored both rules and keepers; successfully, too.

During the week she spent in the isolation chamber, they took so much blood from her that she became weak. Each time they took some they came back and fed her more chemicals, poisonous brews some of which contained living creatures. The ones put straight into her veins did not make up for loss of blood. They said she would make more quickly. They had to get it right, though it would be impossible for her to walk among human beings until she came home and the work was undone. They were stripping her of her immunity to certain dangerous organisms at large in human society, because in some way she did not understand it was incompatible with immunity to common Uskosian equivalents. Rubee and Awnlee, separated from her for now, endured the process in reverse.

Hanna did what was asked of her, and otherwise withdrew from human intercourse. She had planned the withdrawal, not consciously, for a long time; she understood that almost as soon as she entered quarantine. The isolation chamber was built into a habitat in orbit around Luna. The accommodations were spare but comfortable, and though she could not touch another human being (except those swathed in protective garments), she could talk freely with anyone she knew at any distance. She might have said her good-byes then. But she had planned, not consciously, to get that done beforehand. She was finished because she had sensed a subtle internal warning that she would need this space of time in between Earth and embarkation, though she hardly knew for what.

The reason unfolded as the quiet days passed. When first she stepped into her chamber she sighed and felt relief; thereafter all her thoughts turned away from Earth. She did not so much think as feel; feel Earth drop away from far under her feet, not physically, not yet, but in importance; feel Rubee and Awnlee as lodestones close by; feel her thought change as her body changed to something that could no longer stay whole among humans.

* * *

In a year Nlatee said to his sire, "With fire we might warm ourselves in winter, and the path to the land of the mountains of fire is not long."

The path was discouraged by the Master of Chaos, however, and Nlatee's sire and all his sire's selfings and all the people sought to dissuade him. They said, "Who knows what will happen to us if you take that path?"

Nlatee on a night therefore broke open the winter stores and took what he needed, and he set out alone on the path to the land of the mountains of fire.

On a day of his journey the Master of Chaos came to him and said, "I see that you travel, Nlatee. Where are you going?"

Nlatee, because the Master had discouraged this path, answered, "I am going to the great river yonder, to steal fish from the persons who live there."

"That is forbidden by treaty, Nlatee."

"Then I will take care they do not catch me."

The Master signified amusement, and disappeared.

Nlatee thought it would be best for the Master to see him no more; yet how could he not be seen? Who knows what the Master sees?

*While Nlatee pondered this he saw a beast. He killed
it and skinned it and while he ate its meat he said to
himself, "This path is not discouraged to beasts. If I
were a beast, the Master would not notice me."*

*An so he put the skin of the beast on his shoulders
and its horn on his head, and went on his way clothed
in the hide of the beast.*

*Nlatee went on his way and the land was warm though
it was winter, because he came near to the mountains
of fire and they warmed all the land about them, so that
green things flourished forever. He came to the mountains of fire and there he kindled a flame, and he returned with it to his land.*

*When his sire and all his sire's selfings and all the
people saw that he had tricked the Master of Chaos and
that no evil had come to them as a result, they took the
fire and warmed themselves, and would have made Nlatee head huntsman. But Nlatee refused.*

*"I am going back to the land of the mountains of fire,
and there I will bring forth my selfings and rear them,"
he said.*

"But why?" said all the people.

*"It's warmer there," said Nlatee, "and if the fire
goes out you can rekindle it easily. I don't like it here
any more."*

*So Nlatee returned to the land of the mountains of fire
where all was green forever, and in later years his descendants warred with the descendants of his sire's other
selfings and with the descendants of all the people, and
the descendants of Nlatee won because if their fires went
out they could easily be rekindled.*

*And the Master of Chaos came, and signified amuse-
ment.*

* * *

From her position deep in the interior of the habitat,
Hanna could not see Luna or Earth or any stars; yet
paradoxically, though she was confined and enclosed,
her awareness of infinity outside grew and grew. She
did not need to look out to see stars. They were there

when she closed her eyes, rank on rank of them, blazing in spinning islands. Always deep space had drawn her, from the first; always her desire had led her there; she had commanded her first Jump at fifteen. *I am an exopsychologist. That is what I do.* Being an exopsychologist was a fine excuse for straying on the edges of space. Was that the real reason for the paths she had chosen? The knowledge of her connection to the great void expanded daily, hourly it seemed. The universe was in motion, it vibrated, it shouted with joy, thunderous. She stood stock-still in a bare sealed room and listened to it. She was an arrow in the instant before release. She heard a great heart beating, and she would fly to it as to a homecoming.

On the very last day before launch Starr Jameson came to see her. It was day where he had come from; in Hanna's chamber, attuned to the rhythms of the *Far-Flying Bird*, it was night. A transparent barrier separated them, and there was dusk on her side of it. Rubee and Awnlee slept; Hanna heard them sleeping. She stood at the barrier and watched Jameson pretend to find her normal. It was hot inside the chamber, as it would be on the *Far-Flying Bird*. Hanna's concession is to Earthly convention were sloughing off one by one, she wore nothing but scraps of fabric molded round her breasts and hips, and her body distracted him. It was something to get a physical reaction from a man futilely desired for so long.

He talked dispassionately enough. He told her about all the precautions Contact and I&S had taken. It did not matter now that there would be no armed escort for the *Bird*. The course program was secure; it was more secure than any other knowledge in human space. All the anxiety had been over a rumor, a wisp, a nothing. He had come to reassure her so she would not be afraid.

That was considerate of him. Hanna listened, and thought that here was someone else who had taken blood from her. The fullness of the freely, generously given self was a memory; her love had gone wrong somehow; it had become thin and acid and if she let it would only leach the life out of her. After tonight she could put it far behind her. She was eager to be gone.

At the very last he said, "I will not see you again until you return. Rubee rejected the idea of a formal leavetaking."

"I know. He wanted to be alone with Awnlee. They have spent much time in meditation."

"So I hear. An attitude of prayer, I'm told."

"Oh, no, it's not that."

"No? I'm afraid I've never gotten it straight about the Master of Chaos. None of us have yet."

"I wrote a paper about it."

"But no one understood it."

"I'll try again when I get back, or while I'm gone. But you must have understood that they don't worship the Master. They recognize his hand, they beseech him, they curse him—but they do not worship him."

"That seems very wise of them," he said.

Because he could not touch her to say good-bye, he put his hands against the barrier. She set her own, much smaller, against them. It seemed that a trick of dimension had set him far away. Before he went away finally, he turned to look at her once more. He hesitated. She saw herself just for a moment as he saw her: beautiful, unique, a creature who moved freely through strangeness and somehow always came back to being Hanna. He had known her for a long time, he had watched the shaping of her, and he was so used to her that the fresh perception of the moment surprised him profoundly. It seemed to her that he might come back.

Hanna turned away. She melted into the darkness of her chamber and did not sleep, and waited for the hour when she could come to the *Far-Flying Bird.*

* * *

"There's the bastard," Shen said after the last Jump. It brought them out close to Revenge, compensating for the season so that they were at the right place in the planet's orbit and even looking at its dayside. It was still a million klicks away, and they boosted magnification for a better view. Cloud and ice made it nearly all white; it reflected back the light of the determined star and never got warmer, it was ice and ice and ice. A surge in the sun's radiation might make it productive, that or terra-forming. But nobody needed it badly enough to bother with terraforming. It was left to the People of the Rose.

"Got something on infrared," Shen said. "Just vul-canization, though."

Michael said, "*GeeGee*. Is it day or night at the set-tlement?"

"Night," said his ship laconically.

"Check again when it comes around," Shen said. She got up and stretched. *GeeGee* would handle the final approach. Michael stayed where he was, looking out at the sterile brilliance of Revenge. Presently he began to sing. It was a measured dirge.

> *There were three ravens sat on a tree,*
> *Downe a down, hay downe a down;*
> *And they were black as they might be,*
> *With a downe.*
> *One of them said to his mate,*
> *When shall we our breakfast take?*
> *With a downe, derrie derrie down . . .*

Shen made a rude noise and disappeared. Michael sang on.

> *Down in yonder green field,*
> *Downe a down, hay downe a down,*
> *Lies a slain knight under his shield*
> *With a downe . . .*

Lise unpeeled herself from the wall of *GeeGee's* con-trol center. She was pink and gold, the walls and car-peting were the color of a ripe apricot, the light was faintly golden and suited Lise well. She belonged here; Michael and Shen, grim and dark, did not. No wonder he had thought of ravens. She came lightly to the seat Shen had left and dropped into it. She said, "Why doesn't Shen like the song? I like it."

"It's a sad song."

He leaned back and put an arm around her thin shoulders. She had gotten it into her head that he preferred grown-up women, and accepted him happily as a kind of older brother; though, "I will be grown up someday," she had said.

"What are ravens?"

"Big black birds."

"Like swans?"

"No, and what you're thinking of aren't really swans. They just call them that on Carrollis. Ravens aren't that big."

"What did they have for breakfast?"

He turned his head and looked at the fresh, pretty face, into the bright blue eyes. He said gently, "They didn't have breakfast that morning."

"It isn't good to be hungry," she said seriously.

"I know."

They sat in companionable silence for a time. *GeeGee's* motion was not perceptible, but Revenge was a little larger. Presently Lise said, "Why didn't Shen want me to come? This is fun."

"She didn't want you to come because it might be dangerous. She's right, too. If we hadn't left so fast, if I'd been able to think of anything to do with you, you wouldn't be here. I'm telling you right now that you're not getting off this ship until I tell you you can. Do you hear me?"

She looked rebellious, but she nodded. She said with a startling switch to adulthood, "What's all this about?"

"None of your business, little puss."

"I will find out," she said placidly.

"I bet you will." He grinned, but quit at a vision of Lise in the hands of the man he hunted. She nestled in the crook of his arm, excited by her new status as a traveler. Once upon a time he had taken responsibility for Theo, and once again for Shen. A lump of defeat that could not be called a man. A madwoman who had tried to kill him for a handful of cash. This was different. But probably he would not be on Revenge anyway, Chrome-Maxwell-Pallin-Anyname.

Must have had a thousand names in thirty years. B they called him thirty years ago, just B. Saw him once in

Shoreground later. Putting together the stake then. Looking for the chance. Knew it was Tonson, didn't know how. Thought about that, nothing else, wasn't room for more. Coming out of Flora's. Mind's not on your work, she said. Lady had complaints, Mike. Said you were bored. Sorry, won't happen again, pretty boring lady you know what I mean. Walked out and there he was. Looked at me straight. Knew me. Smiled I knew that goddamned smile take it off with his face with a blade if I see it again. Went round the corner, I got there he was gone. Almost had him in my hands and he was gone.

"Mike? That hurts." He looked down at Lise and saw pain in her eyes. His fingers clutched her shoulder too hard. He let go quickly.

"Sorry, puss. Didn't mean to do that."

She said, dismissing it, "Can I watch the landing?"

"Sure you can."

"When?"

"Later. When it's day there."

She smiled, the ache in her shoulder forgotten. They watched Revenge come closer.

Michael knew what to expect of Revenge. Theo had not been there before; he began making noises of displeasure as soon as the *Golden Girl* came to a landing outside the city of The Rose. It was early in autumn, but the red rock jutted in patches from a layer of ice; there were clouds over the city and it brooded bitterly under the gray ceiling. The city was scattered over the rocks instead of the snow-covered fields close by, as if the settlers had chosen to make things difficult for themselves. There were some seven hundred buildings, all low and making no use of the ubiquitous rock; they were premanufactured structures of varying ages and designs, some welded together, badly married. At the end of the descent they had seen people moving in the city, and the *Golden Girl* must have been seen also; in a place like this the ship could only be an object of wonder; yet they landed only half a kilometer from the nearest modules, and nothing moved outside them.

Michael said, "Come on, Theo. Let's go see if we can find somebody to talk to."

"Looks nasty. *I* should go," Shen said.

"They're harmless—at least they always have been. I've never done anything to get them mad. I wouldn't take a woman with me, though, not and expect any cooperation."

"Me," Lise said softly. She tugged at Michael's arm.

"Not you. Especially not you."

He detached himself and went with Theo to find winter gear, warmcoats, heated boots. When they left the *Golden Girl*, they still had not seen a single inhabitant. The walk was short but not easy. The *Golden Girl's* landing site was the only flat place among the rocks; a hundred meters from the ship they had to begin climbing over them or skirting them. There was ice underfoot, and stones that turned treacherously. When they passed the first buildings, there were people at last: half a dozen small boys, bundled in black. One held a ball, another a tapering metal rod. Perhaps they had been playing with the objects. Now they stood and stared.

Michael said, "Hello. We come from the Polity. I want to speak to an elder."

Theo muttered, "Polity?"

"I don't know if they've heard of Valentine. They know about the Polity."

For a minute there was no reaction at all from the boys. Then one moved; he took off at a dead run into the town.

"Is that an answer?" Theo said.

"I don't know. Maybe. We'll wait."

They waited a long time. The children did not go back to their game. They stayed where they were and stared. Michael felt a prickly wrongness and tracked it down. He got on well with children and knew their ways; he and Theo could not have come in such a way to another such isolated place without being surrounded by children and besieged with questions when the first shyness wore off. But not here.

The boy who had run away did not come back. An adult came finally, moving without haste through a stony

channel that could not be called a street. A cap covered
his ears and clung to his skull. He was heavily bearded
and dressed, like the children, in a loose black tunic
and trousers. There was no warmcoat, though, nor any
real protection against the cold. The season would not
be cold for him.

He said a word and the children moved away, walking
quickly but not running. One disappeared into a house
nearby. The others straggled on and vanished among
the rocks and structures beyond. The word had been
unintelligible; even Standard was changing here, where
contact with the linguistic mainstream was so rare.

The man said nothing else. He did not look as if he
were going to. Michael had prepared a speech; he made
it. He regretted intruding on the peace of the People of
the Rose. He would disturb them for no more than a
few minutes' time. He wished to join his friend, a red-
haired man who might have come here in recent months.
The world was large. Might the People of the Rose have
word of him? Might they know where he had gone?

The silence when he finished was so long that he
wondered if the man had understood him, or, understanding him, would not answer. *Answers one way or
another.* He glanced at Theo. It might be necessary to
come back, and bring with them Theo's answer kit. And
indeed, when the elder had stood for a time in silence,
he turned around and walked away.

Theo stared after him. "Hard to carry on a conversation with, isn't he?"

"They weren't this bad when I was here before."

Michael started after the elder, Theo following. When
they had gone a few paces the elder turned. "Begone!"
he said.

"I would like to do that," Michael said. "I intend
to. Will you at least tell me if my friend has been here?
I only want," he added truthfully, "to take him away."

He had worn no gloves and his hands were cold. He
folded them under his arms and waited some more. The
elder said finally, "If you do that, the Lord will bless
you."

Michael's heart jumped so far he thought the jolt must

show in his face. He heard Theo draw a breath. He said carefully, ''He will go as soon as I find him, and so will I. Are there others with him? They won't stay after he goes. And I'll tell the Oversight Service you want them gone.''

The elder thought it over and said, ''I am Elder Rann. Come with me.''

They followed him through icy pathways to a building perhaps a little larger than most. Inside there was a bare hall, unheated, with doors on either side. The elder opened one of them. Past it there was a flurry, but when Michael and Theo went in no one was there. A woman of the house, Michael guessed, had slipped away. Inside the room were a table and six hard chairs. There were no ornaments, and no other furniture except a case set against one wall. This held two roses carved in stone, a third of some softer substance, and six books.

''Wait here,'' Rann said, and left them.

The room was stuffy, and no sound came into it. ''What's he gone for?'' Theo said.

''Man-eating dogs,'' Michael said solemnly.

''They have those?''

''No. Of course not. They don't have any animals. It's against their beliefs.''

He looked closely at the roses. He had taken the central one to be made of fabric, but now he saw that it was molded from a plastic with the texture of flesh. The lines of the petals were obscenely suggestive. He lifted an eyebrow and took down one of the books, listening for the elder's return. The book was covered in fine linen and had been bound by hand. The pages were handwritten. He opened it and read:

''The one-hundred-twenty-sixth subclass of the sixty-seventh class of knowledge is this. The land which is given by the LORD is HIS and HE gives a small part of it to man. It is the will of the LORD that man encroach not on the land under HIS sway.

''The one-hundred-twenty-seventh subclass of the sixty-seventh class of knowledge is this. The hand of man is heavy on the land, but less heavy than the hand of the LORD.''

He heard a sound outside the room and shelved the book quickly. The elder came in carrying a long scroll. He put it down on the table and unrolled it: an exquisite hand-drawn map. Michael bent over it and saw that it showed the city. Every shabby building was on it, with a name or a function written neatly from corner to corner, and the gradations of rock were indicated in shades of rose and red.

"You landed here," Rann said, pointing. "We are now here. They are *here*." He set a blunt fingertip on a rectangle larger than the rest. It was at the side of the city opposite *GeeGee's* landing site.

Michael said incredulously, "They're in the city?"

"They are not here now. They have gone."

Gone. He was paralyzed. One faint lead after another, traces, guesses—where the hell could the trail lead from here? Theo glanced at him anxiously. But Rann said, "They will return. They said they will return. They said if we touch their possessions we will die. We do not want them. I have seen them. There are tawdry, frivolous things and offensive machines. When the Fleet ship comes, it will drive them away. But the ship will not come for one hundred days, and the Lord has sent you to expunge them from his land."

Michael breathed again. "I will certainly do my best," he said.

The warehouse was booby-trapped, but at a primitive level that suited B's assessment of the People of the Rose. The safeguards gave Michael and Theo no trouble. Inside was a great empty space, but also, stacked against one wall, a mound of crates. They broke into some of them and found that the "tawdry, frivolous things" were treasures. There was a silver tree that swayed and sang. A portrait of a lady came to life in pearly-rose flesh. When Michael reached out to touch her he felt softness, but saw without surprise that his hand came out her back. A plain black cube when touched produced a symphony of color and sound accompanied within a small radius by gravitational variations that made them dizzy. Near to it a crystalline complex of shapes winked in and out of real existence. There were many more beautiful things. Nearly all were marked "ones"; the creators of some were known throughout human space.

Against silver-gray walls the wonders stood and moved and sang. He looked at them with wide eyes. Kia's hand pulled him on, but he hung back, staring. It was the first time he had seen beauty like this, and he had no word for it.

"Mike? Mike!"

"Yeah." A thick sound. His eyes cleared. He was back in the warehouse on Revenge, and Theo stood among the crates, apprehensive. He was pale, and he looked at Michael with something like fear. Michael took a deep breath. The blood-deep rage retreated to the place where it lived, mocking him; frightening him, this time. It had stayed where it was supposed to be for years. Yet in a few hours it had shown itself twice, leaving the bruise on Lise's shoulder, the look on Theo's face. A name hung in his mind: *Kia*. There was nothing else with it. Whatever it meant was gone back deep inside him with the fury.

Theo said slowly, "If he's stored all this here, if it's got to be gone before Oversight comes in a hundred days, do you think . . ."

They looked at each other. Michael finished it. "That he'll be back soon?"

"We could be close, Mike."

"Could be. Could be."

He had the priceless ability to think of one thing at a time. He put everything out of his mind except the coming days.

"We got some luck," he said. "Now we wait."

II.

The setting forth of the *Far-Flying Bird* was a stately processional. Cheers accompanied it, wrenching Rubee, Awnlee, and Hanna from their seductive detachment. It seemed there were human beings on every bit of rock or ice in the stellar system of Sol, and all of them had something to say. "I did not know there were so *many* of you!" said Rubee, but he had known the number, twenty billion, from the start, and knew that eight billion occupied the home system.

"Talking germs," Hanna said. It was not her habit to disparage humankind, not even the nontelepathic majority D'neerans called collectively "true-humans"; but she had hoped they were done with this.

She was the more derisive because the bombardment of talk was not necessary. The *Bird* might have Jumped from Lunar orbit directly into deep space, there was no need for this sequence of in-system Jumps, it had been planned for political reasons. Rubee and Awnlee were not to escape without a formal leavetaking after all; only instead of getting a single banquet of platitudes, they were getting it piecemeal.

They were also widely seen. The Polity could not pass up the opportunities for propaganda provided by this quick peace with friendly aliens. Hanna thought the citizens of the Polity worlds must have seen enough of Rubee's and Awnlee's mild lumpy faces, but somebody, somewhere, did not think enough was enough. There were many requests for visual transmissions from the *Bird*. When Hanna played back edited versions culled from assorted newsbeams, she found the public eye was directed rather too much to herself. Someone discovered where she had gotten the opal that gleamed provocatively between her breasts, which Starr Jameson had given her long before. The old gossip about the two of them revived and was flung about human space all over again, titillating God knew whom. Were true-human lives so dreary that the long-dead affair of an aging man and a demolished woman could be some kind of entertainment? She listened with her lip curled, but she took off the opal.

She did not take off the other thing she wore close round her throat, a worked silver strand that was not a present to Hanna from anyone, but one of the gifts from humankind to the peoples of Uskos. The others were stored in the *Bird's* cargo hold. They were precious works made by human hands and brains, and they were (thought Hanna, who had seen them on one ceremonial occasion) very beautiful. The Uskosians would like them. She liked better the filigree chain that for all its look of delicacy could be used; a thing of practical import she could cup in her palm. It held secrets to be read with the proper tools. It was a key to the Outside, and it traveled to Uskos warmed by her skin, stirred by the surge of her blood.

"I *could* remove it, if I wished, if I tried, if I knew the proper codes," Awnlee said, his fingers impossibly thin, prying gently at the chain. He teased her to remove it, she could do that, the invisible clasp was keyed to her voice; she laughed and refused, teasing him. The scanners sent the picture to every part of human space.

It seemed to her obscurely that something would change when Sol's system was left behind, but the border was passed, and it was not enough. Voices still fell into the Bird like music, men's voices or women's, in Standard speech accented more or less strangely. The accents all together sketched the settlements of man, and all of them were official. Hanna thought: *That is noise.* To escape it she prowled the ship. When the optics were finally blanked, she reclaimed her opal. The hot air of the Bird comforted her skin.

Another Jump, another and another: for all the distance the *Bird* ate so quickly, the pace seemed slow to Hanna. Yet once it had been slower, because new. Someone had come this way a first time, without foreknowledge; before Willow was found; before the Founders of D'neera, fleeing genocide, escaped to a new world; before the ragged bands settled Nestor and Lancaster and created from the dirt and rock of one world a sickness, of the other a pastoral dream.

That was history. Hanna did not care much about history. Starr Jameson had tried without success to teach her its importance, "because if you do not understand it," he had said, "you will be its blind tool."

She was then working on Zeig-Daru, coming home to him and Earth at the intervals she herself had prescribed as mandatory for any D'neeran whose work meant being lost in the People. To communicate with the People meant, by definition, giving up the separateness of the self. Hanna said to him: "Contemplation is the luxury of the detached." She could not be detached and do what she did so successfully that when Rubee and Awnlee came, he begged her to do it again: saturate herself in an alien culture until she was more alien than human.

Now detachment was her only wish, though she did not understand why. She only knew that the increasing distance between herself and humankind was not enough. And so she waited restless and impatient and trapped by the murmur of human voices in a space that seemed not empty, but crawling with life.

On one day of the voyage through this busy waste, Rubee called her to the central command module from which he directed the *Bird's* Jumps. Thi was a circular platform in the center of the circular bridge, bordered by a skeletal structure made of thin columns of light. The light was composed of mathematical symbols that changed rapidly when the *Bird* was in Inspace mode, and Rubee monitored them by eye all at once. When Hanna passed through it to Rubee, the hair on her arms and the back of her neck stood up. In the center of the module a column of golden metal rose from the floor to the height of Rubee's waist. Its top had only two features: a ring of flame-green jewels surrounding a well of darkness, and below that a small indentation.

Hanna asked, "Do you wish me to see a thing, Rubee?" She was fluent in Ellsian now, and no longer used a translator.

"I do," he said, "and I will have pleasure in your perceiving it. I wished to do this sooner. But I have not because it is a thing among we three only, you and Awnlee and myself, and we have not been truly alone. The surveillance skills of your people are admirable."

Hanna laughed out loud. "You are courteous to speak so, Rubee. I do not know if 'admirable' is the word I would use. But now that we are alone, I will serve you in any way that I can, and it will be an honor to do so."

"Indeed, part of my intention is to ask you to give a service to me," he said, "and if you will undertake it, the honor will be mine. Yet also I have in mind a token of friendship between our peoples, but even more a token of the bond among we travelers, and especially the amity between you and my selfing. When I brought him forth on a winter day, I did not know that he would befriend a creature of another star! Therefore in a year I will make the story of the Friendship of Awnlee, and so it will be remembered forever like the friendship of Porsa and Awtell. But this story is not ended yet, and it will not end in my time, for I am no longer young, Awnlee coming to me late. And the service I ask is this: that if it is your fate also to survive Awnlee, you will finish the tale for my people. I would charge you with this; for our friendship is such that if you will, you stand to me as a selfing, and Awnlee's close kin. Will you accept this charge from me?"

"With gratitude, Rubee," she answered, but she was startled. Uskosians did not take kinship lightly nor speak of it casually; on the contrary. She said uncertainly, "Have I heard more than you have said?"

"You have not," Rubee said. His fingers rippled with pleasure. "I used those words with deliberation: 'You stand to me as a selfing.' They are the words of formal adoption in the second degree. Though you may reject my choosing, if you wish," he added.

"No! I am more honored than I can say. Yet I did not expect this, sire."

"No one will expect it because it is new," he said with some complacency. "I do not know what my people will think. You will be a citizen of Ell now, though an alien, and it will be interesting to hear what will be said. Perhaps they will say: if Rubee wished to adopt a selfing, could he not have chosen a person of our world? It is known among my friends and farther kin that I will bring forth no more selfings, to my sorrow, and that I have long wished that Awnlee might not be without close kin. It is an old loneliness for him, and for myself as well; and who better to assuage it than one who shares with us what no one else of any race will share? By that I mean the circumstances of our meeting, which had great significance for those of both our worlds, and this our journeying together. And perhaps in time you will think of this, and have less loneliness, too; you, the ever-homeless traveler."

Hanna stared at him. *The ever-homeless traveler—* she wanted to say, *Rubee, isn't that going a little far?* She had a home, D'neera was her home, she had a house upon it near a lake in a cold climate—

A house cared for by others, a house in which she could not remember where the light switches were.

Her hand went slowly to the opal at her throat. The occasion surely called for an exchange of gifts, as most Uskosian occasions did. But she had never been fond of having many personal possessions, and in the last years she had left behind those she had one by one, so that all she had of her own on the *Far-Flying Bird* was the jewel Jameson had given her.

She said, "Sire, I give you all my gratitude, and I would gift you with treasure; but this is all I have. And it signifies a bond that was broken."

"Then we will defer gifting," he said. "I will own with pleasure whatever you choose to give when the time is convenient; but indeed, I cannot give you now what I wish to give, because it cannot yet be spared."

He bent and touched the green jewels on the column between them. "Look!" he said.

She came around the column to stand beside him. He touched the darkness centered in the stones and she saw that its surface was not, as she had supposed, a miniature screen for electronic display, but a transparent covering over blackness. She leaned closer, and looked into an infinite depth clouded by silver webs whose threads appeared and disappeared at random and directed the eye to—where?—she could not tell, and she could not take her eyes from them. They were beautiful, and cold.

"What is it?" she whispered.

"It is the visible aspect of a confluence of dimensions. There are eleven at least; no doubt there are more."

The remote lights absorbed her. "I do not understand . . ."

"It is a portion of what you call Inspace," Rubee said.

"Of Inspace. . . ?" Hanna looked up, with some difficulty; the depth attracted her powerfully. She said, "How can this be?"

He was proud, and pleased by her wonder. He said, "I have learned that the making-visible of the confluence of dimensions is not a skill that humans have. We possessed it nearly from the time we learned to distort the dimensions and so cheat the limits of lightspeed. In the designing of the *Far-Flying Bird* it was deemed suitable to place here what you see; but when we have come to my home, I wish it to be yours."

Hanna said, "Sire, my people have never made a thing like this. We use Inspace, but we have never made any of it visible. The value of this gift is precious beyond words to say, either in your language or in mine. I cannot think of anything I might give you that is not small in comparison."

"Yet its true significance lies in more than its intrinsic value," Rubee said, "and I will show you that it is already yours."

He touched the phenomenon, the ends of his fingers thin as blades. He slipped them under the green jewels and pulled; the stones proved to be fastened to a thin cylinder that came up smoothly from the column. He gave it to Hanna. It was no longer than her hand and felt weightless. It was finely engraved with glittering spirals, and when she looked at it closely she saw that script was woven through the spirals, some of it Standard, some Ellsian. The Standard words said, with many formal flourishes, that Rubee and Awnlee of Ell, on a day aboard the *Far-Flying Bird*, had set into the molecules of this metal a program that marked in the symbols of two planets completion of the course from Uskos to Earth, the homeworld of their honored friend. If they had not assigned Hanna quite the correct birthplace, that did not matter; they regarded Earth as the homeworld of all humans, and they were, Hanna supposed, essentially right.

She said, "My dear friend, when did you make this?"

"We did not 'make' it," he said. "It has been a part of this ship from the beginning of our journey, and we had only to refine the programming contained in the surface when your Fleet gave us the end of our course. As to the embellishments, and addition of your name, I began them, in our script, soon after you joined us on this ship. Awnlee, when he had learned your script and mathematics, did the remainder; also he entered the course in a form a human ship can read, for your sake, when one day you wish to come to our home, which is yours. The gift you yourself bring to Uskos, the course which is contained in the fillet you wear, proves that the ways of thought of our peoples are not so different. Yet this is not a gift of state, but for your possession only. It is yours although you cannot possess it wholly yet; we stand over the main course computer at this moment, and this is what it reads. But at our journey's end it will be altogether yours, and it will be a memento forever of our travels together, and of our trust which is that of sire and selfing."

Hanna turned the precious thing slowly in her hands. She could not find words adequate to thank him, and so she touched his thought: *There is nothing like this in the universe. It is unique. It is both yours and mine. I*

*shall have no other comparable gift, ever. And I will
remember you forever.*

They moved rapidly through the remainder of human
space. They followed the route Fleet had given Rubee
when he came, a clear, well-charted path, though first
Hanna had been rushed to meet him so that a telepath
could examine his thought for hostility or hidden motives. After that the Fleet vessels surrounding the *Bird*
had become in fact what they pretended to be at first:
the escort of an honored guest.

Hanna resumed her restless tours of the *Bird* and
counted the Jumps and the good-byes, checking them
off against an invisible list in her mind. When no more
were left, it would mean escape. Among columns of
crystal and silver in the *Bird's* engineering section she
asked: *Escape from what?* And answered the questions
in the banner-bright lounge where Jameson had met her
some weeks before: *From Starr. From humankind and
its rules and demands.*

She did not know why this was so. Perhaps she only
needed a vacation. Perhaps she ought to have gone to
Valentine. With Rubee and Awnlee in tow?—the thought
of the stately Rubee astray on Valentine made her laugh.
But laughter left her quickly. The *Bird* seemed hotter in
the "nights," and she slept badly. The list of Jumps
and farewells dwindled each hour.

On the last day there was a final farewell from Lancaster. After that the messages stopped, except the routine transmissions from Fleet stations monitoring the
Bird's progress. They had come to the edge of the
greater gulf, past which all was unknown, except for
the thin thread of their course and Uskos' small sphere
of space at the end.

Here they paused for final systems checks. The light
of the command module faded; the free-standing columns of numbers dimmed. Rubee and the *Bird* and
the voices of Fleet technicians talked together, examining life support, servomechanisms, data banks, plasma
engines, navigation, course computation, quantum-

dimensional mechanics; they went over all of it again and again.

While that went on Hanna paced, unable either to be still or to leave the bridge. Apart from the central module, the bridge was not exotic to human eyes. The predominant color was a soothing cream. The interior semicircle was thick with displays and work terminals all along the wall; the exterior curve was transparent, so that those on the bridge always could see, in a sense, where they were going. Hanna passed back and forth behind the padded benches that rimmed this section of the circle, and kept looking out, looking Outside. The *Bird* pointed in the direction of its next Jump. Already far behind it lay a relay whose number no one used any longer. In conversations with Fleet it was Omega, the last, the end; Uskosian tongues turned the word into Oneba. The vagaries of space-time made it safe for the first Jump past Omega to be long: four light-weeks, a liberal beginning for their journey. If its liberality could be taken as an omen it could mean, in Uskosian terms, that the journey was not discouraged.

But it would be a Jump into silence. From the next position an Inspace communication would stretch beyond its limit and never reach Omega. Radio or microwave or laser communications would get there—but not until four weeks after they were transmitted. Hanna felt that she looked toward a final, outer limit, into a place where the ubiquitous voices of humankind did not go. Somewhere ahead was an invisible but real barrier. Perhaps she was not the first to pass it here. Perhaps long ago in the great exodus from Earth, some ill-prepared colonists had gone this way. But if so, no one had ever heard of them again. They had vanished into the great silence.

She shivered at the thought in spite of the warmth of the *Bird*, and rubbed her bare arms. There was a movement at her side; Awnlee joined her just as the hum of the *Bird's* Inspace mode began. The air sang with it, the floor, the walls. Through the clear sound a last human voice rang through the *Bird*: ''Logoff from Omega complete. Fair winds attend you!''—and then it was gone.

Her heart lifted. She took a deep breath and came closer to Rubee. The light about him was brilliant; through it she saw dimly that his hand hovered above the golden column. When he touched it, the Jump would come. He seemed to have grown larger, though that was a trick of her eyes and mind, for he was the same stumpy personage she had known all the time, not much taller than herself. But now he was where he belonged. He did not need to be careful and diplomatic; without any diminishing of his native courtesy, he had become the pure traveler, the master of starflight, himself, the essential Rubee. Hanna knew that look. She had seen it in certain human beings, and in the Explorers of Zeig-Daru. The wind was up, and Erell trimmed the sails.

At the proper time by his reckoning, and not a moment sooner, Rubee said to the *Far-Flying Bird* in his own language: "Prepare to ride the gales of the stars!"

To ride the gales of the stars . . . Humans did not talk to their spacecraft that way. Rubee at the center of a cylinder of pulsing light, standing, was not ugly or misshapen, he was magnificent. Hanna stood also, as if at attention. Awnlee beside her wrapped his fingers around hers, all the way around. Hanna said directly to his mind: *We have this in common: I, you, all intelligence; naught else in the universe feels and does this.* The *Bird's* common sound, a low sweet humming, grew louder, higher, louder. The ship under Hanna's feet gathered herself; poised on the edge of space and time; lifted her wings; in a chronon was somewhere else. Hanna turned to the transparency and looked in all sense Outside. The configuration of space had changed; the stars had shifted. All the worlds she knew were at her back. Awnlee chattered as the *Bird's* song faded sweetly. "Five of your weeks, a short time, till the fourteenth day of Strrrl. Think of what I will show you! There are forests like scarlet plumes under skies as blue as yours. There are ruminants big as your house. There are sparkling wines colored like the grain, and pink insects sweet to eat. There are—"

"Awnlee, come here," Rubee said in a voice so ordinary that Awnlee suddenly silent was at his side before Hanna registered the movement. Then came a knowledge of something she had not felt before in Rubee: not fear, but a kind of deep concern.

She followed Awnlee to the central mandala. It no longer glowed; that should not be. The omnipresent humming dropped to silence. The *Bird* should not be so quiet, not in Inspace mode. Rubee was intent, Awnlee apprehensive, and Hanna saw that they were concentrated on the ghostly columns of numbers which were all that remained of the brilliant light.

All of them showed, uniformly, the Uskosian symbol for zero.

Rubee and Awnlee forsook the central mandala for the work stations that lined the bridge. Hanna did not speak. It was not easy to refrain, but she could not interrupt their urgent absorption. She only said once, "Is there a way in which I might be of service?"

But Rubee said, "No. We are grateful, but you have not the necessary skill with our vessel."

Therefore she listened with all her senses. With her mind she perceived that Rubee was worried and surprised; in Awnlee there was a chill of fear, and he kept reassuring himself in terms that in words would translate to: *It is not so bad, we will be safe will be safe will be safe!* With her ears she heard them talk of technical matters that baffled her. Their hands flew over glowing banks of keypads which responded with unintelligible schematics and columns of numbers. The *Bird* talked back to them, sounding anxious; or was that Hanna's imagination? She stood at Awnlee's back and watched what he did until she could endure it no longer. She must ask what had happened. Before she could do it he said, not to her but to Rubee, "That is the thing, then. It is a simple electrical malfunction. Simple, yet extensive; it is the power infrastructure for the distortion of dimension. I have not heard of such a thing before, neither in the prototypes nor the test voyages. I do not know how it could be."

He looked at a many-colored pattern that looked like (and, Hanna now realized, was) a wiring diagram.

Large portions of it blinked on and off. Two meters away Rubee sighed, watching an identical image.

"There will be no quick journeys without repair," he said, "and repair means retracing our course. We will not come home on the fourteenth day of Strrrl; not this year."

Awnlee was still tense, but he said with the appearance of cheer, "If we must have this trouble, it is good that we have it at once. The conventional engines are unaffected. We are near Oneba, some thirty light-days; a long journey, yet not impossible nor more than inconvenient."

"That is true. Yet it will be best to remain here and signal distress, for the searchers will come quickly when our call comes to Oneba. That will use only thirty true days, and in one day more someone will come. And what are thirty-one days?—a grain of sand."

Hanna absorbed it slowly. They meant that the Inspace system was out. The *Bird* could not Jump. Without the Inspace option, the *Bird* was months away from Omega. They were, it appeared, marooned, for at least a month. Then she thought, surprising herself: What of it? Here was light, warmth, air, food, companionship. The *Bird* had not suffered a disaster. It was only a routine breakdown in space; it only meant delay. *It means rest*, she thought, and said half-consciously but aloud, in Ellsian, "There will be nothing we can do. There will be nothing we must do."

But Rubee had made a negative with his hands. "It is true that we have no present danger," he said. "Yet I am troubled because of the error that has occurred, and I wish to study it further. Also I wish to investigate the systems that continue to function. The failure of dimensional manipulation has bereft us of much power. If the old-style engines should fail also, only emergency generators will be left to retain life support—and I do not like having only one system as our defense against death in space."

Hanna knew well the perpetual caution of starship captains, whatever their species or form. She said,

"That is proper. Yet how could two such errors occur, Rubee?"

"How could one occur? Yet there is not one, but two; there are two already. There is the error that effected the malfunction. Therefore I must deduce that there is an error also in a diagnostic program, or else we would have been forewarned. What else might there be? What else might fail? We will work until we find out."

He said this with finality, and he did not intend to wait; at once, Hanna and Awnlee following, he rose and took his way to the "wing" that housed the *Bird's* Inspace systems, which Rubee and Awnlee accurately called the distorters of dimension. Hanna had spent little time in this part of the *Bird*. It was a world of soaring silver spaces, arched and dizzily high. It was impressive, but it was not designed for comfort.

Hanna was not comfortable, and there was nothing she could do to help the Uskosians, except to stay out of their way. She did that for a long time, watching the units of time the aliens called hours go by on the strange chronometers. She was left to her own thoughts, which were not comfortable either. At about the time help could arrive, she had expected to be making a ceremonial, mythic landing on Uskos. She had expected a period of such intense work that it might produce the most brilliant results of her life. All her expectations had led to this, a profound anticlimax, and she was—not distressed. It even seemed that she might be treacherously relieved.

"There are erasures I do not understand," Awnlee said suddenly and very loudly. His voice echoed in the curved spaces, solitary in the great expanse.

"But what is the cause?" Rubee said.

"I do not yet know. They have not the appearance of randomness."

Hanna listened absently. A smile twitched at her lips. She was unquestionably released from the expected, at least for a little while. No human voice could follow her here for a month. She formed phrases and turned them over in her mind, trying them out: *I'm very sorry, Starr.* But they did not have the ring of truth.

Rubee, peering over Awnlee's shoulder at a console a few meters away, straightened with a gesture of disappointment.

"It is garbled beyond retrieval," he said.

"It is not," Awnlee said. "I will need some days, but I will reconstruct it. I will start at once."

Rubee said, "Do not begin now. Night has come. No reason has occurred to hurry us. I wish to observe what you do, but I do not wish to do it tonight."

The tendrils around his mouth drooped. Hanna remembered what he had said of his age. She said, "Indeed, Awnlee, it is time to rest."

"Then I will wait," Awnlee said, though it was plain that he longed to begin, and Hanna left him to talk to Rubee and take "one look more" at the mystery.

Hanna slept uneasily in the hot night. She dreamed too much, and woke often. The dreams were all a confused medley of the past. Here was the governing House of Province Koroth, vast and cool. "Do this," said the Lady of Koroth, "do that, you must, it must be done." The pale face altered; Hanna looked into her own blue eyes. She would be the Lady of Koroth one day, a magistrate of D'neera, lawmaker, law-abider. The People of Zeig-Daru thought to her, fondly accepting. Their great hands held instruments of torture. Hanna woke sweating; turned, and slept again. She rested comfortably in Starr Jameson's arms. She was loved. "Not yet," he said. "There is something you must do first." He turned into the Master of Chaos and then into Rubee, who lectured under a tree.

"Details change," Rubee said. "Grand designs must not, except by the hand of the Master. The honor is greater that way. By honor I mean sureness and security. Nonetheless persons make designs, and the Master enters in their alteration."

Rubee's face changed in its turn; first to something cruel with many pointed teeth; then to a human face that looked at Hanna with a pleasant smile and gold-flecked eyes. It said in a stranger's voice, "No one can hear you out here."

"No, no!" Hanna cried, trying to scream. Her own muffled shout woke her up. She sat up in the dark and pushed at her hair. It was wet with perspiration.

She turned on a light and looked about with an eerie sense that all that surrounded her was unreal; that she still dreamed. The room had been made over for her in blue and lavender, as comfortable and human as her own fading home. The air circulated with a faint whisper. Except for that there was silence, and Rubee and Awnlee slept deeply nearby.

She lay back uneasily. The face with the gold-flecked eyes was still nearly visible. An old sensation gnawed her, as if she whispered to herself, "You have overlooked something!" But it was associated only with danger and fear; and what was there to fear?

But she had thought that, too—sometimes, before.

She made a face and thought: Be paranoid, then; think of the worst; think back, seeking anomaly; think.

There are erasures I do not understand. They have not the appearance of randomness—

She felt vulnerable and exposed. She got up and put on some of the skimpy clothing she had brought with her. The tight singlet and shorts clung to her; her skin was clammy.

Think.

The programmed distortion occurred, the *Bird* had told Awnlee. And then the Inspace failure. *No one can hear you out here*.

She paced the room. Her bare feet trod the resilient floor without disturbing the silence of the *Bird*.

Suppose there was no random error. Suppose what appeared to be error was the result of a skillfully implanted series of commands.

The course program had never been touched. For that it need not have been touched. There were people who had studied the *Bird's* Inspace engineering systems. Hanna did not remember Jameson saying anything about those persons being investigated beyond the common bounds of security clearance. It was just possible, therefore, that the engineering failure had been planned. And the route from Earth to Omega was available to anyone who wanted it. It was standardized, part of the common programming of Inspace navigation. Given such detailed knowledge of the *Bird's* course so far, and knowledge of its general direction beyond, which had never been a secret, anyone might have extrapolated the *Bird's* approximate location after the first Jump past Omega. After that first Jump the possibilities for error would a grow exponentially, but the finish of the first must be within a reasonably confined radius. The calculation could not be precise, however, without possession of the course program; and without precision, even if someone were searching within that radius, there would be a margin of safety for the *Bird*. But Hanna could not estimate its extent.

Should she go to Rubee now and wake him from sleep? She leaned against a lavender wall and pressed her cheek against it. It was the wildest speculation, but she thought of how it could be done. Someone who was not afraid to go out past Omega could do it, exploring in weeks of small patient steps the logical path outward, until the data were complete and the leap as safe as any inside human space. Given the necessary skill, it needed only time. And Awnlee and Rubee had been in human space nearly a Standard year; had someone come this way while they went with Hanna round the worlds?

She closed her eyes and shut out the lavender light. Reached out, out, past Rubee and Awnlee, beyond the sleeping *Bird* and farther still, in all directions and no direction. In the isolation of the *Bird* she might, with all her skill and all her mind concentrated, touch a familiar presence although it was light years away. There ought to be nothing else for her to touch. There should be no stranger near at hand.

There was something. She brushed against it and jerked away, chilled. It was in space and thought of the *Far-Flying Bird*. It thought of the treasure in the *Bird's* guts.

"God damn it," she said softly, scarcely able to believe in what she had felt. But it was there. It was close by, and purposeful.

She did not know exactly where it was. Telepathy could not tell her that.

She went to Rubee's room and pounded on his door. He answered at once. He wore a sleeping robe that brushed the floor and he adjusted it punctiliously as the door opened. Hanna felt his surprise. She said, "I am sorry to wake you, Rubee. But I must, and *now*."

"Enter. Enter—"

She was already in the room, talking as quickly as the need to think in Ellsian allowed. He did not understand her at first, so that she had to back up and repeat her knowledge and surmises; when he grasped them his eyespots worked and shone.

She finished, "All that would be necessary, would be a command for the system to fail upon completion of the first Jump after Omega. I think that was done. Our position is exactly what they would wish. No signal from us can reach Omega for one Standard month. We cannot Jump to get away. These humans can be sure that we will transmit a distress signal that includes our exact location, which is all that they need. Perhaps they even believe it will be directional toward Omega, and will confine their search accordingly. I think we had better not do that, Rubee. I think we had better not send a signal at all, and begin the long journey to Omega as soon as the old-style engines are at power—and not in a direct line, either."

Rubee said, "I will activate the engines and set course at once. But I wish one of us had thought of this more quickly. The signal was initiated some time ago. I saw no reason not to do that."

"Directional?" She watched the margin of safety shrink.

"Yes. How long will it take a human spacecraft to find us if all that you say is correct?"

"Hours."

"Hours have gone by already."

"Then we had better think of evasion instead of escape," she said. "They may be nearly here."

He went quickly to the bridge and she followed him. He did not speak again, but manipulated a work station without explanation. She understood that he ordered the *Bird* to extend its scanning range. The display at this station was blank and black at first. Then it showed one thing: the arrowhead-shape of an atmosphere-efficient spacecraft. Rubee's fingers stretched to pointed threads and touched tiny keypads in a blur of speed. Numbers appeared beside the image.

"What does that mean?" Hanna said.

He said, "They are moving in from the direction of Oneba, and they come with great speed. They have scanned the *Bird* as we slept. This vessel could not match the speed of that one even at full power; not in a hunt; it was not made for chase or pursuit. There is no hope of escape."

He turned away from the terminal and started out. Hanna called after him, "Where do you go?"

He answered without stopping, "I go to wake Awnlee. They will arrive in one of our hours; less than one of yours. We are caught completely."

Awnlee, so calm until now, lost his composure and his courage all at once. "This was not supposed to happen!" he said over and over, and all efforts to soothe him were ineffectual. Hanna wished to learn what she could of the distant presence that was perceptible in this waste of isolation, but she felt only Awnlee's agitation. Rubee took him away again so that she would not see his pitiful terror. It made no difference. To close him out she had to shut down telepathy altogether, as a true-human might close his eyes, and then she was insensible also to the presences she wanted to touch.

Shutting consciousness to all of them had one advantage: she was able to think of their situation coldly and without distraction. It came more easily than she expected, as easily as even Jameson might have wished. Alone on the *Bird's* bridge, she thought about that. She felt no fear or uncertainty. That was new. In D'neera's brief war with Nestor, and even more in her first agonizing contacts with the People of Zeig-Daru, she had lived on the edge of madness. This was different. It was as if the years of order and protocol had not passed; as if, in her official life of courtesy, she had grown more callous to danger. Yet she had not faced danger for a long time, so that what she felt could not come from habituation. She traced it, and saw that its source was anger. This event was too much. She had gone obediently where she was sent, produced what was wanted, done as she was told by D'neera, by the Polity, by all the human voices, for a long time, all her life. Now she must stop and surrender to—well, to the Master of Chaos, if it came to that; Rubee surely discerned that unpredictable hand. After all she had done it was going too far, after all she had done for Polity; could they get nothing right? But she knew she was unfair, that at least Jameson had tried to ward off what was coming, and that it was her own skepticism, conspiring with the aliens' stubbornness, that had brought her to this position of helplessness.

Then she thought with more logic of other things. And the first thing logic told her was that they could not escape or get help.

The next thing was a question. How far should they go in defending the cargo of the *Bird*?

She did not have to think about that much to come to a decision. The robbers could have it. *Here, take it, is there anything else you would like*? Precious it might be, irreplaceable even, but it was dust next to the lives of Rubee and Awnlee. And Hanna did not want to die either, not defending a crateful of baubles.

The last thing was whether their lives were in jeopardy in any case, and whether anything could be done about it. She was no longer critical of Jameson's urgency in educating her about Michael Kristofik. She wished she had paid more attention. Twenty years ago on the *Pavonis Queen* no one had been harmed. With luck it would be sleepygas again. But men change in twenty years. Probably Kristofik did not know that he was already suspected, in advance, of something he had not yet done. He might think that eradicating the *Bird* and her passengers would be the safest measure; that the *Bird* would be presumed lost in space on a course that was nearly untried. It seemed to Hanna that murder was the logical step for a man capable of taking it.

Was he, then, capable of taking it?

She sat on the bench that girdled the *Bird's* bridge with her chin on one hand, and retrieved certain statements from memory. Honoria Hood, twenty years ago: "At no time were lethal weapons used . . ." Jameson, drawing on sources that went back that far and farther: "There were incidents on Alta and Valentine and later everywhere. He was dangerous. He is still dangerous." Her own voice, casual, dismissing the threat: "I suppose if you assume your subject is a monster, and then he doesn't act like one . . ." But here was Jameson again: "He must have known every worst thing there was to know about men . . . don't forget the man he's believed to have killed . . ."

It was so sparse, there ought to have been more, but she had not wanted to listen. And now she must estimate the extent of her danger, and she did not know enough to do it.

A communications module that ought to have stayed silent for weeks made a sound. Hanna scrambled for it. "Acknowledged," she said tightly.

A man's voice said, "This is the trader *Avalon* out of Lancaster. We've picked up a mayday from your location. You in trouble?"

You could say that.

Hanna said, "We're the *Far-Flying Bird* out of Terra on special mission for the Polity. What's a Lancaster trader doing out here?"

"Just looking around."

The voice was thin and toneless. It disturbed her. She said, "Nobody comes out here. You're well out of Omega's range. I don't know if coincidence goes that far."

"You want help or don't you?" said the voice.

Rubee came in. His comprehension of Standard was limited. He said, "What have they said?"

"They play a game."

"Do you play?"

"I will. To discover what we may expect."

The light voice outside said, "Talk Standard."

Hanna said, "We don't want help. We'll handle it."

"Not good enough," said the voice.

Only three words. The hair stood up on Hanna's arms, she had heard nothing like them before, nothing like the irony and finality in the slow light voice. If this was Michael Kristofik, Jameson's assessment had fallen short of the dreadful truth. Her hand shaped itself for a weapon, though she had not held one in years.

She said coldly, "Let's work with the truth. I know what you want."

It must have startled him. There was a pause before the voice said, "Yes?" so softly it was nearly a whisper. There was a suggestion of hollowness, of echoes in empty spaces, a trick of acoustics.

"Is it whom we feared?" Rubee said.

"Who else could it be?"

"Tell this person to take the cargo and leave."

Hanna thought of her own estimate of the reasonable thing to do. She had qualified it before: murder was the logical step for a man capable of taking it. The reservation no longer counted. The man who owned this voice was capable of it.

The voice said, "I don't want to hear any more of that alien noise. I said: Standard."

"All right. I'll talk Standard." Some of her fury might have gotten into her voice. She hoped it had. "Listen to this. The Interworld Fleet and Intelligence and Security expected trouble. You got by them, I don't know how. But this isn't going as smooth as you think. They've got an idea who to look for. The Uskosian envoys don't want trouble. They want you to take what you came for and get out. So do I. You come right aboard and get it. We'll stay out of the way. But believe me, you don't know what trouble is. Trouble is what you get from Fleet and I&S if you touch an alien envoy. I'm not talking smuggling, Earthside Enforcement, port patrols, that kind of garbage. I'm talking top-level Polity Admin. If you're smart, you'll make sure nobody gets hurt. How does that sound?"

The voice said, "That's fine. Glad you take it like

that. Just remember what you said about wanting trouble. The kind you get if you ask for it, is a battery of Fleet surplus wide aperture laser cannon. Give us an airlock and stay where you are. We're coming in.''

The approach took an hour. The *Bird* waited dead and silent. Awnlee appeared on the bridge, apologetic and calmer. He said he did not know what had happened to him. He sat between his sire and Hanna and held Hanna's hand.

"I thought I was brave as Bistee!" he lamented.

"I don't think it was an unnatural reaction," Hanna said.

"But you and my sire did not act so!"

"We are older," said Rubee.

"Yes," Hanna said, "and I don't know about Rubee, but the last time I was in such a position, I was jelly. And I may yet forget myself before we are done."

"I wish I were like Sirsa of Sa," Awnlee said with a return of his natural enthusiasm.

Hanna opened her mouth to ask what had happened to Sirsa of Sa, or who Bistee had been, for that matter, and shut it again. This was no time for legend.

She said to Rubee, "We must think of defending ourselves."

"Do you think we will have need?"

"I think it is very possible."

"We came with weapons; a small number only; meant for defense against beasts if we met such danger. You saw the weapons destroyed, all of them." Rubee hesitated. "Did you know then why I did it?" he asked.

"I did. I gave you then my gratitude, even before I gave you my love."

Awnlee said, "It was a token of good will when 'Anarilporot joined us."

"It was another thing also," she said, watching Rubee over Awnlee's head.

"You had great fear," Rubee said. "I then knew nothing of your kind of speech, thought to thought. There was no other common language and when words came to you I did not know what they meant. But there

were pictures. You stood here, where we are now, and
remembered another meeting. I could not endure your
memories. And so I put our weapons into space. I knew,
because of you, that we would not need them."

"It was a token of good will indeed, and has been so
ever since. But now we may need weapons, Rubee."

"Is there not an accommodation?" said Awnlee.

"I would not give my trust to these men," she said.
"I do not wish you to have alarm, Awnlee, but I think
we had better think of the worst case. We have tools.
Perhaps we could use them. Even something to throw
would be better than nothing; better still would be tools
that could harm from a distance."

"There is nothing," Rubee said. "There are objects
we might modify, given time. But there is no time."

The air lock was open. The *Bird* would announce at
any moment that it had been entered. Hanna's mind was
busy with possibilities that she rejected as quickly as
they came—close the lock, seal the inner one, trap them
inside it—but the cannon that could punch holes in the
Bird as easily as a fist smashing through paper rendered
all her ideas useless.

Awnlee's grip on Hanna's hand felt strange. She
looked down and saw his fingers change. He said, "Tell
me of this accommodation."

Hanna could not answer. She had not laid out all her
conclusions even for Rubee. But Rubee said, "I think
'Anarilporot and I are of one mind. I think our danger
is great." He touched his selfing gently. "We are in a
tale, Awnlee. We thought it another telling of the Tale
of Erell. That was what we wished and planned. But
the Master has come to us. The danger was there always. It is present always, and especially in a great undertaking such as ours. And now we are in a new tale,
a dark one."

"They have entered," Awnlee said. He moved closer
to Rubee, looking at a schematic that showed new points
of light where none had been. "There are four. I wonder if that is all?"

Hanna watched the blips of light. When the lock finished its cycle, they moved out and turned for the

bridge. She said, "There are probably others on the *Avalon*, if that is its name. But now that these are aboard, they are not likely to use the cannon. As long as they are here, our only danger is from whatever weapons they carry with them."

"Perhaps we should attack at once," Rubee said. "Yet there are four of them and three of us, and we have no weapons."

He was icy: a good being to have by you in a fight. Hanna said, "Yes. We must wait and find out their intent. It would be foolish to provoke them if there is a chance they will not harm us. If there is no chance—then an attack may give us only a small one, but it will be the only chance."

The blips were almost at the bridge. Awnlee quivered. Hanna put her arms around him suddenly and said, "Do not be afraid, my friend."

"I wish you could give me some of your courage!"

"All that I have is yours," she answered, which was an expression of deep love at any time. She felt Awnlee formulate a response, *And all that is mine I give to you*, but there was no time to say it; four spacesuited figures came onto the bridge, two by two, and quickly.

They held stunguns, which gave her a moment's hope. Then she saw that each also had in his belt a disruptor or a laser pistol. So they were prepared to wound and kill. That was not good. Worse was the transparency of the faceplates of their suits. They did not care who saw their faces. They were not worried about being identified.

Hanna said to Rubee and Awnlee, silently: *They mean to kill us. We will have to fight.* Rubee made no sign, but Awnlee started and looked at her, and one of the men stepped forward.

"D'neeran," he said, and she almost shrank away; this was the man with the voice. But the face was not the one she had expected to see.

He said, "We don't like D'neerans. We don't like what they do with their heads. You have anything to say, say it out loud. Or else you're dead. Understand?" He looked at Rubee. "You. How's your cargo secured? Open it up."

Hanna said, "He doesn't understand Standard very well."

"I will translate," Awnlee said in a steadier voice than Hanna expected to hear from him, and he did so.

Hanna listened to their conversation and assessed them. The man I&S had expected to be here was not here, but he might have remained on the *Avalon*. There was the man with the voice, red-haired and fair-skinned; there was a towheaded giant; there was a thin brown-black man whose fingers were nervous on his weapon; and—hanging back a little—there was a smaller man with a straggling mustache and eyes that looked anywhere except at her and the Uskosians. The red-haired man talked with authority and clearly was the leader. I&S might have been wrong. They might have wasted all their worry on Michael Kristofik, and while they researched and watched him, this other man with the empty eyes might have crept in undiscovered. Which did not change the basic situation, and Hanna wished I&S had been right. She would rather face the man who had taken the *Pavonis Queen* with sleepygas and stun-guns, rejecting a massacre.

Rubee went to a work station and began the procedures for releasing the cargo hold locks. His back was to all of them. Hanna said to him: *Rubee, if they are divided, if some go to the hold and others stay here, it may be our best chance.* His hand moved in a way that meant assent. It would be meaningless to the intruders.

She said to the red-haired man, "What is your name?"

"Castillo," he answered, his eyes on Rubee. Hanna's skin prickled. It was a lie. But there were overtones she was not used to finding in the perception of a simple lie; a glimpse of a depth not uninhabited, into which she would not care to descend. It went with the voice.

She said casually, distractingly, "You've done this very well. I&S was looking in the wrong places, and at the wrong man, too, I think. You can laugh about that when this is done. But there is one thing you might have forgotten that might increase your profits. I meant what I said about trouble from the top. We're worth much more to you alive than dead, especially the aliens. You could name your price for their safety and the Polity would pay instantly. Have you thought of that?''

He said without looking away from Rubee, ''Hanna ril-Koroth bargains for her life.''

''That's right. Half of what you've heard about me—you've obviously heard of me—isn't true. I don't want to be hurt and I don't want my friends hurt.''

Rubee stepped back from his station. Awnlee said, ''It is done. The hold is open.''

The red-haired man put away his stungun and drew the disruptor. He did it casually and with no trace of emotion at all, so that Hanna had no warning, she did not even know the moment had come until he lifted the disruptor and fired it at Rubee. The beloved ugly body jerked and fell. It happened in only a second, which for Hanna was an eternity of paralysis. The muzzle turned toward Awnlee and she threw herself at it, but she was too far from Castillo to reach him and he fired at once. She heard a single sound from Awnlee, higher-pitched than anything she had ever imagined coming from an Uskosian throat. It was not as clean a shot, and Awnlee's shock hit her like a wavefront, and then so did something else. Not a disruptor beam, though she thought it was at first. In a heap at Castillo's feet, still trying to think in the moment of terrible grief, she felt Awnlee die crying for his sire, felt the weakness and tingling that meant light stun, and tried to get up again. Something else hit her, in the side of the head: a boot. Her vision swam.

Awnlee, Awnlee! she called hopelessly, knowing there would never be an answer.

The voice said, ''She's dangerous. I told you to knock her out.''

The last thing she saw was the thin man standing on the command platform, bending over the golden column, attracted by the jewels. A heavier blast from a stungun hit her, and all of them went away.

She thought of the ship ever after as the *Avalon*, and of the events that occurred there as things that happened

on the *Avalon*, though that was not its name any more
than the red-haired man's name was Castillo. In memory, later, the ship and the man would be unreal. That
was because during her time on the *Avalon*, Hanna held
on only to the edge of the real.

She had been stunned so heavily that it was many
hours before she woke. When she did, at first, she was
aware only of bodily misery. All her muscles were
cramped from the stun effect and hours of not moving.
She was cold, frozen. Her head was a weight of pain,
and trying to move made it worse; the throbbing started
where she had been kicked and radiated outward to fill
her skull. She was also desperately thirsty.

When she had identified these things, she remembered the rest: Rubee and Awnlee. She called to them
from her misery, without hope, and though thinking
minds surrounded her, the dear shapes of Rubee and
Awnlee were not there. She had known they would not
be.

Finally she moved. She was not a stranger to suffering. She did not welcome it, but she knew what could
be endured: more than she had once thought possible.
She also knew the value of hope. And so she moved.

Very slowly she got up, holding on to a wall because
her knees kept giving way. The room where she was
had one dim light overhead. It was not large, and all
the surfaces were bare metal, but there were outlines on
the metal showing where fixtures had been stripped
away. There were two doors. She tried them both, feeling her way from one to the other along the wall. The
first was locked. The second opened into a claustro-
phobically small bathroom with no other exit. So probably at some time this had been some kind of crewmen's
quarters.

She splashed cold water on her face and drank from
her cupped hands with gratitude, though when she bent
over she thought her head would tear apart. Still, she
could think more clearly.

About Rubee and Awnlee?—no. She would think
about them later. Instead she must think of questions.
Why was she still alive? Where was the *Avalon* taking

her, and why? She could not answer the questions. Her head was only clear enough for sorrow, not for reason. Now if ever was the time to put to use the disciplines of the D'neeran Adept. But entering trance would not be easy. Once pain had begun, attenuating concentration, it was harder.

She went back to the icy cubicle that had once been someone's room and eased cross-legged to the floor. Tremors ran through her from the cold. She closed her eyes and prepared to control breath and blood. But then the door opened and she knew the room had been watched, they had seen her wake, and she would not get her chance, not yet.

She opened her eyes and looked up at Castillo. The blond giant was behind him, and the thin man from the boarding party. All three had stunguns pointed at her. It was flattering—and devastating to any hope of escape.

Castillo squatted in front of her. There was an empty smile on his lips. The pale blue eyes were empty, too. He said, "You said I&S knows about this operation. Tell me about it."

She thought it might be a good idea not to tell him. She thought that if he had kept her alive in order to ask her that question, it would be advantageous to put off answering as long as possible. She said as much.

He said, "You're going to stay alive for a while anyway. If Fleet's tracking us, you'll come in handy. I don't want to play games with the Polity, but D'neera might pay well for you—without getting the Polity involved."

He did not go on, but in the minds of the other men she saw that there would be another, sexual use for her. Because she was there and helpless, had been thrown into their path like a bonus and there would be no retaliation because no one would ever know; that was all.

She was sick, and knew it showed in her face. She knew also that Castillo lied casually, indifferently, about D'neera. She would never see it again.

"Now tell us about I&S," he said.

"No," she said, as an experiment, to see what kinds of threats he would make so she could learn more about him.

He did not waste time with threats. He stood up and stepped back. The blond man jerked her to her feet and held her upright while the other man, the thin man, beat her. He enjoyed it; after a while his eyes glazed, and he panted. Castillo watched, the smile unchanged on his lips. She threw at him once a desperate silent plea for mercy, a cry of stark pain. He still smiled and she did not do it again, she would not beg again, never in what was left of her life. But she had not known that unaided hands could bring the unendurable so near. Her flesh broke under the fists, her body felt as if it disintegrated. "Yes, yes!" she cried long before it was over, but the only thing that happened then was that Castillo said, "Don't break her jaw." So when the giant dropped her on the floor she could have talked, if she had had breath to talk with; but then there was another boot that smashed into her right side so hard that she heard a crack, felt the balanced structure of bone shift, and passed out again in agony.

The little man with the mustache was a medic of some kind. When he brought her back to consciousness she answered questions in a wilderness of pain, unable to think clearly enough to lie. Castillo held out the promise of painblocks as a reward. She was lucid enough to know he lied, that they were still afraid of her and would do nothing to make her competent. Strangers had joined the group, the room was full of silent men. They would not make it better, but they could make it worse. She did not want that to happen. And it did not matter if they knew the truth. I&S had been wrong, they would look for the wrong man, Castillo had done what he set out to do and it made no difference if he knew it.

When she said Michael Kristofik's name, Castillo laughed aloud. "Him! We're clear," he said. So he knew Michael Kristofik. There was a connection after all. That made no difference either.

Then Castillo got up and went out. The little medic disappeared, too; the others stayed. Her clothes came apart under more hands, her legs were forced apart and agony ran right up into her chest and choked her. The pain in her side stopped everything, rage, disgust at this casual rape: "Nothing personal," she thought one said, and the pain in her side held her down so she could not even move to kick him. It could not get worse but did so in improbable peaks, until it was finally, surely unendurable and she escaped into darkness again. She was unconscious when the last one left.

"Be quiet, don't say anything, don't move—!"

She turned her head at the whisper. Her head seemed to be full of something thick, so that she could not hear or think very well. She was not cold any longer; she burned. There was a dull ache in her side.

"Be quiet, be still, I can't stay long . . ."

It was hard to focus her eyes. The face of the little medic danced and divided and came back to being one face. She said something in a drowsy mumble.

He said, "That's all I can do. I'll come back if I can. If I can!"

He edged away from her. She tried to call after him, but her tongue was as thick as everything else in her head. She could still think to him. *Wait, wait!* she cried, and he did, compelled by something in the thought, maybe despair.

He said, "I gave you enough for a few hours. I can't do anything about the fever. I don't know what it is. In a few hours we'll be on Revenge."

She listened with more than her sluggish ears. Revenge? The end: a place to die. That was where it would happen.

Why there. . . ?

Telepathy made him nervous. He twitched. "He kept you in case of trouble. If they came after us somehow. We won't be there long."

Why did you. . . ?

He jittered, moving toward the door. "I don't know. I was a physician once. I learned some things too well to forget. Like relieving pain. You hurt. You're going to die, I know that, it could be easier. I don't know if I can come back again. Don't tell him I did this. Please!"

Him. . . ? She formed a picture of the red-haired man. The medic shuddered and was gone.

Heat not cold, fever not pain. On the whole a better set of problems. What fever? Could be anything. Reconstructed my blood, who knows what's got in?

The pain was easy to manage now, though she staggered when she got up because her head floated. She tried moving as if in free fall, but that didn't work. She kept lurching against walls no matter what she tried. She gathered up the rags of her clothing and made knots in them and put on the result. A glint caught her eye in the dim light: a gold chain, broken on the floor. The opal was gone. The other chain was still around her neck, unbreakable. They had tried to break it; the skin under it was tender.

She drank water, a lot of water, the thirst was worse than before. Then she sat down on the floor again. The heat and the fever were nothing. The pain was in abeyance, and that was all that mattered; she could anesthetize herself before whatever the medic had given her dissipated.

And then? They would think her helpless. She would not be helpless. At the first sign of a chance she would act. As she had not acted on the *Far-Flying Bird*. They had waited, she and Rubee and Awnlee, civilized, rational, for an optimal opportunity. And so Rubee and Awnlee had died. It was necessary to forget about the civilized. There was no place for it out here.

She put herself into trance easily. The fever helped.

* * *

"Getting bored," Shen's voice said from Michael's left wrist. "Every hour, every half hour, kid says—" her voice rose to a whine, " *'Can I go out?'* Theo's gonna start doping pretty soon. How much longer?"

"You ask me that every hour, every half hour. *'How much longer, Mike?'* "

He tried to imitate the whine, with fair success. Shen snorted. He added, "Long as it takes. Stay there. I could need you fast."

"Know that."

"All right. Check in again—when you're bored."

Shen signed off, grumbling. He leaned back against a rusty rock, bundled against the cold of an autumn night outside the City of the Rose, and stared into the darkness.

He was bored, too, and perpetually cold. A week ago he had had all the warehoused beauties put aboard *GeeGee*—from motives of pure malice. *Hope I see his face when he finds out it's gone. GeeGee* lay behind another pile of rocks at the horizon, far enough away, he devoutly hoped, to be missed unless B made a detailed scan of the region before coming in to land. Michael meanwhile lived in the rocks outside the warehouse like a rat, never really warm, as close as he could get to B's customary landing site. Michael gambled B would use it again. His plan was simple: to stun everybody in sight as soon as B appeared, get him onto *GeeGee*, and run like hell. Subtlety was not the way to deal with B.

He scanned the sky once more with goggles adjusted for infrared. Nothing. The sky had been empty all week. The planet's single dim pocket-size moon was below the horizon. The sky was clear and stars spilled across it like sand.

He pulled up an all-season tarp to cover his mouth and got ready for another uncomfortable night. He did not sleep well with rock for bed and pillow. For the sixth night running he slipped into the same interminable half-dream that was also half-waking, so that he could think *oh no not again;* slipped back through the chain of years on Valentine, back to Alta, inexorably back. It was like watching history run in reverse. He had to go through the part with B at the center all over again: the empty smile, the soul-killing, inescapable demands. Back: the night spared him none of it: flames and death and the agony of his shattered hands. *You'll carry no more messages, boy.* Then memory ended and he stood on the edge of a void. Maybe there had been happiness there, but he did not know; would never know, without B.

The transmitter on his wrist burped and pricked the skin, hard. It was the signal he waited for.

He kicked away the tarp and grabbed the goggles. He had been sweating, and the icy air bit his face. *I'm ready to sell out the whole operation for a hot bath,* he thought, but he watched the spot of heat come in from high in the south. One fast coded answer to Shen and then silence, prearranged. He pulled the stunner, tested its weight in his gloved right hand, and crouched behind the rock, waiting.

* * *

It had grown easier, with the years, to become a machine. That was one of the pitfalls on the path of the Adept, the teachers said. It was easier not to feel, not to cry, not to rage. It was easier to turn aside from rejoicing. The disciplines were seductive to certain spirits, and Hanna might be one of them. It came too easily to her. She was very good.

Burning with fever and caged in ice she felt nothing. She held her broken bones upright and monitored the pain as if she watched a visible gauge. The pain was separate from her. No time passed. It was always the present moment. The sick life of the *Avalon* was visible to her as if she watched a play, though she did not use her eyes. Castillo was an empty black hole in which the commonest thoughts turned into things that crawled, more alien and more terrifying than any animal or sentient being she had known. She acknowledged the fact and filed it away without emotion. Gaaf the medic twitched inside all the time. He thought of Hanna with misery. The big blond man, Wales, wondered why he had wanted to take her, ugly from the beating as she was; he must have been too long in space. The one called Suarez thought with ordinary pleasure of someday going home, and what he had done to Hanna was a footnote to memory. Juel who had beaten her slept heavily. He always did after something like that. The release would relax him for days. She had no names for the other two. One was impatient: *Get the rest of it and get Outside, get paid, head for Valentine, spend it all. God, how I want to get drunk.* The other thought: *That might have been too much. But they were only aliens. And a D'neeran. So what?*

No time passed for Hanna, but she watched time shrink in their perception as they came close to their destination. Revenge. The Rose. There was a great stir of landfall and night. They stopped thinking of her. But soon they would come to kill her, said the voice of pure reason. The landing pods screamed through the hull, and she saw or imagined there was dust blowing, rocks flying. The ship was down. The scream fell to an already hum. Men went out.

She monitored, distantly, consternation and rage. Something was gone. That did not matter. What mattered was that someone thought of her. There was a use for her, a last use before she died. They would take her into the open. That was good.

When Juel came for her, she walked passively through the *Avalon* with the muzzle of a disruptor jammed into her back. He would have to be induced to move the muzzle. But it stayed against her skin and stayed there when they stopped. They had come to a lock in the side of the *Avalon*, open to the night. A short ramp led to the ground.

She looked straight ahead into the night. There were presences.

Castillo: "Look at this. Look at her. This is what your wives and daughters will look like when we get done."

From the ground, a shadow just starting to be afraid. "I tell you the truth. We did not touch the things. There are others on this world. I do not know what they did with your goods. I do not know!"

In the darkness at her left, another presence, silent, invisible to eyes. Watching with animal alertness.

Slowly she turned her head and looked into the dark at the tail of the ship. She said clearly, "Who is that?"

The muzzle of the disruptor shifted away from her. Remotely, in no-time, she twisted and turned. Her left hand hard as a steel blade caught Juel on the side of the neck; her right had the disruptor and fired and he fell. In no-time she turned it on Castillo—and jerked at a jolt of stun from the shadows at her back. She staggered down the ramp. In trance she could even fight stun, a little, for a while. The Castillo-target was gone. Running feet came toward her from somewhere and she swung the disruptor toward them, but it weighed more now than herself. Another wave of stun: the end. She did not get off another shot.

The ice of Revenge was in his veins, holding back the fury. He kicked the dead man aside, useless meat, whatever he knew was locked in the dead brain forever. The woman was another matter. He thumbed the emergency summons for *GeeGee* and pulled the woman away from the storm of coming liftoff, counting on darkness and luck and surprise. He threw her down behind rock and ducked just before light split the darkness where his head had been. The light quested, found its range, and began to melt away the rock. He measured the distance to the next one. Might make it. The high-pitched howl of *GeeGee* moving fast in atmosphere filled the night. The killing light blinked out; the ship without a name took off with a roar.

He forgot it instantly. His blood had turned to liquid fire. He knelt by the woman and got his hand on a light; it shook. His ears rang and he instructed himself: *I must not kill her. I must not.* The light swung wildly and settled on her face. Crouching in the darkness, watching the shadowplay at the lighted lock, he had thought her skin strangely mottled. The mottling was as fine a selection of bruises as he had ever seen. Somebody didn't like her much.

Shen was out of *GeeGee* before the ship was fully down, running and yelling. "Goddamnit, answer! You all right?"

"Yeah." He touched the battered face with itching fingers. He said, "He got away because of her."

Shen stopped at his side and said with interest, "What is it?"

"I don't know, but I hope it can talk."

The body stirred a little; eyes gleamed through swollen slits.

"You can talk, can't you, yes you can," he said.

"Later," said Shen, but he did not hear her. The fury came out of its cavern and he lifted a hand high, all his strength gathered to strike. Another movement caught his eye and he stopped because it might mean threat. Lise stood on the edge of the light and they stared at each other. Her chin lifted and she took one small, perceptible step backward. Away from him.

He let his hand fall, got control of his voice, and said, "What the hell are you doing here?"

She said nothing. She kept looking at him with bright blue eyes, betrayed. Then she melted into the darkness, back toward the *Golden Girl*.

Michael did not move. Shen knelt beside him and waited, silent and stony. The noise in his ears died away with the rage. He was sick and exhausted and his head throbbed.

Shen said finally, "Cold out here. Turning blue." She pointed at the body on the ground.

"Yeah. We have to go. He thinks *GeeGee's* armed, I guess. If he comes back shooting, we're in trouble."

He felt a violent aversion to picking up the stranger. When he did, it was worse; she was too light, too limp, too helpless. When he reached the *Golden Girl*, it was a relief to hand her over to Theo.

It was night on *GeeGee*, adjusted to the cycle of the City of the Rose. The gentle light in Central Control was made for amusing conversations, leisurely journeys in luxury. He appreciated it. He never stopped appreciating it. Lise was tucked into her place against the wall. He tried to talk to her, *I would never hit you, I would never do that to you,* but he got only silence in return. Lise had learned early what kinds of evidence to trust.

First things first. He took *GeeGee* into space and made the first Jump on a common route chosen at random so that for all practical purposes they were unfindable. When that was done, Shen said economically, "Well?"

"Wait a minute . . ." He leaned back, soaking up warmth, sorting out what had happened, getting used to the idea that there were no more reasons to hurry.

"There was a lot going on out there," he said. "They landed without spotting me. A couple of them came out. They were starboard-on to me and they opened up portside. The ship was between me and the warehouse and I couldn't see what was happening. I worked my way around behind the rocks. Took the last hundred meters without cover. Good thing they came in at night. There was a lot of coming and going. They'd found out about the warehouse. One of them took off into town and came back with one of the elders, Rann, I think. Poor old Rann. What happened to him, anyway? Think he's all right?"

"See his body?"

"Good point. I was at the tail and coming up along the side by then. B was talking to Rann, accusing him of taking the stuff. Then they brought that woman out. Who the hell is she, anyway? I got in range and I was ready and she told them I was there. I swear I hadn't made a sound. She was standing in the light and it was pitch dark where I was."

He hesitated, replaying the blur of violence. He said slowly, "There was another one holding a disruptor on her. She got it away from him and killed him. I was starting to fire at B. But she was going to kill him. So I stunned her first. It was *that* close." He held up two fingers close together. "And while I was doing that, B jumped back in the ship. And then she almost got me before I stunned her again. Shen, there's something wrong with the power pack in that gun. I shouldn't have had to hit her twice."

Shen said, "Recruit her."

"One of his monsters? You don't know what you're talking about."

Shen shrugged. Michael got up and said, "I'm going to go see if Theo's got her up to talking."

"Need help?"

"Maybe later. Somebody'd better stay here for a while."

He had not told Theo where to take the woman. There was a medlab on *GeeGee*, as sophisticated as everything else on this ship. He went there first; when he opened the door the equipment hummed at him, but no one was there. He went to the two unoccupied staterooms, to Theo's room, and to the smaller quarters over the engineering section before he decided that he should have asked *GeeGee* in the first place where Theo had gone. Now there were not many places left, and he went to his own cabin with some indignation.

He went in and said bitterly, "What's she doing here? Bleeding on my bed."

"It was the first one I got to," Theo said simply. He stood by the bed and peered at a reader in his hand, scowling. A scanner pointed at the woman's right side, looking more deadly than helpful. A tube in her left arm snaked across the bed and out of sight. Half a dozen metal cases of varying sizes littered the bed, some talking quietly to themselves. Theo had cut away what passed for the woman's clothes. The bruises ran into one another, except in one place. Michael said, "Nice of them to leave her jaw alone," and the body twitched for the first time, startling him. He said, "Can she talk yet?"

"No."

"How long?"

Theo looked up and shook his head. His eyes were watchful. Michael cocked his head and said, "You can't talk either?"

Theo said in an odd voice, "Maybe in a few days."

"You can do better than that."

Theo braced himself. "Her temperature's forty-two-point-four. That's critical. She's got broken bones. She's dehydrated and I don't know how long it's been since she had any nourishment. She might be dying."

"There's heavy life support in the lab."

"I don't know how to use it. I never got that far with the courses. You know that."

''Then I want you to wake her up now. I can't talk to her if she's dead.''

''If I juice her nervous system now, she could be dead in an hour.''

The reader trembled in Theo's hand. Michael said experimentally, ''I'm going to talk to her. That's what I want. Wake her up and the hell with it.''

''No,'' said Theo. It was barely audible.

After a while Michael sat down on the bed and rummaged in one of the metal cases. He found a pouch and opened it and took out the saturated pad inside. He began swabbing the woman's bruised face. ''I liked you better when you were a worm,'' he said.

Theo took a deep breath. He started talking, not quite in a normal voice. ''She's got Dawkins' fever. I don't know how she could, but she does. She's got two broken ribs. I'll have to go in. I'll need your help. Shen's, too, probably.''

''Blood all over my bed.''

''There won't be much blood. That's the other thing, her blood. I can't make any sense out of it. I'll have to take some to the lab where there's more to work with. Somebody has to stay with her.''

''All right. I will.''

Theo was silent for so long that Michael finally looked up. He said, ''What's wrong with that?''

''It's just—look at her. Think she got that way falling downstairs?''

''I won't hurt her,'' Michael said, shocked.

Theo said, ''You haven't been yourself lately.''

''So tell me something new—'' He waited a minute to make sure his voice would be steady. ''Consider me under orders. Just tell me what to do.''

Theo looked into his eyes and relaxed. He said, ''Keep doing what you're doing. Stay away from the right side. I don't want accelerated healing there till I've done the bones. Don't worry if she wakes up. There's no pain in the side, I took care of that, and what you're doing will block out the rest.'' He started out with a vial of something red in his hand. At the door he said over his shoulder, as an afterthought, "I think she might have been raped, too."

When Theo was gone the room was quiet, except for the boxes talking to each other. Michael touched the woman's side; the flesh had a spongy feel. How could he ever have thought of beating her? She wouldn't be the first terrorized innocent to escape from B.

The full impact of the possibility hit him; he dropped the swab and was still. When some time had passed, quite a lot of time, he felt heat under his hand. He looked at it and saw that it was cupped about the woman's cheek. Her skin was on fire.

He found a fresh swab and went on with the job very gently. When he touched her thighs, her eyes opened and she made the first sound of protest he had heard.

"It's all right," he said. "I'm just trying to help you. That's the only reason I'd touch you."

Her eyes focused on his face. He did not know if she had understood. He leaned closer to her and said softly, "Don't worry. We don't do things like that here. It's different here."

She understood that time. She looked at him with intelligence; he might have said with recognition, if that were possible. Her lips parted and she said something he would not have heard if he had not been so close. It was: *"Not much improvement."*

He drew back and stared at her with astonishment, and then with appreciation. He said, "Look, I've got enough consciences hanging around here. I don't need another one."

He thought she said something else, but her lips did not move and he did not know what the word was. He almost thought she had thrown a giant question mark into the air. That was impossible, too.

"What was that?" he said, but her eyes were closed again, and he did not think she heard him any more

* * *

B returns to Revenge with caution. Sweeps land and sky for a trace of technology beyond that used by the

People of the Rose. The other ship has gone. They hunt down Elder Rann again; the city prays and quakes. Rann cannot talk fast enough. "A golden ship, a man with a companion, he called himself your friend—"

B has a visual on the marauder. Enhanced, it shows name and registration clear on the bow. The Golden Girl *out of Valentine. Who is her master?*

* * *

Theo said, "You have to clean up."

"Huh?"

"Nobody comes in my surgery that dirty."

"You never had a surgery."

"I do now."

The picture of what was happening on Revenge faded. It was accurate; Michael was as sure of that as if he were there.

He said, "She's dirtier than I am."

"Shen's going to clean her up."

"My bathroom looks like a biosyn supply house. Thanks to you."

"Use mine."

Theo was implacable. Michael looked at him quizzically. He said, "Sure you're up to this?"

"It's not that hard." To Michael's surprise Theo blushed. He said, "I was pretty good, you know. Before I got thrown out. I can handle this. But we ought to be heading home. She's really sick."

"Before we go home I want to see what she says."

"If she lives long enough to say anything, you mean. Look, I can only do so much. We need to head for Valentine and we need to get Rescue out for rendezvous. 'Cause I told you, I can't use the heavy stuff. And she might need to be on it real soon. If her heart stops."

Michael looked at the face of the unconscious woman. It was less swollen, but she had not stirred again. He thought of her single-handed ruin of the plan that had almost succeeded. There was nothing to do but accept it. They could not go back to Revenge; B had heavy arms and was warned. He would watch the empty sky.

There had been no time to think about the size of the disaster, the waste of two years' work, the hunt that should have ended on Revenge. So close. So goddamn close to the secret, the path that led back to the start.

"We have to do it all over again," Michael said. But Theo did not know what he was talking about, so he said, "God knows where he'll turn up next. Maybe he'll go on Outside. It might be years before we pick up a trail—before I do. You're out if you want to be."

Theo shook his head. "No."

"Think about it."

"I already know. I've been with you six years. Where would I go? I'll never do what I wanted to do, I doped it away. No med faculty in space'll let me back in. What would Shen do? Go back to Nestor? You're stuck with us. Mike, it's not as bad as you think. We can get something out of this woman. We have to keep her alive. Let me contact Rescue. Please. You said you were under orders."

He was right. He was also anxious about Michael. Michael's face was treacherously transparent; he was desolate and it showed. There were limits to what he wanted even Theo to see. He could not smile, not yet, but he rearranged his face somehow and Theo was relieved. He would have to fight the rest of it out later, when he was by himself.

He went to Control and called Rescue. He told a voice from Valentine there was a sick and injured woman, unidentified, aboard. Would Rescue pick her up? The voice balked. *GeeGee* was outside their customary range. They were shorthanded. Michael went on talking. He quoted regulations (making some up) and precedent. He appealed to humanity. Shen listened with a sneer and Lise, her interest caught, forgot to be afraid and came close and took his hand. Finally he did what he ought to have done at once. He reminded the voice who he was and mentioned a Valentine Ecomanager whom he knew personally. When it was over, he had what he wanted and Shen was as close to smiling as she ever got. "All right, all right," he said. "I forgot the Kristofik theory of social structure."

"What's that?" Lise said.

"Money always wins."

"Ah," she said, enlightened.

He gathered clean clothes and went to Theo's room, walking the corridor as if the stone of Revenge had gotten into his feet. The game he had played for the last two years was over. As soon as B knew who was after him, it would be a new game: not a private hunt but a private war. It would start soon. It might have started already.

* * *

The People of the Rose have no use for Inspace communication, but the relays come near Revenge, as on all norm-pattern routes in human space. The Interworld Fleet has sown relays like seed for centuries. B puts a query to a common-access information network. The request has low priority and traffic on the relays is heavy. Access is skewed by the demands of Fleet, which often commandeers great chunks of the system's capacity for an hour or a day. B waits.

* * *

Hot water did not relax him; it only reminded him of his weariness, and of too many nights of half-sleeping on rock. *Had it all, Kristofik. All that money. Couldn't you just enjoy it?*

* * *

The answer comes, the name. Maybe it means something; maybe not. The man with a thousand names puts little stock in them. He gets a picture, too. He knows the face. Twenty years ago: a boy on a street in Shoreground. Thirty years ago: a terrified child.

Then it is war. And B's first object is the elimination of Michael Kristofik.

* * *

Dressing in Theo's darkened room he jumped at a movement on the edge of sight and spun to face it. His savage reflection looked back from a mirror. His hands were clenched. "Quick with our fists today, aren't we?" he said to the mirror, but there was no humor in the face that looked back at him. And after all, he thought irrelevantly, the woman was probably property of the pack that ran with B this year, willing enough to watch a night of flame.

He saw inside his eyes another fist from long ago.

Never again. Not any man.

"Shut up," he said to the voices inside his skull, wondered why he had ever started the hunt; but he knew the answer to that; only he had not known how hard it would be.

When he knows it was me, he'll wish he'd killed me years ago in Shoreground. Seeing me there must have been a shock; but he thought I couldn't be a threat. Just another kid fallen into Valentine. And lost. Like the troubadour's song—"Since the soul in me is dead, better save the skin"—knew what that meant first time I heard it—

Hanna thought it might be time to come out of trance.

The cool voice of reason said it was time. The disjunction of consciousness should not be maintained past necessity. It drained the body, especially when it was held, as she held it, against the body's sickness and wounding. Necessity, said reason, was gone. This was medical treatment she was getting, no worse; unorthodox, perhaps, but competent. If she stayed in trance, she might find a way to overpower the men and women who held her, and then?—without them she would die.

Reason also warned her of the consequences of letting go. Everything was there, waiting its time—pain and fear, grief overdue and thus strengthened, some particularly revolting memories from the *Avalon*, and the knowledge that she was lost outside—no longer human space, perhaps, but certainly human law. Not even reason could assess her exact position; she had missed some important facts. The stun effect had made her

memory patchy, like her consciousness as she fought it.
She had escaped the *Avalon*, but she did not know what
she had come to. She remembered an upraised fist and
brutal rage, somehow averted. She remembered indifference to her death, provided she remained alive long
enough to be useful. It was all connected to the face
she recognized and the gold-flecked eyes; that made
sense; but she also remembered pity and a soothing
touch, and it was all the same man, and that did not
make sense at all.

While she thought about this, she was touched again.
She gave herself up to the hands with indifference. She
knew without opening her eyes whose hands they were;
they belonged to the woman and the girl. They washed
her carefully and renewed the healing salve. The woman
did not like it. *Babysitter, medaide, nurse: didn't sign
on for this: he'll want me to cook for them next!* The
girl might have been caressing a doll endowed with
imaginary life, healing its hurts and her own with nar-
cissistic devotion. *Poor baby, poor darling, I'll make it
better, oh help me, oh hold me!*

Hanna opened her eyes to see what they would say
when they knew she was conscious.

The woman called Shen did not say anything. She
thought: *What a constitution. We could use her.*

Hanna turned her eyes on the girl named Lise. She
could not see Lise very clearly. Lise did not know that,
and it made no difference anyway. She responded with
the egocentricity of her age. She leaned over Hanna, a
sudden jerk. She said, ''He didn't mean it.''

''What the hell?'' Shen said.

Lise said in an urgent whisper, ''He wouldn't have
hit you. He wouldn't. He doesn't do that. He won't hurt
you.''

It was overpowering love, it was worship that excused
and did away all faults. Hanna thought that the child
deceived herself. But Lise said, ''It's hard for him. I
don't know what it is, he won't tell me anything, anything at *all*. But he won't hit you. He won't.''

She touched Hanna's shoulder lightly, mindful of the
bruises.

Hanna acknowledged without emotion that all of them were careful with her, even Shen. Reason said they would care for her; that it was time to submit to the body's claims and let herself be healed.

Since reason anchored the trance, and the balance of reason urged leaving it, she did so.

The first thing she thought as her mode of thinking shifted was that the concept of the Master of Chaos was more clear to her than it had been before.

The next thing was that she wished she were safe within the strictures of Polity Admin.

The last was a question even reason had not raised. She knew the Polity well, and especially how Jameson thought. Admin had the course to Uskos. Fleet might have tracked the course of the *Far-Flying Bird* as a precaution, a day or two behind, listening for messages of distress. If they had done that (a thing that would suit Jameson), they would know something had happened. The context of her situation would be changed, and she would not be as alone as she felt; the power of five planets waited to help her, if only she stayed alive long enough.

It was her last conscious thought. Exhaustion waited outside the trance, and took over.

* * *

GeeGee sang:

> *The hounds they lie down at his feet,*
> *So well they can their master keep;*
> *His hawks they fly so eagerly*
> *No fowl dares come him nigh . . .*

"I don't think that's exactly what I want to hear," Theo said. His face was shiny, but his eyes were intent, and the fingers that manipulated the instruments were steady. The living bone quivered, an artist's medium.

"I thought it would help you with your incising," Michael said gravely.

"Incising? There's no such word."

"Sure there is."

"How do you know?"

"I'm educated, remember?"

Down there comes a fallow doe
As great with young as she might go.
She lifted up his bloody head
And kissed the wounds that were so red . . .

Theo said, "I haven't done anything like this in years. Shut it off, all right?"

"Remind me not to let you touch me, if I get hurt."

"Dammit, Mike—"

"Yessir. *GeeGee*, the music is not appreciated. Turn it off."

The sweet voice stopped in mid-song. All of them were in Michael's room, leaving *GeeGee* to tend to herself. The room was brilliantly lighted, especially the bed where the injured woman lay in a cone of blinding light. Movement had a sharp edge in the light, and some of the sharpness was tension, but imperceptibly it drained away. That was because Michael so far had not slipped, to all appearances was himself, and the others were reassured.

A splintered end of bone shifted a millimeter and a metal box said suddenly, "Optimum match."

"Not quite as good as the other one," Theo said. "Still. She can be grateful. It should have punctured the lung." He used a spindle-shape the size of his thumb to fuse the fixative saturating the bone. The metal box chirped and displayed patterns of relative binding strength. Theo touched up his handiwork and the chirps steadied to a hum. Theo said with satisfaction, "That's good. Sealed tight. It waited too long. This must have happened two days ago."

Lise, watching avidly, said, "Ow."

"Mike?" said Shen. She was at the woman's feet, watchful. Theo had not wanted to burden the weak body further with a general anesthetic; he had stationed Shen and Michael so that they could restrain sudden movement if the unconscious woman stirred. It had not been necessary. Michael still held her right hand, stretched above her head and out of Theo's way, but his grip was light. Her left hand lay on her breast, puffy in spite of quick care; that came from the blow to the man with the disruptor. How had she managed to do it, painful as it must have been to move?

Shen said, uncannily echoing the thought, "Two days like that, she did what you told me? Couldn't."

"You wouldn't think so."

"What did she do?" said Theo, who had not heard the story; and when Michael told him he would not believe it. He said, "She couldn't even have walked without screaming."

"She did. I saw it. She might have been doped. It would've had to be a hell of a brew."

"She wasn't doped. She had a broad-spectrum anesthetic at some point, but that was a long time ago. There was just a trace left when I looked at her blood, not enough to make any difference. There was a high concentration of endorphins—still. She couldn't have," Theo said, firmly rejecting fact.

He put away the spindle and selected a slim object with a bulge at one end. He drew it carefully along the edges of the incision. It made no sound, but the layers of fat and muscle quivered. Michael looked away, queasy. There was no difference in kind between what had happened to the woman already, the beating and the rape, and this even more intimate invasion of the flesh. *What nonsense,* he thought, and heard faint clicks; he looked again and saw Theo with a handful of clamps. "That's a good job, if I say so myself. Ready to close," Theo said in a strong, efficient voice that was an echo from some past time.

Michael said, "You said you couldn't make any sense out of her blood."

"I finally did. In some ways. You know what I can't understand? Dawkins' fever. Nobody gets that."

"I've never heard of it."

"You're immunized against it, though. Everybody is. It came out of Colony One at the beginning of the Explosion. You've heard of the Plague Years, I know; well, that was Dawkins' fever. Ever since then you can't even get a vital signs readout without having your immunity tested. It's still around, but you don't find it very often. It would be just possible for her to get it if she'd always been in some isolated place and never had any medical care. But she's had the best—there's evidence of a massive regeneration effort in adulthood—and she's been around. Has she ever been around!''

The edges of the incision melted together under Theo's hands. When he was done, there was only a red line cutting across the inflamed skin. He ran a finger over it with a craftsman's approval and said, ''Rescue can worry about scarring. That's good, though. You can let go now.''

Michael held on to the right hand anyway. It had escaped the general destruction and was smooth to the touch, but it radiated heat. He said, ''What did you do? The same kind of profile you did on my blood a couple of years ago?''

''Yes, and she's been everywhere. All the Polity worlds. Valentine. And the Outside worlds, too, which is very rare—Girritt, F'thal, even Zeig-Daru. And there were some other things the tracking program couldn't match up.''

''Maybe there's something wrong with it. That doesn't sound right about Zeig-Daru. Nobody's been there except a few D'neerans.''

''Well, the base pattern is D'neeran.''

''It's *what?*''

''D'neeran.'' Theo, puttering among metal boxes, stopped and looked at him curiously. ''What's wrong with that?''

''Well—it's just that getting anywhere near B would have to make a telepath sick.''

He was shocked and it must show; Shen was too still, Theo looked too uncertain. He pulled himself together and said calmly, ''If she's D'neeran, she wasn't with him by choice. She might not have much to tell us. Are you sure?''

''That's what it said,'' Theo said stubbornly. ''And if she's not D'neeran, why would she go to D'neera? Nobody goes there either.''

"I did once," Michael said reminiscently. "I was spaced. I thought I was going to D'ning on Co-op, from a town an hour away. I couldn't figure out why passage cost so much and why it took so long."

Theo looked at him suspiciously, but the story was true. It had happened in the years just after the *Pavonis Queen*, when he had spent money wildly and the drugs and the women were interchangeable, the craving for something unidentified insatiable, the fights a constant in every spaceport bar. Twice he had nearly killed men with his fists, and later bought them off. And lately it seemed he had not changed so much since then as he had thought. *Not much improvement,* she had said.

Theo cleared away equipment. He left a monitor bracelet on the woman's wrist. He studied the readout module at her shoulder, frowning.

"She's no worse," he said. "You said three days to rendezvous, if we start now? I hope she holds out."

Shen said, "Mike, they called back just before I came down. Want to talk to you."

"Why?"

"Want to know what happened."

"They don't have to know."

"Told 'em you'd call."

"Forget it."

She shrugged. Theo said, "Mike, I said let go of her hand. You'll confuse the monitor."

Michael released the hand with a twinge of reluctance. "Think she'll make it?" he said.

Theo said, "Somebody help me take this stuff back to the lab."

Michael watched him gather up instruments and load them onto Shen and Lise like pack animals. He did not repeat the question.

When the others went out, he stayed where he was. The woman on the bed looked more like a human being now that some of the bruises were clearing, and he was uncomfortable. After a minute he realized that her nudity disturbed him, and drew a sheet over the limp figure. It was not possible for her to be an object of desire, and he had known more than his portion of naked flesh; it was her helplessness that troubled him.

He thought of Theo's judgment of her origin. D'neer-ans were no more faultless than other human beings and had some faults of their very own, but they were too sensitive to psychic pain to live willingly with evil. This woman could not be one of B's pack. Instead she had had the bad luck to become his prey. And she did not think Michael was much better.

He thought: *Live. So I can tell you that wasn't me you saw. He just drops in sometimes. Please live.*

The dark lifted a little from time to time. When it did, she thought she was in a nightmare. Past, present, and future bounced around inside her skull in urgent jolts—

Contact the Polity Admin Starr Starr Starr! they must not find out who I am—hide from them!

Michael slumped with his head on one hand, half asleep. The room was dark except for a pool of light around the bed. The iris that opened on space was shut to the shifts that came with each Jump. The edges of the room melted into the dark, and Lise slept in shadow on a padded couch, her fragile legs in an awkward sprawl. Theo sat near the bed; he did not sleep. He got up often and looked at the patient, the monitor readouts, the tubes that fed into her arm all the help that was left to give. Shen had shrugged and left them to their vigil. There was no sound except for the whisper of *GeeGee* at night, and the sick woman's difficult breath.

I must do it, I must. But in nightmare one cannot move, the body has no strength, I cannot breathe, I feel nothing . . . nothing . . .

Michael brooded on the face that healed before his eyes. The lesser bruises were gone, the others disappearing. It was like watching a blurred image come into focus; as if it were not her face that changed, but his eyes that cleared. In the slow hours he saw the clear arch of the brow emerge, the mouth soften to delicate curves. A silver chain that could not be removed glistened against skin turning to pale brown satin. Once, her eyes opened. When he leaned over, he saw that it was reflex and she was aware of nothing near her; he saw also that her eyes were the deepest blue he had ever seen. They closed and he drew away, troubled. She had begun to look familiar, but he did not know her.

—oh no I have failed all alone with the dead I feel NOTHING—!

Six years of Hanna's life vanished. She fell into the past. The People of Zeig-Daru tore her apart, humans regenerated her, and she woke, a disembodied consciousness in null-space, sightless, paralyzed, disconnected from muscle and nerve—

Lise stirred and moaned. The sides of *GeeGee* rushed in and sucked out with a roar. The air went with them. Michael woke to the dark, paralyzed. He could not lift a hand, could not breathe, there were weights on his chest. "*GeeGee*!" He was choking. "Life support! Air!"

"All systems A-OK," *GeeGee* said, "don't you like the atmosphere mix?"

He flailed at stifling darkness and then it was gone. His heart pounded and he breathed in gasps. He felt something he had not known in years: panic. He was incredulous. Lise lifted herself with a struggle, dazed. Theo said, "What was—?"

"I don't know—" His heartbeat eased. Nothing was changed. He must have slept and dreamed something terrible—but Lise and Theo had felt it, too—

D'neerans learn before they are six to suppress unwilled projection of thought. In extremity inhibition gives way.

Oh God they are big so much bigger than I cruel and ruthless oh agony no—! No!

The room filled up with ghastly shadows. Michael got a good look at them, impossibly there, bestial figures of malignant intelligence. Lise flew across the room and into his arms with a terrified cry—right through the shadows.

"Theo!" He shouted into a well. "Something on Revenge, what did we pick up!"

Shen tumbled into the room. She held a knife and yelled, "Where are they, where!" *Oh help help help me!* Hanna screamed, but silently, dreadfully, and Lise shrieked an echo in Michael's ear.

The monstrous shadows touched the sky. The sick woman writhed in a pile of sheets and tubes, center of a storm. Michael fell on her. "Stop it," he said, "stop, stop!" He took her face in his hands, took her shoulders and shook her. Her eyelids flickered. He saw her face and nothing else, shadow was everywhere. "Wake up! Stop it!"

She shrank away from his hands and lifted her own and struck at him. He felt the effort as if it were his. He thought she clawed his eyes, chopped his neck—but that was only her intent; she had not touched him. A strong woman with a newborn's strength.

The light came back.

Lise cried in great gusts, howling. Michael held her tightly with one arm and kept the other hand on the stranger's shoulder. Over Lise's head he saw Theo and Shen shaken, staring, waiting for him to say it was all right.

"All right. It's all right," he said, and disentangled himself from Lise. He did not want to loose his hold on the woman. He brushed a lock of tangled hair from her face and she made a pitiful sound, still lost in a private horror. But it was private again.

"It's her. Telepathy." His fingers were tight on her shoulder, but he made his voice light. "Wonderful thing, telepathy. What do the books say about this, Theo?"

"Huh?"

"Go check the lab library. Or call Rescue. Find out what this is about." He let go of the woman cautiously. Lise crowded against him and he held her and stroked her hair; she snuffled against his chest. "Theo, it could start up again, go find out what to do!"

Theo, an automaton, looked first at the tubes and readouts. "But the fever's down," he mumbled, and stumbled out.

Michael looked at Shen and said, "Put the knife away." She growled and shoved it into her belt. She took Theo's place and stared at the patient balefully.

"What the hell?" she said.

"I told you. Telepathy. I thought for a minute we'd all been doped or something, got some kind of mind-bending bug on Revenge—but all that came from her."

"Those things? In here?"

"Not real. Illusions. Some kind of shared hallucination that started with her."

Lise said with a last sob, "What were they?"

"I don't know. Something she made up. Or maybe saw . . ."

It was past. He began to relax. He sat on the bed and watched the woman's face. Lise wound herself into a ball, her head on Michael's knee; she looked at the telepath fearfully. Michael thought about the shadows. What kind of mind could think them up? But they had had the detailed immediacy of experience: the gray skin, scarlet garments, paws with long curving claws.

He said restlessly, "I've seen those things before. Not them, but pictures of them."

It was just out of reach, as if someone had just told him the answer and he had already forgotten. He went on thinking out loud: "Nothing looks quite like that except—well, Zeigans do a little; they might be exaggerated Zeigans. They might be, she's been to Zeig-Daru, Theo said. And she might think of them like that. The first person to make contact, a D'neeran woman, had what you might call a bad experience—"

After a minute of dead silence Shen said, "So?"

He got up, dumping Lise out of his lap. She retreated quickly from the bed. There was a library terminal in the room and the library was well stocked. He sat down at the terminal with some reluctance. He kept wanting to look back at the unconscious woman, as if it were dangerous to turn his back on her.

The guess had to be wrong. There had to be some reason for her look of familiarity besides his reading about Zeig-Daru.

But the search took no time at all. When he asked the library about Zeig-Daru, the first answer was a woman's name. There was a portrait with it. He looked toward the bed once, quickly, without needing to; now he knew why it seemed he had seen her before. He had seen pictures of that face over and over in the months just past, because of the envoys from Uskos.

After a while he got up and went back to the bed. He looked down at Hanna ril-Koroth and said tiredly, "This is very bad."

Shen lifted an eyebrow. Lise was frightened; she did not understand, but his tone warned her something was wrong.

"This is an important person," he said. "I knew a lot about her once, at the time of the Zeigan contact. Which she made. Among other things she's Contact's darling and a commissioner's lady. Former commissioner's. I don't know what the hell we're going to do with her. I thought she belonged with B, thought she was nobody, nobody cared what happened to her, we could question her and hand her over to Rescue and that'd be the end of it—but we're going to be looked at like I haven't been looked at in fifteen years. Like I never wanted to be looked at again. There's no way to keep this quiet."

Theo came in, steadier. He said, "There's not much we can do if it happens again. One of us can try to keep her attention and focus the projection, so we don't all lose our minds. In D'neeran medical centers they keep mindhealers on staff for that."

Shen said, "You got it wrong."

"What?" Theo said, but she was talking to Michael. "Wrong? How?"

"About quiet." The knife was in Shen's hand. She touched the blade. "Cancel Rescue. All they know is the bitch died. We jettison the body. She never had a name."

Michael said, "Theo, what did you do? Contact Rescue?"

"No, it was in the library. I'll do that, though. I'd better do that."

"No. Don't."

"No?"

"No." He looked at Shen. "If she dies, all right. No

name. Some stranger from anyplace but D'neera. But we don't do anything to hurry it along.''

Shen hissed. ''Gonna run *Gee* with those things around?''

''I'll try what Theo said. Try to keep her attention on me, keep her mind focused.''

''Dangerous! What if she lives?''

I don't know, he started to say, but there was no time. The figure on the bed moved with a moan. Lise whimpered. Nightmare moved in.

Hanna crept through a maze of stone. The People of Zeig-Daru were at her heels; she kicked at a flat-muzzled face. ''I am a friend!'' she cried. They answered: *Thou hast killed he with whom thou wert bonded, that is one; his spouse, the lady of the dawn, that is two; the persons of his crew, that is four others; the spouses of three of these, altogether nine; likewise he who took thee to selfing and thy close kin Awnlee. That is eleven; oh thou human who communicates with We who differ from humankind!*

She called for Jameson, for her mother, for the Lady of Koroth. *Starr, Cassie, Iledra, help me!* she cried, and beat with her fists against stone. The air was hot and close and stifled her. There was no end to the rocky passages.

''We could go somewhere nicer,'' someone said cautiously.

The stone diminished; the People receded; there was a blur of light. She was just as hot and the breath on her cheek was scalding. She pushed it away impatiently.

''Think of something nice,'' the voice pleaded.

''But what?'' she said, or thought she said; she could not have named the language.

The voice said hopefully, ''Springtime? Flowers. Raindrops.''

She thought a burst of millefleurs and smiled at their color. Trees she had never seen before arched over them: alien vegetation. She was confused. The stone half-materialized again. She said, ''Whose spring? D'neera's,

Earth's? Zeig-Daru's or F'thal's? What planet, what place on it, what latitude, where?''

''Pick one.''

Her hands were gritty with dirt; they held a plant with naked mud-caked roots. She set it carefully into the hole she had dug. Its tight-coiled buds were shaded with pink. The slanting springtime afternoon light bathed her house in gold. She patted dirt gently around the plant, anticipating its blooms with pleasure.

''That's better,'' the voice said in relief. There was a body to go with it now, rangy and well-knit. The face was pleasant, though it was sometimes a man's and sometimes a boy's. The eyes had vivid flecks of gold.

''I have tangentially conjoined you in past!'' she said in F'thalian, and knew that he understood it to mean *Why, I know you!* and knew therefore that she had not said it at all, but thought it.

''So I see,'' he answered. ''But how?''

''They thought you would attack the *Bird*,'' she said, the ''they'' encompassing I&S, Fleet, Contact, Jameson, Figueiredo, and Rubee and Awnlee.

His shock nearly bowled her over; she clung to the dream, she did not want to fall back into the wilderness of accusing stone.

''Why?'' said the voice. ''Tell me why they thought that!''

Her house slipped away, though she held on as hard as she could; flat on her back she looked up at a blur of a face. She said weakly, ''The computers said so.''

''Computers,'' said the voice. ''Oh my God, their damned computers!''

She could not find her home again. She had escaped the stone, however. She wandered in the summer of another Home, the People's Home. The lady of the dawn, Hearthkeeper of a Nearhome, dead these five years, walked with her. *Thou killest my spouse and my self,* Sunrise said, *and whom else? Not the beings of F'thal; but you did not make that contact; it predated you. Fortunate F'thal!*

I did what I had to do. Thou wouldst have killed me. He whom we both loved would have done so.

*And thy sire and sib-selfing? There also thou didst
what must be done, heedless of precautions wise men
urged.*

*Rubee's wishes were fulfilled. I did what he would
have me do.*

Sunrise laughed. That was an anomaly, the People
did not laugh. Therefore Sunrise was not really here
and it had to be the fever. And it was, she had been
dreaming, she was awake now and trapped in a cube of
metal on the *Avalon*, in great pain; she waited in rage
and disgust for her clothes to be torn away. The hands
had not yet touched her flesh, but she felt them crawl
on her body anyway. And screamed, outraged.

"No, please," implored the voice. It was shaky. One
chaste kiss touched her cheek. She held hard to a hand.

*It doesn't matter you know I can endure it what I have
to do have to do have to do—*

"Oh, think of something else!" he begged. There
were tears on her cheeks; not her tears. A child sobbed
at her side. They were in a spacecraft without a name,
which both was and was not the *Avalon*. She turned to
the boy although it took all her strength, and put her
arms around him.

"It was over long ago," she said grieving.

"I thought so, too. But it wasn't. In a way it only
started later."

The amber eyes widened. Tears were caught in the
long lashes. "You're not supposed to know about that!"
he said, more surprised than angry, but she shrank away,
he had grown up suddenly and smelled of jungle.

He vanished in a lingering fashion. A blurred outline
remained which was somehow palpable to the touch, so
that she could hold on to the disappearing arm. There
were other voices. She could not understand them, but
she heard them:

"You all right?" Shen said through her teeth.

"I think so—"

He tried to move his arm, but Hanna held it fiercely.
He moved enough to give his cramped muscles some

relief; yet surely he could not have been long in that shadow world. He mumbled, ''She's too strong for me.''

''Then stop it,'' Shen said, bending close. ''Stop it now!''

He had forgotten why he had begun this. The abyss of dream was close, easy to slip into again, and tempting—and suicidal. Some part of him knew that it could strip him of secrets without meaning to, without even wanting to. It was the danger he had avoided for a lifetime. Why, then, was it so seductive?

Brother Martin, all white stone and smoldering eyes: ''There is a joy in degradation. The freedom from all rules. Cry to Heaven: I do not care! Let go. Wash away . . .''

Theo and Shen talked. There were echoes; he heard with two sets of ears. The words had meaning for him, but not for the other personality of which he was so powerfully aware. She seized from him whole and unbroken the meaning she could not sort out for herself.

Shen raged; that was some of the meaning. Theo said, ''I don't think there'll be long-term effects. I think it's harmless.''

''Mike? Mike?'' whispered Lise. The sound was close. He opened his eyes to a dazzle of light and felt his solid body with surprise. He had thought himself immaterial. Lise hung over him. Her anxiety and fear were blows, channeled by the sick woman.

''Don't be afraid,'' he said.

''But I am!'' she wailed. ''Why don't you just let her die?''

''It's all right, little puss—''

Not for her. Silly. Can't you see she's afraid for you? Aren't you afraid of anything? Weren't you afraid on the Queen?

''No,'' he said. They stood in the docking bay of the *Pavonis Queen.* It was empty and its angles and substance were unreal. Hanna understood that where they were was in fact an engineer's diagram. Every symbol was reproduced on the intangible surfaces. He had a laser pistol in his hand and held it competently, thoughtfully.

"But where did you get the plans?" she said.

"You know how I got them."

"Why weren't you afraid?"

"What was there to be afraid of?"

"Well—being caught. Of course. Prison or Adjustment. Even death?"

"The Polity never executes anybody."

"Prison, then?"

"I would have chosen Adjustment. They let you do that."

"But why? That's death, too."

"Sure it is. It was worth the risk, that's all."

"How could it possibly be?"

"Freedom is worth any risk."

"In theory, yes—" The snow fell outside her house. A fire sang on the hearth. She served tea: a polite accompaniment to polite conversation. He was urbane and relaxed. Too relaxed; his eyes were too knowing; they had seen too much of the other side of civilization.

"The best you can do," he said, "is choose your own parameters—choose, that is, which game you'll play. What I had in mind required money. I got it, too. Got my choice."

The glass wall dissolved; snow blew in with a howl. Hanna, teeth chattering, served tea.

"You sit here in this storm and tell me that?" she said.

"I didn't plan the storm," he said.

The wind cut through her with knives. Hanna stood in a drift of snow. Beyond the long black line of false-oaks, in the direction of D'vornan, the sky was red. She turned to see him bent in agony, cradling his wrecked hands close to his body. "You see it never stopped," he said. His voice shook with the pain. The glimmering snow parted and a crevice gaped black at their feet, bottomless. She fell to her knees in the snow, weeping; took the twisted hands and kissed them.

"You don't have to do that," he said.

"I want to. Nobody else ever did it, did they."

The crevice pulled at them. He knelt before her and they pressed close together, turning their faces from the abyss as if, unseen, it would go away. It did not; it moved under them and they fell gasping, clinging together, through its deeps. They landed not ungently in a blood-red sky filled with shooting stars and long measured howls. Hanna cried out in a nightmare that was not, this time, her own. Black ruins stood stark against a wall of flame. A face leered from the fire: the man she knew as Castillo.

She cried, "What's burning?"

"Everything. My mother. Oh, my poor mother!" He wept again.

"I can't bear this. We have to stop," she said.

"Yes," he said, but the tears ran down his cheeks all the same, and she understood that this landscape that was new to her was one he visited only in dreams and never willingly. But he had lived in it. And suffered in it.

"Where are we?"

"I don't know!"

He vanished and the light went with him. "Michael!" she called. "Michael, I'm lost!" And he came to her at once, but now they were in a forest of scarlet plumes which beat together with a sound like rattling bones.

She held to him and said, "The Master's here."

"He always is," said the man at her side.

"You know about the Master?"

"I didn't know that's what he was called."

"I'm tired of him. I don't want it any more."

"There's a choice?"

"I'm *tired*. I didn't want to kill again, I didn't want to fight, I didn't want to hurt and grieve. I'm tired of pain, I had enough!"

"I know," he said. "Me, too. Could we help each other?"

They were on another spaceship: "Welcome to *GeeGee*," he said, she was in his arms and they lay close together; had she taken a lover after all?

"I didn't want that either!" It came out in a strangled

cry, but they were still in a place where speech blurred into thought, and he understood.

"You choose what you can and the rest is just there," he said.

He seemed to know where they were. Hanna did not; she tried to go home and was on the *Bird* with Awnlee dead at her feet.

"I will not do this any more!" she said, and he put his arm around her shoulders. He was concentrated and alert.

"I've been lost a lot," he said.

"That's good," she said, because it was preposterously reassuring.

"Why don't we just go home?"

"I don't know where it is," she said painfully.

"I don't either. We'll find it, though. Let's go see my friends first."

"But where are they?"

"Here. They always are," he said, confident. The *Bird* got lighter and lighter, dissolved, and resolved into:

Ordinary light, most extraordinary of all things. Blurred faces floated in it. She turned her head and looked into the amber eyes. They were wary and exhausted. "Hello," he said, and she felt a great astonishment in him.

She whispered, "Can you control that woman who wanted to kill me? And her apprentice. The little girl."

"Sometimes."

"Try."

He said something to the faces and they retreated. Hanna sank toward sleep. Before she got there she felt him twine around her comfortably, possessively. It felt good.

We have to sleep, she said.

"Can I dream my own dreams this time?"

It struck her that he was true-human and had no right to accept so equably what had happened. But she answered, *Yes, I think so, good night.*

"Good night," he said. He put his cheek against her hair and fell asleep.

* * *

Watson Sellers was an experienced officer of the Fleet. This was not the first derelict he had boarded, spanning the space between ships in free fall, suited against zero and vacuum; behind him the bulk of a Fleet vessel—*Comet*, this time—and his team strung out in a wavering line; before him a dark hulk whose luck had all been bad.

The *Far-Flying Bird* was not dark, though, and not silent. Uskosians built windows into their spacecraft with abandon; the *Bird* looked from close up all light. And it broadcast a continuous mayday, not the sedate rote of a human spacecraft in trouble, but a frantic shout. A ship this noisy and this bright should not be derelict. It should answer *Comet's* call. It did not even drift or spin; it stood to unmoving, nose lifted toward home as if it smelled the way.

An air lock was open. Sellers already knew that; everyone on *Comet* knew it. The noise and the light and the lock made them think of old spacemen's tales that had once been seafarers' tales of undamaged vessels found with lights burning, meals cooking, gliding calmly before the wind with no one aboard and nothing to say where everybody had gone.

Sellers had not been on the *Bird* before. He was a man of some aesthetic sense, and when the boarding team broke through he walked through the *Bird* stunned by the sweeping lines that made small spaces look large and large ones vast, and by the palettes of color. Then they came to the bridge and found rags and swollen fleshy bags: Rubee and Awnlee. The *Comet's* skipper heard Sellers grunt inside his helmet and said, "Well?"

"We've found them, ma'am."

"And?"

"They're dead. That's the aliens; Lady Hanna's not here."

"Keep looking. How did they die?"

"There are no visible wounds. We need a medical team here."

He heard her give the order. Then she said, "Getting

word to Omega is first priority. Find out as much as you
can as quickly as you can, and find Lady Hanna. I shall
wait only for a preliminary report before Jumping to
Omega. You'll remain there in charge of investigation
until relieved. Understood?''

"Yes, ma'am," Sellers said. He split up the party to
search for Hanna and set off in the direction he had
asigned himself. In his helmet he heard the controlled
bustle of the *Comet's* bridge. The skipper speculated
with her officers on disease; Sellers knew that she was
wrong. There was the open air lock, and the aliens had
the look of beings who die suddenly and in pain. He
listened, unconsciously at first, for sounds besides those
transmitted from *Comet*. Then he found himself trying
to adjust the audio pickup of his suit and knew what he
was doing. The pickups were working fine. There was
nothing for them to hear. When the sounds of the *Comet*
were gone, complete silence would descend. Sellers
thought for the first time in twenty years that he was a
long way from home.

* * *

Michael drifted in and out of sleep. He had been very
tired even before Hanna's hallucinations began, and
those had gone on for a long time. In his dreams scenes
from Hanna's life and his tumbled together. He thought
at first that he saw pictures from his own imagination,
made-up events from a life inferred from the dream-
truths she had shown him. Later he knew they were
real. He had not been to Koroth, but if he were set down
in its House, he would know where each corridor led,
he would know the women's faces, fair or aged with
ironic eyes: *The child has left us*. White whispers of
F'thal in crazy-angled chambers: *Poorly the creature
gyres!* Polished echoes in emptiness, a deep voice colder
than any unhuman's: *Do not ask if I love. What's all
must be enough*.

Someone dreamed: *I am lost*. He did not know who
dreamed it.

Theo shook him from time to time, talked quietly and

went away, full of worry. He ought to tell Theo there was nothing wrong with him, he only needed sleep, there would be time enough for waking. And meanwhile the woman in his arms was a firm anchor to reality, a sensuous burden that differed from the others he had known in feeling just right, tailored to his comfort. Or had they all felt that way in the deep contentment of half-sleep?—perhaps they had. But he could not remember any of them. There was only the tent of warmth he and Hanna made together, a cathedral-space of sufficiency.

But there was the other part of her and what she represented: the implacable hand of the Polity.

The last thought woke him fully. He let go of her, startled.

Don't leave me, please don't leave, she dreamed, and her longing overwhelmed him. The longing was for somebody else, but that did not matter. *I am empty, fill me,* she dreamed, a powerful erotic plea; he kissed her throat and touched her, unresisting, unresisted; he nuzzled and nestled into the hollows of breast and flank. His cheeks burned and her skin burned his urgent hands. "Oh, yes!" he whispered, but her memories rose between them. Powerless, hurting, revolted, she felt other hands, and *No!* she said, and "No!" she moaned aloud, so that he separated from her and left her, aching with desire.

He turned his face away and waited until the faint sounds of disturbance ceased and she was quiet. When he looked at her again, she was profoundly asleep.

* * *

Jameson found out about the *Far-Flying Bird* from Gil Figueiredo. He got the news late at night, in the dark, and once or twice during the recital he thought he heard echoes of Hanna in the stillness of the house she had loved. Figueiredo's face glared from the white light of a video screen, and he was furious, apportioning blame, assigning some to the commissioners of the Polity for permitting the *Bird* to depart unescorted, some to the

Uskosians for their folly. Jameson, it appeared, was exempted. His anxiety was well documented, and the efforts he had made to communicate it to others. But he was appalled when Figueiredo said, "We should have probed Lady Hanna. She's gone. The treasure's gone. She had access to the course. There's an implication of complicity."

Jameson said bluntly, "You're mad."

"I'm objective. I don't think you're objective about her."

Jameson did not argue. He regretted those two spontaneous words; there was no chance of Figueiredo's accusation being taken seriously, and when he found that out he would drop the idea.

Later, in the morning, he tried to reach Edward Vickery, but Vickery had no time for him yet. It was not like the old days when he could reach whomever he wanted whenever he wanted, whether it was convenient for them or not. Now he only learned what was going on at the pleasure of others, no one rushed to tell him anything, no one asked him what to do. He told them all what to do anyway, transmitting urgent memoranda that dealt with approaching Uskos. "Send a mission at once," he wrote. "There should be no delay in carrying news of an event which the Uskosians will understand as an irruption of Chaos. They will look favorably on an attempt to appproximate, insofar as the event permits, the legend-determined landing date set by Rubee and Awnlee."

But Vickery finally called him and said there would be no mission until Michael Kristofik had been caught, so that human justice could be displayed to Uskos.

It did not occur even to Jameson that someone besides Kristofik might have been responsible for the rape of the *Bird*. The only objection he made was: "What if you don't catch him?"

"We will. He doesn't know we came up with his name before it happened," Vickery said with satisfaction, "and he doesn't suspect anything, because he arranged rendezvous with a Rescue craft out of Valentine."

"I beg your pardon?"

"Evidently there was a casualty. He contacted Rescue a day ago with some story about picking up a sick woman somewhere—he wouldn't say where—and we'll have I&S and Fleet personnel aboard the pod when it makes contact."

"A sick woman?" Jameson said with interest.

"The *Bird* is not a safe environment for human beings. One of his crew probably caught something."

"It's not that dangerous." Jameson wondered how much of the material on Uskosian-human biological analogs Vickery had read.

"There were injuries, too. There might have been a fight. *Comet's* gone back to get a report from the team on the *Bird*. We'll know more about it soon."

"The aliens and Hanna were unarmed."

"It doesn't have to have been a firefight," Vickery said impatiently. "Lady Hanna knows unarmed combat, doesn't she? We'll find out when we get him."

"Valentine has agreed to switching the Rescue craft's crew?"

"Oh, yes. There were token objections. But this is not an internal human affair. This concerns relations with a sovereign nonhuman species. We made it plain we had to have compliance. We mentioned travel sanctions, and that was that."

Jameson murmured, "I should think so." Valentine's one-trade economy would fail overnight without the Polity's millions of visitors to its pleasure domes.

After that, acknowledging reality, he stopped urging an immediate expedition to Uskos. He had time to think about Hanna. Michael Kristofik would hardly show himself so quickly if he had not gotten rid of her. Yet it was odd that no one from D'neera had contacted him, Hanna's frantic mother perhaps, nudged by a daughter's ghostly awareness of impending death, or by the disappearance from the universe of the entity that was Hanna. D'neerans were strange about things like that; they always knew. But it might be that Hanna, in her long absence from home and her increasing detachment from the persons there and elsewhere, had come to maintain such a tenuous place in the hearts of her friends that when she left them altogether, they had not know it.

As for himself: should he not feel something more than concern about relations with Uskos?

Then he realized that he did not believe in Hanna's death, regardless of probability. She was clever and aggressive, he had made her learn a little about Michael Kristofik, and she was amazingly good at staying alive. She did not have as many scruples as a peaceful D'neeran ought to have. The Hanna who had said in the safety of Admin that she did not want to fight again was one person. Hanna alone, out on the edge of law and life, was someone else, as she had proved in the past—though she might not wish to admit it.

He might have loved her better if civilization had sunk deeper than her soft skin. But then she would not have been Hanna.

* * *

GeeGee sang in an archaic tongue with glee, but not much sense:

The bay horse is in the pasture, hurrah!
With two unshod feet, with two unshod feet.
She goes at a sweet ambling gait.
The bay horse is in the pasture, hurrah!

Michael sat at Hanna's bedside, an invalid himself. The bay horse had a blaze down her nose; on cool days she was frisky, snorted at pockets for sugar, danced when you got on her back, not enough to throw you off, just enough to tease you so that you laughed, and so did she; when she was really in a snit she swerved to trot under low branches, tried to scrape you off and made you duck and yell. He knew the feel of the saddle under his thighs, the reins in his fingers, the partnership of human and beast.

He had never ridden a horse in his life. He had never even seen one that was close enough to touch.

Theo pottered among the tubes and metal boxes. The light was dim now because Michael, waking, had tried weakly to shield his eyes, which were filmed and unfocused; he might have been drunk. Hanna's temperature was in a safe zone, but Theo worried over the incision, which had suffered in the tumult of her first panic. At intervals he asked Michael questions. "What's the name of this ship? What's your name? What's my name? Where do we live?" The answers were accurate, but they came slowly.

"I'm not crazy," Michael said.

"Of course not."

"I just feel a little funny."

"Sure."

"It's like double vision."

"Really?"

"Or like—like being expanded."

"Expanded," Theo repeated with a glint in his eye.

He waited for more, but Michael shut up. He slouched by Hanna and stared at her. He knew more than how to ride a horse. He knew what it was like to communicate telepathically with an alien intelligence; he knew what F'thalians and Zeigans and Uskosians were like in ways his reading had never told him. He had a name for the hand that had striven with his for control of his life: the Master of Chaos. He knew what hid behind the library's portrait of Hanna. He knew what he looked like to her: half threat, half comforting guide.

There was a sound like the ocean in his ear.

Shen came to him and said, "She's better. Gonna live. Cancel Rescue?"

He looked at her helplessly. Somewhere in his slow brain he remembered learning something that made canceling Rescue a good idea. He could not remember what it was, though, and he said, "No."

"She doesn't need 'em."

"Does she?" he asked Theo.

"Need Rescue? Maybe not. I'd feel better if somebody else looked at her, though, and she's so weak she could get worse again, or get sick with something else.

Anyway, you said yourself we can't keep this quiet. She's got to be identified sooner or later.''

"Later!" Shen said.

"How long to rendezvous?" Michael said. He was dizzy.

"Two days now," Theo said, "You slept a long time."

Sleep still sounded good. "Stay on course," he said.

Shen said, "Wish she'd died."

"I don't."

He eyed the space beside Hanna with longing. Lise said from the corner, "Wish she'd died."

* * *

Emma Maurello was an assistant to Valentine's chief liaison official in Admin's External Trade Affairs Department. That department was a cell of a larger congeries that dealt with nuances of trade within and outside of the Polity. Somewhere there must be a clear organizational chart, but in two Standard years Emma had not found out to whom, in the long run, External Affairs answered. In any event Emma's offices ordinarily did not care. It was enough, said the transplanted citizens of Valentine in Liaison, to go along at a quiet clip, maintaining routine without expediting it unnecessarily. The work was easy, the surroundings comfortable, there was more talk of leisure than of work, and Emma lived a quiet life which had nothing disturbing in it.

Today was different. Today was an uproar. And Emma, when she had found out what it was about, got away. She slipped away from the towers of Admin, not without frequent glances over her shoulder; she skulked (or felt that she did) through the walkways, the parklands, the structures that housed services for Admin, to a public message center looming against the hazy autumn sky. Here she took a cubicle, placed a call to Valentine, and watched the charges mount against her credit. Private interstellar calls were expensive and Emma was not rich. There went a dress she coveted;

there went all her luxuries for a week, and for another week—

She took her eyes from the racing figures. It was a hot morning, though in the fall of the year. The message center's environmental system was poorly programmed and the cubicle was hot, too, so that her hair stuck to the back of her neck. She looked anxiously behind her again, because she was doing (or supposed she was doing) an illegal thing for the first time in her life.

In Shoreground it was (she remembered too late) the middle of the night. When Kareem Mar-Kize answered, there was no video and she knew from the sound of his voice that she had gotten him out of bed. He sounded as if she had better have a damn good reason for this.

"It's about Mike," she said, and in the silence she heard the unspoken answer: *Reason enough.* Because her voice must give it away, her face which Mar-Kize could see though she could not see his.

She plunged into her story with no other preamble. Halfway through it he activated video and she saw the bronze face, the intelligent black eyes robbed of sleep. He asked questions. She answered them as best she could for her nervousness. She was not used to listening for footsteps behind, or waiting to be caught in an illegal act.

At the end he said, "Why are you telling me this?"

"Because I know Mike—"

She felt herself blush. Mar-Kize had been at Mike's house that night, must have seen some of the evening's long flirtation. Mike was not easy to get: as if she had ever thought in those terms before! As if she would! Finally the others left. She went with Mike into the garden, helped him extinguish the glittering starpoints of light in the big old trees, and he kissed her just as she began to think she would have to start it herself. They stayed outdoors. The sea pounded distantly, the wind sighed through the long night hours, the thick moss was soft on her bare skin. Near dawn she said, "I must go." "Dear Emma, stay and rest. You've had no sleep." But she went, not wanting to face the mid-day light later, the disinterested courtesy of the persons of his house, the amicable acceptance of the animals (who had come to the trees from time to time to see how they got on)—

"—very good of you," Mar-Kize was saying.

"I can't believe he'd do what they say. Can you?"

"Good God, no. Does anyone know you've called me?"

"What? Oh. I don't think so, I'm at a public call center, I don't think I was followed or—they don't tap these places, do they?"

"Not routinely. Do they know you know Mike?"

"Everybody knows Mike. Don't they?"

"Seems like it. All right. Thank you. I'll try to get a message to him."

"Can you? Do you think you can? The I&S people, I heard they said they've got the ship's access codes tagged, so if the relays pick up any transmission for Mike it can be stopped. Can you do it anyway?"

"I'll try," Mar-Kize said neutrally, but Emma did not know how much hope he had.

The call was over. Emma sat in the heat, afraid to find out what it had cost her but not regretting it. It was the right thing. Even if the affair had been brief, even if Mike had not been her lover for long; because better than that, he was her friend.

A hand fell on her shoulder, and when she looked up she was more afraid than she had known she could be. The man behind her wore the uniform of Admin Security. Behind him was a woman, not uniformed but with the look of I&S; and behind the woman was a robot with a Domestic Enforcement patch where its head should be. It was the end of Emma's future. *Maybe Mike will give me a job.*

She went with them without protesting. She thought that if she were docile, what happened to her could not be as bad as anything that would happen if she fought.

She was wrong.

Kareem Mar-Kize placed Emma when the call was finished, not before. He had met her at one of the par-

ties Mike occasionally gave for a handful of old friends
and new acquaintances. Maurello was one of the recent
acquaintances. She had had a hard time keeping her
eyes off Mike; that was not unusual, though hers was a
worse case than most. What was unusual was Mike's
response. It was (Kareem had decided then) sweet innocence that did the trick. Mike was adept at dodging
the predators, the sophisticates with hungry eyes, but
Emma had made him helpless for a while.

Kareem's wife, who had waked near the end of the
conversation, said, "What's wrong?"

"Mike's in a little trouble."

"Trouble? What kind?" She sat up in bed suddenly.
"It's not that old thing, is it?"

"It's related. Never mind. Go back to sleep."

"I won't be able to now. Where is he?"

"Somewhere in space in that flashy toy spaceship.
I've got to get in touch with him—and the Polity's fixed
it so I can't."

He told her everything Maurello had told him, on the
principle that two heads were better than one. He was
right; she said immediately, "Some of those luxury craft
scan all the newsbeams and flag the crew if there's
something interesting. Does *GeeGee* do that?"

"Of course. That's common for a ship that class.
Why?"

"Well, will what the Polity's doing prevent Mike from
getting information that way?"

"Shouldn't, but I don't see— Wait a minute. One of the
things she scans for is his name. He set her up that way.
I told him it was paranoia. He said he was being realistic.
This is top secret, though. It's not out on the 'beams."

"Not yet," said his wife, "and wouldn't any 'beam
service just love to get it first?"

He gave her a hearty kiss and made a call. It only
took one.

* * *

Shen shook Michael awake. He came up out of a deep
sleep, without dreams this time; it was a black cave,

and it sucked at him. The tension in Shen's hard right hand was a warning. He turned to Hanna in anxious reflex. The room was dark, but there was a soft glow near the bed. It showed Hanna's face and he saw that she slept in peace, her breath coming easily.

"Gotta hear something," Shen said. Her mouth was tight. He got out of bed reluctantly and found that his knees shook. So Theo had been wrong and what he had done with Hanna had hurt him somehow after all, at the least had drained him.

Someone had relieved him of his shirt and boots. He found them in the dark, fumbling, and put them on while Shen waited impatiently. Lise and Theo had disappeared.

"What time is it?" he said.

"Fourteen hundred hours. *GeeGee's* back on Standard time. Another day to Rescue. Rescue!" she said bitterly.

"What's wrong?"

"Come on."

He followed her to Control. The brighter light outside his room hurt his eyes and the climb up the spiral stairs seemed long; his strength was not at norm. Lise was in control, her nose almost touching a display surface as she scowled at the words there. She could read, but not well. Shen flipped a switch and a perfectly modulated voice (robo, he thought automatically) said, "Rigorous identification procedures are in effect for incoming traffic to Nestor and Lancaster as well as Valentine. Private vessels approaching Polity ports should be prepared for security checks and possible boarding."

Shen stopped it and said, "Newsbeams." He didn't know what it meant; he didn't want to have anything to do with it. He looked at Shen, baffled. She touched another key and he saw a face that made him blink; it was gaudily painted and the eyes glowed with artificial light. It was human, though. He had seen it on the 'beams before, slashing at more or less deserving targets. It said, "My contacts inside I&S admit Kristofik is the man who robbed a Polity vessel in deep space of a fortune in '23. They don't say why he's been allowed to spend it unmolested all these years. They say there was advance warning of danger to the *Far-Flying Bird*. They don't say why Kristofik wasn't detained before the *Bird* started her flight.''

Shen shut that off, too, ''More?'' she said. Michael shook his head, a reflex action; he was dazed. What he had heard percolated and sank in slowly. So they'd found out what had happened to the *Far-Flying Bird* and—

His head was stuffed with dust. He needed to think clearly and could not.

He said, ''They thought I was going to do it ahead of time. They don't know about *him*.''

Shen said incredulously, ''You knew? About this?''

''No. Yes. I mean, I should have realized what it meant.''

Shen stared at him; so did Lise. He could not be making sense. Shen said to Lise, ''Go wake Theo up.''

''No. Wait—'' A connection made itself without his volition. He picked words carefully. ''They knew somebody was after the aliens, I don't know how. They'd made up their minds if anything happened it was going to be me, and they don't know anything about B. So now they're after us. How long to Rescue?''

''A day. Told you. *Was* a day. Changed course soon's I heard this. Good thing I didn't kill her.''

''Huh?''

''Witness. Tell 'em we didn't do it.''

''Yeah. All the same. They'll want to know what we know about B, why we were after him, how we knew he was on Revenge, lots of questions. Questions I don't want to answer. Don't want to get near it, Shen. Too good an excuse to shove me under probe.''

His mind was working better. Shen relaxed. She said reflectively, ''Can't go home. Or anywhere.''

''Right. Until she's in condition to talk.''

''Take real good care of her,'' Shen said warmly, and the turnabout should have been funny. It was not. With Hanna dead the only way to prove his innocence would be to go under probe. If they got him under probe, they would not be content with his ignorance of the present

crime; they would go on to the *Pavonis Queen* and that
would be the end. Without Hanna there would be no
escape. Not even Valentine would shelter him from this;
surely Rescue cooperated in a trap. So all his life had
hung on the thread of Hanna's, and in saving her he
might have saved himself; though he had done it for no
charitable motive and almost in spite of himself, because of Lise and Theo. Left to himself he might have
killed her, he would have killed her in a frenzy of rage
or obsession—Hanna who was part of him now.

Shen misinterpreted the look on his face. She said,
"Big trouble."

"Not so big," he said, although it was; but also there
it was, and there was no point thinking about the size
of it. He looked for ways out. Best would be a way that
did not mean running, a way to sidestep I&S. He said,
"I want her to talk to the Polity as soon as she can. We
stay lost until then. See if she can keep them off our
backs. If she will. Maybe she'll do it. She's not interested in us. She never used to care about anything but
her work, although— But maybe she'll want to get back
to Contact and the hell with I&S."

He saw that Shen was astonished by the implied
knowledge of Hanna, and became tongue-tied. Shen
said, "Maybe. *Can* she do it?"

"I don't know," he said after too long a pause. "It's
worth trying. She's got influence. The council of magistrates on D'neera gives her anything she asks for. In
the Polity there's the Contact director. Jameson. He
knows all the commissioners. Some of them are hold-
overs from when he was on the Commission. He knows
everybody in I&S, too. And he owes her. God, does he
owe her! But he won't care about that."

Michael sat down suddenly and put his head in his
hands. He wondered if Hanna knew as much about him
as he knew about her.

She had forgotten. She woke without strength, still
fevered, and alone. She was not altogether awake. With
enormous effort she propped herself on her right elbow,
swaying. There was something on her left wrist and she

lifted her hand, which seemed heavier than rock, and looked at it intently. It was close to her face, brown and out of focus; it seemed to have floated there. She examined it as well as she could for the blurring. A medical monitor bracelet gleamed at her, silvery. She reached suddenly for the chain at her throat, lost her balance, and fell back.

The bracelet had done its job and signaled someone. She was lifted and there was a steady arm behind her back. A hand held a cup to her lips. She swallowed clear water, the sweetest draught she had ever drunk. Her mouth was sand-dry and she sucked at the water greedily. Pieces of the world came back one by one. She looked into Michael Kristofik's unmistakable eyes. She remembered doing it before—but the memory slipped away. *I will help you,* she thought. Or was it, *Help me!*

He moved so that her head, which she was not strong enough to hold up, lay against his shoulder. Fogged with fever, unsure where she left off and he began, she felt his pleasure in holding her. She thought that was odd. And sorted through the broken pieces of the recent past that came back a little at a time. And remembered.

"God. Oh, God."

"What? What is it?"

Awnlee. Rubee. I must contact—

She made pictures of Awnlee and Rubee dead and alone in the *Bird*, and the hive of Admin waiting for her call. He said, "They've found the ship. They know."

There were tears in her eyes. She had not cried for a long time and the wetness was strange and awkward. She cried for Awnlee, her friend, and Rubee, who had extended kinship to her. It seemed the event had happened a moment ago. She knew it had not, time had passed, and there were things she must do, if only she could stop crying. But she could not, it was beyond her strength, and she was angry. Michael held her and made sounds of consolation. She remembered that he was connected with Castillo. She tried to push him away; she hated him. She made him feel it, and knew it wounded him.

He said in distress, "Oh, no, I had nothing to do with it, I only came later and found you," and it was the truth, but how could it be? He knew Castillo. He had known the monster for lifetimes, the beast of flame.

Don't touch me, don't touch me! she cried, and heard him swear. He let her down gently and leaned over her, painfully anxious. It added to her confusion; he treated her as an intimate might.

Short as the episode had been, she was exhausted. She could not lift a hand again, not even to wipe the tears from her face. He did it, uncannily responsive; then he kissed her eyes, each in turn. She was paralyzed with rage; she threw it at his head like a weapon. It hurt him. She did not know why. How could he do that to a stranger and then be surprised by her fury?

She could not sustain anger; she drifted away. She wondered if she would ever again in her life be strong enough and well enough to do anything besides sleep.

Michael stayed beside her until he knew she had gone back into the dark. It only took a minute. He thought that he would keep away from her. Perhaps when she was stronger and rational, he could explain. Perhaps by then he would be himself again.

* * *

When it was "night" he slept in the lounge. He dreamed of Claire, Claire of the moonlit hair and milky skin, Claire who had agreed to marry him. Then he dreamed a dream that was an accurate memory, except that he was in a dark, threatening emptiness instead of the comfortable dome-mounted flat he had occupied ten years ago.

"I disobeyed a direct order," Kareem said. "You can do what you think best about that."

He looked so peculiar that Michael was alarmed. "It's that serious? I'm poor, or something?"

"You told me not to run confirmation on Claire's background. Because if she found out someday, she'd be hurt."

A light answer died on Michael's tongue; he looked

at Kareem's face and could not say a word. Kareem said, "I did it anyway. You have to know. She's an I&S agent."

When Michael could speak again he said, "She can't be."

"She's not even real. They made her up, she turned herself into what they thought you'd want. I'm sorry, Mike. I'm so sorry."

He woke sweating. No one else was in the lounge. The video screen was in the middle of a biography of Hanna. He did not look at it. He knew enough about Hanna. No wonder he had dreamed of Claire; he had thought that he knew her well.

* * *

Early each "morning" Shen, faithfully grumbling but faithfully, went to bathe Hanna. This morning while she was gone, Lise brought Michael and Theo coffee in the lounge. The video screen yammered on. Starr Jameson answered questions about Uskos. Michael watched him with unfriendly eyes. The man had not wanted Hanna. Only an idiot would not want Hanna. Therefore Jameson was an idiot. Simple logic.

GeeGee finished with Jameson, searched, and landed in the middle of a statement by a woman of D'neera. She spoke with a faint accent, as if, among themselves, D'neerans shifted Standard pronunciation to suit their own ideas of correctness. Michael had heard no such accent in Hanna's speech, but she had spent much time on Earth. The eyes of the image were eerily like Hanna's, widely spaced and the same deep shade of blue. D'neera's founding population had been small; those splendid eyes might be common there. H'ana's intimates, the woman said, were convinced she was alive. She was held hostage, no doubt. D'neera had complete faith in the Polity's ability to rescue H'ana from her captors.

"That's us," Lise said, excited.

"So it is," Michael said.

Theo said, "Maybe we should go ahead and contact I&S. Tell them what happened."

"I want her to tell them. Think she could do it today?"

"No. Maybe tomorrow, but I'm not even sure about that."

"She's not out of danger yet, is she?"

"Not weak as she is. Don't push her."

"Can he kiss her?" Lise asked.

Theo blushed. He mumbled, "That was just because of what they were doing with their heads."

"Not that time. Later."

"Later?" Theo said. He looked at Michael suspiciously.

"Where were you?" Michael said to Lise.

"In the door. You didn't see me. She didn't like it."

"No," he admitted.

"You shouldn't do it again. She's too sick. Theo said so."

"I suppose you're right," he said.

GeeGee kept music going behind the anonymous noises of the 'beams. A choir of male voices chanted in unison in a long-dead language. The solemn songs had echoes behind them, as if the singers stood in a cavernous space and drew deeply on the hollow past. *Nostra corda fove laetitia prabe praesidia,* they sang: Warm our hearts with happiness, offer us thy protection!

The structure of Michael's life in these last years had been carefully planned. He had worked hard to make it as it was: peace, freedom, security, beauty. It had not been enough, but he had valued it.

It disintegrated and dissolved.

Kareem Mar-Kize, having proved uncooperative, was restricted politely to his home. Michael did not try to call him. It could not help; it could only harm.

Emma Maurello, apprehended for unspecified reasons, had disappeared into I&S custody—into, no doubt, the half-world of the probe. It would take from her the details of their sweet shared nights and they would never be hers or his again.

The banking officials of Kingstown, where most Shoreground money went, froze all of Michael's holdings. It was possible that they would be irrevocably seized with an eye toward reparations. His credit was rescinded so that even if he were fool enough to land somewhere and try to use it, he would be a pauper.

I&S personnel from offworld overran his home. If he closed his eyes he could see it as clearly as if he were there: cats glared from trees and stairways, dogs whined outside closed doors, the F'thalian tourmaline balled up under his bed and hid and starved.

Fast little Fleet scouts fanned out through human space to every habitat, mining station, or satellite that supported a human settlement. Revenge would be on the list. The People of the Rose would show an incredulous I&S that Michael had been on Revenge during the taking of the *Far-Flying Bird*. The hunt would be widened to include B, but it would not slacken for Michael. B would know that, too; know, when he heard this, that his time was gone. Then he would flee forever. The secret would go with him, while everything that might have been left to Michael here vanished, too.

He heard again and again about the *Pavonis Queen*. If five years' grace between the event and his linkage with it had not saved him from the scrutiny of I&S, at least it had kept him from the attention of the public. Now the crime was resurrected and greeted with a clamor. It would not be forgotten again.

The Fleet scouts got to Carrollis and someone added up the facts of Prissy's murder, the brass-colored ship, and the dark man from offworld who had been in Town on that day and no other. They talked about the fate of the child Prissy had owned. She had not been on Valentine long and her presence in Michael's household had gone nearly unnoticed, so that now she was said to have disappeared. There were speculations on Michael's reasons for taking her away from Carrollis. He did not recognize himself in them.

After that he thought: *I had some good years. I knew it could end.*

He looked up and saw that Theo watched him. He tried to make his face indifferent, but Theo said, "For a while there I thought you didn't know what it all meant."

Michael was silent. Presently Theo went out.

Nostrorum scelerum tolle maliciam—lift the weight of our transgression—

He wondered if, even after he was cleared of the present crime, I&S would take him from home one dark night and he would wake up in a cell on Earth and find out he had confessed to every unlawful act he had ever done, and everything he had ever tried to hide.

Probably.

The monks of a world far away from Alta, treasuring the ancient music, sang on.

Miserere nobis: Have mercy on us!

III.

It took Hanna a week to wake up fully. At first she understood only the music that surrounded her, which was not like any music she had heard before. The instruments were strange to her, and the oddly suncopated rhythms, and when there were voices the languages as well. On some level she knew they were very old. They reached into history, and even those presented in Standard breathed no modern spirit in their phrasing. *Sweet Robin, lend to my thy bow,* a man's voice sang; *I must a-hunting with my lady go . . . With my sweet lady go . . .* That time there was no accompaniment; the song was not recorded, and the singer was nearby. Hanna rested in the music, at peace.

Later her eyes cleared and she saw the room she was in. It was colored in tones of earth and sun, and there were spaces filled with a patchwork of furnishings, paintings, fabrics, and oddments sifted by a curious, acquisitive hand. For sky there was a polished ceiling etched with bronze traceries of leaves like the shadowed roof of a forest. The little world breathed a personality: sunny and clever and brash.

And later still the anonymous hands that cared for her had faces with them, and the faces had names: Theo and Shen. The blue-eyed half-crazy girl, Lise. And finally Michael, *the one with the eyes,* Hanna thought, the man who was supposed to be dangerous. He wasn't dangerous now; he sat by her bed with lines of strain around those eyes, and the lines disappeared when the others were around, and she felt the effort it took to make them vanish and the reason behind it: the love. *Everything's fine,* he told them with his smiles. And therefore, for them, it was.

By the time Hanna began to think again, she had forgotten that she was supposed to be afraid.

"You're not a monster," she whispered when the slow swell of thought finally crested in speech, and the man by her bed started, worry thick in his eyes, heavy on his mouth.

"You're not going to hurt me," Hanna said.

"Of course not," he said. He looked at her with diffidence. His mind was on what had happened to her on the Avalon—not so much the beating as the rape. She was too weak to explain that where she came from the two were considered much the same. It was not as large a thing as he thought. Killing Castillo's men would satisfy her.

For economy's sake she held to the important fact. "You almost did hurt me," she said.

"Yes, well," he said. His eyes pleaded with her. Gold filled her vision; her small stock of strength was exhausted. "That was a mistake," he said. Hanna went back to sleep, unafraid.

Lise said, chattering: "You look pretty in that." She meant the gown Hanna wore, a fragile white shift that slipped softly across her skin. "It's mine, that's why it's too small for you. But even Shen said you're pretty. Only she doesn't say much. It's because her tongue was cut out."

"What?" Hanna said.

"Theo told me. Her tongue was cut out and when Mike found her he made her go to the Polity. He made Theo go with her because he couldn't go. And she got a new tongue. But she still didn't say anything for a long time."

"Naturally," Hanna said.

"How long have I been here?" she asked later, when she felt strong.

Michael counted on his fingers, childlike. "Eight days," he said.

She was sitting up, propped up by pillows. She had decided it was time to ask questions. It had become apparent that Michael knew exactly who she was and what had happened to her. Therefore he must know that the Polity would be searching for her desperately; but he had not mentioned it.

"You haven't said anything about getting me home," she said.

"There's a little problem," he said, looking hunted; she had never seen so expressive a face.

"What problem?"

"Your friends in I&S think I'm responsible for what happened."

"I can tell them otherwise. That isn't a problem."

"It won't be enough," he said. "They'll want me all the same—to find out about *him*. If they do—thirty seconds under probe and I'm finished."

"Because of *him*?" she said, and answered herself: "No. Because of the *Pavonis Queen*. But what good does keeping me do?"

"Maybe you could persuade them not to probe me," he said, looking away, not liking to ask. "And maybe"—this came harder still—"if that doesn't work, you could be used. As a hostage. If it comes to that."

"Used," she said, tasting the word. It had a familiar feel. "I don't want to be a hostage. I just want to get back."

But that was a lie. She didn't want to get back to anything yet. The rest and the music were good. They were better than anything waiting for her in the Polity.

"At least I can tell them the truth," she said.

Night: the eighth night? The ninth? She woke often, thinking of what she would say when the time came to speak. Her thinking kept sliding away from the point she wanted it to have. Her memory of the union into which she had drawn Michael was dim, but there was a bond she wished was not there. And he had a swimmer's body, broad-shouldered and sleek; his skin was

the color of burnt sugar, his hands beautiful, the curve
of his mouth a pleasure to her eye. *Oh, stop it!* she said,
ordering herself, denying the bond and an astonishing
physical pull. *Remember the point!* The point was that
he had not asked much of her. Only to use her influence. She had enough, had some with people who had
more. He had only asked her to help him survive.

And if he gave something in return? Told them what
he knew about B? But she knew already that he would
not tell it all. He would answer only to a point. A point
of his choosing; not too far back. Would he go far
enough? No.

She turned in bed, sighing. He would not tell them
enough. Castillo would escape. Saving Michael Kristofik somehow meant saving Castillo, too. And that
meant her duty was clear.

In the morning Michael came for her. Shen had
brought clothes and Hanna dressed and tried her legs,
but they were unreliable. She had to lean on Michael's
arm, and when they came to the spiral stair that connected *GeeGee's* two levels—a pretty, impractical con-
ceit far beyond Hanna's strength—he carried her. He
carried her into Control and said, "What are you going
to say to them?"

"I don't know," she said.

A little later she was telling her story to Gil Figueiredo. Figueiredo admitted (angrily, defensively) that one
of the team that had studied the *Bird's* engineering was
missing. Michael stood nearby, but far to one side and
out of Figueiredo's line of sight. Control was nearly
dark, and Hanna saw him as a shadow on the edge of
vision. His head was bowed and he looked at his folded
arms.

"He told you his name was Castillo?"

"Yes. That's not right, but I don't know what it is.
Michael Kristofik," she said, "knows more about
him."

"How much does Kristofik know?" Figueiredo said.

"Everything about him, I should think. It goes all the
way back to—"

Michael moved as she started the sentence. She struck at his left hand and hit it as hard as she could. The effort made her dizzy; his right hand found its object, and Figueiredo's face was gone. *GeeGee* floated unconnected to anything.

He was rocked, tottering closer to death or Adjustment. "Why the hell'd you do that?" he said.

"It's your fight. Not mine."

He did not take her back to his own room. He took her to another, smaller chamber that blazed with reflected light. There were many mirrors. There was no feel of habitation. There was a bed, though; he put her down on it. It pulled at her like sand.

He said, "It seemed like a good idea to get this room ready, so we did. The only thing you've got for communication is intercom. The only thing it talks to is this." A wafer of metal appeared in his hand, disappeared into a pocket. "*GeeGee* won't respond to you. The lock's voice-controlled and you'd need a laser to cut a way out. If you want something we'll get it for you. There's a gymnasium on the upper level and you can use it when you're stronger, but I'll be there, too."

"I did what I had to do," she said.

"I thought you might."

"What I said didn't have anything to do with you anyway."

"It did and you knew it. I asked you to help me keep out of the probe."

"You go back a long way, you and that man."

She felt a flash of pain. It showed on his face, too, so naked that it was indecent. But he said nothing. He left her there alone, to think about what she had refused to do.

* * *

The voices drifted windy and murmurous; through air, space, night, invisible; swirled into currents, spilled into windrifts; were patience, dedication, efficiency. The dark between the stars hummed with them. They made up a single thing, a thing in itself, a web or a net vibrating in the night.

One voice was light and toneless, except where the edges were rough. That was Figueiredo's.

A woman's, soft, with a smile in it: the psyche expert from Admin, the negotiator.

Furred and slipping toward the guttural: Denkovitz, head of I&S.

Even, staccato, edging toward high harmonics: Edward Vickery.

A voice that was a deep bass bell: Starr Jameson.

Others. A woman's voice like the clear note of a violin. A man whose speech was a breathy sigh.

The voices cut in and out in a dance between Earth and points outward, points of light in the dark.

"What will he do now?"

"Bargain."

"With what?"

"Her life."

"He is innocent."

"Only of this."

"And maybe not this."

"Conspiracies . . ."

"Plans gone wrong . . ."

"A struggle for mastery within . . ."

"He planned it and meant no loss of life, perhaps."

"And lost control."

"Even if innocent—"

"They are connected."

"Clear on the evidence."

"So Hanna said."

"But how connected?"

"We'll learn how."

"He has no power."

"Nowhere to flee."

"No escape this time."

"Valentine will comply."

"And her life?"

"We'll trade. After that—"

* * *

Michael sat in the lounge, which was lit up brightly, as if to shut out the spread of night and the Jumping stars. It was still littered with hand-held readers, music cubes, clothing and blankets, though it was no longer necessary for Michael to live in it.

He held a reader that showed the first page of a stores inventory. He held it for some time without scrolling onward. Lise perched on the edge of a chair nearby, as if she had drawn an invisible line between *too close I'll annoy him* and *too far he's too far away*. Presently Theo came in, looking about casually but not at Michael or Lise, as if they were not really there, as if no subtle pull had called him there where Michael was. A little while later Shen, abandoning Control, came in, too; she glared at Michael *(What are you doing here?)* and sat down.

They turned to Michael in silence and made a circle, shutting out everything else with their backs.

GeeGee sang with great unhappiness:

Now, oh now, I needs must part;
Love lies not where hope is gone!
Now at last despair doth prove
Love divided lovest none.
Sad despair doth—

"*GeeGee*, shut up," Michael said.

He looked at the others one by one. "There's one thing left," he said. "We've got a hostage; we'll use her. I don't expect it to work. If it doesn't, it's not the end. Remember that, all of you. I want you to remember it. If we have to, we'll head for D'neera. They've no great love for the Polity there and they'll settle for getting Hanna back. I'll get rid of her and leave the rest of you there. No—" The movement caught his eye. "Don't say it, Theo. I'm not taking flak from any of you. That's the way I want it. You can do more for me that way. When you get off D'neera they'll probe you, but they'll let you go. Theo's clear with Co-op. They won't send Shen back to Nestor, they never make anybody go back there, and it won't matter what happened on Carrollis. The less attention Carrollis gets from I&S the better they like it. When you get to Valentine, you can start helping me. Work with Kareem. He'll know what to do."

He heard himself with satisfaction; his voice had less expression than *GeeGee's*. They looked at him warily. Theo said, "What do you do in the meantime?"

"I go back to space and wait. *GeeGee's* powered and provisioned for years."

"Years!" Shen repeated, incredulous.

"If necessary."

Lise's face crumpled, but Theo and Shen looked at each other with grudging accord.

It was working. What he said made a kind of sense. They saw the picture he wanted them to see: *GeeGee* glittering here and there in human space, disappearing and reappearing, outwaiting I&S.

But it was not a real hope. No one ever outwaited I&S. Instead he would take *GeeGee* out, out, on a hopeless quest that would end only with the end of his life, or of his sanity. But he would not take anyone with him.

He left them to look at the illusion with hope, and went to call I&S again—without Hanna, this time.

* * *

Figueiredo's voice said: "We have contact. Make it quick."

"Make him wait," said the expert's smile.

"Is Hanna with him?"

"I think not."

"Dead perhaps?"

"I think not."

"Why did she. . . ?" The violin.

A sigh. "A warning of some kind."

"Suicidal," Denkovitz growled.

"An old pattern." The deep bass, rarely heard.

"Not quite," said the expert, light and sweet. "That is, yes and no."

The voices hushed to respectful silence. The expert went on.

"She was shattered once. I think not whole since.

There are ways to give warning. Ways and ways. This might have been one. So public? So direct? Inviting attack? Consider what happened. Besides the deaths. The trauma. Her instinct is: become rigid. Cling to what's known. Those near breaking make shows of strength. She is not well. Perhaps not quite sane.''

"No good, then.'' Disapproving. Vickery's voice.

"Those who do what she does must somehow be split,'' said the bass.

"This is different,'' said the smile. "There's nothing solid, she stands on air and swings at nothing; it's been long since there were foundations, else she would not have risked what she risked. It may mean her time with us is past.''

After a long silence the bass said, "And next?''

"I do not know,'' the expert said.

"How do we find out?''

"Watch,'' she said.

* * *

Hanna was dozing when Michael came to her again. She had not been able to turn off the light because *GeeGee* would not answer or obey her, and it was a vicious glare even to his eyes. He noticed the cold for the first time also, and spoke to his ship. The light dimmed and a current of warm air brushed his face. Hanna did not stir. He sat at her feet, which were bare; he took them in his hands to warm them and she came awake all of a sudden, kicking at him by reflex, savagely.

"Sorry. Sorry!''

She had been on her stomach. Now she was upright. She put a hand to her chest, where her heart pounded too hard. Michael raised both hands in the ancient peacemaking gesture.

She waited to see what he wanted.

"Don't kick,'' he said cautiously. He touched her feet again and she jerked and said, "What are you doing?''

"I didn't mean to freeze you to death.''

His hands fell easily into a pattern of massage. He

knew what he was doing and the blood moved into her icy toes. He talked quietly, eyes on his task.

"We've Jumped. Several times, in fact. I'm talking to someone on Earth. Not the man you had before. They say there might be a compromise, but they want to see you first. So they'll know you're all right. You'll have to come up. I hope you'll keep your mouth shut. If you don't, there's not much I can do about it. But if you think about it, you'll see that the sooner we get it over with, the sooner you can leave . . ."

He went on talking, but Hanna ceased to listen. Something was happening in the soles of her feet. The warmth went straight up her legs and into her belly like current carried on a pair of wires.

She thought: *This man was a Registered Friend. He has forgotten nothing.* She had entirely forgotten it, however. Until now. He did not look up. If he met her eyes while his hands were busy in this way, it would be a challenge. Somewhere in the training (and how was he trained? What else had he learned?), he had been taught when to challenge and when to submit, or appear to submit.

She drew her knees up suddenly, pulling her feet away from him. He looked up. His eyes were innocent; he had only wanted her to be warm. But something else came into them now.

He said, "Just once I'd like to meet a woman who didn't know. I might as well have stayed in the trade."

"It must be a great burden for you," Hanna said politely. "The curiosity. The expectations. You must have to say no all the time. What a pity."

The corners of his mouth twitched. She was right, and he nearly laughed. He stopped it, but his eyes danced; somewhere there was a well of merriment hard to suppress.

"Come talk to I&S," he said.

The spiral stair was not long, but Hanna's knees felt the climb halfway up. In Control she sank into a seat with relief. In front of her she saw, first, a chronometer engaged in some kind of count. It was counting up. Then she saw the face of the I&S negotiator, the dark brown face of a woman with a mild, almost sweet expression. The brown eyes were lustrous and made her look very young. Her hair was styled in yielding curves and there was a frill of lace at her throat.

Michael said, "Hanna, this is Colonel Stiva Waller. As you can see, Colonel, Hanna is alive and well. Shall we get on with it?"

"And how are you being treated?" Waller said, ignoring Michael.

"All right," Hanna answered uncertainly, and looked at the gentle face with wonder; then she understood. How like I&S; how like the Polity! This would not be a straightforward negotiation if they could help it. They would tip the balance in any way they could, they would use a pretty woman whose smile and soft voice might disarm Michael and confuse him; might, even, suggest this affair was a peccadillo that did not threaten him and need not be taken too seriously. Did they hope he would flirt with her? Or be distracted by a subliminal mother-image?

"Would you like to tell me what you've been doing?" Stiva Waller asked sweetly.

"Doing. . . ?"

"Are you well? How have you been treated since we saw you last? Some hours ago?"

"I've been sleeping—" Hanna's voice wavered. She pulled her scattered thoughts together and said, "I was very sick, you know. I've been cared for well."

"It must be nice to know you're in good hands," Stiva Waller said.

Hanna did not say anything. She felt Michael behind her, unmoving. Waller said, "And have Shen Lo-Yang and Theodore Jadinow helped in your care?"

Hanna did not understand the reason for the question. She said, "Theo saved my life."

Michael put his hands on Hanna's shoulders and said, "All right. Tell her, Waller. You're dying to."

Hanna screwed her head around to look up at Michael. He watched Waller's face and for once she could not read his expression. Disgust? Contempt? His fingers moved a little. It felt like a caress, and she was still;

but the invisible watchers on Waller's side would see those graceful hands near her throat.

"Shen Lo-Yang," Waller said, "was an executioner in the service of General Greenway on Nestor for many years. She loved her work. So much that when she fell from favor—the punishment, I believe, was mutilation—she turned to robbery with murder to support herself. Theo Jadinow enjoyed a lucrative and illegal medical practice—gypsy practices, they're called—on Co-op's frontiers. He was motivated by the need to procure large sums to pay for his use of—well, of nearly any drug you care to name. He does not seem to have killed anyone, at least not personally, and he was not remanded for Adjustment. His medical training beforehand was minimal. Yet you feel safe?"

"Quite," Hanna said.

"I see. That being the case, Mr. Kristofik, we can talk about terms."

"Mine are easy," Michael said.

"Let's hear them."

"Safe passage to Valentine. A personal guarantee from Ecomanager Mejian that when I go back there I won't be handed over to I&S. Restoration of my property. I want you to quit harassing my friends and I want you to let go anybody you've got in custody because of me. In exchange I'll give you Hanna—and everything I've collected on the man she told you about. The places he's been and the names he's used and his contacts for the last two years."

"That will do for a start," Waller said.

"It'll do for a finish, too."

He did not say anything else. The tips of his fingers shifted and rested softly on either side of Hanna's jaw, on the pulsepoints under her ears. It was a blatant bluff and she was astonished—first, that he thought he could make anyone believe he would harm her, with that transparent face; and secondly, that she had not denounced the fraud at once.

Before she could make up her mind to do it Waller said, "We'll discuss it. I'll contact you later."

"No." He glanced at the chronometer. The call to

Earth had given away *GeeGee's* position, and he would not linger. "We're moving on. I'll contact you."

That was the end. As Waller's image disappeared, Hanna turned and saw Michael's face as she had not seen it before: stone. Perhaps they would believe him after all.

He changed; he looked only tired. He dropped into a seat beside Hanna, forgetting for a moment that she was there. She put out her hand and touched him of her own accord for the first time. The golden eyes turned to her face and she saw that this desperate bargain was not what he wanted to do; he was not doing anything he wanted to do. She took her hand away, surprised at what she had done.

"I have to lock you up again," he said.

"All right, if that's what you want. But—" She hesitated. "It's hard for me to believe all the things I heard about you."

"They're probably true," he said.

He got up and took her back to the mirrored room. It was dim and warm now, and she fell asleep quickly. She was not present two hours later when he settled the details of the trade with Waller.

* * *

The voices considered details.

"If it fails—"

"It won't fail."

"If it does—"

"Then what would he do?"

"He has nowhere to go."

"D'neera," said the bass.

"D'neera?"

"D'neera's mad enough," someone sighed.

"Not that mad!"

"If she is," said the bass. "And she is."

They were quiet.

The expert said, "You watched. You know her well."

"I did. He touched her. You saw it."

"Yes."

"That was threat, was it not?"

"It was."

"Was not. She was not afraid. More important: she was not angered."

"How do you know?"

"She would not hide it if she were. When she lived here," said the bass, as if it talked of a long-ago time, "she met eager men excited by her beauty, or by the ease with which, it's said, D'neerans contract affairs, or by, perhaps, her belonging to me and the challenge that meant in the games of men. I've seen her touched against her will—more ambiguously than this. The look in her eyes freezes blood. What happened, she says— the beating, the rape, most especially the rape—well. I wouldn't like to be one of those men, if she meets them again. Wouldn't touch her myself, old friends that we are, without care. But *he*—what did you see in her face?"

"Surprise," someone said. "Only that."

"Only that. She did not dislike it."

"I thought so," the expert said.

"Thought what?"

"She's unstable. Old wounds reopened."

"And so?" someone said.

"D'neera," they breathed.

"D'neera might shelter him. At her request."

"Not for long. There's no life for him there."

"When it's done—"

"When it's done, then what?"

"Their cobweb plan is done. Hers, the aliens'. When it's done we'll do it—"

"Correctly," said the bass, weary now. "By rule. A mission staffed with those she's trained. Not her."

"No?"

"No. When we get her back, she can help us—if she will. But I do not think I will trust her. I think," he said, "her loyalties are suspect. Does she know it herself?—perhaps not."

* * *

The rendezvous was fixed for six days hence, even though they were near Earth at the start, at the heart of the network of common routes humanity had developed in the course of seven centuries. The intercom in Hanna's room, as Michael had promised, worked—after a fashion; when she used it to ask if anyone was there it did not answer, but soon afterward Theo appeared to make sure she was all right. She did not need to use it again. Theo came at regular intervals, solicitous of her health. But the solicitude was mingled with resentment, as if Hanna alone were responsible for what was happening to Michael and his household.

When Theo was not there, and Hanna had done all the sleeping she could, there was nothing to do except listen to silence. In the silence she "heard" fragments of thought. From Theo: *I can do without the money and all. But how can I do without him?*

From Lise: *He is so sad. He doesn't want me to see.*

From Shen: *I will kill for him if it helps. Or die for him. But I will not say so to anyone though they take my tongue again.*

But Michael only thought: *Why in hell'd this happen? Bad timing. Pure dumb luck.*

One day she asked Theo, "Why do you love Michael so much?"

He was reading what her blood had to say; he looked up and looked at her as if she were a nonperson with no right to ask such a thing.

Hanna said, "I'm trying to understand. Why won't you tell me? Is it something to be ashamed of?"

In fact he looked ashamed. He muttered, "Only for me."

She waited. It was plain that he ached to tell someone. And she had asked.

At last he said, "You heard what they've been saying on the 'beams? About me?"

"No."

"You didn't hear anything?"

"I can't make anything in here work. I haven't heard anything at all."

"Oh." He was still trying to make up his mind; he fidgeted. He looked at her slantwise and said, "I used to use a lot of dope, you know."

"I didn't know," she said, not quite truthfully, remembering what Stiva Waller had said.

"Well, I did." His skin was very fair, almost transparent. The blood climbed behind it in a violent blush. "I got into some trouble trying to support it. They're saying, they say, Mike's mixed up in the traffic. Or was back then. He never was, though. You'd think as hard as they've tried to find out things about him they'd have gotten the truth about that."

"How did you meet him, then?"

He stared at her for a while. Finally he said, "Like I told you, I got in some trouble. When they let me go, I couldn't—there wasn't anything for me to do. I'd been studying medicine on Co-op but I couldn't—well, I'd been thrown out. And deported to Valentine. They're not that particular on Valentine. And I was, as soon as I got there I started doping hard again. I didn't have much money and it ran out. I was in Port of Shoreground, that's where it's easiest to get the stuff, you understand? And Mike—"

He stopped, looking at her uncertainly. Something about her attention reassured him. He went on: "I was sitting on a curb in the port. In the rain for God's sake. Wondering if I was strong enough to pick up a few hours' day labor. If anybody'd hire me even for that. I'd slept on the street the night before, a lot of nights actually. Some people came by, they were eating something from one of the market stalls, one of them didn't like it and he threw it down in the street, some kind of meat roll. Half eaten. I hadn't had a meal in a couple of days. I couldn't wait till they were out of sight, I jumped on it. There was this dog heading for it, you see. They saw me and they started laughing. I was sitting there eating it and thinking about the ocean. I can't swim. I wouldn't have had to go out very far. Somebody sat down next to me, I looked over and it was Mike, he'd seen the whole thing. He said, 'You want a job?' I went with him. At first I thought he wanted the obvious thing, and I would've gone along with it, I guess, but it wasn't that. Then I couldn't figure out what he did want. He never said. He never has said. It's been six years and he never said why he did it.''

He added after a moment, ''He took the dog along, too.''

'' 'There was only the hunger,' '' Hanna murmured.

''Huh?''

''Something someone said. Nothing . . .'' She looked at him thoughtfully. ''You never thought of leaving him later?''

''There wasn't any reason. At first it was just because I had it good. Later he picked up Shen on Nestor and—'' He blushed again. ''I didn't trust her, actually. I thought she'd cut his throat some time if I wasn't around. After that I just sort of never thought about leaving.''

''Why did he take Shen on, anyway?''

''Don't ask me. Never made any sense, far as I could see.''

''Did you ever ask him?''

''Sure. Never got an answer, though. But we're not the only ones, me and Shen. Mostly they take him for what they can get and move on. Steal him blind sometimes. He's thrown a couple out. It never stops him, though. Once I told him he was crazy and he reminded me what he'd done for me. It's the only time he ever brought it up, he just wanted to shut me up. So I quit asking questions. You're a telepath, maybe you can figure it out. I can't.''

Hanna was not done with surprises. Perhaps as a result of her attention to Theo, Shen came to her some hours later. ''Want a drink?'' said Shen, slouched in Hanna's door.

''Why not?'' Hanna said.

''C'mon, then.''

That was how Hanna got to Shen's room, which looked like military quarters. Worse; it was entirely bare, as if, when Michael refitted the *Golden Girl*, Shen had said: ''Strip a spot for me.''

Shen produced brandy and told Hanna, in blunt language, what Michael had saved Lise from. This appeared to be the reason for the invitation, and after that there was not much to talk about. Hanna asked certain questions, but with the greatest caution. She did not want Shen to feel cornered. Shen would be dangerous that way. Hanna knew it; she was impressed.

All the same, with care, she got some information about Shen herself, though most of it was only a terser version of Stiva Waller's accusations. When Hanna spoke of Shen's fall from the Nestorian hierarchy, she thought she had gone too far. She was alarmed at the look in Shen's eyes. Shen was hard as primal rock, she had the balance that comes from knowing how to fight, and she was healthier than Hanna, who still was disgustingly weak.

The shotglass in Shen's hand was full of brandy. She drained it without taking her eyes off Hanna; then she refilled it and handed it over. It seemed Hanna was safe after all. She drank, refraining from making a face. She had an anthropologist's approach to dreadful tastes.

"So they didn't treat you so good," she said after that—and reflected that the brandy, her third, was having an effect; she was beginning to talk like Shen.

"Not good," Shen said.

"Cut out your tongue."

"Yeah." Shen's eyes glittered.

"And then?"

"Can't talk, can't do much."

"Robbery with violence." Hanna added hastily, "That's what the Polity said."

"True. Bastards," Shen said obscurely.

"So how'd you get here?"

There were indefinable ripples in the sullen face. "Picked the wrong one," Shen said. "Picked Mike."

"Wrong how?"

"Bastard looked easy. Big, yeah. But rich. Soft. Careless." Shen said with disapproval.

"And?"

"Wasn't easy. Ended up, he hauled me off over his shoulder. Had a nice place. I stayed. Went back to Valentine with him. That's all."

"All," Hanna repeated rather helplessly. "Why'd he take you away?"

"Dunno."

"You don't know? After all this time?"

"Never asked," Shen said.

She drank more brandy, filled the tiny glass, and gave it to Hanna. Who drank, afraid to refuse.

Michael had locked himself in his room. He saw the others occasionally, fleetingly. He knew that Hanna was free. *Of course she is. They would like her. I could love her.*

He was studying charts. One wall of his room could be turned into a bank of video screens, and he filled it with representations of Outside. There was a lot of it. In seven hundred years the human species had barely stuck a toe in this sea. There was the Polity, there were the other scattered worlds that would support terrestrial life, there was a lot of rock and gas, and then there was—everything else. Which was everything there was.

The charts in which he was interested had two things in common. They showed areas that were largely obscured by interstellar dust, and, because of the dust, they were guesses. He was going to pick one.

About the middle of the last night he dragged himself out of the dust and relieved Shen in Control. There was solitude enough there after Shen left; only Lise had been waiting for him to appear, and now went to sleep curled in a seat nearby.

Between Jumps he made a handfall of calls. All of them went through without interruption, but somewhere, surely, they were monitored. There was no overt evidence of a trap. Stiva Waller's promises were being fulfilled. Michael was a rich man again, and Kareem Mar-Kize was free. Kareem talked with enthusiasm of Michael's coming home. But he said, "Why do they have to link up with you in space? Why not here?"

"Guess," Michael said.

His last call was to Earth. He got a lot of people out of bed while he traced down Emma Maurello. He found her at a medical center near Admin and the caretakers there got her out of bed, too; it seemed that notoriety gave Michael a certain importance. Emma was a tear-stained wraith. She was not recovering as she ought from the I&S probe. She would not meet his eyes and when he spoke to her with tenderness, she wept. She said something he could not disentangle from the sobs. "What was that?" he said. "What is it, dear Emma?"

"I hate you. I hate you," she said.

After that he sat for a long time with his face in his hands. *Dear Emma, good-bye.* The sound of Lise's breathing disturbed him. He had wanted to be to her, at the least, what the monks of St. Kristofik had been to him; he had meant to watch her grow up. *Good-bye, little puss.*

A few hours later, after all the waiting, it was time.

Hanna sat in the lounge where Theo had put her and looked out at the stars. If she were to go closer to the transparency and look torward her left, toward *Geegee's* nose, she might see the ship of the Polity that had come to rescue her. She sat on the edge of a divan with her fingers gripping it as if she might fall off. She had no possessions to take with her; she owned none. There was only the silver chain at her throat. She knew nothing of the procedure for transferring her to the Polity vessel. Now she wondered about it, and when Theo put his head into the lounge, to make sure she was still there, she asked him.

He said, staying where he was, "Somebody's boarding with a suit for you. We don't have any to spare."

"They can't dock a shuttle—?"

"No, of course not. We're not big enough to take one in. Why? Can't you use a maneuvers pack?"

"Yes, of course. I just thought—wouldn't it be easier to dock *GeeGee* in the other craft? Or is it too small, too?"

"It's big," Theo said. "But that would be stupid. Once they had us in there we might not get out. No, this way we keep some distance between us and them, see?"

"I see. Will I see Michael before I go?"

"You wouldn't if it was up to me," Theo said honestly.

"No?" She looked at him closely as she could from where she sat; he still had only one foot inside the lounge, as if he were impatient to get away from her.

"It's really not my fault," she said.

"No, I guess not, but the result's the same."

"He has some kind of plan, hasn't he? If it goes wrong?"

"If he did, would I tell you?" Theo gave her an incredulous look and withdrew.

She waited, thinking of nothing except anxiety. It ought to be only for her own safe return to civilization, but it was not. Presently Shen came and led her to Control, and there was Michael. He was not quite calm, but Hanna saw that what he felt at this moment was not unpleasurable. There was excitement in him, a bright edge of daring. He was going to see what he could get away with.

She began to understand more about the *Pavonis Queen* affair.

The Polity ship lay not far from *GeeGee's* nose, outlined in light. No one in Control was doing anything, but one display module showed the two ships and, between them, a pinpoint of light that moved. Hanna shivered. It did not take much effort to find out why. The last time she had watched a blip of light approach, Awnlee had been huddled at her side.

She moved at the thought, and Michael glanced at her for the first time. She said awkwardly, "I guess it's time to say good-bye."

He said, "Think so? We'll see. He's supposed to be unarmed—" Michael pointed at the dot of light—"but we've got no way to tell. *GeeGee* doesn't have detection sensors for things like that. They said we had to be all together up here. I don't like that."

"Couldn't you refuse?"

"Sure. Then they would have had to think of something else. I hope this is as obvious as it looks."

GeeGee said suddenly, "He's approaching the lock. He says the agreement was, you all have to be visible to the craft standing by. Except the one who comes to get him.''

''All right. Link us up. Go, Theo. Fetch.''

Theo left them. *GeeGee* said they could be seen by the Polity vessel's crew, but the transmission was one-way; there were no voices or faces from the other ship. They waited in silence, Hanna and Michael and Shen.

Hanna opened her mouth to say: Where is Lise?

Then she shut it without speaking.

Theo came into Control with a spacesuited man behind him. A patch on the shoulder of the suit showed a name: Mencken. Mencken had removed his helmet and it hung loosely from his hands. He looked at the others clustered at the farthest point of Control and said, ''How are you, Lady Hanna?''

''I'm fine, thank you.''

''Everybody's here? Good,'' he said, and dropped the helmet. There was a stungun in his hand. He said, ''Come over here with me, Lady Hanna.''

But she stood beside Michael and said, ''I hoped you were acting in good faith.''

''Necessity, ma'am. Please come over here.''

And still she would not have moved, if Michael had not given her a push. She went then to stand beside Mencken. She looked at Michael anxiously. If he were going to do anything, he had better not wait much longer.

''That's right,'' Mencken said. He lifted one wrist to his mouth and said, ''All right, Commander. You can send the others over now.''

Hanna thought she had made a grave mistake. She thought she had overestimated Michael's intelligence. Nonetheless she turned in a single swift movement, kicking. The point of her toe caught Mencken's hand and the stungun went flying.

At the same moment he grunted and went down like a rock. Lise stood behind him, another stunner held in both her hands, her eyes wide with responsibility.

They moved fast after that.

''If you shoot,'' Michael pointed out to the faceless

commander from the Polity, "your own man goes up in atoms. Not to mention Hanna. And you want me alive, too, right? So don't shoot. And you'd better put some distance behind you because we're going to Jump. Now."

"What about Mr. Mencken?" said a cold voice.

"I'll think about it. That's nice EVA stuff he's got. Did he even bring gear for Hanna? I guess he did, that's where he hid the gun, wasn't it? Maybe we'll dump him at a relay someplace."

The voice said, "Where'd the kid come from?"

"She's been here all along. What did you think I did? Carved her up and ate her? Get moving. For your own good."

"Lady Hanna?"

Hanna did not answer. *GeeGee* broke the audio link; the two ships moved apart. They were alone again, except for the unconscious Mencken sprawled in the door.

"They're clear enough," Shen said. "Now, *Gee.*" She touched a switch and the field of stars changed and the Polity ship was not there any more.

Michael stood looking at Hanna as if he had never seen her before. She said, "I don't know why I did that."

"Fair play," he suggested. He said it as if the idea were funny. "All you had to do was nothing."

"You didn't tell me that. You didn't trust me."

"True," he said. "But there was something else, too. If you were caught the way he was, they couldn't say you had anything to do with it."

"Now's a little late to be telling me that," she said.

Hiero-volan Mencken of I&S was shut into a small cabin over engineering. There were three such rooms there, former servants' quarters, bare and isolated. He made a lot of noise at first. Presently he was quiet, but no one on *GeeGee* forgot he was there. His anger was spread from end to end of the *Golden Girl*, a subliminal thunder that underlay all their hours. When it was time to take him food, Michael and Shen went to him together, armed and implacable.

Hanna, unable to account for herself, turned to other

things. She wanted no part of keeping Mencken locked up and she wanted no part of whatever plans the others might make. To keep from thinking, she found her way to the gymnasium on *GeeGee's* upper level. It was dark there, not because it was supposed to be, but because Hanna turned off most of the lights as if to hide from herself her own lingering weakness. There she stretched, pulled, bent, reached, until her muscles ached and trembled and she was covered with sweat. The small chamber was deep inside the *Golden Girl*, entirely enclosed, and the only stars Hanna saw were those exertion floated in her field of vision. The only other things to see were padded walls hung with mechanical devices that looked like weapons, or like instruments of torture. She had always been bursting with health, taut and fit as a sleek young animal, except when the People of Zeig-Daru had taken her apart. She had not liked weakness then and she did not like it now, and struggled with it bitterly. The work kept her from listening to immaterial echoes of Mencken's fury, but it could not stop her from thinking altogether. This still was not her fight, or her flight. She was not needed; Michael and Lise would have managed quite well without her.

She caught herself thinking, was enraged, and punished her unfaithful body. She could not let it continue to be weak.

She did not give up until she hurt everywhere, every muscle throbbed; there was also a pain low in her abdomen that made her straighten, panting, at a new thought. The medic at Halber in Province Koroth, where she had gone briefly on assignment for her House. When had the trip been? Exactly when?

(". . . *and so after regeneration, nothing was done about fertility control. It was not necessary. I had only one lover afterward, and he was sterile by choice. Not that I did not want—but he did not—"*

"*I understand. And now you wish—?*"

"*Yes. Please.*"

"*You're celibate, I hear. Then why—?*"

"*Why not?*"

"I don't recommend implants unless there is need. I have, oh, a prejudice against tampering unneeded."

"But the bother. And the aches. Every thirty-five days!"

"You don't need an implant to control that; only as a guard against conception."

"But I want it! I'll go elsewhere."

"No, I'll do it. For how long? Three years or five?"

"Twenty?"

"At your age? That I won't do."

"All right, then. Five years.")

Five years Standard, or D'neeran? If D'neeran, she was safe, she could not have gotten a child by rape. If Standard—well, if Standard, she should be safe, too, though the margin was terribly narrow.

Safe or not, she stood with her back to the door and rubbed her belly cautiously. She had stripped to briefs and tied a scarf tightly around her breasts, but otherwise she was naked, and the skin she touched was hot and slick with sweat. When she looked down, the scar of Theo's surgery stood out like a red beacon.

The lights came up, startling her. "Are you all right?" Michael said.

She turned quickly, thinking that she was safe nowhere. The people of the *Golden Girl* appeared and disappeared at random like particles subject to continuous creation and demolition, as if they had some basic right to materialize in her life.

"I'm fine. Why?"

"Oh, nothing. I just—"

His eyes were peculiar. *I just saw you touch yourself like a woman suspecting new life*, said his thought.

"You ought to have a pool," Hanna said at random.

"Huh." He was distracted; his eyes danced. "I went to Earth on a Dru once, years ago when I was a Friend. It had a pool. Halfway between Valentine and Earth something went wrong with the grav stabilizers. One minute we were three times our weight and the next it was free fall. There was water everywhere pretty soon—except in the pool. Ever thought you'd drown in your own bed?"

She saw his memory of the sodden luxury craft and the bedraggled passengers, nearly laughed, then bit it off. She stood stiffly, a sullen droop to her shoulders. So he could surprise her into laughter; it was good to know. She could guard against it.

He watched the smile fade from her eyes. "I want you to tell me about D'neera," he said.

"Why?" she said.

"I want to dump you. Also him from I&S. Also my friends. I go alone the rest of the way."

"What way is that?"

"I've got friends on Valentine; maybe they can get something done if I hide long enough."

He might as well have put out a sign that said "evasion," though he had lied to Stiva Waller with flair and precision. But the first part had been true. He meant to go alone from here.

"Why D'neera?" Hanna said, but guessed the answer. "A more humane place for your friends to be caught?"

"I hope so. Will it be?"

"It should be. Especially if I'm there."

"Then tell me this," he said. "Suppose we turn up at the closest possible Jump terminus to D'neera. Shen estimates—if I push *GeeGee* to the limit and slow down for nothing—*GeeGee* can land, offload passengers, and get back to Jump-legal space in thirty minutes. What I want to know is what's going to stop me."

"D'neerans aren't." The sweat had dried; she was getting cold in the blazing light. "What do D'neerans care about you? There's nothing to stop you."

"You're wrong," he said. "You gave your sympathies away, back there. I always meant to go on to D'neera if they tried something like they tried, but it wouldn't have been an obvious move before. After what they saw you do, it is. There'll be a welcoming committee from the Polity waiting for me."

She said after a long pause, "I've got no way of knowing the exact situation. I could call D'neera. Find out."

"Then they'd know for sure we're coming. The only chance is speed. And no warning."

"Yes. Of course."

"Can you even make a guess at what they'll do?"

"Speed," she said half to herself. "Maneuverability; that's what you've got. No guns. They must know it. Wait." She thought about D'neera's defenses. They were taken seriously since Nestor's short, vicious attempt at conquest several years before. "You'll have to identify yourself. You can put it off for a little while. Not long, or they'll shoot; D'neerans will, I mean. Then if the Polity's there, their people will know who you are, too. They'll let you go down, but they'll have you targeted by the time you hit the ground. Have you thought about where you'll land?"

"Koroth, that's all. Your own House is least likely to risk you, right? You tell me where to touch down. *GeeGee* can do the rest."

"There's prairie west of—no, don't try the prairie. City Koroth's got an Outport. Land there; there won't be any shooting. Too many people around. They'll get you going back out. If I were a Polity commander, I'd have a lot of small, fast gunboats there. With atmospheric capability, as many as I could get the magistrates to agree to. They'll be faster than *GeeGee*. And I would—I don't know. Try talking you down, I guess. If it didn't work—it won't work, will it?" She saw the answer in his face and said, "Then I'd start shooting. Sharpshooting. Not to destroy *GeeGee*; just to disable her so you'll have to land. But if that doesn't work either—well, then they might shoot to kill."

After a minute he said, "I'll try it. Just make sure your own folk know who I am. I don't want them thinking I'm a Nestorian kamikaze who's forgotten the war only lasted a day."

He turned away. After a moment Hanna went after him. She was very cold now. He glanced around and waited for her; she came up beside him and looked up with troubled eyes. It was too easy to see him riding *GeeGee* down the sky in a burst of flame, plunging toward Hanna's native soil.

"Mike. . . ?" The friendly diminutive came by itself. She had not wanted to use his name.

"Yes?" he said.

"Do you have to do it that way? Are you sure you can't go back to Valentine?"

"Oh, yes. We hooked into a relay a little while ago. I tried a transmission to Valentine. It didn't get through; I got a Fleet officer instead. That's all I get to talk to from now on, Fleet and I&S." There were shadows under his eyes, but he was tranquil. "A Jump later I scanned the 'beams. Valentine's officially turned over ownership of *GeeGee* to I&S as reparations for the *Pavonis Queen*. I&S got an order waiving trial; did you know they can do that? *GeeGee's* stolen property now. Valentine's cut me loose, Hanna. And believe me, when Valentine's bankers don't back you, you're done."

She said, "Let me try talking to Starr."

"Who?" He was blank; she nearly laughed again, but it would have been bitter. "Oh," he said. "Would it help now?"

"I could try. Even," she said, looking away, "if it's a little late."

And she was still a person of some importance, because the censors permitted her to do it. There was a delay that seemed endless, and she shivered in Control. Michael disappeared briefly and came back with a blanket which he draped over her shoulders. "I wonder just how close the nearest Fleet ship is," he said, watching the chronometer. *GeeGee's* mass detectors were at full power, and she was ready to Jump the instant they registered anything larger than a hydrogen atom. "Traps," Michael said succinctly. Hanna waited, listening to unknown voices murmur through the great distances. She thought of the *Pavonis Queen*, and of the outrageously simple approach to the trap Michael had just escaped.

"Have you always seen traps everywhere you looked?" she said.

"I always looked for them," he said, "but I only saw them when they were there." He paused, and when he spoke again his voice was grim. "There were one or two I didn't see."

She would have asked what he meant, but the light-raddled screen in front of her cleared, and there was Jameson. Her heart rose up all in one piece. There was stability, there was everything she had craved; it was in the irony in the gray-green eyes, in the imperturbable mouth.

"Well?" she said.

He looked past her, looking for Michael, but Michael had faded into the shadows. "Yes?" Jameson said.

"What about that bargain?"

"It didn't work very well, did it?" he said. Hanna studied him carefully. This was not a private conversation; many ears would hear what they said.

"Why don't you just take him on his terms?" she said. "There's information you could use. Take the bargain or you get nothing."

"Stop saying 'you,'" he told her. "Don't use that word. I have very little to do with this."

"Why are you talking to me, then?"

"You asked," he said; she saw amusement.

"Well, say what they told you to say," she said. It went home, but he recovered.

"Enough is enough," he said. "You're valuable. So is Mr. Mencken; possibly more so. A mistake was made. Mr. Figueiredo is willing to start over again. Give him the information that was promised, and Mr. Kristofik can go free. He has only to return Mr. Mencken. As for you: your position seems ambiguous. You can do as you please."

She was watching him intently. The amusement had not gone away.

"We'll think about it," she said, and broke the connection. She did not hear Michael come up behind her, but as she stared at the blank screen, he spoke almost in her ear. She did not take in what he said.

"Starr was lying," she said. "He was saying what he was told to say, and it was a lie. And he knew I would know it."

"You don't mean they'd try the same trick again!"

"Probably not the same. Not exactly the same. Maybe this time they would do just what they undertook to do, and then when you got home to Valentine and walked into your house, they would be waiting for you. They'd do something like that, this time."

"You said he knew you would see through the lie," Michael said. "Why would he be so careless?"

"He's not careless about anything." She stood up, letting the blanket fall from her shoulders, feeling the bite of cold air. "He wants to see what I will do," she said. "He's curious. He wants to see what will happen now."

She went out then, back to her room, where she could try in solitude to set her thoughts in order. They resisted. All she could think was that the rules for domestic order that she had accepted as necessity on civilized worlds had turned into a cold machine. They were meant to protect people like her. They were meant to protect her from people like Michael. Maybe that was right. She supposed it was.

The journey to D'neera night have been made in three days. Michael extended it to ten for misdirection's sake, to weary the watchers' eyes on D'neera and make them wait and wait. *GeeGee* had not gone in a straight line to anywhere since leaving Revenge. She went in no straight line now; she zigzagged across human space in a butterfly dance. All the space outside looked the same: black with sparks and the swathe of the Milky Way.

Late on the first night Hanna came to Michael's room, and to his bed. Throughout the rest of the flight she kept coming back. Sometimes he looked at her eyes and thought they saw too much—inevitably she saw the charts that haunted him—but she did not ask questions. They did not say much to each other at all. But when she was with him she made these last days a time of pleasure and peace, and to give her something in return he played songs for her, the antique music he loved: dances, madrigals, melodies of courtly love, a solstice song two millennia old. She did not make him feel that he had to talk with her, nor did he feel that he had to pretend anything.

With Shen and Theo he pretended, exerting all his strength to appear natural—cheerful, confident, filled with light. But then he would let it slip when he was alone with Lise, and with Lise, he talked. He had promised to teach her to cook, and he used the promise as an excuse to keep her with him in the galley for hours at a time. He meant to teach her more than cooking, and ten days was not long enough. *Love life,* he said, *it is precious no matter what happens.* And, *Don't gamble with money,* he said, *it's not important enough. Gamble with your life, your happiness, your health. They're the only stakes worth gambling for. Remember that,* he said, *repeat it back to me.* And, *Promise you'll remember. Promise. Promise,* until she promised, her eyes so troubled that he was forced to check himself, smile, pretend his intensity had been a mistake.

On the last night Hanna woke briefly to see Michael like a shadow at the wall, studying the dim glow of his charts. She slept again and dreamed that Starr Jameson came to see her. At first they were on the *Golden Girl,* but then they were in mountains, in the heart of a D'neeran range Hanna knew well. They were near the top of a peak, but Hanna could not see anything because the morning was filled with mist. Water dripped from shrubs to the ground, and the fog was so low it barely cleared Jameson's head. He wore an expression she had never seen on his face before; he looked both hurt and outraged.

I can't help it, she said, *you knew there must be someone else one day.*

I knew, and it comforted me. But why this man?

Can't you see how beautiful he is?

Since when has a beautiful face meant anything?

There's more to it than that. He gives, he gives with every breath.

Why should that matter to you? You are cold, as cold as you need to be. I was able to give you that. Now you can think—at least, until now, I thought you could.

But I don't want to think.

Then what in heaven's name do you want?

She told him explicitly what she wanted to do, and that she wanted to keep doing it with Michael. Jameson was not jealous. But he said: *You wouldn't be able to keep him. He came from nowhere and that's where he'll go. He has no center—love, you'll say, but love is way-*

*ward; you need law and custom as well. You could have
kept me, were it not for your pride. But you won't be
able to keep him.*

You go to hell, she said.

In the morning Hanna saw Theo, and he talked with
some tension of what would happen on D'neera. Hanna
thought again of *GeeGee* racing through the sky, carrying only Michael, going out and out. The charts of
nothing rose up before her. They came together with
Michael's silence and with something she had guessed
without explicit awareness. She knew.

Theo spluttered at her; her face must be bleached.

She brushed him away and went in search of Michael.
He was in the galley with Lise, who sat on a high stool
and dropped pellets of produce into a very large pot set
on a very small cooking flat. Lise giggled as the pellets
expanded, resuming vegetable shapes. Michael stood
beside her, talking of spices.

Hanna thought she was going to be sick. She rocked
on a wave of panic, the first she had felt in years.

I have to talk to you, she said, not in words but on a
gust of fear. There was a clatter on the polished floor.
The ladle he had dropped dribbled streamlets of aro-
matic broth.

He got the ladle back and gave it to Lise. "Just keep
stirring," he said.

Hanna led him to his own room in silence. She felt
fragile, breakable; her hand sliding the door shut was
not steady.

"I know what you're going to do," she said.

He had no answer. He was silent, watching her.

"You've lied to all of us. You're going Outside, aren't
you?"

"It'll be all right," he said.

"Oh, you're mad!" she said, and he moved toward
her and touched her, stroked her face and hands, was
concentrated on her comfort; she saw abruptly, with the
force of revelation, what he was. Time came and went,
the Master's hand was light or heavy, and always it was
all right. He believed it; that was how he convinced

others it was true. And if it were not all right he would
make it so, if he could, asking nothing in return. She
looked at him with a kind of terror. She had never
known anyone like him before. She did not think she
would know anyone like him again.

"Why?" she said. "Why?"

"Hanna, there's nothing left for me here. There is
absolutely nothing for me here."

"There's nothing out there either!"

He said gently, "There's something I'll try to find.
I've been looking for it for a long time."

"What?"

He shook his head, smiling.

"Listen, oh, listen," she said. "I might still be able
to keep them from changing you, from Adjusting you.
And I might, I could still, D'neera would be sanctuary,
I only have to ask. Koroth would take you in, you could
stay there, you could be at the House or at my home—"
She hardly knew what she said. She was thinking: *You
can't go, I don't know you!*

"Think what it would be like," he said. "Could you
guarantee Polity treachery wouldn't extend even to
D'neera? You could get Koroth to shelter me, but I'd
never be safe. I've looked over my shoulder for twenty
years. I won't do it again. And think what it would be
like for you. D'neera would be the only place where I'd
have even a margin of safety, small as it was, and I'd
never be able to leave. Can you see me there, an outsider in a telepaths' society, dependent on you? Going
slowly crazy, I'd think, and following you around. No,
I'll do it this way. Maybe someday I'll come back."

"You won't."

He could not console her. He smoothed the hair at
her temples, and she felt a great tenderness in him.

"Hanna, nothing lasts," he said. "Nothing lasts."

She shook her head, but it was hardly a denial at all,
so great was his conviction. It had always been true for
him. And he might have been a madman—she thought
then that he was—but he was not bitter or cynical or in
search of pity. Instead she felt only his compassion—
for Hanna, looking toward loss she could not even gauge

accurately yet; and for all the others who hoped for shelter, and when they had found it, saw it blow away.

There was no formal countdown. There was only, as the time neared, a slow move toward Control; Hanna joined it. *GeeGee* Jumped just as she entered Control. The stars outside were achingly familiar. Dead ahead, brilliant but not yet a naked-eye disc, was Hanna's own sun.

"One more Jump," Theo said. He fell silent as a strange voice sounded in Control, calling for identification. No one answered. Soon the air rippled with D'neeran voices, first startled at this unscheduled arrival, then impatient at the absence of response, and at last exceedingly cold.

Michael talked over the murmur, running through the plan one last time.

"At ten minutes before landfall, Theo and Lise go down to the main passenger hatch. Theo, you use manual override to open the inner seal so there'll be no delay on the ground. At five minutes, you two—" he looked at Shen and Hanna, "—get Mencken and take him down. Don't take any chances with him. Pick up stunners on your way and drag him out feet first if you have to. I'll pop the outer hatch from up here when we're down. Don't waste a second. Get out and run like hell. I'll be monitoring you and I can't take off till you're clear, understand?"

Hanna was bitter with resentment. That last was unnecessary; he did not need to play on their anxiety for his clean escape to make them move fast. But perhaps he had said it because of Lise, who was already in tears at a parting she thought temporary. Theo stayed close to Lise; Hanna thought he was assigned to keep her under control.

Shen said, "You're at optimum for atmospheric moves. The landside program's laid in."

"Jump her, then."

And there, without a whisper or sensation of movement, was the world of Hanna's birth. The light of its sun, a near-twin to Sol, shone into Control. D'neera was between the ship and the star so that they saw the planet's nightside, the great black circle rimmed with light. Hanna was coming home. To blue and lavender, dew-washed meadows, the horses on the fields of morning, the duties of her House—

(—*and the voices,* said a whisper, *that send you here and there; submitting to the Polity, treading amongst its rules; what else is there? See what happens to those who step outside, oh yes Outside indeed—*)

GeeGee started her preprogrammed descent, an arc of wild speed that would take her round the planet fully three times before she braked for landfall on the dayside. "Start talking," Michael said to Hanna urgently, she remembered what she had to do and heard the shocked voices now, the men and women wondering if they would have to shoot. She identified herself, stumbling over the words, unreasonably giving the birthname unused since childhood instead of her name in Koroth's House, by which she was better known: "It's H'ana Bassanio, don't fire, I'm just coming—"

Home. She could not say the word.

GeeGee skidded through the terminator and leapt into full light. Below there was dazzling white cloud. Hanna heard herself talking, making sense maybe to someone but not to herself. Because there were other voices at her back and she heard them as if they were the only sounds in the silence of deep space.

Lise said, "But can you fly *Gee* by yourself?"

"You could fly *Gee* by yourself."

"If they shoot at you, they'll only make you land? Sure?"

"I'm sure. Go on, little puss. It's time to go."

"But what if they hit something else?"

"They won't. They're good."

"But if they do, you'll *crash.*"

Hanna's head jerked right around. She said brutally, "He doesn't care if he does."

GeeGee flashed into the dark again. Control was full of shadows. Michael walked purposefully toward Hanna. She saw the gold-flecked eyes with clarity in the half-dark, as if they had a light of their own. It took him perhaps two seconds to reach her, but for Hanna time slowed and stopped and the world she had always known turned over. She heard his intent to shut her up, and his rapid calculation of the changes in plan that must be made to offload an unconscious Hanna.

In the last split second, in a single devastating pulse of thought, she told the others exactly what Michael meant to do.

He heard it, too; he knew what she had done and what it meant. They would revolt as soon as they grasped it. They would not let him set them free.

And here it was: the rage she had forgotten burst out like an oily cloud with screams in it. His face changed. *Not Mike. I don't know who this is but not Mike.* A creature hardly human leapt for Hanna's throat. She dived and rolled. Her mind ticked over in an endless second, analyzing. If he knew anything about fighting, the fury had wiped it out. He was fast, though, and she barely got out of the way of the next lunge. Time still was slowed and everything in it was preternaturally clear. Lise wailed, paralyzed with a terror that was half longing to help Michael and half animal recognition that this was no longer Michael but a thing that ought not be helped, a thing he would not wish her to help. Theo was white as a corpse. Shen was busy with *GeeGee*, looking over her shoulder as often as she dared.

She was going to have to hurt him to stop him; if she could; before he caught her and killed her with his hands.

She picked a direction. Two more lunges; two more calculated, dangerous dodges that brought her up with her back to the swiveling seats before an auxiliary control console. When he came at her again, she caught the outstretched arm, bent, shifted—and heaved him over her shoulder headfirst. She spun and pounced like a cat. He was wedged between two seats, struggling to get up, all coordination gone in the passion to destroy. She kicked him on the jaw without compunction and it had no effect at all; so she sprang to the top of the console and crouched and waited. When he came up at last, back half turned to her, she hit him at the base of the skull with the edge of her hand. She had to do it twice more before he went down. Then he was still.

GeeGee skimmed back into the light. Shen swore, hissing.

"Gotta pull out," she said. "Theo. Come help."

Hanna slipped from the console to the floor. She pulled at Michael to turn him over, and Lise helped her; when he was on his back, she got his head into her lap and held him. His mouth bled where her foot had smashed it. The pulse in his throat faltered under her fingers and her own heart nearly stopped; then the beat steadied to a slow but strong rhythm. She nearly wept with relief. Control was full of voices, it seemed that all of D'neera and the Polity were shouting at her. It was dark again, and then light as *GeeGee*, no longer on her programmed course, broke out over one planetary pole; whether north or south the disoriented Hanna could not tell. "H'ana!" said a woman's voice, she knew the sound of it, the Lady of Koroth called her. Shen's lips were drawn back from her teeth; that was, Hanna saw with astonishment, a smile of sorts. Shen fed *GeeGee* a Jump order; they were nearly away. All the Polity's gunboats had been plunging for projected landing sites, and the change in course had taken them by surprise.

Michael's eyes opened, their color strangely faded; all Hanna saw was the gold. Almost at once he looked up at her with knowledge. She smoothed his hair and it felt like silk to her hand.

He pulled himself to his feet just as *GeeGee* Jumped. Hanna gave him her shoulder to lean on. He did not reject it; he needed support and so he accepted it, eternally the realist. He whispered, "Stay here," and she let him go. The tall figure staggered and she thought of the spiral stairs. Theo started after him and she said: *No. He'll be all right.* She added aloud before Theo could respond, "How is he after that happens to him?"

"After what happens?" Theo was puzzled. "Getting beat up by a girl half his size?"

Shen muttered, "Told him he'd got soft."

"The fit, I mean. The craziness. When he turns into somebody else."

Theo looked as if he wanted to deny that anything had happened. He said, "I never saw it before."

"I saw the start of it once and I haven't been around very long. You must know what I mean."

"All right. All right. I guess I've seen the start of it, too. But I never saw him lose control before. I mean, he could always stop it. He told me, once he told me there were times before when he didn't. But I never saw the whole thing before."

Shen looked at a scanner and said, "We're clear. Nobody around." She made an evil noise that Hanna recognized, after a moment, as a chuckle.

"I have to look at his head," Theo said.

"Not yet. Unless you want to handle him if he starts up again."

"No," Theo said with alarm. "No, I don't."

Shen said abruptly, "Good thing you did that, told us what you did. Outside, huh? If he wasn't shot down first?"

"That's right." Reaction was setting in. He could have crushed her skull between his hands; the thought made her weak. The silver chain bound for Uskos was chokingly tight.

"Can't get rid of us that easy," Shen said. "You're all right."

Hanna did not say anything to that. Shen would not expect it.

She made herself wait a little longer. When five minutes had gone by, she passed through *GeeGee* to Michael's room, stopping on the way to take a stunner from the cabinet where *GeeGee's* small store of arms was kept. But she knew at once, when she went through his door, that she would not need it. The room was dark except for the glow of starlight; he lay on the bed looking up into the dark. She came to him and touched him, and found that his hair and face and shoulders were wet. He had put his head under cold water.

She stretched out at his side, but he did not speak. Hanna ached as if it were she who had been hit.

"Michael," she said, but there was no answer. She turned and leaned over him in the dark. She put her

hands on him and his body was foreign to her as an
alien substance. In his rage he had fallen into a dream;
he was in it still, and in Hanna, seeing it, recognition
woke. Snow and flame and a blood-red sky. A child
crying with pain.

She whispered his name at intervals, until finally he
moved, remembering her. She could not say anything
about what she had done. Intead she said as steadily as
she could, and practically: "When did you start having
those attacks?"

To her surprise he answered, perhaps because he was
so beaten that it did not matter. But he talked as if
speaking hurt.

"The first time was—the night I got away—onto Alta."

There was a jolt of fear and flight. Castillo.

"Got away from *him?*"

"Yes." The quiet voice was hoarse, as if he had been
screaming. Perhaps he had, down here where no one
could hear.

"How long were you with him?"

"I don't know. Months, I think . . . There were never
any clocks. I guessed about day and night. I got bigger . . .
I knew we'd landed somewhere. He went out and came
back drunk. He forgot to lock the door. It was the first time
he ever forgot and I tried to run out and he caught me. It
was always bad, but it was worse that night . . ."

His voice trailed away. She saw a picture of explicit
sexual brutality, an agonized child caught in terror and
helpless rage. She said, her own voice not quite steady,
"He gave me to the others, but he never touched me
himself, not once. I never thought about it. If I had, I'd
have thought he only liked men."

Michael said, "Only when he can't get little boys."

"You must have been an exquisite child."

"That's why he took—" The ragged voice stopped.

"Took you away from where, Mike?"

The silence lengthened in despair. She was whispering again, and shaking. "You don't know, do you?"

He turned his head away; he was trembling, too. She
said with urgency, as if the quick question let her leap an
abyss without looking down, "How did you get away?"

"He passed out . . ." So faint she heard more thought than words. "There was something—heavy—I can't remember what it was. I got it—somehow I got it up. I couldn't hold things, I, my hands—"

She thought he was going to choke. She stroked his cheek, willing him to breathe. "Your hands were injured. Did he do that?"

"He saw it done. When he—took me on board—he tried to fix them. So I could use them for him. On him. He was, he was satisfied with how they came out. He liked, liked ruining things, I think. And so I dropped it on his head—" He was entirely unaware of a disjuncture. "I didn't remember until later. That was the first time."

"And then you ran out?"

"Yes."

"Got off the ship?"

"Somehow. I don't remember. Hanna, don't you see what you've done?"

Another whisper. "I know what I did . . ."

"I can't take the rest of you Outside." He was trying patiently to explain. "Lise and Theo and Shen, they've got a right to a real life. We can't just fly around forever with no place to land. But they won't let me give myself up. That's why I had to leave them behind . . ." His voice trailed away. *GeeGee* closed in on them, claustrophobic.

Hanna's fingers went to the chain at her throat. The links pressed into her skin. "There's Uskos," she said.

He shook his head, uncomprehending. She said, "I'm a citizen of the nation of Ell. There's a story I promised Rubee I would tell. Would the Polity risk an incident to get us back? I don't know. I don't think so."

She waited while he absorbed it. She knew when he had grasped it, because she felt a little of the laughter revive in him. It was a giant joke on the Polity, and he turned toward her in the dark, almost smiling.

"I'd rather run toward something than away," he said. "But I seem to remember the course was secret."

"They gave it to me, though." She lifted a hand to her throat and spoke a word in Ellsian. The silver chain parted and slid into her hand, shining in the faint starlight. She held it out to him.

"It's in here," she said.

He did not take it at once. He said, "You know what you're doing?"

"Yes. Take it."

"I know what you had back there. You can say good-bye to all of it if you do this."

She was barefoot and wore another woman's clothes. The last thing she possessed was in her hand.

"I know," she said. "Take it."

After a minute he did. He did not speak again. She lay close beside him and presently he fell into a quiet sleep, still holding the chain. Hanna did not sleep; she looked out at the stars and seemed to hear the blowing of a clear strong wind.

Hiero-volan Mencken was told nothing. He had been told nothing from the moment he woke, tingling and dizzy, in the dark little room he identified as part of the *Golden Girl's* staff quarters. His shouts did no good, except perhaps to relieve his own feelings, his head hurt and he stopped shouting quickly. There was nothing in the room or on his person that would help him get away. If he ever got his hands on Hanna ril-Koroth—

He did not know what had happened. He thought it was Hanna who had stunned him somehow. But perhaps she had been doped, drained, brainwashed and filled up again, her personality altered; no other explanation was conceivable.

He waited for ten days, subject sometimes to concerts his captors may have considered entertainment, or torture.

J'ai trove qui me veut amer;
s'amerai, quant la brunete au vis cler m'a dit,
que s'amour avrai,
bien me doi de li loer . . .

"What the hell does that mean?" he said when it broke in on his lunch, and got nearly the only piece of information he was given on the *Golden Girl*, for what good it did him. While he drank the excellent soup—the food was good, he had to admit—Michael Kristofik smiled and translated: "I've found one who wants to love me; if I should love, as the dark lady with the bright face told me I'd have her love, I'm to be praised for her."

It made no more sense in Standard than it had in whatever the original language was. Kristofik looked happier than he had any right to be. He had only put off the inevitable, he was a dead man so far as his present antisocial personality was concerned, but he looked as if he'd forgotten that. But Mencken could not take advantage of the lapse because Shen Lo-Yang did not take her eyes off him, she did not even seem to blink, and the stunner she leveled at him was set for full power, which at this range could be fatal.

The next thing Kristofik told him, when he had been there nine days, was that on the morrow he would leave the *Golden Girl*. He was told that someone would come for him when it was time, and he was advised to go quietly. He was told he would then be safe, and free to pursue justice as he chose.

So he waited through the next day, but nothing happened; at any rate not to him. For a time the sounds of the ship changed in a way he recognized as a difficult but slickly accomplished set of maneuvers; the self-contained gravitational field of the spacecraft did not waver, but Mencken thought they were in an atmosphere. This was it, he thought. But then it ended and time went on and on into the night, hour after hour without activity or news; he did not even get any dinner.

Went wrong somehow, whatever they planned. He had mixed feelings about that. Some of it was grim satisfaction; was Hiero-volan Mencken to be shoved off a pirate ship with a gun in his back, while the pirate laughed at him? Never. On the other hand—the other hand was not good to think about. He had a family waiting for him. He did not like thinking of how long they might have to wait.

"What happened?" he said next morning when they brought him breakfast. There was a lot of it, as if they were making up for the meal missed the night before.

Kristofik and Lo-Yang did not answer. They looked

at him as if—he saw this acutely—he were a problem. He was by no means a coward and he ate his well-made omelet with deliberation, studying the black-clad man and woman who had his life in their hands. He thought he detected in Shen Lo-Yang a certain pleasure, which was a nasty thought, considering her history. Kristofik was pale and his mouth showed the trace of a shallow cut. Trouble from outside?—but the *Golden Girl* had not landed anywhere or been boarded; he was sure of that. Perhaps Lady Hanna had slipped out of control, a heartening possibility.

Some hours afterward the *Golden Girl* stopped. He had not heard for some time the characteristic stresses and puffs that meant Jumps; instead there were the louder but less abrupt sounds of movement in realspace. Suddenly there was almost silence, as all movement ceased; life support alone did not make much noise. His door opened. In it this time there were three people, not two, and all of them were armed. They wore spacesuits, but their helmets were not in place. Kristofik and Lo-Yang, of course; but the third was Lady Hanna ril-Koroth. She looked beautiful and calm. He said, "Are you sure you're pointing that gun the right way?"

"Come on out," she said.

They marched him toward the tail of the *Golden Girl*, not leading him but telling him where to go, staying a safe distance behind. Michael Kristofik said, "You're getting out of this safe and sound."

"What did you do to Lady Hanna?"

"It's what he *does*," she said sweetly. "Several times, when he's having a good day."

Mencken glanced around. He did not understand, but Kristofik evidently did, and looked scandalized. Kristofik said, "Your own suit's waiting for you, and your maneuvers pack. We're next door to a relay. I'll tell you the number if you want to know, but it doesn't matter; you can't broadcast from on-site anyway. We'll wait till you've got yourself anchored and then we'll move out. We'll contact Fleet and tell them where you are. You should be picked up in less than twenty-four hours."

"How'd he do it?" Mencken said to Hanna. "Drugs?"

"Is that what they're all going to think?" she said. "Tell them this. Tell Lady Koroth and Commissioner Vickery and Gil Figueiredo and Starr Jameson especially, tell Starr in person, give him this message: I quit."

The suit was outside an air lock whose indicator lights showed ready. Mencken put it on and waited while the others fastened their helmets, one at a time, so two of them always had him covered. There was no haste or confusion; the teamwork reminded him of his colleagues in I&S. They escorted him into the lock and out of it. Free fall caught at his stomach and he fumbled for the maneuvers pack, switching it on. He saw that they were indeed close to an Inspace relay, close enough for a searchlight to pick out the details of its platforms and antennae.

He could not help saying, "I hope you really are going to contact Fleet."

We will, said a voice in his head, so clearly he might have mistaken it for speech, except that he had had contact with telepaths before; also it carried the absolute assurance of truth that speech could never have.

He gave up, having no longer any choice. They stayed where they were while he glided the short distance to the relay. He had no way to tell when the others went back into the ship; the *Golden Girl* did not move and kept the searchlight shining while he hooked his utility belt to a steel stanchion. After that the searchlight blinked out. The *Golden Girl* moved away; its other lights became fainter and disappeared.

He only had to wait seven hours. It was not even long enough to get hungry, after the breakfast he had had; it only seemed like an eternity.

IV.

Gaaf the medic, a former physician of Fleet, was trapped in the *Avalon*, and trapped by more than metal. There were the dreams, and waking nightmares, too.

First there was the uproar on Revenge. Gaaf watched it. All of them went to the warehouse to retrieve the treasures stored there, but all the things were gone. Castillo made certain statements about what would be done to the People of the Rose. There would not be much living in the City of the Rose when he was finished. Gaaf would have preferred not believing the threats, but he believed them. Castillo's face was scarlet and he screamed at Suarez to bring him the headman of the town. While he waited he paced and snarled, and then he said more about what he was going to do. Gaaf started to go away but thought: *What if he notices I'm gone? What if he knows I left because of him? What if he gets angry at me?*—and so he stayed. He stood just inside the *Avalon* and watched Castillo interrogate Elder Rann. He saw the D'neeran woman again, walking in front of Juel to her death, and turned away as if that would make it not real and sink it into dream.

And then there was the shocking end of it, he heard the sounds outside and hesitated, thinking he ought to go see, and Castillo came back, running and yelling orders through an intercom to Wales on the flight deck. Gaaf was in his way and was shoved aside. The push was hard enough to knock him into the wall and bruise his shoulder, and the first instant of shock and pain brought tears to his eyes. He collected himself and fol-

lowed Castillo slowly to the flight deck. But they were
taking off when he got there, in a hurry, jabbering. Later
he found out Juel was dead.

The *Avalon* left Revenge behind and moved out into
space. There was no more talk about the People of the
Rose. Instead they talked about the *Golden Girl*. The
Avalon had gotten a good look at her: a pretty ship, an
expensive, sophisticated toy. A Dru-class yacht. Gaaf
had never seen one before. He stared at the pictures and
tried to imagine the luxury inside. You had to be born
to wealth to have one, he thought. But why would anyone who could own one be on Revenge? What interest
could anyone like that have in stealing Castillo's store
of trade goods?

Far away from Revenge, in deep space, the *Avalon*
waited. The men asked: for what? But Castillo kept his
own counsel. Besides Castillo there were five of them
now that Juel was dead: Suarez, Wales, Gaaf, Ta, and
Bakti. They passed time with gambling and watching
the 'beams. What the 'beams had to say was going to
be crucial. What was the golden ship going to do with
the woman who was the only witness to the aliens'
deaths?—it was a mystery. The *Avalon* filled up with
the stink of fear. If Oversight had come to Revenge
between scheduled visits, if a Fleet representative had
been there to warn them off, that would have been one
thing. But the golden ship could have nothing to do with
Fleet. And nobody knew about Castillo and Revenge.
Except—Castillo in those early hours looked at the men
of his crew with (it seemed to Gaaf) something new in
the ice-blue eyes—

They waited, watching the 'beams. They waited for
information about the golden ship. It did not occur to
any of them that Hanna might be dead and the secret of
their identities gone with her—to any of them except
Gaaf, the only one who knew how sick she had been.
He did not tell the others, because he did not dare tell
Castillo that he had eased her pain and thus, surely,
helped her turn on them. But he was haunted, and his
dreams were haunted, too, by the swollen brutalized
face, the stripped fever-hot body; by knowing he had

played God and given her (though he had not known it then) a chance at life. A voice echoed in his mind, fuzzy with fever and drugs. Equally without fear or gratitude she called to him: *Wait!* Still he was afraid that she was dead. But she might get treatment in time. But from whom?

The name of the *Golden Girl's* owner came finally. Gaaf was on the flight deck when it came. There was a picture with it, a routine identification shot. Gaaf looked at the face and wondered what it would be like to be handsome and rich. The man in the picture looked gently amused. Castillo barely glanced at it. He knew the name; he did not have to look at the face that went with it. Suarez also knew it, and cursed bitterly. Castillo only said: "Him!"—as he had said once before, laughing then.

"Who is he?" Gaaf asked, but softly, so that Castillo could choose to overlook the question. And he did overlook it, or did not hear it. He looked at the image with cold hate.

The *Avalon* went nowhere for a time. "What are we waiting for?" said the others.

"You'll see," Castillo answered in his soft voice.

Gaaf wondered if that meant Castillo didn't know, had no ideas.

Castillo and Suarez talked together privately a great deal. They did not tell anyone what they talked about.

Twelve hours after Hanna's escape:

Gaaf slept fitfully, an hour at a time. The aliens died over and over in his sleep. Hanna's eyes were blank with shock and blue as meadow grasses in the clear morning light after a night of storms. She threw herself at Castillo and Wales turned the stunner on her and she fell, the distant sleepiness of stun softening her face.

Twenty-four hours:

Castillo was calm. There was nothing on the 'beams. The men gambled and drank. "If he's smart, he'll kill her," Suarez said. "He doesn't need the attention."

"Worst thing he could do," Castillo said. "They're looking for him, not us. She said so. He needs her."

''He might not know that.''

A smile of real pleasure. ''If he finds out too late, when she's dead—that's best for us. More time.''

''They'll drag it out of him, though. That he had her. Where he got her. Us.''

That was not a private talk. Gaaf heard it, but it was too complicated for him. Every place in the *Avalon* seemed dark. There was shadow on all the faces. He went once to the room where Hanna had been imprisoned and saw the gold chain on the floor. He saw its provocative gleam against smooth skin—until the skin bruised and bled. He had not been able to watch the beating, but Wales had come to get him to wake her up, and so he had to see what they had done.

He put the chain into his pocket. When he revived her, she had been warm under his hands . . .

Suarez had been with Castillo a long time, longer than any of them except the dead Juel. Gaaf was the new man. He had been on the *Avalon* for six months, buying medical supplies for resale, and this was to have been his first run to the place they called Gadrah. He supposed it was something like Revenge. When they got there, he was to perform some kind of service, act as physician to some vague population of colonists. There was a great deal he had not been told.

He came across Suarez in the common room. Suarez, drinking alone, was talkative. Gaaf asked him who Michael Kristofik was.

''A mistake,'' Suarez said. ''That's what he is, a mistake.''

''What kind of mistake?''

''I remember,'' Suarez said in a confiding voice. His eyes had a secretive look.

''What do you remember?'' Gaaf said, bolder.

''Prettiest little boy you ever saw. Got away one night on Alta.''

A nightmare that was not a dream swept over Gaaf. Cries in the night months ago, no dream; in space near Colony One, which they had left in a hurry for no reason Gaaf could see. They were a child's cries, but in the morning no child was aboard. Later, on Willow, he watched Castillo watch a fresh baby-fat boy, maybe ten years old; the dilated eyes came out of a bad dream. The boy was with a crowd of family. He left with them, safe, out of reach. You could not forget nightmare when the pieces added up by day. Castillo's expression. Cries in the night. The pretty boy who got away.

"Mikhail," Suarez said.

"What?"

"That's his name. Wonder if he remembers."

Gaaf thought about something else, retreating. He put his hand in his pocket, and the chain rubbed against his fingers.

Slight as the wisp of a dream and with burning flesh. The black bone-deep bruises on her thighs. *I couldn't do what they did,* Gaaf thought. *I'd be gentle. So careful—*

He dreamed about it, smiling a little. But Suarez said, "He went to whoring on Valentine. Then he pulled off a big one. I mean big."

The lights in the common room seemed dim. It was darker and darker. Chairs, tables, everyday objects thickened; they had sharp angles in the dark, were unrelieved cubes.

"What's the mistake?" Gaaf asked.

"He's still alive," Suarez said.

Thirty-six hours:

He slept again, a little. Hard fists on soft skin. She cried out, tears of agony stood in her eyes, burst out, coursed down the discoloring cheeks.

"Oh no. Oh no—" He woke again and stumbled to the common room. They were listening to the 'beams. The hunt was up. Not for them. But only not yet.

"We have to go," Suarez said.

He sat at Castillo's right hand. Castillo sat at the head of a long table. He had something in his hands. Gaaf had seen it before: a cylinder of densely engraved gold. At one end there was a rim of flashing jewels round a circle of blackness. Castillo turned it over and over.

"Go where?" said Ta. His nails were badly bitten; he was subject in some moods to something like remorse.

"Gadrah," Castillo said. "As planned."

"They'll get us there, too!" Ta said with violence.

"They won't," Castillo said. The faint smile covered his whole face. *I know something you don't,* it said.

"Fleet'll be everywhere for this. There's no place they won't go."

"Not Gadrah," Castillo said, and he said it with absolute certainty.

"Why not?" Ta said.

"You'll see. But our cargo's incomplete. We were robbed," Castillo said without irony. "This is the last run. We're trading for more than payload this time. There's not enough to trade."

The things stored on Revenge had been purchased legitimately. There was no chance of replacing them.

Wales said, "You're not thinking of another raid someplace."

"We might not need one." The smile stayed in place. "We might be able to get somebody to give us what we need."

"How?" Wales said.

Castillo explained. He kept turning the golden cylinder in his hands. The engraved letters on it, the ones in Standard, said plainly where it could take them.

Space fled away behind them. Now they had an itinerary, and the first place they would go was Outside. Gaaf, though ten years with the Interworld Fleet, shrank from it. In Colonial Oversight the stops had been far apart, the isolation profound; each tour of duty was like being Outside, or so he had always thought, and he had never been sure the Fleet would return. To avoid thinking of it he made his head be full of Gadrah: a simple puzzle, a place an Oversight veteran should know.

Suarez showed him pictures of two children of Gadrah and their mother. He said they were his children and their mother's name was Nekotym. She was a plump creature with bad teeth and extraordinary eyes of warm amber flecked with gold.

"I never heard of the place," Gaaf said. "Is it called something else?"

"Maybe."

"What's it called?"

Suarez grinned. Gaaf persisted. "Why's he so sure Fleet won't pick us up there?"

"You'll see when you get there," Suarez said, sounding like Castillo.

Gaaf spent a long time ciphering it out. At least he evolved a satisfactory explanation: that wherever Gadrah was, Castillo's cover there was impenetrable. It was the only possible explanation.

Still Gaaf ought to know about the place; ought to have heard of it, at least, by whatever name.

* * *

He tossed and turned in the dark nights, doping himself to sleep when he was desperate for rest. The rags of his life flapped around him in the dark. He had not meant to come to this. He had not meant to witness murder and break bread with murderers. Yet inexorably he had come here. He had never made one single right choice, had not even been a very good physician. There had been too many deaths in the backwaters of a star-spanning culture, and too many of the bereaved had shaken his hand and thanked him, like God, for his failures. His progress from a failing farm on Co-op to greater failures on lesser worlds had been—no progress at all. Increasingly furtive, increasingly alone, he had garnered no good memories to take along on the longest journey he had ever made. He had done one brave thing in his life, and only one: in a sudden access of good taste where a woman was concerned, he had tried to make dying easier for Hanna ril-Koroth. The pathetic inadequacy of it ground at him and gnawed his dreams. There had been a stunner in his hands. A brave man with a stunner could have saved her. But he was not used to saving people; he was only used to helping them die.

* * *

And yet she had survived. They heard it on the 'beams as they hurtled toward Omega. The news came out of D'neera somehow, on the heels of the news of the hunt for Michael Kristofik. No one was surprised, except Gaaf. He had to stay away from them, he could not let them see it. Someone else had saved her. The bruises and fever must be gone. She must look as she had when he saw her first, seated between two lumps of alien flesh, holding one by its thready hand. Steady sapphire eyes: *she* knew what she was doing. Gaaf did not even know where he was going, he did not even know what Gadrah was. But first he was going to the planet of the aliens. He did not know anything about aliens either, except that he did not like them. *She* knew about aliens. *She* was not afraid of the Outside. She was supposed to have gone there. He was going in her place, and someone else had saved her; a criminal, it seemed; a braver one than Gaaf.

They passed beyond Omega and heard nothing more.

It started to seem as if pieces of the *Avalon* were missing. In the dark; it was always dark. Sometimes what the other men said made no sense, as if they spoke an alien tongue. They gave Gaaf peculiar looks at times. He stayed in his cabin, but it was dark there, too. The nightmare went on without end. But when it ended, they would be where the aliens were. After that—Gaaf's mind skipped ahead, passing over the aliens. After that it would be Gadrah, where there were people.

Sometimes, when he had the energy, when the men of the *Avalon* looked like people, he tried to find out about Gadrah.

He was afraid to question Castillo, and Wales was as secretive as Suarez. So he approached Ta, but Ta had made only one trip to Gadrah in three years. He said Castillo and the men of the *Avalon* were important at Gadrah, that Castillo was a powerful man. Ta said there was a city of white stone that shone in daylight, but the sky always looked cloudy at night. The inhabitants of the city dressed in fine garments and jewels, the finest the Polity could provide. The girls were lubricious, the liquor strong.

It did not sound like any place Gaaf had seen or heard of in his years with Oversight. But after a while it was plain that Ta was nearly as ignorant as Gaaf; that at Gadrah he had been too preoccupied with spirits and girls to look around much, and the memories he had were unreliable.

Gaaf wanted to ask if Ta had ever heard the others talk about the way to get there, but he was afraid to. He was afraid Castillo would find out about his questions.

The other man on the *Avalon* was Bakti. In ten years he had been to Gadrah three times. He did not know much more about it than Ta. But one night, hunkered in the dim corridor near the black room where Hanna had been held (her blood still spotted the floor), he said to Gaaf, "I don't think we're going back."

"Back where?"

"Civilization," Bakti said. He talked as if he knew what it meant.

"What do you mean, civilization? Gadrah's civilized, isn't it?"

The other man's face was uneasy in the shadow. "It's a long way out."

"So?"

"A *long* way."

Bakti looked at Gaaf emphatically. Gaaf shook his head and Bakti hunched closer.

"Listen," he said, "I don't think anybody else knows where it is. It's out past Heartworld, I know that. And there's no charted settlements out there. I looked it up. I don't think anybody knows except *him*. And maybe Suarez. Juel knew. The other trips I made, they didn't let anybody else onto flight deck. You couldn't pick up a relay transmission. It was like it is out here. They said it was us that was shut down for security. I don't think so. I don't think there was anything to pick up. It was a lot like this. A long, long trip. And there wasn't anybody else out there."

Gaaf looked at Bakti blankly. Bakti was hinting the

impossible, a trap for the credulous. An Oversight veteran would know. The disbelief showed on his face.

Bakti said, "Listen. Most of the people there, they don't even speak Standard. Most of 'em don't read it. Most of 'em can't read at all."

Gaaf grunted. That was unusual even for an isolate like Revenge.

"And they keep slaves. Would the Polity put up with that if they knew?"

Gaaf refused to take the statement literally. "It's not much better on Nestor. They've never done anything about Nestor."

"Nestor's got a fleet of its own. This place doesn't. Even on Nestor there's Polity observers walking around. I never saw anybody from the Polity on Gadrah but us. They talk like nobody ever comes there but us."

"Oversight does," Gaaf said. What Bakti proposed was unbelievable, so Gaaf did not believe it.

He would see it for himself, and in the meantime he was going to see the aliens.

Hanna's face when the aliens died was painted on his dreams. She had tried to save them. She had suffered for them. Nobody had ever done any of that for Gaaf. Nobody had ever looked at him like that. He did not think anyone ever would.

The journey of the *Avalon* went on for four weeks, which was as long as any point-to-point journey inside human space ever had to last. Then it went on for another week, and another. After that it was impossible for Gaaf to disregard the truth that he was really Outside, and he stopped counting. The others had, perhaps, less imagination; they were not as disturbed as he. Or maybe they were reassured by Castillo's calmness. The red-haired man was as tranquil as if he were native to Outside, as if the dangers of the flight were insignificant. To be so he must be a masterful pilot. Whenever Gaaf saw him, the empty half-smile was in place on his lips, and his eyes were calm to the point of vacancy. Their light blue was transparent at times. But Gaaf, when he looked into that window (when he dared), looked through it, saw nothing: blank vacuum.

He seldom saw Castillo, or any of the others. They lived on packaged rations and did not come together to eat, only to drink or gamble or watch dramas of human lives from standard recreational programming play out in the walls of the common room for hours on end. Otherwise they moved in separate orbits, colliding accidentally and not often.

The *Avalon* seemed more dark each day. Gaaf secretly brought more lights to his room from other places, and tried to make the shadows flee. But they lurked at the corners of his eyes even when the room was bright as a star. So in the glare of light he closed his eyes and thought of Hanna to keep from thinking of other things. Old habits reasserted themselves and he stopped thinking of the reality of pain which he had witnessed, and remembered the beauty she had been at the very start, an untouchable ideal, like all beautiful women. But they were not untouchable in fantasy, and so she played a part in the limited reach of his sweaty imaginings. There was not much to do on the *Avalon*, and it was a long voyage.

One day when he had gone straight from fantasy into sleep, he woke with a sense of alarm. He knew immediately what had caused it: a change in the background noises of the *Avalon*. It took him a minute longer to realize that the ship had stopped. He went into the corridor with dread. Ta and Bakti huddled in a dark corner and talked in low voices. They fell silent when he came close.

"What happened?" he said.

It was Bakti who answered. "We're there."

"Where?"—for a minute he thought they meant Gadrah. That was how little he wanted to go to Uskos.

"Alien country," Ta said.

Gaaf went to the flight deck. He had been there frequently throughout the flight, and so had all the others; on this trip it did not appear to be, as Bakti had said of other journeys, forbidden. Castillo and Wales and Suarez were there. Castillo talked. His voice was strange and what he said was a rasping gabble. Then Gaaf saw the transparent shield of an automatic translator in front of his mouth, which damped the vibrations of his voice, twisted them around, and turned them into another language.

Almost as soon as Gaaf came in, Castillo switched off the translator and looked around. "We're landing," he said.

The *Avalon* was guided to a city of great stone buildings, all identical and so massive they seemed monolithic. Gaaf was on the flight deck for the landing. The *Avalon*, accompanied by (or strategically surrounded by) an escort, glided over the city for a long time. It went on and on, the truncated tops of stepped piles of masonry all alike ticking away beneath them. This was the City of the Center, by which was meant it was treaty ground, and here came the beings of Ell and Sa, of Ree and Naa and other lands, to settle their differences and have peace. Gaaf looked out on the City of the Center with blank eyes. Before the landing Castillo turned off the translator again. He said, "We'll be traveling a lot. I told them we want to. Look out for what we need."

Gaaf thought that meant there had been a promise, and whatever was asked for would be given. So maybe the crazy scheme would work and Castillo would get what he wanted from the ignorant aliens. He trembled with relief, hoping no one would notice. Quite apart from other dreadful suspicions, after what had happened to the aliens and Hanna, Gaaf had come to understand that Castillo dealt out death casually and apparently without fear. It meant nothing. It only meant something had gotten in his way. Gaaf did not want to see any more of it. He had never thought himself a violent man, and now he knew he could not strike or wound or risk his life even to save someone else's more valuable life. That was why, when they needed him to wake up Hanna, they had had to come and get him after his flight from what the others did, and why his hands had trembled when he lifted her bleeding head.

There was a great commotion at landing. There were

translators enough to go around, both ear- and mouth-
pieces and the processing modules for the hand or belt.
What was the *Avalon* doing with all these translator
units?—nobody used them in human space, they were
only used by people who had business in places where
Standard was unknown. No one on the *Avalon* asked
Castillo about that, but Ta said, "How'd we get the program?"

Castillo gave him an amused look, but he did not
answer. It was Suarez who said, "Got it soon as we
decided. Hook into any relay and tie in with D'neera.
Ask for D'vornan library. That's all."

"They just give it to you?"

"Anything you want."

They came off the ship all together. They were armed.
Just before they went out Castillo said, "Don't answer
any questions. Not now, not later. I answer the questions."

Outside the air was stunning in its brightness and
clarity. Gaaf was blinded; he put his hands to his eyes,
shielding them from the light of the star. Nothing
shielded him from the heat. Yet he was only in the sub-
tropics, and they were only a little more hot and more
brilliant than comparable latitudes of Earth. But the *Avalon* had been very dark, and Gaaf had sprung from a
cool climate.

Finally he took his hands from his face. Eyes blinking
and watering, he saw Castillo hand the golden cylinder
to the aliens. He called it a token of faith. He said Rubee and Awnlee of Ell would not return, but men who
would have been their friends, though too late to save
them from beings alien to humans as well as Uskosians,
had made this journey in their place and come to initiate
friendship. After that they climbed into wheeled vehicles and were taken through the towering city. But
Gaaf's eyes kept watering, so that he did not see anything.

It was not so bright in the chambers of Norsa. Norsa,
a personage of indeterminate position and age, appeared to be in charge. Gaaf knew that was his name

because he said "I am Norsa," but his description of his function was beyond the capability of the translator. He wore a garment that looked like a brilliant, lavishly embroidered blue barrel. Other Uskosians were there also. They talked with Castillo. At first Gaaf did not listen, but looked in horror at the aliens. They were unutterably ugly. Their skin was dank and leathery, in color a dirty brown. The depressions of their eyespots were filled with an unstable colloid that made him want to retch, and the agitated cilia round their mouths made his skin crawl. Their hands were variable and blunt; he looked for the long thin strings of fingers that had been wrapped around Hanna ril-Koroth's small human hands, but he did not see any. And they stank. The whole place stank. The walls of Norsa's chambers were golden, except where they were streaked with bands of other colors, some bright and some subtle. The bands were horizontal and strapped them into the room, which seemed to shrink.

Gaaf began to hear the conversation. Norsa said: "It is a strange tale you tell."

"Your emissaries indeed met with misfortune," Castillo answered.

"Is it possible to obtain their bodies?"

"We could not find them. They were put into the sea."

Gaaf's eyes wandered to a sweeping window on the city. It was as impressive from here as it had been from the air. The gleaming towers marched away into the sky, making him small.

He heard a name he recognized and his attention sharpened:

"—and this creature of another people, to whom this gift was made—this Hanna ril-Koroth—betrayed honored Rubee and his steadfast selfing?"

"That is what we learned."

"But why?" Norsa said, and even in the mechanical impersonality of the Standard words fed into Gaaf's ears, there was a tone of perplexity.

"Zeigans are not like humans," Castillo said. "They hate those of other species, even humans. Humans do not often go there. Humans went there this time only because there was word of your envoys landing there. But we were too late for anything except vengeance.''

When Castillo finished talking there was silence. But after a time Norsa said, ''Your people will have the gratitude of mine for the vengeance you took. Also we must have gratitude that it is you, the human beings, who have come to seek us; rather than those others who would wish us only to die. It was too much to think that we would find only peace in the stars. Yet that was our hope.''

They were given a spacious place to stay, which, however, was well guarded. Surrounding it was a garden. Many of the flowers were tall, coming higher than Gaaf's waist; they had great blossoms made of flat petals; they were in color bright yellow, deep gold, and vivid pink, and glowed so brightly, and were so perfect, that at first he thought they were artificial. Before the first evening was over there would be more meetings, but for a short while they were alone. They left the house and went to the garden, ''In case the walls have ears,'' Castillo said, and they walked among the flowers.

''All of you listen,'' Castillo said. He looked around, shepherding them with his eyes. Some of them were nervous. The reality of their presence on an alien world getting its first sight of humans was sinking in.

''Don't answer any questions unless you have to,'' Castillo said. ''If you have to, say as little as you can. Don't even talk about it among yourselves, in case they're listening. If you have to talk, keep the story straight. Their envoys first made contact with Zeig-Daru. They got killed there, Fleet heard about it, that's how we got the course and why we're here. They were killed by Zeigans. Remember that.''

''What about the D'neeran woman?'' Ta said.

''The name's right on the course module, says she was their friend. I had to bring it up. They think she was a Zeigan and we executed her for what they did.''

''They won't swallow it,'' Ta said, ''the Zeigans are

telepaths, they can't pretend to make friends first and kill you later, they just kill you right away.''

Castillo said, ''They don't know that here. So forget you ever knew it.''

Later there was a banquet at which the food looked terrible and tasted worse. Suarez and Wales went back to the *Avalon* and returned with real food, but Gaaf did not eat; the drinks had been all right, and he was asleep. Only in his dreams Hanna protested bitterly, as she had not protested, not once, aboard the *Avalon*.

They began traveling at once. Despite Castillo's strictures the men talked among themselves. ''He said we don't have much time before the Polity comes,'' Bakti told Gaaf.

''He told *them* that?''

''No, no, I don't know what he told *them*. That's what he told Suarez.''

''You heard Suarez say that?''

''No, that's what Ta said Suarez said.''

So it was impossible to know what could be believed. That did not stop the men from talking, and it did not keep Gaaf from listening.

They did their traveling in the *Avalon*, though transport was courteously offered. What explanation could Castillo have given the aliens for this? How did he explain their going armed—and why did he want them to be armed? How did he justify keeping their hosts off the *Avalon*? Why did he keep them off?—Gaaf did not hear all the lies and so he never knew if a lie were at issue, or an omission. It crossed his mind that the same thing was precisely true of what Castillo told/lied about/ did not tell the men of the *Avalon*. There was no use listening to words at all. The range of certainties shrank from hour to hour. To: food and drink to go into the mouth. A smelly cubicle on the *Avalon*. The physical existence of the other men of Castillo's crew. Gaaf's own body was less certain than it ought to be; it had tics, twitches, moments when it seemed to fade. As for the outside world, the alien world, it was all a single shining piece, like a peculiar dream to the meaning of which there was no point of entry.

Two beings were assigned to him, him personally, to assist him (or maybe to watch him or both). He was nearly afraid to speak to them at all. Their names were Biru and Brinee, and whenever the *Avalon* landed in its travels they were there, like personal demons. Gaaf dreaded stepping off the ship and seeing them, inescapable. The other members of the crew had their personal devils, too, and Castillo had several. But Castillo's face, unlike Gaaf's, never altered at the sight of them. In their presence he was impassive, and at other times he never spoke of them except to make coarse jokes about the presumed sexual practices of this species.

All time was a single piece to Gaaf, a seamless tissue. There were events, but it did not seem to him that they marked a progression. The events might as well have coexisted all together: until the very end.

There was:

A day of rain like the rain Gaaf remembered from the poor fields of Tarim on Co-op, the water coming down in a curtain like a solid substance. Without being able to see anything because of this cataract, he entered, with the others, a building that grew out of the rain. The water poured down with such power that inside it could be heard pounding the structure's roof, though the building was substantial. Gaaf was dizzy with the stench of the aliens. There were hundreds of them here, spots of gaudy color in their overdecorated garments, though they sat in shadow on long benches. Only the foremost portion of the great chamber was brightly lit, and there, set well to the back of a deep platform, were two black cubes. The human beings were taken to the front of the hall and given cushioned seats. A being dressed in scarlet came to the edge of the platform.

"I am Balee of Ell," he said, and began to speak or to declaim, and presently Gaaf realized that he was attending some kind of memorial service for Rubee and Awnlee of Ell. When Balee was done, music began: a kind of irregular drone punctuated by scrapes and squawks. More beings came onto the platform, until it was filled with them. They were masked, and they glittered and dripped with jewels.

Suarez sat at Gaaf's right, and Castillo beyond Suarez. Gaaf heard Suarez whisper, ''Those stones real?''

Castillo breathed, ''Find out.''

Balee of Ell said, ''And this is the story of the Fate of Relell.''

Gongs sounded, setting up vibrations in the walls, the furnishings, the bones. The beings on the platform moved in the stately ritual of the Fate of Relell.

''On a day,'' said Balee, ''Relell of the tribe of Relell in the land of Ell set forth with his selfings and all his kinsmen to settle on the far shore of the land of Naa. For in that time the coast of Ell was torn by great storms, and against those storms the Master of Chaos aided none, but watched.

''And Relell and his selfings and all the people went forth in fair ships well made, yet scarcely were they out of sight of land when the ship of Relell's selfing Uprell foundered, and all who traveled in it were lost. Yet when the people looked behind they saw that the storms were worse than before, and so they could not go back; yet when they looked before them they saw the Master of Chaos. Therefore they went on.''

There was a good deal of noise on the platform-stage. Balee's voice was amplified, the stiff robes of the players crackled and swished, they chanted and cried out, and the droning went on, too, interrupted by other raucous noises. Under cover of all this Castillo and Suarez talked softly together. Gaaf leaned toward them, trying to appear as if he did not.

''Where do they keep it?''

''We'll find out.''

''Find out where it is from the air.''

''It won't be enough.''

''Mark one, though.''

''And they came after great peril and loss to the shore of the land of Naa, and it was summer. Yet the Master of Chaos had caused the season to sicken, and though summer it was cold, and nothing grew in all that fair land. And so when the people sought to plant the seeds they had brought, the seeds died in the ground, and nothing lived and all the land was barren. And there was an end to the food that had come on the ships, and there was great suffering. And the Master of Chaos walked among the people of Relell and watched, yet he did not signify amusement, but was grim and did not answer those who cried to him.

"The winter came, and Relell, though starving, was gravid, and his time came upon him and he brought forth a selfing whom he named Senu; for he wished the Master to be unaware that the youngling was of the land of Ell or the tribe of Relell or that he was the selfing of Relell, and thus he hoped that Senu would be spared. But the Master came to him as he suckled the babe, and it died at Relell's teat, and the Master watched. And Relell cried out to him, but the Master did not answer, and disappeared.

"At length the winter passed and spring came, and of those who had set forth from the land of Ell, only the twentieth part remained, and they had scarcely strength to hunt or fish. Yet they did, for they said to one another, 'Now at last the winter is past, and surely now the Master will cease to discourage our endeavor.' And they grew stronger; but one day there came storms and wind. The wind blew down their huts and blew away their ships and weapons, and they ran from the waves that came onto the shore. And Relell with his last strength tied himself to a tree so that he might not be washed away.

"But then he looked out to sea, and on the sea he saw a wave as big as a mountain, and he knew that his end had come. And in the wave he saw the lineaments of the Master of Chaos, and he cried out to the Master of Chaos, 'Why? It was a brave undertaking done correctly. What is the reason for these things?'

"But the wave overcame him and he was swept away and drowned, along with all the people. And when all of them were gone the Master of Chaos looked down and said, 'There was no reason.' Yet he did not signify amusement.

"And so," said Balee abruptly, "it is until this moment," and everything stopped.

After that the players went one by one to the black cubes and took off their jewels and laid them on the cubes. They grew into blazing heaps which Castillo watched with concentration; Suarez's mouth was open. Then it was over.

There was:

One more standardized tour of a manufacturing facility. Gaaf was on the flight deck again when the *Avalon* landed near it. Castillo and Suarez talked. Gaaf listened, and as he listened there filtered into his comprehension, too slowly for alarm, the reasons Castillo used the *Avalon* for local transport rather than accept the transportation the aliens offered. One reason was that here they could talk among themselves. Another was that this way they could build up detailed maps of where they had been so that, if they wished, they could come back to a place quickly.

Gaaf was not sure what that meant.

They got off the ship and there were greetings. Here were Biru and Brinee, and here also were the other beings of the official party of escorts, the devils who shadowed Castillo and the others. Here were the beings who managed this particular facility, and at their heels something else: a small furred bright-eyed creature on all fours, with a kind of embroidered saddle on its back. It made ambiguous noises the translator could not render into Standard.

The factory was built in a brown countryside. There was warmth in the sunlight, and Gaaf did not know if this country was always brown, or if it was only not the season of growth. The factory made no pretense of fitting into its surroundings. It had cupolas, and its enameled facade was indigo and maroon. Gaaf's bitter youth on Co-op had convinced him that all factories ought to be underground. The Uskosians were proud of this one, though; it pleased them; they talked as if they were amused by its effrontery.

Castillo acted amused.

They went through the factory and the thing with the saddle got interested in Gaaf. It sidled up to him, pranced around his feet, tripped him up. He kept thinking it would bite him, he dodged it, he made tentative kicking movements, and finally he ducked into a dark passageway to escape it. It followed him. So did Brinee, who found him leaning against a wall, sweating, trembling, and cursing the beast in a whisper. His agitation was apparent even to nonhuman eyes, and Brinee shooed the thing away.

Brinee said, "I am sorry. It is only a pet."

Brinee stood between Gaaf and the end of the passage. Gaaf looked past him longingly. Where were the other human beings?—he had to catch up with them. But he could not bring himself to walk toward Brinee in the dark.

Brinee said after a while, "My far-kin Awnlee had such a one as a child. He loved it dearly."

Gaaf knew which of the dead aliens was Awnlee. Hanna's mental cry of anguish at his death had been perceptible to all of them.

The passageway was murky as the middle of a night. Something seemed to tug at the leg of Gaaf's trousers; he looked down in a frenzy, kicking. But there was nothing there.

"Are you well?" Brinee said.

Gaaf passed a shaking hand over his face and said, "This is hell."

The word came out of the translator in unadorned Standard. Neither Ell nor any other Uskosian land had an equivalent concept or a comparable word.

"Ell?" said Brinee. "No, today we are in the land of Ree. Let us join the others."

Throughout the rest of the tour, Gaaf felt animals snapping at his ankles. There were never any animals there, though.

The factory produced fine liqueurs the color of ripe grain. There were jars and jars of them stacked, shelved, crated, awaiting shipment.

Castillo tasted the liqueurs and nodded. He said to Suarez, with no attempt at concealment, "Mark two."

The aliens had no idea what he meant. Gaaf was beginning to guess.

* * *

They were given certain gifts, as Castillo had predicted. Half a dozen jars of the exotic liqueur; a pyramid of spun-crystal many-colored balls that made sweet sounds when the wind blew over them; stiff ceremonial gowns and masks in primary colors; a handful of other things; not much.

"They took a fortune in presents to Earth," Ta complained aboard the *Avalon*.

"They expect a return before they do that again," Castillo answered.

That was enough to satisfy Ta, but Gaaf, emboldened by this rare communicativeness in Castillo said, "Did they come out and say that?"

"Hinted."

"That's a hell of an attitude," Ta said, aggrieved.

Wales said, "The funny thing is we've got what the Polity was going to give them right down in the holds."

Some of them chuckled, but Gaaf did not see the humor in it.

"Don't say so when they're around," Castillo said. "Not a word."

They were traveling toward a city in the heart of Ell where they would be welcomed by an agrarian guild. Suarez said before they landed, "Won't be much here, I guess."

"You never know," Castillo said. "There's something they want us to see later, some kind of museum. Might round us out, if it's as good as I think it is. It's time we went. Long way to Gadrah. Back to Omega, a good six weeks; a week to Heartworld sector; then another five. Three months. We might pass the Polity on the way, I guess," he said and the smile came again.

They had now been on Uskos for two Standard weeks, and Gaaf had thought himself adjusting to it. By that he meant that he had learned to blank out the nonhuman landscapes, beings, language, and artifacts. He clung instead to the interludes on the *Avalon* as if they were life, and all the rest a dream to be endured. In this life a single image suddenly stood out, clear if not technically accurate. It was the course Castillo projected: a course through the waste of Outside, then into and out the other side of human space to another void. In the middle—to be crossed with casual haste, touching nothing—was all the space Gaaf had ever known before: Earth and Fleet's headquarters at Admin, the amusements of Valentine, the roiling network of Polity culture, even the outposts to which Oversight ministered, even (God help him) Co-op. And everything outside that was barren: a few alien civilization that were patches of terrifying light; and Gadrah, the unknown.

He put his head down on his knees because he felt faint. "You sick?" Bakti said.

He mumbled, " I don't feel so good."

"That's a joke," Suarez said. "The doctor gets sick."

He thought of saying: *Maybe we can catch what they have here.* But he did not, because he suddenly did not want them to have an overriding reason for wanting a physician aboard.

He still had his head down at the landing. He said, "I have to stay here. I can't sit through one of those God damn shows the way I feel."

"I don't know if I can get through another one either," Wales said, but they were indifferent.

Castillo said, "If somebody's here, at least we don't have to secure the ship. Just keep your eyes open."

"Yes," Gaaf said.

They were down and the others filed out to the farmers' guildhall and a dignified spectacle of sowing and reaping, to the some-kind-of-museum which might be—what? Mark five? Mark six? Mark the last, anyway.

Gaaf did not raise his head until they were gone. When he did he had real difficulty doing it, because of the fatigue that dragged at his bones all the time. From the flight deck he saw that the sky outside was gray. The town of Elenstap was spread out before him on a series of gracefully folded hills. Many of the structures in it were brightly colored, so that it presented a festive air. But the colors all ran together, and it was not a human spectacle, and Gaaf shrank away from it, back into the dimness of the *Avalon*.

The unknown. He chewed the palm of one hand. His head ached.

He thought: *I can't do it.*

He thought of what would happen if he begged Castillo to leave him somewhere, anywhere, in human space.

He would be killed. That's what would happen.

He looked toward the controls of the *Avalon*. He had been in Fleet too long not to know something about them. For centuries the human species' desire for many spacecraft had run head-on into the complexity of interstellar flight, and the result had been standardization. A brave man would hijack the *Avalon* and—

But Gaaf was not a brave man.

The Fleet would come eventually to this world of aliens. They would take him and probe him and punish him for his part in what had happened to the *Far-Flying Bird*.

Unless. There was his Fleet record: adequate if not outstanding. There was what he had done for Hanna.

And if the impossible was true? Then there might be more. If it was true.

Desperation gave him a small cunning. He crept toward the controls after all. Trembling, looking over his shoulder, he researched the course to Gadrah.

And there it was, as he had feared but not quite, not really, believed until now: a lonely track past the limits of known space, bumped off the inner edge of the spiral arm that had in it not only Earth and her offspring, but all the habitable worlds supposedly known to any human beings.

Aboard the *Avalon*, standardized, were data storage modules no longer than a finger and a centimeter thick. Gaaf knew where to find them. He put onto one what he wanted to take, and ordered the *Avalon* to forget his tampering.

Then he sat back, quaking and twitching, to wait.

The Treasure Store of Elenstap in the Land of Ell was a fair, proud structure three stories high, with two wings set at angles to the main bulk of the building, which was the older portion. Ell had been essentially at peace for a thousand years, and its people's lively interest in the arts for those thousand years and longer was reflected in the land's Treasure Stores, by which name was meant public treasures that belonged to all the people who came to admire them. The newer wings of the Store of Elenstap had been constructed to complement the Old Store. They were made of white marble streaked with russet, the marble having come from the same quarry that had supplied the stone for the Old Store. Set into the exterior walls at intervals were palimpsests representing the most important works within, and the representations, though stylized, were masterpieces in their own right. Also the cartouches had been treated with a substance, invisible by day, that absorbed the daylight and shone at night. The Store stood by itself in a grove outside the city, and visitors to Elenstap came there at night to regard a sight no visitor should miss: the radiant images floating in the dark, seemingly unsupported, a catalog in light of the chief treasures of that place.

The *Avalon* remained at Elenstap that night. The crew rejected the hospitality of Elenstap and stayed on board. If the townsfolk or the official party from the City of the Center were offended, they did not say so, and the humans could not read the nonhuman faces or tell what the movements of the heavy bodies said.

At twilight it began to rain. There was a sharp burst of wind and water which declined to a settled drizzle. No one would come to stand outside the Treasure Store that night, though it glowed brightly as ever in the rain.

Before dusk changed fully to night, Castillo began to detail certain plans he had been formulating since the *Avalon's* arrival. Not even Gaaf was surprised by them. But his lack of surprise was of a different order from that of the others. He had made a vague guess at what would be done, deducing it from what Castillo said. The others had not had to guess. There was something that they needed on this world, and it had not been given to them. Therefore they would take it.

Gaaf listened to them talk and they turned into aliens—strange smooth-skinned beings with flexible mouths. This terrified him, and the *Avalon* was very dark. His simple plan for escaping them seemed a hopeless thread. He was afraid they could read his mind, that someone had read it all along, like the woman who ought to have died on the *Avalon*. He even thought he saw her at a corner of the dark room.

Don't give me away! he begged, but she did not hear him; she disappeared. He knew she had not really been there, he was not crazy. All the same his body twitched. The Uskosians were no good either, anatomical freaks with muscle in the wrong places. They were the only link he had left to the Polity, though; to real human beings.

The briefing was over and he had not heard a word of it.

In the middle of the night the *Avalon* lifted into the air. It flew straight over Elenstap and came to the Treasure Store, and it pushed fire before it. The end of the new west wing blew away. The *Avalon* hovered at the broken end and the men threw down a ramp to bridge the gap between the ship and the smoky second floor of the Store. Gaaf shoved through the men at the end of the ramp. He did not remember going there. Wales yelled, "You're supposed to be up with Suarez!" but they were in a hurry, they did not have a second to spare, and no one else questioned Gaaf. Castillo looked at him and the pale blue gaze looked through him; then Castillo turned away.

Gaaf prayed to something and ran after the others, across the ramp, fleeing from darkness into the dark.

The others had lights and wore masks to protect them from the dust and smoke. Gaaf had no equipment. He ran in the dark, tripping over broken stones, falling. His clothes ripped, his hands bled; he got up again and ran into a wall. But he fell on it weeping with relief. He fumbled through the dark with his hands on the wall, bumping into things and knocking them over, or bruising himself against heavier objects that would not move. A door opened under his hands and he fell inward into a blacker darkness and the door snapped shut behind him; the air was cleaner here, but he could see nothing and crawled in the blackness, clawing for the door. He found it and crawled out into the smoke again—and saw a light bob as a man ran back toward the ship with something in his hands.

He kept dragging himself along the wall, stumbling and choking. He was dazed, he had forgotten why he was doing this (but he knew he could not go back); it was blind flight propelled by blind hope, but the hope was light years distant where there were human beings. Another door opened, on light this time, and fresher air; Gaaf saw a staircase, and he half-fell down it. The stairs were painted like the rainbow and gracefully railed, lit by lamps shaped like miniature starbursts, though this way was for emergencies and seldom used. It was pretty, for a nightmare.

He could not read the strange alien signs. But the aliens left nothing to chance, not on a route designed for frightened beings trying to get out. The door that led outside was transparent, the blessed wet night showed through it, and it opened outward as soon as Gaaf fell on it. He stumbled out into the rain. There was a terrible howling somewhere, horrible screams far away but surely louder than any normal throat could make—he did not recognize it as machine noise, fire or disaster control devices racing to the Store of Elenstap and making their ordinary sounds. It seemed that something living and huge and ravening was coming for *him*—

A dark shape passed overhead, accelerating to another target. If Gaaf had been missed from the *Avalon*, no one had bothered looking for him.

He stumbled through the grove of trees with wet branches lashing at his head, and out into the soggy fields.

In the night Gaaf began to understand about the Master of Chaos. Rain pattered on trees he could not see in the dark, and the wind moaned through them. He walked zigzag and blind, falling when stones and other objects turned under his feet, capricious and malevolent. The ground kept falling away or rising up in front of him, so that he moved in a drunken lurch. He could not see anything. He could not even see the lights of Elenstap reflected from the clouds. He did not know if

he were walking away from the town or toward it, he
went in no direction but randomness.

He kept his right hand in his pocket much of the time,
clutching the precious wafer that might buy his life from
the Polity. The gold chain was there, too. And maybe
she would plead for his freedom as she had pleaded for
the aliens' lives. And when she learned of his flight
from Castillo and learned of this journey in the dark she
would say, *How brave you are, Henrik Gaaf.* The blue
eyes would rest on him gently and—

He talked to her in the dark. He talked to his sisters
on Co-op also. But they said, *Quite whining, Henrik,
shut up and work.*

The rain slackened and stopped. After that there were
new noises in the dark as nightbeasts crept from hiding
and set about the hunt. There were not so many trees,
and then none. The ground was more even and things
grew in it in rows which Gaaf followed because it was
easier walking that way. Sometimes there were no rows,
but solid masses of vegetation that caught at his legs
and feet like snapping animals. He stumbled on, wet to
the skin, cold and hungry and very tired.

When he could go no farther, he sat down on the
ground. He tried to imagine Hanna beside him, the
warmth, but he could not. He was too cold.

He fell asleep without knowing it, and when he woke
up it was light and an alien bent over him. He yelled
and squirmed away from the touch and then he saw that
he was surrounded by a ring of them. He began to weep.
He wept all the rest of the day; they looked at him without comprehension. There were no translators and they
could not talk to him, though they tried; they tried very
hard. And they took him back to the City of the Center
and put him in a bare locked place, he had not expected
anything else, he had not expected anything, and he was
passive and only wept; but when they took the wafer of
data away from him, he howled so desperately that they
gave it back to him again.

V.

A long space voyage is the ultimate reach of boredom; any Fleet cadet will attest to that. The leaps of starflight pall after a time, the dark outside has no end, and all parts of the universe look the same. Library terminals and holoshows are finite resources; one's companions rub on one's nerves. The journey is not an end, but only a means toward one. Getting there is a state of stasis to be endured, and it seems as if the end will never come.

But there are also people who seek space with passion. With freedom from planets and solid ground comes a freedom like that of the sea. For these persons, where there are no other beings, there can be no obligations. Time is measured not by the tyranny of regulated clocks, but by Jumps; a very different matter, since no two are of the same length, and the exact point of terminus is increasingly hard to predict as routine paths are left behind. For those who absent themselves further from the human race, avoiding use of the relay system, a season in space can be as close to perfect freedom as any human being will get.

In order to take up the course to Uskos, the *Golden Girl* first had to go to Omega.

That was the hard part. Humankind was universally unfriendly, and the sense that it was so grated on everyone but Michael, and the others grated on him.

Theo spent too much time with the newsbeams, helping no one's mood. There was nothing to be heard about Mencken, but there was news from D'neera, since

245

D'neerans talk profusely about everything they know or think they know. The magistrates of D'neera clearly had been lied to. Hanna's message had not been delivered to Lady Koroth, and the magistrates, in ignorance of the facts, clamored for Hanna. A flower of their civilization, beloved, needed and missed, Lady-Koroth-to-be, dutiful daughter of her House, she could not be spared: the magistrates appealed at large to the Polity and the man it sought. They said Polity clumsiness in trying to trap Michael had caused him to abort, what other reason could there be?—they wanted Hanna too badly to engage in games or duels, there would be no more traps, if only Michael would bring her home where she belonged.

Theo told Michael about this, and told Hanna, too; she got a pinched look around the mouth and disappeared into the room of mirrors. She would not come to Michael's bed and she would not talk about it. He did not know what to do for her and she would not tell him.

One living D'neeran who can keep her mouth shut, and that's the one I get—

Lise was pale and quiet. She had not understood the events at D'neera when they happened, but Theo of the flapping tongue explained. She was outraged. Michael tried for hours to tease the reproach from her eyes. She forgave him finally for trying to abandon her, but in a flood of tears. "Don't do it again!" she cried, and charged into a full-blown tantrum in which he saw, to his horror, imitated elements of the display he had put on three days before. At the height of it Hanna flew out of hiding, cheeks burning, her sensitivity to emotion exacerbated past bearing. She pounced on Lise and shook her; Lise retaliated with fingernails; Michael at the risk of life and limb was about to dive into the melee when Shen, watching with calm interest, caught his arm.

"No harm done," Shen said.

"What the hell are you saying!"—they rolled on the floor now, spitting.

"See what she's doing. Look."

And when he made himself be still and look, he saw

that Hanna, though her hair nearly stood on end, did
nothing more than passively defend herself, blocking
blows and guarding the hair Lise pulled.

It did not last long. Lise went limp and cried again
and Hanna held her. Michael came up to them cautiously; they paid no attention to him. "I know," Hanna
was saying, "I know, I know, it hurts so much . . ."
She laid her cheek against Lise's and they cried together. Michael did not know which of too many kinds
of abandonment Hanna grieved for—what she had just
done to D'neera? What had been done to her in the
past?—or Lise either, for that matter. The range of possibilities was chilling. He thought of Claire, Emma, Kareem, the dogs, the cats, the tourmaline faded and dead
by now; he was sick. Hanna lifted her tear-stained face.
"Come here," she said, and held out her hand. He sank
to the floor with them and they drew him in, and he
bowed his head and wept, too, for a good life made at
great cost and senselessly destroyed. Whatever happened now, he would not have it again.

In the hours before they came to Omega, Hanna,
sleeping in the arbitrary predawn, slipped in and out of
slumber. She had discovered that some of the mirrors
could be made transparent, and she could look out from
this room as she could from Michael's next door. In the
absence of artificial light, stars reflected jaggedly everywhere. Each time she opened her eyes that night, she
floated in a bath of diamond-dust. It was beautiful, but
not restful. It seemed that somewhere another Hanna
moved parallel to this same track, approaching Omega
with Rubee and Awnlee once more. The voices channeled through Omega bounced off the cradling stars.
Nearby was a ship of the Polity; on cue it would come
sailing to the ravaged *Bird*.

The sense of time slightly askew was very strong.
Hours later at Omega it still wrapped her in dream—the
kind of dream which makes waking welcome. But this
time there was no wait at Omega, no systems checks
with Fleet cooperation. "Ready as she'll ever be," Shen

said briefly, when *GeeGee* was on the edge of the long
Jump that had marked the Bird's end.

"Let's go," Michael said, and they went, *GeeGee*
making the Jump without the histrionics in which Uskosian spacecraft indulged. There was a certain tension
in Michael and Shen. It was possible that the *Bird* was
still out here somewhere, with official company. She
was not, she must have been taken away. There was
nothing out here: no people, no relays, no voices, no
habitats. Nothing.

GeeGee clucked away at the calculations preceding
the next Jump. Lise, curled against the wall, returned
to her absorption in a doll. She ought to be outgrowing
dolls, but this was one of the sort whose appearance
could be manipulated in detail. Not long ago it had
looked like the pseudo-Zeigans of Hanna's hallucinations, and had suffered a good deal as Lise avenged the
fright she had gotten. Now it had human features, light
brown skin, and long black hair. Lise worked on making it beautiful, and on making its blue eyes exactly the
shade of Hanna's. Shen put her feet up on a control
panel and almost smiled. Michael and Theo talked seriously together. Hanna thought that was a good thing;
someone had better be serious about this great step into
silence. She went closer; they were discussing what to
have for dinner.

The dream-cloud of threat vanished from her mind
quite suddenly. She went to Michael and waited until
Theo went away. Then she said, "I suppose I ought to
move in with you."

"Of course you should," he said, and that was that.

The beings on the *Far-Flying Bird* had expected to
reach Uskos from Omega in approximately five Standard weeks. The *Golden Girl's* capacity for data manipulation was not as great, and for *GeeGee* the trip would
take seven weeks. It was a long time to live between
the dubious past and the uncertain future.

Michael did not think much about what he had lost.
There was nothing he could do about it.

The future was a different matter, but he could do

nothing about that either, yet. It would come as it would come. You took the opportunities you had and made more when you could. That was the deal the universe handed you. It was the only one you got.

He liked hearing Hanna talk about futures. They were not futures you would expect from a woman who had tried to kill you with a colloidal disruptor at first sight.

"Before the Polity comes," she said, "we can move on. There are places out there like D'neera before the Founders came. We could find one and start all over."

"Inventing fire," he said wryly, "unless you can re-create technology."

"I'm a technological idiot. I only know how to make things work if other beings put them together right. I'm a specialist, you know."

"How do we start over, then?"

"With babies, of course. What else do you need to start over? Yours and mine. Theo's and Lise's. And Shen—Shen—"

"Shen as a mother doesn't quite—"

"No. No, it doesn't compute. Are you sterile?"

"Not for much longer."

"Me either. That's all right, then."

* * *

Lise wanted to pilot the *Golden Girl*.

"You said even I could fly her alone. You said that."

"It was true."

"Teach me, then. You're teaching Hanna."

"You can't read well enough."

"But all you do is talk to *Gee*!"

"Not quite. That's not quite enough."

She said that she would learn to read better if he would teach her about *GeeGee*. At that time she had become interested in remarks Hanna had dropped about the place where they were going. Hanna, to encourage Lise, wrote a lively synopsis of what she had learned about Uskos from Rubee and Awnlee. It began as a primer, but because part of Hanna was a scholar, it was comprehensive. The others read it, too, and talked about it a good deal.

Hanna instructed them: "The first thing to remember is that Uskosians are friendly."

But Shen said, "Never seen human beings. No reports. First thing we tell 'em is the envoys got murdered. Second thing, we're in a stolen ship, hope Contact never shows up. Stay friendly? Huh."

"Well. When you put it like that—"

There was a past, too. It could not be excised from the future.

Hanna whispered endearments in four languages, panting. The small fists dug into his back, the little claws of her fingernails nearly pierced his skin. She treated his mouth as her personal property. These moods were like an exorcism, as if past and future could be made to disappear if only the present was narrowed to sensation. "Darling Michael, sweet Mike—" He kissed her throat and she trembled; he licked droplets of moisture from her breasts and she shivered and sighed, an animal with swollen blank eyes. "Mikhail," she cried, "Mikhail—!"

He froze so sharply she must feel it, then thought she had not noticed; she closed around him like a vise, strong arms wrapped around his neck, strong legs pinning his hips. The name echoed in his head.

"Never mind," she said clearly. "Let it go."

"But—"

The shock got worse as it sank in. She felt him soften, and remarked on his failure coarsely.

"I'm not made of stone," he said, distracted.

One hand tangled in his hair; the other slipped between them and took up a purposeful caress.

"Where did it come from?" he said.

"I don't know. Not now, darling."

His cultivated detachment slipped under her slippery hand. "That's right," she said. "Oh, yes."

"Right," he said, it was the last articulate sound he made for some time; he could worry later about the pitfalls of loving a telepath.

* * *

Theo studied medical texts. Sometimes he had questions, and each time he started for Control. The first time he went all the way there before he remembered there was nobody to call, and the only library to which he had access was the *Golden Girl's* own. After that he never got out of his seat; but he half-rose, a reader clutched in his hand, more than once.

He also haunted the medlab, which since Michael's purchase of the *Golden Girl* had been used only for analyzing Hanna's blood. He spent hours becoming familiar with the equipment, going back and forth between the electronic instruction manuals and the mechanical and computer controls. After a while, at times, he thought he could use some of it; at other times the equipment laughed at him, if crystal and metal could be said to laugh.

His chief comfort was that all *GeeGee's* passengers were healthy. He had even reimmunized Hanna against Dawkin's fever—though that might have been the worst thing he could do. Who knew what was waiting on Uskos?

"Nothing," Hanna said with finality, finding him one day in the medlab; she wandered about, touching polished chrome.

"Why'd the Polity go to so much trouble with you, then?"

"They always overdo the wrong things. Can you deliver babies, Theo?"

He stared at her in disgust. They were at this time approximately halfway through the time to Uskos (rather more than half the distance), and there were long intervals when Hanna and Michael disappeared from the life of the *Golden Girl*, to reappear softened, blurred, and shamelessly devoted. In six years Theo had seen Michael through half a dozen affairs, but nothing like this. There had always been a trace of unwillingness in his surrender before, something withheld; but this woman was affecting his brain, there was more than gonads involved.

She looked at him and he thought she had felt his disgust, but she only smiled in an absentminded way.

"It was because of something that happened with Zeig-Daru," she said. "There was a cut on my arm. Here." She showed him the inside of her right forearm. It was smooth and glossy; her skin glowed, these days.

She said, "They finally found out what the infection was, but they never could cure it. They ended up cutting out the whole chunk and regenerating down to the bone. So they decided, when the Uskosians made contact, to be extra careful. But they admitted we're not likely to trade diseases."

He was relieved to hear her talking in practical terms. "How'd you get the cut?" he said.

"It was a knife wound," she said. "But I won. Killed 'em all."

She smiled at him again and walked out, leaving him gaping.

He pulled himself together and got back to work. If anybody got hurt or sick, he was all they had. That went for all of them, even a bubblebrain who talked in one breath of babies and killing.

They kept a sort of erratic Standard time, and erratic half-regular watches in Control. Michael, as the paid companion of some traveler in the past, had picked up enough knowledge of spaceflight to obtain pilot's certification for most ships of *GeeGee's* class. Shen had a sound background in military training, and had refreshed her skills with *GeeGee*; she and Michael between them had browbeaten Theo into learning enough to follow *GeeGee's* own precise instructions. That was good enough for the common routes of human space. What *GeeGee* did now was not so easy. There were questions to be answered and decisions to be made. There was also, fortunately, Hanna. She had begun intensive spaceflight training in her teens, she had been a pilot before she was anything else, and she could fly (she said once, casually) anything. The result was that in practice her watch was flexible; it began whenever there was a question and ended when the hard parts were over. She was the acknowledged authority on the journey, and on call all the time.

Her "watch" ended one night near the middle of the night. Theo had taken over in Control, and Shen and Lise were asleep. Hanna rested with Michael in the smaller lounge, which was quite dark. Even the ports were dimmed, so little light entered from the field of stars. Hanna sat at one end of the small room, Michael at the other but not far away. Each was visible to the other only as a shadow. Michael had said something about Uskos, and then they had been silent for a time. As if a couple of meters between them made a difference, Hanna began to think of Michael as she had never thought of him: objectively. He had essentially relinquished command of the *Golden Girl* to her. In the timeless round of their days and nights he was almost a passive presence, anticipating her wishes and meeting all her desires. He was sunlight uncomplicated by shadows; a pattern of simplicity, all surface. It would be easy to think of him as weak.

And yet. Her very first perception of him had been as a presence of shadow crouched beside the *Avalon*. He had been in grave danger; but there had been no anxiety or fear in his thought. Afterward there had been that night of intense emotional union. Most true-humans could not have done what Michael had done. Most true-humans, fearing dissolution in her madness, would have knocked her out with drugs or otherwise, and almost certainly killed her. And then there was the rendezvous with the Polity and what he had done to meet it, and the decision to flee Outside to nothing less than death.

She thought of water, sunlit, dappled with the shapes of leaves. If you slammed into it, it slammed back and broke bones and broke skulls. If you came to it gently it shifted, accommodating. It crept into corners, changed shape silently; it sank through sand and found crevices invisible to eyes. In heat it evaporated into gas and dissipated; in cold it froze to crystalline solids of great beauty. It adapted infallibly to circumstance; but it was very strong.

But the metaphor did not hold up indefinitely, because in Michael there was also a black place where Hanna could not go. Michael could not either, not at will. He only endured it, when he had to. It had nothing to do with sunlit water. "I guess," he said into the dark, very quietly, "we ought to learn how to be polite to the Uskosians."

"Polite?"

"To say 'please' and 'thank you' and so on. In Uskosian."

"Ellsian . . . That's not a bad idea."

"It's a little late to start learning the whole language. Is it hard?"

"Not very. Not like F'thalian. These beings think in the same patterns we do, at least, and the linguistic structure—of Ellsian, anyway—is comprehensible." She thought unwillingly that she was going to have to start working again. "We could have tapped into D'vornan and picked up the language programs."

"Could we? But we don't have any translators to use when we get there."

"It would have helped, though. My accent's not perfect; human throats and tongues aren't made like theirs. The Polity translators were programmed with Awnlee's help, and I can't duplicate what he did. I can make a basic phrasebook for the rest of you, though."

"Have to do."

"Yes. I guess it will."

Once or twice she used the name again: "Mikhail." She did not mean to do it, and knew what she had done only after she had said it. The first time she paused, surprised at herself; she looked quickly at Michael for his reaction. There was also a certain invitation in her eyes. If he wanted to say more, she was ready to hear it. But he smiled and shook his head, and she picked up a cushion and threw it at him. "All right," she said. "Who needs to know anyway?"

The second time she did not even hear herself say it. He did not know where it came from, how she had dredged it from his memory, why it slipped from the

end of her tongue. She said it half in her sleep as she
drifted away. Michael could not follow her; he was immediately awake. He lay with his head on her breast,
so restful, such a restful place. What was he going to
tell her, how much, when, and what did it matter now,
the little he knew? B was gone, must be gone forever.
The hopeless quest into dust was postponed, at the very
least; he would not pursue that path if Hanna could
produce, magically, another life for him. He was entirely in her hands, hers and the hands of chance. The
hands of the Master of Chaos.

He sighed and turned his mouth to her skin. She woke
a little; her fingers ruffled his hair.

"But if you'd told the Polity," she said, "they would
have searched."

He stopped breathing. She was more than half asleep;
not even half awake. The compulsion to speak to her
dream was strong.

Why not? She would find out anyway—

And so he answered, and relief, like the release of a
long tension, made him weak, and his speech was
slurred.

"They wouldn't have believed it. Not without a probe.
With one they'd have had me."

"Then you didn't know yourself . . . until after the
Queen."

She was a sleepwalker, an oracle, and he was not sure
he heard her words with his ears.

"It was hard," he said. "Nobody knows how hard.
A kid in the dark . . . Didn't know there was anyplace
else. Thought Alta was part of the same world. Later I
knew there were more, but then I thought it was someplace like Revenge. Didn't dare ask questions. Afraid
they'd send me back. Thinking they could. Didn't guess
the truth till long after the Queen. Too late."

"Yes," she said. She was awake now. Her arms tightened around him, or around the lost child he had been.
She did not ask any more questions. But he thought that
for the first time in his life there was a certainty in it:
Hanna's flesh and blood, the beating of her heart.

Hanna lay still. The words bubbling up to conscious-

ness stung her, connecting. With the speculations of an
aged monk; with a vision of flame in a silver-shot sky.
The questions she did not ask trembled in her mouth.
Who should know more about Lost Worlds than she? It
was Hanna who had brought back the news of one Lost
World in the first terrible weeks of contact with Zeig-
Daru: a message of destruction, a tale of a colony long
dead. Almost, in this moment, she believed the old abbot had been right.

Then sense asserted itself. *"If he got to Alta from a
Lost World, it couldn't be considered lost . . ."* The
voice of ultimate common sense; Jameson's voice. The
fire had to have been on Nestor where such things could
happen at the hands of the so-called law; or maybe,
even, on Co-op, in the great riots a few years before
Hanna was born. It was easier to believe that this
strange, exquisite man lived with one great delusion than
to believe in Lost Worlds.

Finally she said softly, "Mike? Where could it have
been really?"

But now he was asleep, at peace, and she would not
rouse him to talk about yesterday.

* * *

Then they were there, a new world broad before them:
Like a feast, Michael thought, watching Hanna's intent
face. And he stood by her place in Control and felt
regret for what would be finished today, the honey-
moon. Past now.

Hanna had no time for regret. She was worried.

GeeGee had moved in slowly, broadcasting a simple
speech Hanna had recorded in Ellsian. It said: "I am
the friend of Rubee and Awnlee of Ell, she who traveled
with them: an alien, a visitor, a guest. As gifting I bear
the story of the Journey of Rubee. I will have great
honor if you will speak with me."

Hanna liked this speech. It was dramatic, it was designed to provoke curiosity (a fact the Uskosians would
recognize and approve), and it was courteous. Hanna

had spent some time concocting it. Uskos should fall
at once into a frenzy of welcoming.

Instead there were flat acknowledgments in harsh-
sounding voices that had the half-familiarity of a dream,
followed by a command for the travelers to do exactly
as they were instructed. There was no threat, but also
there was no welcome, not even the most formal of
courtesies. When *GeeGee* landed at last—it took a long
time to get permission to land—they were directed to a
desert, a place of dried watercourses in a red-brown
land. And an escort of Uskosian vessels landed with
them, gently as a fleet of butterflies, surrounding the
Golden Girl.

They went through *GeeGee* to the starboard lock, and
Hanna went out with the others behind her. The sky
was vast and opalescent and a cold wind came from it.
There were sharp stones on the rusty soil, splintered by
heat and cold, and scrubby plants that bent in the wind.
Five streamlined vessels flaunted gaudy insignia in an
arc in front of Hanna; the others had landed behind her,
to *GeeGee's* port side, completing a precise circle with
GeeGee small and impotent at the center. Between
GeeGee and the ring of aircraft a single Uskosian
waited, a spot of vivid color in the gray wind. Hanna
led her little party toward him. He stood without moving; even the stiff fabric of his bright blue uniform did
not sway in the wind.

The humans came up to him and stopped. When they
did, other Uskosians came out of the other vessels, so
colorfully garbed they might have been sifted through a
prism. Hanna looked around and saw that her party was
surrounded.

She said to the blue-clad being in Ellsian, with all the
courtesy Uskos had taught her: "I am she who was the
companion of Rubee and Awnlee of Ell, and was present at the end of their journey. I have news of them,
though grievous news."

The being did not answer at once. There were
pouches and a slackness in his face that showed he was
about Rubee's age, and there was something of Rubee's
stateliness in him. The advancing Uskosians in their

bright uniforms stopped. It was wrong, all wrong, a
Polity mission must have gotten here first, and at any
moment humans must show themselves and seize Michael and Hanna, too. Yet she sensed no human presences except those she knew, and though she did not
probe the thought of the being before her, there was no
hint that he acted on behalf of humans.

At last he said, "I am Norsa of Ell, a maker of agree-
ments."

Hanna answered politely, "I am 'Anarilporot. My
companions are named—"

She stopped. At the sound of her name—which she
had rendered as an Uskosian would say it—Norsa had
lifted his hand. The aliens converged, each holding at
ready a glossy shaft of metal. The weapons were not
stunners. They could release a force that punched holes
in flesh.

She had not meant to shock Uskos with telepathy at
once. But she used it to say unhappily to Norsa, because
it carried conviction more powerfully than speech: *I did
not expect this greeting for the friend of Rubee and Awnlee, Rubee's selfing in the second degree of adoption,
Awnlee's near-kin!*

Norsa was sufficiently shocked, the tendrils round his
mouth squirmed with it, but he took Hanna away anyway. The other humans also were removed, separately,
except that Lise and Michael were permitted to remain
together; that was because the child shrieked and clung
to Michael, and Hanna, seeing weapons leveled, said to
Norsa, "But they are sire and selfing!"

Shen who had made a sharp movement toward Michael also was in danger. "No!" he said, and Shen
stopped in mid-stride. "Hanna will fix it," he said, but
his voice was strange.

Hanna was led away. She got a last glimpse of Michael standing in the waste, looking at her over Lise's
curls. Shen and Theo also watched her go, and they
looked after her mistrustfully. But Michael's eyes were
as strange as his voice: without hope. She could not do
anything about it then, she could not even stop to comfort him, and had to walk away.

* * *

On a day (said Hanna), *Rubee of Ell set forth with his selfing Awnlee to seek the persons of other stars; and the vessel which bore Rubee and his selfing outward was the* Far-Flying Bird, *which was the pride and flower of the land of Ell and of all Uskos. And Rubee and Awnlee sailed on and on, and the years went by; for space was dark and empty, and it seemed there were no other persons among the stars. Yet they did not fear, but felt themselves better acquainted with the Master of Chaos than they had been before.*

They came at last to a place among the stars where other persons were, and these persons called themselves Humans, which Rubee and Awnlee rendered '' 'Unans,'' and this meant in the tongue of the 'Unans, ''persons.'' And the 'Unans sent to Rubee and Awnlee one 'Anarilporot to be their friend and guide, and they were feasted and made welcome, and they made gifts to the 'Unans and were given fine presents in return, and they traveled widely among 'Unans, and always they were welcome.

Yet one day Rubee said to 'Anarilporot, ''The hour approaches when we must leave, for we wish to come to our home on the fourteenth day of Strrrl.'' But certain wise 'Unans sought to discourage the departure, for they had heard the whisper of the Master of Chaos. But Rubee was firm, and set forth as he had decided, and he was accompanied not only by his selfing Awnlee but by 'Anarilporot, even as in past times Erell and Awtell were accompanied by Porsa of Sa. And there was great friendship among these three, and especially between 'Anarilporot and Awnlee, so that Rubee claimed 'Anarilporot as his selfing in the second degree of adoption. And Rubee made the beginning of the story of the Friendship of Awnlee, which now is lost; yet in truth it is the same as the story of the Journey of Rubee.

And when the Far-Flying Bird *had been on its journey only shortly, certain 'Unans came and took away the gifts made to Rubee and Awnlee, and they killed Rubee and Awnlee in the sight of 'Anarilporot, who grieved for them and grieves for them and will always grieve for them. And 'Anarilporot also would have died, except that the Master of Chaos was present, and because of certain things 'Anarilporot said to the 'Unans with the Master's encouragement, they did not kill her, but took her away from the* Far-Flying Bird. *And nonetheless she would have died, but she was saved by certain other 'Unans who were enemies of those who had killed Rubee and Awnlee.*

In time 'Anarilporot came to Uskos without Rubee and Awnlee, but with the 'Unans who had saved her, and also with gifts which the Master had placed ready to her hand. Yet when she came to the land of Ell, 'Anarilporot was received without courtesy, and concluded therefore that the Master of Chaos had come before her; yet where is the Master not present? And so the story of the Journey of Rubee, which is also the story of the Friendship of Awnlee, and yet also the story of the Fate of 'Anarilporot, is not ended; for its ending lies in the hand of the Master of Chaos, which even now moves to write it.

* * *

Past Norsa and the other beings who examined Hanna, there was a window. While daylight remained she could see the towers of the City of the Center through it. Later, when it became dark, the tops of the towers were still visible; they were illuminated at night, and hung in the black sky like a fleet holding steadfast over the city.

She answered every question that was put to her without hesitation or evasion. She was not allowed to ask any in return. "Later, perhaps," Norsa said, "if we are satisfied." He asked most of the questions, but the others also participated; they were, Hanna recognized, a committee.

Night deepened, came to its turning, and began the slow progress toward morning. The persons of the committee melted away one by one. Hanna was given food and drink, but they did not interest her. She began to

feel the weight of exhaustion in every muscle; she kept
her head upright with conscious effort. There was weariness in Norsa's face as well. At last there were pauses
between questions, and the pauses grew longer—and in
them Hanna saw that the tension attending her presence
had eased. Therefore during one halt she said, "I wish
to offer only cooperation; yet I do not understand the
reason for this sparse welcome. Since first we met in
the wildlands I have known there is in you hostility and
mistrust. This was not what Rubee gave me to expect,
and therefore I knew that the Master had come here
before me; but the shape of this occurrence is not
clear."

Norsa regarded her with caution. He answered, however, "Other 'Unans came here before you."

She let out breath in a little puff. Now that her fear
was confirmed she was nearly too tired to react. Yet she
must start now, with Norsa and the Polity's representatives, to insist on her rights of kinship—though in the
face of this reception, they seemed dubious.

"Where are the other 'Unans?" she said. "It is necessary that I speak with them." Absurd that they had
not come seeking her!

"They are gone," Norsa said. "I do not know where
they have gone."

"Gone?" She did not understand him. "When will
they return?"

"I do not think they will return," he said in a curious
tone.

Of course they would. "Why did they go?" she said.

"Their reasons were excellent."

Hanna said, "I feel that I play the Game of Scant
Deduction. Will you speak to me plainly? I have made
it clear that we are not the official representatives of our
people, and I have had the thought that those representatives might have preceded us here; yet you have asked
many questions which those persons would have answered fully, and in your description of their actions I
perceive anomalies."

"Those who came *said* they were official representatives," Norsa said doubtfully. "Yet they did not be-

have as we expected such representatives to behave. Also they said that 'Anarilporot was dead.''

He rose and went out of the room, leaving Hanna to the care of guards. She was groggy with fatigue and was not sure she had heard his last words right; what she thought he had said made no sense.

All the other persons of the committee had gone away to bed. Two silent guards were left; perhaps they always worked at night, because they did not seem tired, but regarded Hanna with lively interest. If she moved aggressively, though, no doubt they would react quickly enough.

Norsa came back with a small enameled box in his changing hands. He put the box down in front of Hanna and opened it and took something out. "Do you know what this is?" he asked.

She stared at the golden cylinder with its ring of jewels at the top. She knew what it was but rejected the notion; it was preposterous. She put out her hand and Norsa gave the thing to her. She looked at the engraving and saw that she had been right in the first place.

"But this is mine! Rubee gave it to me! How did you—? It must have been the official party who came and—"

An explosive memory rose into her mind, shocking her so that she transmitted it to Norsa without warning. *Half unconscious, she lay stunned with loss while a thin man reached for the circlet of jewels—*

"*They* came?" She was incredulous. "Those who murdered Rubee and Awnlee?"

"That is how it appears," Norsa said. He added, "Please do not startle me like that!"

"I regret . . ." The words of apology came by themselves; it was hard to absorb the truth. Norsa regarded her calmly, though with some wariness, as if he expected her to fling another memory of violence at his head.

She said, "This gives me great amazement, Norsa. Now I know why you did not give us any welcome. These persons may have behaved grievously. Will you tell me of their acts?"

Norsa debated within himself, and Hanna saw that he was about to embark on a catalog of grievances. She waited with considerable apprehension.

Norsa said at last, "We made them welcome. There were doubts from the first. They did not ask the questions that would be expected of beings come first to a new world; yet we had no experience with such beings, and thought our expectations perhaps were wrong. Nor did they wish to answer questions; I have learned more in this night with you than in many days with them. And when they had been here for a time, at the end, they set about destruction. They took precious goods from Ell and also from other lands. In this endeavor they destroyed all that was in their way; and at the last, in the burning of a great costumerie, several hapless persons who labored in that place were killed."

Norsa had seen some of the destruction at first hand. Hanna saw it now in his thoughts. She bowed her head.

"After they did those things . . ." Norsa looked at the object in Hanna's hands. "There is the course," he said. "It was evident that we must set forth and follow it, and at the end find out their reasons. But we have not yet done anything, because there has been much discussion of what we might find. Some among us have said: 'Withdraw; give up space; stay at home!' Others have said: 'We must have vengeance, and assert our honor and vigor!' And others have said, 'These persons in the depths of space know of our existence, and also our whereabouts; and so, if we do not seek them out, they will continue to seek us.' And still others have answered, 'Indeed that is true, and they will prey on us.' And so we have debated, and done nothing. Yet perhaps now that you have come, you can tell us the motive for these events, which we do not understand."

Hanna was vividly reminded of Rubee. She could have wept.

She said, "I do not know the reason. Perhaps they wish to sell the precious things they took, as surely they meant to do with the gifts which were taken from the *Far-Flying Bird*. I do not know how they could sell them, or where, for already they are hunted by the true

representatives of human beings for their actions on the
Far-Flying Bird. They would have to go to a far place
indeed, far from law; and there is no place so far as to
evade human law, not in a matter such as this. There
can be no escape for them, Norsa. It must seem to you
that humans have little regard for law; do not even my
own actions, as I have described them to you, indicate
so? But indeed there is in humans a great impulse toward law, and the humans who did these things will be
found and, at the least, confined. But I cannot tell you
more than that, because I do not know any more.''

She spoke with her thought as well as her tongue, and
when she was finished she saw that her simple honesty
had convinced Norsa. They had come to an understanding at last. There were no more difficulties in the way.

But Norsa said, incredibly, ''One of those who came
before is still here.''

''Still here?'' she repeated.

''One of those who came remained behind. Was it by
his choice? Was it by the will of another? I do not know.
I have been unable to determine the truth. None of those
persons spoke any Uskosian tongue, but used devices
which translated their words into those of Ell, and the
language of Ell into words they understood. They took
all the devices away with them, and we have not been
able to ask questions of the one who remained behind.''

''I must see him,'' said Hanna in a dream.

''Immediately.''

They went out into the night. The guards accompanied them; Norsa might be softening, but he was not a
fool. It was summer in the City of the Center, and night
closed around Hanna like warm water. The air was clean
and before she got into a shiny vehicle with Norsa and
her guards, she stopped and breathed deeply. She had
been in space too long. The air of a living world caressed her cheeks. In her weariness she could have fallen
asleep in the gentle night, floating in it.

Yet as they rode through the quiet streets, and she
thought about what she was doing, her chest was tight.
Which of the men of the *Avalon* would it be? Not Castillo, surely; more likely a man he had deliberately

abandoned. It could not be Juel, whom she had killed. *One down:* the palm of her hand itched. She wished for a weapon. Not a stunner; something deadly.

They drew up before a great building which looked just like the one they had left, and walked through its spacious galleries. Norsa spoke and Hanna answered at random, until they stopped before a door and he said, "Have you too much weariness? You do not hear all I say."

"It is not weariness."

"Ah?"

"It is rage."

"Rage? Why?"

"It is because of a thing that was done to me. I wish to kill," she said honestly. "I may kill this human, Norsa."

Norsa said, "We will not let you kill this creature. If that is your desire, I will not even let you see him."

She wondered where her sense of civilized behavior had gone. Then she thought: *I will be civilized. I will not kill him now, whichever it is. That would be an insult to Norsa. I will kill him later.*

"Let us go in," she said. "You may observe me. If I do something that causes you agitation, you will stop me."

They went into an antechamber where they waited for some minutes while the nightwatch went to wake up the man in a farther room. But presently the watchman came back and said, "He will not come out."

"Then we will go in," Norsa said, and they went into the next room and Hanna saw Henrik Gaaf.

She was startled. He was not. He was far past ordinary surprise.

The room was sparsely furnished and there was a pallet which might have served as a bed, but Gaaf huddled in a pile of coverlets on the floor. He had his back to a corner. He was emaciated and pale, and he blinked at her and a slow smile spread over his face.

Hanna took a step toward him. Norsa said quietly, " 'Anarilporot!''

"I will not harm him," Hanna said. "This one gave

me a kindness. The Master encouraged him to do so and therefore I lived, though it was meant for me to die as Rubee and Awnlee died. I will not harm this one.''

She took another step, though with reluctance. It seemed that something was going to happen that she would not like. It did. Gaaf came up out of his swaddling and threw himself on her feet. She backed away and he caught at her legs so that she lost her balance and sat down abruptly face to face with him. She had looked once into a lava lake that seethed and boiled. It came back to her because that was what she saw inside Gaaf. He pawed at her face and hair and she wanted to hit him and escape—but she did not, though her skin crawled. She ground her teeth and set herself to endure him; she studied him through her revulsion. He smiled and crooned and his eyes had an expression she had never seen before. He patted her shoulders and then her breasts; she twitched violently and caught his hands to keep them off her. He was content with holding her hands. He whispered and whispered and she sorted out the words that ran together. ''Came for me, you, you. . . ! Not alone. Not alone here any more . . .''

His hands twisted out of hers and caressed her arms. She shuddered. A longing for Michael possessed her, for the touch of his clean hands. She made herself keep still and listen.

''. . . home take me home . . . See? See what I've got.''

He fumbled in a pocket; when he let go of her to do it, she crept away. ''. . . see . . . see . . .'' She looked with disbelief at the broken gold chain; recognized it, and shuddered again. And here was something else. ''Here . . . seeseesee!''

Norsa squatted beside her. ''Do you know that that is?''

She had to try twice before she could answer. ''It is an ordinary data storage module.''

''What is its significance to him?''

''I do not know. I have to get out,'' she said suddenly in Standard. She jerked away from Gaaf, evading the clutching hands; she got to her feet and walked out quickly, though her knees trembled. The ubiquitous guards followed her into the gallery outside Gaaf's rooms. She stood shaking until Norsa came out.

He said with interest, "There is water coming from your eyespots."

"Yes. It will stop by itself in a little while."

Norsa said, "Is that person deranged?"

"I think so."

"We thought it possible, but we could not know. We did not know what to do, and were afraid in our ignorance to attempt any help. We have fed him as best we could, by force, despite the risk; there was nothing else we dared to do. Is there help you can give?"

"I do not know. There is one among my companions who has some skill in healing sickness of the body. I do not know about sickness of the spirit. Perhaps there is help he can give."

"Tell me which it is, and I will send for him at once."

"No. I mean—as you wish, Norsa. But I cannot explain to him tonight. I can give no more help to anyone any more in this night which grows old so that morning has almost come. I must have rest."

"Then you will have rest. Is there anything with which I can provide you for your comfort?"

The tears had stopped, but they started up again. "You can provide my companion Michael," she said. "He is my shelter in the night. I am grieved by lacking him. Surely you know we will cause you no harm. Is it necessary that we be parted?"

"Perhaps not," Norsa said after a pause. "Yet it must be so in what is left of this night, for he is far away. Yet tomorrow perhaps this will change."

"I have gratitude."

She wiped her eyes and followed Norsa back to the street. Tomorrow he would bring Michael to her. Tomorrow also they would have to do something about Gaaf, if they could, if Theo could, but she could not think of it tonight; she was dizzy and her eyes were full of fog. When they came to her quarters she was already asleep and Norsa had to wake her before she could go in. When he touched her to rouse her, she said sleepily,

"Mike?" and Norsa looked at her curiously and thought
of questions that had to do with this odd bonding. But
he was too polite to ask them then; a weary guest must
first be given sleep.

Michael spent the first night in a nightmare of pacing
through the rooms of a place that he took to be a luxurious prison; later he learned it was a private home.
But it was a prison all the same, because he was
guarded. The guards did not try to stop him in his rest-
lessness, but they stood at each doorway that led out
into the night. He paced because he was trembling on
the edge of the terrible rage, which he finally knew had
to do with being impotent and trapped. But he could
not give into it because of Lise; because of her he fought
it back. She held him there with her frightened eyes:
she sensed what the pacing meant, and feared abandonment. And it was because she would not close her eyes,
because she would not look away from him even when
her face was gray with exhaustion, that he finally
stopped moving. He saw that as long as she touched
him, she could rest; so he forced himself to join her on
a pallet meant (his guards made him understand) for
sleeping, and with both Lise's hands clutching his arm,
he, too, slept. But even in sleep he waited for the Polity
to come, waited to be led away in chains.

In the morning they were taken away again. He
thought the next thing he saw would be the face of a
human being from I&S. Instead, after a journey of several hours, the vehicle that carried him and Lise and
their guards drew up before a labyrinth of a cream-colored
house in the center of a garden, and Hanna came out
to meet him. She said that Shen was already there,
and that Theo would come soon but had been called
away to see another human. She told him about Castillo—in shock, he scarcely understood her—and about
Henrik Gaaf. She put her arms around his neck and
talked to him gently.

"It's going to be all right," she said. "But it's not
all right, is it? What's wrong?"

"I don't know . . ." He detached himself from her

and passed his hands over his face. He looked beyond her to the house the Uskosians had loaned their honored guests. The roof shone like copper, the eaves were loaded with gingerbread fancywork. Wide doors stood open to the summer wind, and the interior looked, from here, dim and cool. It was a dream waiting to suck him in. It was the wrong dream, he thought. He had to run, he had to get away, he could not wait on fate though it might come after him anyway.

But Lise had already run down the path to the central door, where Shen had appeared. Hanna took his hand and drew him toward the house, and he followed her into a dream of summer.

By the end of the next day they had begun to fall into natural orbits; at the end of seven days, a Standard week, the process was complete.

Hanna was the first to leave. If she had come to Uskos for sanctuary, she forgot the fact immediately; she was still, and first, a scholar. Norsa gave her workrooms in the city, a vehicle, a chauffeur, and she left Michael each morning and returned at night. Though she saw that a cold hand lay on his heart, it seemed to her that he had strayed into precisely the right dream. If he disagreed, that was his business. So she talked to Uskosians and made notes. "I suspect," she wrote, "that the unusually high rate of mutation on Uskos, which has promoted evolution despite the asexuality of life here, was the origin of the concept of the Master of Chaos; while the identity of generations (though modified by environmental factors and the occasional successful mutation) most likely is linked to the conservative world view expressed in the tales . . . Uskosians handle the physical universe much as we do, but in their attitude toward it there is something else: a perpetual suspense. They do not say only, 'What will happen *if we do this?*' They also say, 'What will *happen to us?*' . . . The Uskosians with whom I talk are becoming aware of this difference between their perspective and ours and, curiously, feel this makes us far more vulnerable than they are. Several have used a phrase I had not heard before. I'm not sure if the best translation is 'children of chaos' or 'the Master's children.' But they meant human beings. I'm sure of that.''

Hanna finished this passage late at night in a room she had commandeered for work in the humans' maze of a house. When she was done, she showed it to Michael. He looked at the last lines for a long time. Then he said, ''Oh, hell, I could've told you that.''

Lise was the next to go. A friendly neighbor's selfing came, then brought other younglings; they enticed Lise from the garden and soon she was running about the town with them in torrents of noise, her slim legs flashing golden among their square brown bodies. Uskosians were indulgent with their offspring, and no one thought it odd that Lise was allowed to run free as she wished. She even followed her new companions to their study groups, the instructors encouraging her visits as highly educational, and her Ellsian improved rapidly.

She came home in tears one day, however; the younglings played many games which required infinitely flexible hands, and Lise could not keep up.

''It can't be helped,'' Michael said. ''I'm sorry, little puss. It can't be helped. You have pretty hands—'' they were very grimy ''—but they're human hands.''

''Then I don't want them!'' she cried.

''Yes you do!'' His voice was harsh and she looked up in surprise; he held her dirty paws tightly.

''Mike?'' she said.

Instead of answering, he bent and gently kissed the backs of her hands. She turned them over and looked at them with greater approval.

''I can run faster than they can,'' she said.

''I know. You run like the wind. Don't show off too much, though. Now run back and watch them so you can tell Hanna what they do. And then when they have a different game, you can play with them.''

She darted out through the garden, brilliant as the flowers. Michael watched her go and thought that she had grown, and at any time now would sprout breasts. Lise had no idea how old she was. This seemed ordi-

nary to Michael, who thought his age in Standard years
was somewhere in the early forties. And when her body
did change, and her mind? He was afraid it would be
hard for her, as it had been for him. When the world
turned out to be different from everything you thought
it was beforehand, you could withdraw from it—or run
at it head-on, no matter how ill-informed you were.
Either course was disastrous. But he would be there to
help her—he hoped—and so would Hanna—

Oh? said a ghostly chuckle in his head. *What have
you ever saved from the sucking dark? Or whom?*

He shook his head, blinking. A cloud must have
passed over the sun.

Think of something else—

—and here in the sunlight Lise was granted an Indian
summer of childhood, among children so alien that her
queer combination of ignorance and sophistication went
unnoticed. The longer it lasted, the better.

That was the last time she came back during the day
except to eat or entertain her lively friends, and she
reported dutifully to Hanna on the younglings' games.

Next Theo went. On the fourth night Hanna came in
and said to him, "You have to talk to them about biol-
ogy. I don't know enough. Medicine, physiology, ge-
netics—I need a whole Contact team. I don't have one.
You're it."

"I don't know enough either," Theo said. He had
not ventured into the city. He spent his days sleeping
or lounging in the garden, staring out at the skyline
beyond the trees. He avoided the others, and reminded
Hanna of a man about to leap into a lake of cold water
and hesitating on the edge.

Hanna was hot and tired, and she had rarely refrained
from leaping into anything.

"You know more than I do. You're an expert, compared to me. Take them to *GeeGee* and open up the
medlab."

"I don't know enough," he repeated.

Hanna looked at Michael, but Michael said, "I'd better see about dinner," and left.

Hanna said to Theo, "Look what you did for me. Look what you're doing for Henrik."

Theo snorted. Henrik Gaaf was present at this conversation: piled in a corner, gazing blankly ahead.

"But he said something today, Theo. He actually said good morning to me."

Theo said, "I haven't heard him say anything."

"Well, I have. Whatever you're doing is working. You know enough, Theo—you just don't believe you do."

He shook his head. Hanna went to where he perched on a shapeless mass supposed to be a chair, and sank to her knees so that she was looking up at him.

"Theo," she said, "where would Mike be without me?"

He did not speak. She went on, "You know the answer. I don't know if you think it means you owe me anything. If you do, please do this for me. For me and for Mike and for the beings who might save him before it's all over. I'll never ask you for another favor. Please."

She had invested the words with an urgency that was more than verbal. He thought about it for a while. Finally he muttered, "I'll try."

"Thank you. Anyway, Theo, you can't know less about humans than the Uskosians do. They won't know when you're wrong!"

So Theo left next day to do his best with a committee of physicians from the nations of Uskos. It was more interesting than he expected, his curiosity was aroused, and he went back the day after that. Soon he only came back at night, too.

Shen got bored and just walked out. She found her way unerringly to a raucous section of the city the Uskosians had not talked about. Somebody bought her a drink, and she liked it so well that she persuaded Hanna to get Norsa to give her some money. He was pleased to do it, but she rarely had to spend anything. She became very popular in certain quarters, and stayed out till dawn some nights, and came home singing, even when she was carried home.

* * *

So they were all gone, settling into courses that circled Michael, the still point around which they swung and revolved, the home, more than the house, to which they came back. He watched them go and come as people had come and gone for years, so sure of his care that they scarcely noticed it. Now in the mornings the house was silent. On the eighth morning Michael stood in it and listened. To silence, except for the quiet wind blowing through the garden trees. Inside the house it was dim and, at this hour, still cool, and outdoors the light poured down.

There were street musicians in the City of the Center. Michael had heard what they played, and though it was strange and harsh to his ears, the games they played with pitch and rhythm had possibilities.

He got his flute and went into the garden, because one still was left, and never would leave by himself. Gaaf sat among the flowers and stared at nothing.

Michael said quietly, "Let's go for a walk."

Gaaf was by no means normal, but he was more responsive than he had been when Theo brought him home. He looked up and mumbled, "Where?"

"I don't know. Anywhere. Come on."

Gaaf climbed to his feet, small and vague beside Michael. They went out together, Gaaf treading close on Michael's heels.

Summer closed over them. The flowers in the garden, instead of fading, grew taller and more brilliant until they were a blaze of colored light. The humans seemed to see them even in the dark, as if some afterimage were imprinted on the retinas of their eyes. The flowers worried Theo. Like flowers everywhere they attracted insects: why? There was no need for pollination.

"Think," Hanna urged.

"I'll ask Ritee and the others."

"No, don't. Think about it."

"You know?"

"I know. I knew before someone told me. Think. Use your eyes."

So he walked in the garden hour after hour, thinking—until he saw it: saw a flower close over an insect, and when it opened later there was nothing left but a little debris.

"I swear I heard it burp," he said to Hanna, and she laughed.

She laughed often in those days, which fell into one another in a golden cascade like the notes from Michael's flute. All the days were alike, so that time seemed to have stopped, frozen at high summer in a great gout of light. The flood of sunlight changed them. Hanna and Michael and Shen turned very dark, and their eyes, blue and amber and green, were startling. Lise was dusted with gold all over, and even Henrik Gaaf turned nut-brown. But the best Theo could do for his own transparent skin was keep it from broiling.

It was the dry season, and there were seldom clouds. The heat was unremitting but not unpleasant, they were dazed with it, in the dusk they sat on a veranda and talked in lazy tones until they straggled off to bed. It was a civilized kind of heat, like their hosts: courteous, attentive to the comfort of a guest. They lived in the safest of sanctuaries—safe in its comfort, safe in its dreamlike separation from any world that had ever been real to them before, and safe in fact—for a time.

No one thought of it explicitly as refuge except Michael, but he thought of it that way less and less. Someday the Polity would come, of course. But if he was only waiting for an end to this world Hanna had given him, he ought to be looking at the sky, and he was not. He looked over his shoulder instead, he looked at the ground at his feet; he did not wait for something from the sky; he waited for the world to be rent and for a look at something deep in an abyss.

Yet his days were as quiet as those of the others. When the morning began to grow hot, he would leave the house with Gaaf tagging behind him, climb into one of the chauffeured vehicles placed at the humans' disposal, and be carried through the city to the place where musicians gathered. Monolithic the city might be, but there were crevices and crannies where gardens had been planted, fountains set to soaring, and parks laid out, each lovely and unique. Through the middle of the day he sat cross-legged and nearly naked in the sun, burning blacker and blacker, in time not a novelty but a colleague. He searched *GeeGee's* library for works on music theory that did not rely on the written word. The leathery beings who played impossible instruments with inhuman hands learned human musical notation quickly, and Michael quickly learned theirs. His Ellsian got better, if somewhat specialized, and he talked fluently of greater and lesser scales. Sometimes he played dances from the Renaissance of Earth's western world, tunes a thousand and more years old, and the beings of Uskos came near and danced, stumping solemnly and rhythmically in circles round the alien with his shining instrument, while one of their number accompanied him on a drum. Sometimes the man and the other musicians played together, the notes of the flute darting silver and gold through the deeper chords. There were strange duets, and when Michael sang he collected crowds who threw money into hollow pots that rang when the coins fell inside. The days together were a timeless dream made of nothing but music; they were rich heavy drops that fell into still water, pregnant with light.

"Indeed all is chaos," said the aliens in their soft growly voices, "yet we of the Musicians Guild impose order on it. It is transitory indeed; all order is transitory. Thus our assertion of sentient being lies in art, which patterns time in beauty."

At the height of each day's heat the crowds dispersed. The musicians drifted away as they had each summer for a hundred years, as they would for a hundred more. Occasionally Michael and Gaaf accompanied individuals to their homes or customary haunts (in one of which, once, they met Shen). More often they sought a shady spot and were quiet under the weight of the heat. Michael talked to Gaaf, dutifully following Theo's instructions: *Let him hear human voices. Talk to him.* Gaaf was a good listener; he never interrupted, never contradicted, never asked difficult questions; he never made a sound. He was motionless, a brown statue with eyes that shifted now and then but never met Michael's. And an extraordinary thing occurred. Michael found there were things he could not talk about. He could talk about now, about quiet, neutral things: how to make a stew, how long the flowers in the garden would grow, a new game Lise had learned; present things. But he tried to speak of the estate left behind on Valentine, how the sea sounded distantly all night and all day, how the peace of it was enlivened by companions of one's choice, and he could not; he tried to talk of how he had bought and fitted *GeeGee*, the pleasure he had felt as the ship became his before his eyes, but the words caught and choked in his throat. Those had been dreams, too, and he was filled with a sense that they had been incomplete, that something was missing and they were unreal. He began to think he had made a wrong choice. Flight and search might have been the better one. He might have found what he sought; then everything would be real again.

Once, though, he spoke of the past, but of a more distant past. It happened on the first day on which he was offered a portion of the morning's proceeds before the musicians took their pay away to eat and drink it up. He nearly refused his share, then remembered just in time that that would be impolite. Later, sitting under a tree whose every branch burst with miniature duplicates of itself which would drop and seek anchor in the soil when the days shortened, he pulled the coins from his pocket and looked at them. They were bright gold and heavy and closely engraved with text that for all he knew might be (and probably was) a legend of the beginning of money.

Suddenly he laughed. So all the riches had come to this, begging to begging, and once more he sang for his bread. He said so to Gaaf, laughing.

"It's easier now, though. Easier . . ." The laughter faded; he talked on; the words came of their own accord. He had never said them to anyone before, not even Hanna. But this was like talking to no one.

"Easier than saying yes yes yes . . . 'Yes, ma'am, I can do that to you, but it costs a little more . . .' 'Yessir, you can do that to me, it doesn't matter if it hurts as long as you pay enough, the docs are good at fixing us up.' 'Yes, Brother, I have spent the requisite hours on my knees contemplating the sin of aggression, only there's some other people I wish you'd told that to, but you wouldn't know them . . .' I would've had to do it twenty years to get as rich as I wanted to be. So I did something else. I invested it. You know how I invested it, don't you? Everybody knows. After that it was easy. The women, all I had to do was look at 'em. Snapped my fingers and down they went. The money had a lot to do with it. So I got radar in my head. Learned to see the ones who looked past the money and the face. Not," he said, scrupulously honest, "that it didn't have advantages. It just wasn't enough. You know what I mean?''

Gaaf did not answer. He did not appear to have heard. Michael looked at him doubtfully and said, ''No, I guess you don't.''

Clouds had settled over the sun; the sky was gray. There was a roll of thunder and raindrops splattered the pavement.

Gaaf lifted his head with an expression of deadly fear. The flute rolled over the pavement with a *ping*; Michael kicked it in his scramble to get to Gaaf. He laid one hand on the man's shoulder, the other on his head.

''It's all right. It's all right. Nobody's going to hurt you. Henrik! It's all right!''

Gaaf breathed noisily. He looked around as if he did not know where he was.

He began to talk. It was the first time he had said more than two consecutive words. He talked disjointedly of the Treasure Store of Elenstap and the night of stumbling through the farmlands. He talked about the morning when the aliens found him, but he was hazy about it. All he could remember was being afraid. He thought they would blame him for what the men of Castillo's crew had done in the night; he thought they would do something to him. He thought that all the time until Hanna came, he expected to be tortured or put to death, he thought they only put it off to torment him. He said all this with surprising clarity.

At the end Michael said, "It's over now."

"Until they come," Gaaf said, meaning the Polity.

"Yeah, well, we've all got that to worry about."

A smile snaked across Gaaf's mouth, a trailing thing of remarkable nastiness.

"Not me," he said. "Everything's been easy for you. It's my turn."

Michael shook his head. "What the hell are you talking about?" he said, but his mind shot on to something else. Gaaf was talking, Gaaf remembered; Michael crouched in front of him; a tremor ran through him, wraiths shifted under his feet.

"Henrik," he said, "where were they going? When they left here?"

Gaaf's eyes settled on his face. He must have heard the plea in Michael's voice, and God knew what was in his too-transparent eyes; Gaaf shrank away.

"Do you know? Do you remember? Henrik. . . !"

But the animation drained from Gaaf's eyes. He fondled something in his pocket, and sank back into silence.

The time sense of a dream is skewed, but Hanna always knew how long she had been on Uskos. When it got to be half a summer, she looked at the sky more often. Where was the Polity mission? Clouds came into the sky, a harbinger of wet autumn. Henrik was getting better.

What time is it? Time. What day? The day was frozen in miniature, as if everything within view was very small but perfectly clear. Not for the first time, not quite; but for the first time Henrik could question what he saw. Directly in front of him, the rangy man with the face carved by an angel. The gentle hands. On his shoulders. *"Here, this way. Don't fall. There's a step."* The music. The man's eyes were closed, he communicated only with the pipe at his mouth. Piercing fantastic

rills. Overhead a gray sky. On every side, an apprecia-
tive circle, the others. The aliens. *Oh no. Oh no.*

He shrank, hiding. No one noticed. *What day is it?
When will they come?* They would come to take him
home. And they would take the musician away; he was
sure they would do that, without knowing why he was
sure.

The wind was cooler today. Cooler than when?—he
did not know. He could not remember. He thought of
the woman, remembering, hand in his pocket, fondling
the chain. And the other thing, the slip of metal. Only
now he remembered something more, without detail.
The woman wasn't alone, she didn't sleep alone; she
lived with the dark musician. There were details now,
disjointed and unplaced in time, but very clear. Blue
eyes distant and cool on poor Henrik's face, turning and
warming to: *Mike. That's his name. I hate him. I hate
him. Who is he? Poor Henrik can't quite remember.
Poor Henrik's not quite himself.*

* * *

Hanna confided in Norsa. Telling her troubles to an
alien did not strike her as an unusual thing to do.

She told him: "My companion Michael has a troubled heart, and I do not know how to give him aid."

"What trouble could he have? For he is well-mated
and also has the love of other companions, nor is he
hungry or ill or enslaved. And by all that you have told
me of 'Unans, he ought therefore to be happy."

"That is correct, and therefore it is all the more difficult to give help to him in his distress."

"Does he fear the law of 'Unans, when other 'Unans
come here? For the gentle hints of my colleagues and
myself ought to suffice in sealing his freedom, if all that
you say is right; and even if we wished, we could not
now withhold them. Else the persons of the Physicians
Guild, and those of the Musicians Guild, will spring,
as you have taught me to say, 'on our backs.' We do
not want that to happen!"

"That is true, and so I have told Michael. Yet it is

not enough, Norsa. And I do not know what to do, for he continues to grow worse.''

The clouds had moved in all the morning, and the wind was fresh, lifting Michael's hair and chilling his bare shoulders. The musicians of the city looked at the sky and tested the wind with dampened fingers. They gave Michael small pieces of paper on which they had written names, places, contact codes: "In the event we do not return," they said, "for autumn is early; yet song flourishes even in winter in warmer climes."

So he sang a troubadour's song for them:

> *Adieu, mes amours, adieu vous comment,*
> *Adieu, mes amours, jusque au printemps!*

"What does that mean?" they asked when he was done, and he translated loosely:

"Good-bye my companions, good-bye until spring; I have naught to live on, not a thing; only air unless I get the favor of a king!"

"Ah, that is a good song," they said, and went away singing it.

The tiny trees still clung to the branches of their sires, stubborn in the gusting wind. There was dampness in it. The vehicle which had brought Michael and Gaaf had gone home, according to custom. They would have to walk whether the rain caught them or not. So they set out through the city with the wind blowing about their ears, for once without the interested participation of spectators who had all withdrawn to await the storm; and they walked through the back ways, the lesser-known paths Michael discovered instinctively. Presently they were walking through a part of the town they had not seen before: by the side of a moss-choked stream that waited for the cataracts of autumn storms.

The heavy vegetable smell of the moss was familiar. Michael had not smelled it for a long time. He avoided the places where it might assault him.

Haven, supposed to be, like this; from myself that time, though. Wasted, worthless human being: what did it? The girl I didn't know in the morning, that last night on Colony One? Crying all night on my pillow, didn't know till I climbed up in the morning from the dead. What I wanted was dope; what was I using then? Saw the bruises on her face, said what the hell did you do. She said: You did it. You did it. You.

He wanted to get away from the stream, but they had followed it into a cut between high banks, smoothly made of concrete and offering no way out. The wind played above, outside this narrow gorge where the air sat heavy and sullen over the dwindling, stinking thread of water.

Find me a place, Kareem. A place to go. Please. No people. No dope . . . And he did, but he hadn't seen it. Hot and dry and the stream drying up so the smell came in—

"Here, he said quietly. "This way, Henrik." Steps cut into the wall led straight up, a hard climb though the bank was lower; near the top a burst of wind shook them. Gaaf swayed and Michael put out a hand to steady him. At the top the monumental buildings of the city stood over them, perpetually falling if you looked up too long. The wind slapped their faces, and then the rain; only a few drops, so far.

Henrick Gaaf said clearly, "We're going to get wet."

Michael was silent with surprise. He stole a look at Gaaf's face. It was different, intelligent, *like a bright rat*, Michael thought, and disliked himself for it.

"It's a long way home," he said.

"Home," Gaaf said in a curious tone.

They walked up the broad street in the wind, in silence. The moss smell was gone, and the memories that had threatened to come into the light had diminished. *This is what I get for not running*, he thought, and put the memories back where they belonged, with an effort.

Think of something else—

Hanna had gone home early to avoid the rain, to her chauffeur's relief. She went to the room where she worked each evening, distilling the observations of the day, and settled to work. The first patter of raindrops swelled to a steady susurration. Thunder growled, but she did not hear it. The room had been dim when she came in, and slowly it got darker. The self-contained processing unit shone with its own light, and she did not stop to illuminate the room. A smell of damp earth came in through the windows.

"Today," she wrote, "I learned through debate with the Philosophers Guild that there is already a movement toward consensus on the significance of this world's very first contact with humans, meaning not Rubee's and Awnlee's journey to our space, but the visit Castillo and his men made here in the *Avalon*. 'That's easy,' they said. 'That was obviously the Master's hand.'

"I asked how they knew. The explanation was complicated, but in essence it seemed to be that this visit was of the same order as natural disaster. It is clear that at the deepest level, Uskos is less concerned with cause than with effect, and the stance, in short, is phenomenological. Still, this is only an explicit, intellectual acceptance of common experience, a shift in emphasis from the human view, which is inclined to subordinate the event to its explanation. There is less detachment from primal experience—"

Hanna had been concentrating intently. Something like a prick between her shoulder blades distracted her. As soon as she was aware of it, it drilled into her back. She leapt up, spun around: pure reflex.

"Henrik . . ." She sighed, relaxing. "I didn't know you'd come home. You startled me."

Gaaf did not answer. He stood and looked at her. She thought suddenly that he had been there for some time, staring at her head framed in light. *A fine target,* she thought absurdly, but it was not so absurd. She had a faint vision of what he saw now. The light fell on her weakly; the curves of her body in its scanty summer clothing were pronounced to his eyes.

He walked toward her, his purpose clear. She took a step backward and bumped into the wall. He reached for her and she said, "Henrik, don't," and called, worried: *Mike!* She was not afraid of Gaaf, she could extricate herself from the unfortunate scene easily enough,

but she might not be able to do it without injuring him.
Gaaf's hands were soft and sticky as slugs and not very
strong. He pressed and smothered her against the wall,
yet there was no threat in him. He embraced her without
violence nor any understanding of her reluctance. Blind
compulsion propelled him, some semblance of love, and
she did not want to hurt him either physically or in
thought. She managed to keep her mouth away from
his, managed to reasonably confine his hands. "No,
no," she said, "I don't like this, Henrik, I don't want
to do this. Please stop, Henrik. Please stop!" *Mike!* she
said again, urgently; Gaaf slobbered at her neck; she
felt sick. "Please, Henrik, stop. I don't want to hurt
you. Please!"

Michael came into the room in a hurry, heard Gaaf's
breathing, saw the shapes struggling in the dark. "No,
please!" he heard Hanna say. He crossed the room, got
hold of Gaaf's right arm, lifted him without effort, and
threw him at a blank spot on the wall. Gaaf hit it with
a thud, slid down it, and was still.

Hanna cried, "Why did you do that!" and plunged
past Michael before he could answer. She flew to Gaaf
and knelt beside him, feeling his pulse, running her
hands over him, testing for broken bones.

Michael said stupidly, "Huh?"

"If I'd wanted to break his neck, I could've done that
myself!"

"But—"

"Did you have to be so rough?"

He swore softly at her back, at the unfairness. Gaaf
was conscious and she cradled his head against her
breast, no doubt, Michael thought, to Henrik's entire
satisfaction. He went to them and squatted beside Hanna
to apologize and help Gaaf up. But when he put out his
hand, Gaaf whimpered and cringed away.

"Don't hurt me," he wept, "don't hurt me, I won't
do it, I won't do anything—"

The sound, the shadow-man, the weak movement in
the dark came together; Michael was somewhere else.

I beg you, said the body in the dark at his feet, bereft

of pride, bereft of triumph; *I won't do it, I swear! Don't hurt me, don't do it, I beg, let me live—!*

Hands grabbed his feet and he kicked them. Another grasped his arm; he threw it off. He did not remember getting through the dark house. But he was in the garden, standing shaking among the drenched flowers. The rain fell and fell, whispering old pleas.

Hanna came after him at once. She came up behind him and put her arms around him, and set her face against his back.

She said softly, "I saw that."

The warmth at his back soaked into his spine, but he was rigid. She felt for his hands and he let her have them.

She said dreamily, "It was dark. Dark and lonely. It was a long time ago. But it was you. Not a child. You."

He shook his head as if he could deny it, and rain ran from his hair into his eyes.

"I didn't want to hurt him," he said in someone else's voice, and Hanna answered in a sleepy trance-tone, the oracle's voice: "Who?"

His voice shook. "This is all for nothing, because of what I did. All you've done won't be enough. But I had to do it. I did what I had to do."

"I know. I know . . ."

The voice was infinitely tender. The softness underfoot, the universal grasses that held worlds together, gave way. He closed his eyes to stop this world from heaving and threatening to crack. But waves ran through the ground as if something alive writhed underneath it. Nothing was solid: nothing except the arms around his waist.

She said, "You are the most gentle human being I have ever known."

It seemed to him mockery. But presently he detached himself from Hanna and turned to face her.

"C'mon," he said. "They think we don't have the sense to come in out of the rain. Maybe they're right."

In the gray light her face was remote and beautiful. "When was it?" she said.

"A long time ago," he said. "When I was somebody else."

They walked back toward the house together, and he began to tell her about it.

* * *

The planning and execution of the robbery of the *Pavonis Queen* had not been easy. Toward the end the details took so much time that there was no time for sleep. Afterward Michael personally dumped the body of the single casualty into space. In those days his face seldom showed what he really thought, and he performed the task without visible emotion. But when it was all over he was very tired. He was (best guess) twenty-three or twenty-four, and he had never been tired before.

It didn't matter, because there was nothing he had to do. For the first time in his life he had nothing to reach for. He hired Kareem to look after the money and make it grow—and was lucky, luckier than his ignorance deserved and luckier than he knew at the time, because Kareem was an honest man.

There was plenty of money to start with, even after the others were paid off, and Kareem started making it increase at once.

Michael had nothing to do but spend it. At first he did not know what to spend it on, but he found out quickly what to buy: any damn thing he wanted.

But it wasn't the way he had thought it would be. He bought fine clothes—and did not recognize himself in them. He was not vain, having come to regard his looks only as a marketable commodity, but he was a realist, and he knew he required no adornment. He gave that up and bought meals that would cost an ordinary workman a week's wages; but they didn't fill him up any better or longer than plain food. He bought places to live and didn't live in them because they always seemed empty no matter how many people came to them (and people came, all right, but he looked around sometimes and saw that they were strangers). Inevitably he tired of the fine homes, and they went on the block. Kareem saw to it that they went for a profit. And Michael bought expensive machines and abandoned them, bought expensive women and abandoned them, bought expensive art—and kept that longer, at least, though years later, acting from an obscure desire for simplicity, he began to rid himself even of that. At a profit.

He didn't buy friends. He bought companions, but he always knew exactly what he was getting for his cash.

He got tired of buying things. There had to be more to freedom that that. So he behaved like a free man; he traveled. He went to all the worlds of the Polity, no longer a smiling guest, someone's pampered toy, but alone (except when he bought a woman to take along). He went to all the great capitals. He found nothing in them except more things to buy.

But that ceased to concern him because he came to see all things through a thickening haze. He drank a good deal, and became indifferent to the quality of what he drank. He was young and strong and the drink was of little consequence. But the mainstream of Polity culture had been notoriously drug-soaked for the last century, and that was a different matter. There was a dizzying spectrum of choices, and Michael, who could afford anything he wanted, started at one end of it and worked his way steadily toward the other. He didn't know what he would do after he got there. But probably he would never get there. He mixed compounds with abandon, for one thing. For another, he developed a penchant for the illegal, which made it a risky business not only from the point of view of the law wherever he happened to be, but also because of the unpredictability of what he injected, ingested, or otherwise absorbed. And then when he was spaced, he got into fights. Somebody would kill him someday, or he would kill somebody else, and that would be the end of it.

The end didn't come and didn't come and didn't come, and he lived that way for five years.

Through all of it he clung to music. The flute went with him everywhere. He had always taken lessons, and now, with the quiet exchange of a great deal of money, he took them from the masters of his time. Not necessarily those he would have chosen; some would not have him as a pupil at any price. He did not resent their refusal, but acknowledged their judgment, which had to do with character not talent. After all, there were days when his hands shook too hard to hold the instrument. But as soon as they were steadier he would pick it up again. And he carried a collection of music cubes, too, compulsively. Here was order, when there was no order anywhere else. Also his inclination led him deeper and deeper into the past, so that he learned, in his pursuit of essential harmonies, ancient history and archaic tongues. He had educated himself with fierce determination and he did not care who knew it, but though he acquired a stunning expertise in this one esoteric area, he kept his mouth shut about it. In all human space he shared this part of him only with a handful of other musicians and scholars. He played sometimes for them, but usually for himself, and never for anyone else, clutching music to himself in solitude—as if it could be taken away from him, if people knew it was precious.

Toward the end he stopped playing. Toward the end he acknowledged that he was not worthy of the music. And so he had been right, it could be taken away. Toward the end he could not even hear it in his head.

He was trying to kill himself. Exactly how the fact came to his attention was unclear, though it had something to do with the girl in his bed on Colony One. He did not know what she had done to trigger the rage in him, and he never found out. It happened at the end of a week he scarcely remembered. He was very sick from doping, he could not think, and so he acted entirely from instinct. He got from her the name of a medic who would not ask embarrassing questions, and he went to get the man and brought him back to take care of her. He was filled with bewildering compassion, he promised to stay with her until she was well, he left her only to obtain some things she needed for the time it would take for the bruises to heal, and he bought presents for her, too; and when he came back she was gone.

This happened in luxurious lodgings in a town whose

name he could not remember. The rooms the girl had left (his rational mind insisted) were bright, clean, and comfortable: worth the high cost of a few days' stay. But in memory they were dim and grimy. He stood in them knowing he was alone.

By merciful coincidence an express flight for Valentine would leave in a few hours. He booked passage and left with nothing but his silent flute, leaving everything else behind.

He knew before he got to Valentine that this time he was really ill. He couldn't sleep, couldn't keep food down, got weaker instead of stronger even though he had left behind his stock of dope. But he was not suffering from the interruption of any addiction. He was not seriously addicted to anything, and he had altered his habits before when his body became insistent. He had never felt this bad. It came to him that he could not go back to his customary pursuits on Valentine, at least not right away, and so he contacted Kareem from space and arranged for Kareem to find a place where he could stay until his strength returned. Kareem agreed, his face expressionless. Years later Michael still would not know what Kareem thought of him in those days. He did not ask; the answer might be too painful to hear.

In the remainder of the passage to Valentine, he began to want certain things he had never valued before: simple food, peaceful sleep, solitude, silence. He wanted them very badly and did not look past them, because it seemed to him a given, inescapable, that when he left the sanctuary Kareem had prepared for him, he would return to living just as he had lived until then. Even when he disembarked at Port of Shoreground (moving carefully because his head was light and his limbs treacherous) and climbed into the preprogrammed aircar Kareem had sent for him, he could not read the future in his overwhelming sense of escape.

The car took him north along the coast and then inland—as he discovered only when it had landed and he asked it where he was; during the first minutes of the flight he had fallen into the first real sleep he had had in weeks.

The place was a lodge by the edge of a stream that flowed north to join the network of tributaries of the Black River, which eventually, much farther north, poured into the sea. He had an idea that this was sportsmen's territory, and the lodge one of a string of similar facilities that dotted the area, but he did not realize until later that he knew that because once he had been told he owned some of them. Later, when he took an interest in what he owned, and went back to see if there were ghosts there (there were), he learned that this was the smallest of them. It had few amenities and was intended for the serious hunter who only wanted a base to come back to at night. It had a single mirror that showed him a stranger with heavy eyes and a thickening middle. The cabin did not talk to him; its intelligence was on the most basic level. It was as isolated as it was possible to be, and as primitive as it could be without being a thatched hut, and no one came there without a reason.

So for a little while he had what he wanted. Solitude: which meant that he could not hurt anyone else. Food, sleep: the absolute foundations of existence, as he discovered in his gratitude for being able to eat and sleep again. And silence: but why did he want that, when he was used to the din of voices and machines?

He found out why. It was so he could hear himself.

The weather was dry and hot and Michael looked at the forest and thought of walking in it, but he was weak, and too many other things screamed for his attention, so he sat on the porch and watched the shadows travel like a compass of the day, pointing west in the morning and east at night. It seemed important to be very still because the ground pitched and yawed whenever he got up. He thought he might be going mad—because though he was alone, somebody asked him questions. Michael thought he knew this stranger, or had known him once, before the dark closed in. He had lived in Michael's head for a long time, but he had been silent or, more likely, drowned out. Now he could be heard. He insisted on a dialogue, and the long conversation went on and on. Michael remembered parts of it word for word for the rest of his life.

''Do you think,'' said the stranger, ''you're any better than the animals who started you out this way?''

''Sure I am. Look at the *Queen*. I said I wouldn't hurt anybody, and I didn't, did I?''

''Oh, come on. What about the spacer who lost an eye in that bar on Co-op? The one whose head you bashed in at Shoreground last year? Not to mention that girl—''

''They're all right. I made sure they were all right.''

''So your bones wouldn't rot in jail—''

The voice took him through every remembered incident of his life. It weighed up, evaluated, and interpreted. He began to learn about accountability, though he grasped the concept only dimly; he also began to learn about possibilities he had never considered before. One of the things you could do with money was give it away. One thing you could do if women fell all over you was take a closer look at the ones who did not; it was even possible that pleasing a woman worth pleasing went beyond what happened in bed. It was possible that the mind that had mastered the *Pavonis Queen* puzzle was good for other things as well. The possibilities might mean there were other ways to live, and maybe even that there were things to live for.

These were new ideas. He grasped them, however, eagerly and easily. He did not attribute his quickness to any special virtue on his part. It was only that he had gotten what he thought he wanted, and it was not worth having. And all he felt, when he thought that he might be able to change, was relief so great there was no room for righteousness—or guilt.

The days ran into each other, and when he came to this point where he began to see the astonishing possibilities, he was not sure how long he had been in the forest. He was not in a hurry to leave. It was taking some time to get acquainted with this person in his head, whose name, oddly enough, was Michael, too. He was likable, not bad company at all; he couldn't do anything about the chasm Michael saw sometimes, but he said *What did you expect anyway?* At least he was a thoroughgoing realist who admitted without hesitation that there were more questions than answers.

But finally Michael knew he could not stay there any longer. It was time to do something else. Get a new place to live, only for a long time this time: on the Carnivaltown dome, maybe, close to where he had started from, close enough to see it, but a little distance away. He would buy it empty, furnish it with absolute basics, and take his time filling it up. He would give some thought to what he filled it up with. And he would find out what Kareem was doing with his fortune, and see if he could learn how to do some of it himself, though starting as the most ignorant of pupils.

He had a vague notion of fishing for his dinner on the last night, and went to look at the stream. But it had fallen much lower than when he arrived, and even in the deeper pools downstream there were thick pads of moss on the stones in the shallows, and a smell of decay in the mud at the margins. He wasn't hungry anyway. He walked back to the cabin in the dusk thinking that he might, tonight, take up the flute again, and see if it would let him play it. And he thought he heard a whine high above as he walked, as if an aircar crossed the sky, but that was unlikely, and he was preoccupied, and dismissed the notion.

He went into the cabin and a man was waiting for him.

He thought the man was someone Kareem had sent to get him, or to tell him something. Not that Kareem had ever done anything of the kind before, Michael being unnecessary to anything Kareem did, but he could not think of any other reason for this stranger to be here.

The man did not say anything, so Michael made some polite, questioning remark.

The man said, "You don't recognize me, do you?"

To the best of Michael's knowledge he had never seen the man before. He said, "Should I?"

"I hope not. Ivo Tonson. Remember me?"

Michael said incredulously, "Ivo?" and the other man laughed. Not even the laugh was familiar.

"They did a good job, didn't they? Know what I did a couple years ago? Went back to Earth and looked up my wife. Walked up and asked for directions. She didn't even blink. So how are you, my boy?"

Michael put his hands in his pockets and looked at Ivo Tonson without answering. It was now nearly five Standard years since the *Pavonis Queen* incident. There had never been any repercussions, and he had gradually left behind the paranoia that had, of necessity, affected every breath he took through every stage of preparation for the crime. But now he felt its old familiar touch. There was no good reason, not one, for Tonson to seek him out after all this time.

He said, "How did you find me here?"

"Oh, that was easy. I called up your headman and told him you'd tried to contact me, left a message saying I was to join you, but neglected to say where you were. I may have suggested there was a party getting ready to happen. He didn't ask any questions. I don't think," Tonson said, "he entirely approves of you, dear boy."

"That's no news . . ."

The air stirred a little, sluggishly. Michael had bypassed the cabin's climate control and opened all the windows, thinking the night would turn cool, but the heat of the day still lingered. The thick smell of the parched stream came in, and the smell of danger with it.

He said, "What do you want?"

"Why, the renewal of old ties, of course. Let me tell you what I've been doing."

"I don't want to know," Michael said.

"Well, you're going to hear it anyway. We'll do this my way, my boy. We always did, didn't we? And so cooperative you always were. Always pleasant. Always smiling. Even when I hurt you. I always thought you liked it, my dear."

Tonson looked around and sat down, making himself at home. He had not had his body structure tampered with, whatever had been done to change the rest of him. He was still a little man with no muscle to speak of. He would be easy to handle; but Michael suspected he was armed.

He stood where he was and no doubt appeared to listen, but he took in little of the talk, which had to do with a series of disastrous investments. Instead of listening, Michael thought of what he had gone through to get this roly-poly sadist's cooperation, the information that was the key to the one big coup he needed to start life over again. It had gotten so he winced whenever he heard the cheery voice across space: "Be in Shoreground in a few days, my dear. You'll be ready, won't you?"

Tonson said something again about renewing old ties, only this time he was explicit about what he meant.

Michael said softly, "I don't do that any more. I'm not for sale any more."

"A pity. Truly a pity. You look just as fine as you ever did, although," Tonson said judiciously, "you seem a little unwell. Not due to this unexpected visit, I hope. Still, if old friendships mean nothing to you, I'm prepared to deal on a businesslike basis."

"I told you, I'm not—"

"Oh, I don't mean that. I don't mean that at all. I came about money. Mostly."

"Oh, yes?" said Michael, and it was as if a string that ran all through his body, out to the ends of his fingers and toes, drew taut. He knew what was happening now. It only remained to hear the details.

He listened. It was worse than he expected. He heard about the hint already lodged with I&S, the promise of more information to come. "It all depends on you, dear boy. I looked for you on Colony One, to tell you it wasn't safe for you there any more, but I missed you. You'd left in rather a hurry." He wanted nothing as simple as cash. He wanted a partnership in Michael's growing network of interests.

Michael considered it. There was enough, God knew, to go around. If it were as simple as that—

But it was not. The man who wanted a partnership today could want control tomorrow. And Tonson suggested, more delicately this time, that there were other things he might want. So Michael still was for sale after all, only now the payoff was silence.

He shrugged and said, "I'll think about it. Want a drink?"

"Delighted. Delighted you're being reasonable, but I knew you would . . ." The man's eyes said: *What else could you do?* "We'll drink to our new relationship, my boy."

Michael nodded, walked past Tonson without looking at him—and turned on his heel and struck. Tonson slumped where he sat, unconscious.

It was the start of another nightmare, the kind he had thought he would never have to live through again. There were enough of them already, more than any human being should have. Unless he were being punished by some ruthless god for unspeakable crimes, though he could not remember committing any that bad: until now. The voice in his head, now when it might have been helpful, was gone. He had been right, Tonson was armed, and with a laser pistol, nothing as harmless as a stungun. Michael took it away, poured water over Tonson's head to wake him, and asked questions. Tonson did not want to answer them. But Michael had to know the answers, the extent of his danger, whether it stretched beyond this one man. To find out he used the pistol, setting the output low, not intense enough to burn through metal but easily hot enough to cook meat. It was (until then) the hardest thing he had ever done and the smell of scorched flesh gagged him, but there was, fortunately, little courage in Ivo Tonson, and not much pain was required to force him to answer. And perhaps in his terror he was not capable of understanding that fortitude, or lies at least, might mean he might keep on living. But he did not even lie, though the truth condemned him. He had not insured his life by leaving his dangerous information with anyone else, and he had relied on the weapon for protection. He had not had anything to do directly with the *Pavonis Queen* and had not seen Michael's cold efficiency there. He had only known Michael in Carnivaltown, and he had not really expected resistance from the compliant, uncomplaining boy he remembered. No one had known he was coming to Valentine, and he had come using another new name.

He had flown from Shoreground in an autocab and sent it back to its base, having expended (the terrified Tonson said) the last of his cash on the long ride, converted from the last of his credit; so he could not even be traced that way. It was possible (he admitted toward the end, with the little breath screaming left) he would not even be missed.

"You're making it easy," Michael said. He was hunched against the wall next to Tonson then. Except that Tonson's hands and legs were bound, an observer would have had a hard time deciding which of the two sweating, wretched men was the victim.

"I won't do it, won't do anything, it's a mistake, all a mistake, you know I couldn't do it, I care for you too much, dear boy, I swear I won't—"

The short night moved on, the sullen air hardly moving. The hollowness under the world was unmistakable, and the lights in the cabin were yellow and dim and resembled eyes. Michael knew what he was going to do. But not just yet, because he could not. And he thought of finding something to use to soothe Tonson's burns, but that was ludicrous, in view of what he was going to do, and maybe (he thought) the pain even was a blessing, because Tonson knew what was going to happen, too, and pain might distract him from the worse agony of fear.

Finally—hours had gone by—he got up, because one thing he had to do was best done in darkness, and the ocean was far away, and morning dangerously near. He got the pistol, which he had put well out of the bound man's reach, and came back and stood over him. Ivo Tonson began to plead. Michael stood there for a long time. The delay was the worst torture he could have inflicted on Tonson, but that was not why he waited. He waited because he could not make himself do the necessary next thing. Where was the murderous rage when he needed it? He listened to the sobs and whispers until they ran into one another and turned into a meaningless babble. He waited until he had convinced himself that the thing at his feet was not human, not even alive, was a bundle of old clothes that did not even move of their own accord but only rocked with the floor, which seemed to move in sickening waves.

Then he knelt on the uneasy floor, put the pistol to the base of Tonson's skull, and burned out his brain. It was a quick business, and very clean.

He loaded the body into the aircar that had brought him here. He would not come back, had brought nothing with him but his flute, and he took that away, too. He also took heavy stones from the bed of the stream. He flew out to sea and just before dawn threw the weighted body into the water, now really a bunch of old clothes, as limp and as tousled. Then he flew back to Shoreground and got rooms at an inn, because he could not remember if he still owned anything that might pass for a home. He had to sleep, but before he did, he took up the flute. To his surprise, it allowed him to play it; or, more accurately, it played itself. He did not think about what to play. The melodies came by themselves, the gentlest and most peaceful tunes he had heard in all his years, and they came for hours. After a while the music began to talk to him. It said that this was just like everything else, one more thing to be left in the past. It said there was now no reason, none at all, not to act on possibilities, because there were no worse places to go than he had gone, no worse things to do than he had done, no worse man to be than he was. And what was done was finally, irretrievably done, and the future would be better because it had to be, because if it were not there was no justification, never would be, never, for the things he had done, especially this last act. But the music was forgiving, and held out hopes of penance. When it finished talking he put down the flute and slept for two days; after which he began to live, but not to live again because that was not what he had been doing before; he only started, for the first time, to live.

* * *

It took Michael a long time to tell this story. Hanna listened to the words, and also to the memories that went along with them. She knew that he had never told anyone about it before, and she knew he was not sure that when she had heard it, she would continue to love him. But it made no difference to her in that respect.

At the end, when he talked of sleep and was so exhausted that he finished the tale hardly awake, she went to the pallet where he lay—they had returned to their own rooms—and sat down beside him. She took his hand, and told him it made no difference. But he wanted to be sure she knew she could not save him, never could have saved him. "Amnesty for robbery's one thing. The Uskosians don't know about this because you didn't know. This is something else."

"Not if the Polity doesn't know either."

"But how can you know they don't know?"

The forgotten chill of the rain penetrated to her bones. She heard a voice from a summer on Earth: *Don't forget the man he's believed to have killed . . .*

Michael had one more thing to say. She bent over him to hear it. "I hate pain," he said quietly, and it was not only his own pain that he meant; and he turned his head away from her and escaped into sleep.

* * *

By next day the rain had begun in earnest. It fell in sheets for hours, sometimes with thunder and lightning and sometimes not. The reason the city was sited on high ground became apparent. The streams that wound through it were not entirely decorative; they were a necessity at this season, supplementing the underground storm sewers which were inadequate for the coming of autumn. The waters were full of miniature shrubs and trees that washed down and down to fetch up at last at high-water mark somewhere else, fresh and healthy after their journey in the nutrient-laden waters. The water also spurred the growth of fine rootlets that would cling to damp soil long enough for taproots to strike into the soil hard and fast.

So the rain was useful and necessary, and it was accepted with such fatalism that the City of the Center essentially shut down. Many inhabitants removed to

drier places. Those who did not stayed in their homes.
Only indispensable personnel were expected to be at
their places of work at this season. The storms were
early this year, however, and adjustments had to be
made for a day or two. By pleading the suddenness of
the onset of the storms, Hanna even got her chauffeur
to take her to Norsa's offices one more time. The chauffeur was depressed about it; he would have been more
depressed if he had known that she went only to ask
Norsa to arrange a journey for Michael and herself. "I
wish to see a place of which Awnlee told me," she said.
"I wish to travel to the Red Forest of Ree."

Norsa had been looking out the window and twid-
dling his fingers, a sight in itself worth the trip.

"But why?" he said. "For the weather in Ree is even
worse."

"Nonetheless I must go, and immediately."

"Then we will all go tomorrow," Norsa said, "and,
at the least, will be over the rain for a time and not
under it."

So Hanna went home through the rain, hoping that
tonight would be better than the night before, that Michael would not wake again and again tense as a beast
of prey that feels the hunter closing in, and that, with
luck, the excursion to Ree would shake him from his
despair.

Heavy cloud brought the evening on them early. After
dinner Shen disappeared into the thickening night, clad
in an Uskosian rain garment that made her look like a
shiny robot not even of human shape. Lise prevailed on
Theo to take her to the home of a friend who lived
farther away than most. When they, too, had gone,
Hanna packed a few necessities for the journey to Ree
and afterward tried to settle to work; but she could not
work. She gave up and wandered through the enormous
house and thought of the Red Forest of Ree, its great
plumes sodden and drooping to the ground. That was
not how Awnlee had wanted her to see it. In his mind,
when he spoke of it, there had been sunlight.

I must get Michael away from here altogether, she

thought; she thought it often. But each time there came
another thought: *There is nowhere left to go*.

Presently the house warbled over the noises of the
storm, startling her: someone was calling in. Henrik
would not answer. Michael would, but he did not, at
least not before Hanna had hunted down the warble in
a nearby room where the utility panel was concealed
behind a bronze plaque more or less in the form of a
being of Uskos. *Aliore as Pure Art,* said an explanatory
legend on the side, which she had to press to open the
panel. She fumbled with the tiny dials behind the
plaque.

Theo's voice roared at her; she jumped and got the
volume down. "What? What?" she said.

"Can't you hear me? I said, young Binell's sire wants
us to stay the night. He thinks it's crazy to try going
home. I think he's right. Listen, if the power goes out,
don't worry. I hear they're putting skeleton crews on
infrastructure and sending everybody else home."

"What? All right. Is it getting worse?"

"This is only the start. Listen, you'll be all right
without the Box, won't you?"

That was what they called the vehicle Theo had taken;
Shen had left in the one they called the Little Box. They
had all learned to drive them, more or less.

"We're not going anywhere."

"All right. You know where we are, if you need us."

"I'll see you tomorrow, then."

But the last words echoed back at her, a yellow light
twinkled from the panel, and the lights in the room at
her back dimmed suddenly. She leaned over and found
that her Uskosian tutors had taught her enough so that
she could just read the engraving. It said: *At present
there can be no connection save with the Emergency
Contact Locus nearest this site*.

What was left of the light began to fade. Spurred by
a memory of something that had not seemed important
when she was shown it, she flew through the house to
an alcove under a stair. She got her hands on an emergency lantern just as the lights went out altogether, and
turned it on with relief. It was shaped like a candle, and

the light at its tip even acted like flame, bending and wavering and casting swooping shadows; but the light was cold.

She stood cupping the light as if it were a real candle, and listened to the rumor of the wind. The air was cooler in the storm, and she shivered, but not with cold; there was a primeval strength to winds like this which demanded notice. And she remembered, fishing it from a dialogue on a long summer day far off on Earth, the reason power was cut off and ordinary pursuits put aside during storms like this. It was not (as Theo had thought) a necessity or even a precaution, but a ritual. In some households there would be talk of the Master's hand, and the younglings would be instructed by the storm. In others there would be no talk—but everyone would stop, and acknowledge the wind and the flood.

She went slowly to the room where Michael was, thinking that perhaps he would be watching the storm, too, his eyes clear with fascination. And she found him in a room adjoining the veranda, and the wide doors were open so that the tumult of the storm came in on a spray of rain; but he was asleep, and did not see any of it. He lay just outside the range of the spray on a lounge that was poorly formed for the human body, so that he sprawled across it like a broken child. There was a music cube at his head, and Hanna came near and heard a shout of summer and sunlight. But outside the night was pitch dark, and she did not see but heard the thrashing of the garden trees.

Henrik sat in a corner on a pile of rugs. He had been watching Michael in the dark.

Hanna knew it; she was revolted. There had been a change in Henrik, as if the moment of violence the day before had waked him from a deep sleep. His new attention was fixed on Michael, and it was inimical.

She sat down at Michael's head as if to shield him from Gaaf's eyes with her body and her light. Patches of the sky lit up from time to time with lightning, and were followed by rumbles of thunder from other places in the city.

Her tension increased. But it was not because of the storm; it was because of Henrik.

Does he think I can't feel his hatred? What if he tries to do something about it?

And if she could see into his head a little? She ought not make the attempt. *Ought* not: a social prohibition against the invasion of the ultimate fortress of privacy. But it was a prohibition that had ceased to trouble Hanna much in these last years, and she might never have so good an opportunity. There was no one near to distract her, and Michael slept deeply. She put her free hand on his forehead and he did not feel it.

And so she made her mind empty in something that was kin to the satya trance, though not so complete or difficult; she made herself hollow, a gong that would resonate to whatever touched it. First the room and then the wind and rain became remote, and she entered a shell of silence; and into this focusing of perception she admitted the point of life that was Henrik.

Thus it was that as the storm thundered on she saw herself, and what poor Henrik thought of her: not much. She was hardly present in his head at all. She was tiny in the map he had made of the world, an appendage to something larger than life that loomed like a threat. It was powerful, detestable, and malignant. It was Michael.

Somewhere far outside the trance she was horrified. Inside it, cool logic operated. It said that under the blankness of the past weeks, an obsession had grown in Gaaf. The burden of uncounted humiliations, the weight of his life, must have a focus; and here, where humankind was concentrated in a handful of personalities, here in a place he did not want to acknowledge as real, Michael had become the focus.

She ceased to hear the storm. Without emotion and therefore unrecognized by Gaaf, she slipped through the perpetual panic of his thought.

Fortune's favored child: that was how he saw Michael. Had Hanna been herself she might have laughed, though bitterly. *How is that?* she asked, but he thought the question came from inside himself, so skillful was

Hanna and so (still) befuddled was Gaaf, and inexperienced in this way of communication; so he answered, and he answered with envy.

She murmured agreement in Gaaf's brain. *He has so much . . .* But she could not have done it if she had not made herself an echo.

The women and the money, the money and the women . . .

There was not much distinction between the two. In Gaaf's eyes they fell into Michael's hands, into his arms, coins and great gouts of credit, a procession of women who offered themselves like shameless animals—

Somewhere outside the half-trance Hanna laughed to herself. Had she been that bad about it? No doubt.

He will pay for it! Gaaf said (he supposed) to himself, with such clarity and certainty that Hanna for an instant lost control, and heard the storm again, and the shadow in the corner stirred, alerted.

Outside the trance she was deeply alarmed. But she could not afford alarm; if Gaaf felt it, even he would know what she did. She wrapped herself in trance like a shield of silence, purposeful and irresistible. She engaged in no casual inquiry now. It was essential to find out what Henrik meant by his smug conviction. And she crept up on him as stealthily as if it meant Michael's life; as it might, if the satisfaction she had read in Gaaf, the sureness of coming revenge, had a foundation in fact.

. . . satisfying! she breathed in the corners of his mind, a vengeful echo.

He gloated: *They will take him away.*

And, *. . . power!* Hanna purred, catching at the knowledge of power in his hand, and there were quick little flashes of events and the burden of all that power:

Michael looking at bright alien coins in his hand, talking of pain.

Michael on his knees, begging.

For what?

The answer was an image of distance and utter isolation.

And I have it! Gaaf thought, triumphant, and she saw

that he had something, she even felt it as he felt in his pocket.

And its name? said the echo in his head, his own thought (he believed), and he answered, thought the word, said it, even said it half out loud.

She pulled out of him then, wrenching herself away from trance. As soon as she did, her stomach revolted; she put her head on her knees to keep from being sick. When she looked up, Gaaf was upright and staring at her. Suspecting. In fact he should know perfectly well what she had done; only he could not believe it.

She ignored him. She turned to Michael and touched him until he woke. He smiled at her as he always did when he woke and found her there.

It did not seem to Hanna that what she had learned could be of any significance, yet it seemed so important to Gaaf, this thing Michael had begged for and Gaaf had withheld. She said hesitantly, even shyly, because she felt ridiculous, "Does the name 'Gadrah' mean anything to you?"

He almost fainted.

When she told him about the module, he took it away from Gaaf. Gaaf resisted, desperate. Hanna was paralyzed with his fury, his fear, her own confusion. She did not recognize Michael. He had gone into shock the man she knew and come out someone else. His shadow leapt on the ceiling as he moved on Gaaf. Hanna was afraid he would kill, though this was not what she had seen before, the passion to hurt, he was only consumed by a single goal; but he might kill to get it. She called to him out loud and in thought and he did not hear, she clutched his arm and he flung her away, she had dropped the light, could see nothing, the tumult in the corner was a melee of violence and noise. But all the noise was Gaaf's. Michael did not utter a sound.

He had what he wanted and ran out into the storm.

Gaaf was conscious and essentially unhurt. Hanna did not waste time with him. She picked herself off the floor where Michael had thrown her and ran after him, pursued by a blast of hatred from Gaaf. The wind hit her

like a wall when she came onto the veranda. *Hurricane!*
she thought, staggering backward, but it was only a
gust, and she got back the breath the wind had taken,
and pushed away from the house.

She did not think about where to go, she ran without
thinking. But when she rounded a corner against the
wind, and struck off without thought down a path slippery with rain that led to the street, she knew what her
destination was, what Michael's must be: *GeeGee.*

As soon as she knew it, she lost her head. Michael
would lift off, he would be gone, no one would know
where he had gone and she would never see him again.
She could not even keep up with him, much less catch
up; sheer weight made a difference in this storm, where
the wind shoved her backward and knocked her from
side to side. She called his name, but the wind blew it
away, so she cried out to him in thought, too. Her feet
slipped on the tiles of the path and she fell with a splash;
it did not matter, she had been soaked as soon as she
got to the door, and now the wind whipped her dripping
hair against her face with a force that stung.

The street was not quite dark. Its margins were edged
with lines of light which the curbs took up in daylight
and released at night. But nothing moved in the street
except water, which made it a stream.

Hopeless, hopeless— The wind slackened and she ran
more easily, though there were gusts that unbalanced
her. She put her head down and threw herself against
it. *Hopeless—* She would (beginning to think again) go
back. She would call that Emergency Contact Locus
and somehow get through to Norsa. There were guards
around *GeeGee* and he would see to it that they would
not let Michael board.

The wind blew her around a corner and she bumped
head-on into Michael.

She wrapped her arms around his neck and pushed
against him as if she could merge her body into his.

"What the hell do you think you're doing!" He
shouted into her ear. "I was coming back. I heard you.
I felt you fall, I was afraid you'd get hurt."

"Oh yes yes yes," Hanna said, not interested in anything but holding him. He looked around; he had to lift his head to do it, and she clutched him. "Come here," he said. She seized his hand as hard as Lise ever had, and he led her to a wall she had not seen in the dark. There was a gate in it. He struggled with it in the wind, got it open, pulled her through it, and crouched with her in the shelter of the wall. It was cold and black, the rain streamed down the wall and down their backs, and the wind still pulled at them, but it was no longer like being beaten.

Michael tried to speak and Hanna interrupted.

"How could you! How could you do that to Henrik? How could you do this to *me?* You can't run away, I won't let you, you're *mine—!*"

She was seized with a possessiveness she had not known was in her. At some time when she was not looking, it had become a law of nature that Michael could not leave her. She shouted at him, cried, pounded his chest with her fists. He let her rave, listening seriously until she ran down; by then the water had formed a puddle around them.

Hanna subsided at last into sobs. "You can't!" had become "You won't, will you? Please?" And she knew she had made a spectacle of herself, fallen into a patch of pure hysteria. She was ridiculous—and wet; a marine creature whose tears were lost in the water it breathed.

Michael leaned forward, put his mouth against her ear, and began to talk.

"I wasn't going to leave you. I wasn't going to take off. I just wanted to take it to *GeeGee* and see. I couldn't think of anything else. I heard you call and turned back. I always would. I always will. Don't you know that by now? Listen to me. Listen. I will never leave you. Never."

But there was something in the hand which caressed her; she felt it burn into his palm.

"That's it," she said, "isn't it. The place."

"I don't know."

"But you have to find out."

"Yes."

She had stopped crying. Her anger was gone; the

weariness it left behind slowed her speech. "Wait until
morning," she said.

"In the morning we go to Ree. We won't come back
until the day after tomorrow. Do you think I can wait
that long? I'll take you back to the house, and I promise
to come back. I solemnly swear it. But I'm going to
GeeGee tonight."

"I'll go with you."

"I don't think—"

"I will. I will."

GeeGee, having been moved near the city for the
travelers' convenience, was not far away as distances
went: an hour's pleasant walk. Tonight it would be two
hours or more, none of it pleasant. In the last years of
Hanna's life she had leapt solar systems with ease. Now
all her journeys had come down to this: a few kilometers of hard going in the rain.

"You think that's the place," she said.

"I don't know." He was part of the darkness, indistinguishable. Only his hands proved he was there.
They had been quiet on Hanna's shoulders, but suddenly they were restless, brushing water from her hair,
wiping it from her face; they felt for her substance in
the dark.

"What else do you think it could be?"

"I'm afraid to think."

"Does Henrik know?"

"Maybe. Hanna, I don't know anything!"

"Let's go back and ask him," she said craftily.

"No. Why? When we can plug it into *GeeGee* and
see?"

She gave up. "I always liked walking in the rain,"
she said.

The irony was lost on him. "All right. Hold tight to
my arm. If the lightning comes too close, we'll lie low
in a ditch."

"And drown!"

"C'mon," he said.

* * *

The wind and rain diminished, though there were periods when the downpour was as hard as ever. The lightning stayed far away. Once Hanna looked toward the city and saw it strike repeatedly at the top of one of the great towers. The glow rimming the streets was subdued in the rain, and they walked in the middle to avoid the rushing, flooded gutters. Time slowed to an endless moment of wet and cold in which Hanna had leisure to be astounded by her panic. She held to herself the thought, like a magical charm, that her fear had found Michael in the storm, that it had broken through the armor of his obsession and that he had turned back, desiring her safety more than this other thing he wanted. But still he had surprised her again. Nothing she knew about him had prepared her for the unforgiving passion he had shown Gaaf. And she was afraid of where it could take him next.

Toward midnight they reached the *Golden Girl*. There were no guards around *GeeGee* after all. But they appeared as soon as Hanna and Michael came into the welcome, familiar dryness, where even the lights were the color of an old friend; they came running from somewhere inside and stopped in consternation when they saw the humans.

Hanna said to them understandingly, "Indeed it is a very wet night."

"Very," agreed their captain. He raised a hand and with great dignity led his crew out to their proper posts; not without some regretful looks backward.

Control had an abandoned look. Michael sat in the master's place, which had been his until Hanna's greater skill supplanted him. In the last hour Hanna had felt a great purposefulness crystallize in him, and he had hardly been aware of her company. Yet above all there was a great restraint. He did not know what he had, and kept speculation to himself.

He slipped the module into a notch and told *GeeGee*: "Read and store." His face and voice were blank. They waited, Hanna as still as Michael. It seemed to be a very long time before *GeeGee* said, "Done."

"What is it?" Michael asked.

"A course in standard format," *GeeGee* said indifferently.

"What's the destination? Compare with what you've got in memory."

This time the pause was unquestionably very long. At the end of it *GeeGee* said, "The destination is not in my memory."

Michael said so quietly that Hanna scarcely heard him, "Give me a schematic." But *GeeGee* said, "I cannot produce visual data from this source. Terminal point lies outside my visual matrix."

Hanna said, "We can get a projection." She leaned over Michael's shoulder, pulled a keyboard into position, and slowly, stopping often to consult *GeeGee*, entered a series of commands. She scaled the display so that *GeeGee's* terminal course referent would be at one side and the unknown destination at the other, and instructed *GeeGee* to superimpose the whole on a map of whatever lay between. The map ought to be accurate enough; it was based on centuries of observation, even though no one had gone out there to look at first hand.

The picture that finally came was a fantasy. The prime referent at the left of the screen was Heartworld, but the star at the other edge was, by *GeeGee's* scale, fully five hundred light-years away. Hanna did not have to ask *GeeGee* to know what it meant. That was unexplored space out there. No one had gone there, not ever—or so all the records said. But here was a course, plain and straight.

Michael did not move. His hair and clothes were partially dry, but only partly, so that he looked half-finished. He was very pale and he looked—Hanna blinked at him—terrified.

"But what is it?" she said.

He said, "That's Gadrah." His voice cracked on the second word. He put his head down on the console so she could not see his face.

They spent what was left of the night on the *Golden Girl.* Michael did not sleep. He lay on the bed in his old room and stared upward as if he would see some kind of path emblazoned in the tracery of leaves at the top of the room. Hanna slept, but fitfully. Each time she woke it was with a start, and with heavier eyes. Once she said when she woke, "You didn't believe it existed, did you."

That was what he had been thinking about. He was used to Hanna; he was not even surprised.

He said, "That's not quite it. I believed it existed, but somehow it wasn't real. Not if nobody else thought it was."

"Except him."

"B. Yes."

"That's really why you needed to find him," she said. This time she did not sound like an oracle, but she might have been the model for one, with her tousled hair and pale cheeks and sleep-haunted eyes.

"It seemed like a good idea at the time," Michael said. He could not interpret her expression. She rolled over and slept again.

Fantasies. They got in the way on Alta, between him and his schooling. Not at first. At first there were only the nightmares, dreadful dreams of noise and screaming and flame, and then, like their extension, the only life he could remember with certainty: the endless time with B, its passing divided into the times when he was locked into a room by himself, and locked into it with B. And the first clear memory that came later was of the Post, and it was no fit medium for fantasy. He would not wish to go there, to that stone-guarded place. Then he remembered a little more, not clearly, without definition. And thought—dreaming over his lessons, washed with sweetness, awash in longing—*When I grow up I will go there.* "There" was a dreambrew of mountains and meadows far from the Post. They would be clean and safe, as they had been before some great event which he thought of one day, inexplicably, as "the relocation." And then—

But he had never gone on from "and then." He only dreamed of the sweet-scented meadows, as if, once there, he could get back everything else still hidden in cloud.

"That's nice," said Hanna, meaning the meadows. He had not known she was awake. "I didn't know there was anything good," she said.

"There was. Before they noticed us."

"Who were 'they'? Who were 'us'?"

"It was so quiet," he said softly, he remembered that, a piece of memory painfully retrieved. He showed her more pieces. "They must have let us alone for a long time, a generation at least. There was music."

"A village." She put a name to something taken from his thought.

"Primitive. But the summers. Oh, the summers!"

The deep shadows of the forest. The cold spray of water on hot days cascading down living rock.

They lay together thinking about summer until Hanna fell asleep again. She nearly pulled him down into it with her.

Flight. From the truth of what it was, forever out of reach. From Alta. From poverty. From memory. From himself.

"But you did stop," Hanna said drowsily.

"No." The quiet space on *GeeGee* was a world in itself, removed from every place he had ever been. Even time stopped in it. "I kept moving farther and farther out of Shoreground," he said. "I worked harder than I had to, for a long time. Thinking it would make a miracle happen."

"What miracle?"

"I didn't know."

"No miracles," Hanna said, and fell asleep.

After a while he answered her anyway. "No miracles."

Compulsion. The history of the Explosion was a nice hobby for an amateur scholar. He even went to all the places it could possibly be. As a dilettante; so he said.

Then a woman named Hanna ril-Koroth met the People of Zeig-Daru. It was an important meeting. But for Michael all its importance lay in the history of the People, who all had once-upon-a-time destroyed a human colony of which humans had no record. Always in his search he had rejected speculation, though rumors of

"Beyond doubt . . ." Under other circumstances Hanna might have laughed. Now it was all she could do to arrange her face in a facsimile of a smile.

She said, "Awnlee told me there were ruminants large as my house. I suppose the ruminants also are somewhat smaller than he gave me to believe."

"I do not know," Norsa confessed, "because I cannot comprehend what was in his mind. Thus may expectation outpace reality!"

"You do not know how truly you speak," Hanna said, staring at Michael. He did not even hear her.

They left after staying only a little while. Just before they passed out of the forest glade, Hanna turned once more. The glades had not gotten their name without a reason. She pictured the place in sunlight, early in the morning or at sundown, when the light was rich and the bronze leaves came to life. It would not take much imagination to infuse the scene with cinnabar and see all it was in red. That was what Awnlee had chosen to do, and how he had chosen to remember it; and so he had made Hanna a gift of his imagination, and with it, beauty.

"Farewell," she said softly, and Michael finally turned his head, drawn from his preoccupation. But she had said the word for her friend Awnlee. She had no intention at all of saying it to Michael.

It was necessary to exchange courtesies with a committee of the Foresters Guild, and after that they went to a lodge where they were to spend the night, first dining with the committee. Michael was entranced, and smiled at things no one else could see. *A sun shone, and flowers shone at night like the light-storing alloys of Uskos, brighter than the flares of meteorites. Iridescent winged creatures no bigger than his thumb flew to perch on his hand and peer at him with faceted eyes, their fine scales light and dry to the touch. The sound of running water filled the nights, and with it music: an old man with a bow. The voices in the next room talked until he fell asleep, and steered him through shoals of dream.*

He scarcely touched his meal. When the persons of the committee departed, he sat over wine with Hanna and Norsa and heard the rain fall. Few visitors came here during the rains, and except for a reduced staff, the travelers from Ell had the lodge to themselves. The refectory was brightly lit, but there were also festive candles, and Hanna had the other lights extinguished so that they sat in the mellow candlelight. Michael watched Hanna and thought: *How beautiful she is.*

When all the correct formalities had been observed, she spoke his name and he followed her to a sleeping room. Once inside, she began to talk to him. She used Standard words and Ellsian, she used terms he had come to recognize as Girrian and F'thalian, and they meant in their various modes the same things: treasure of my soul, thou finest-furred darling, mate desired above all inferiors, more beloved than self; and she called him by his name: *Mikhail.*

"Wait, oh, wait!" she said.

"I will not wait."

She had an unfair advantage if she chose to use it. If she was afraid for him, angry with him, afraid for herself without him, she could batter him with raw emotion and force him to suffer with her. She did not do it, and all he could think was: *How beautiful she is.*

"You have always done everything alone." She had reduced the light here, too, to candlelight, and shadows were caught in her hair. Trickles of water reflected the flickering light, and flame ran down the windowpanes.

"You do not have to do this alone," she said. "You must not."

"If the others want to come, they can."

"I don't mean that. Mikhail, there is a time and place for governments. Don't think of going alone. Wait for the Polity. They'll go at once, and how could they go without you? They'll need you. And you'll have all your wishes that way. Those people, the ones you called 'they,' who did terrible things—they'll be brought down. All your pain will be revenged. Don't you understand that things must have been as they were because of isolation? When the isolation ends, there'll be light there.

It will be a new age. Only be patient, a little patient. Wait. Wait with me, and we'll go together.''

The logic could not be argued. "I'm going all the same," he said, "whether the rest of you do or not."

"It's you I don't want going there. Not like this. I would do it a different way. A better way. This is a world, Michael! A whole world, a strange one! How do you think you can have it on your terms? You need authority at your back.''

He did not know what she was talking about. She watched him try to understand it. But something had been left out of him, or maybe taken out, and he could not understand. Authority was only something to be gotten over or around or past, a part of the environment, to be dealt with when necessary and otherwise ignored: a concrete, null-value thing, not an abstraction, and certainly disconnected from justice. Once he had told her that Alta had seemed like an alien planet with strange gods. So it was, she now saw, with every place. She would never have to wonder how it happened that Michael had moved easily among aliens in these weeks. He had been among aliens all his life.

She came close and touched him. The shadows round her eyes were dark in the candlelight; she looked bruised.

"Is this how you were in the years before?''

"How I was. . . ?''

"Fixed. Immovable.''

He looked at her without comprehension.

"Stubborn!'' she said.

"I don't know . . .''

It seemed odd that Hanna who understood so much should not understand that all considerations were irrelevant beside the course in the module next to his skin; that on the threshold of this last journey, for the first time in his conscious memory, the sense of being in flight had left him. He would stand here and listen to her all night, if that was what she wanted, but it would not make any difference.

She saw that finally. Her hands fell away from him.

She looked up at him from those shadowed eyes and he said, "It will be all right."

"It won't."

"You don't have to come."

"Do you want me to?"

"No. It could be dangerous," he said with no sense of incongruity, and her mouth tightened; but whatever the temptation might have been, she did not let him feel her anger.

"Is there nothing I can do to bring you to your senses?"

He considered the question carefully and answered, "No."

She did not talk to him any more. She blew out the candles and they undressed in the dark, silently. Angry or not, she turned to to him with caresses, and maybe that was supposed to remind him in another way that he need not go by solitary ways any longer; but the dreams were too strong, he could not accomplish the act of love, and though Hanna stayed beside him through the night, he was alone.

She had to tell Norsa that they were going away. It took a long time, and it was evident to Norsa (Hanna did not try to hide it) that she did not want to start on this journey. They sat together in the Scarlet Glades and he made her a remarkable proposal.

"At one time," he said, "upon your arrival, yours and that of your companions, you said to me that 'Unans must appear to have little regard for law; and to support that statement, you adduced the actions of yourself and your companions up to that time. Yet you told me also that 'Unans have a great impulse toward law. And it seems to me that what your companion Nikell now proposes, though not (as clearly as I can determine) unlawful, does not fall precisely within the bounds of law. Is it for this reason you have distress? For I have come to know you well in the fine days of our association, and it seems to me that in yourself, at least, there is great respect for law."

She answered, "Indeed, Norsa, I believe that what

you have said of me is correct; and in regard to my companion Michael, it is not so much that he rejects law, as that he acknowledges none. In these last many years he has had no conflict with law, except as he nearly became its victim, which is why, as you know, we are here; for except in that matter only, the goodness of his heart protected him. Yet it is not law I now fear, but folly. In this matter I would seek the protection of law and the civilization of humans; yet just as this human does not consider law's constraint, equally he does not seek its protection. Therefore he goes forth, I fear, to great peril, and I cannot restrain him."

Norsa's answer was rash, but its source was the pure impulse of friendship.

"It is possible that he could be restrained, and made to wait until the other 'Unans arrive."

"Restrained?" she said, faltering.

"Immediately, at your word. You are kin to the citizens of Ell, and like us a citizen. He is not, however precious he is to you. If that is what you wish . . ."

After a long pause she said, "No. I have deep gratitude, Norsa, but I cannot do that. That betrayal would destroy the affection between us, between Michael and myself, forever."

"Yet you fear for his life, and there can be no greater destroyer of affection than death, which is the end of all sharing and exchange."

"That is correct, Norsa. And yet," she said more firmly, "I cannot do it. I could do it if I knew his death awaited at the end of this path, but I do not know that. I do not know the future. And so I can only seek to persuade. I will not exert force."

"I judge that you choose rightly," Norsa said, "though I share your concern, and always will share it until I know that you are safe. For surely you know the story of the Journey of Nlatee, wherein great benefit came to Uskos, though Nlatee was disobedient and followed a discouraged path."

"Then why did you give me such an offer?"

"It is necessary at times to choose between friendship and right, and right is not always the correct choice.

Likewise, in a matter of affection, as between sire and selfing, some small betrayal may be useful, where a greater runs only counter to the desired end.''

Norsa's cilia and fingers had stopped moving; even his eyes were still. Hanna eyed him cautiously and said, ''I do not know your meaning, Norsa. But it is impossible for me to plan betrayal, however small it may be, at least plan betrayal that must remain secret. I could not, in the long term, hide anything from Michael. I am a telepath, he is accustomed to my free exercise of that faculty, and I could not refrain from the use of it, even if I wished, without his knowledge of my withdrawing. And then I would have to speak truth to him in any case, or watch affection die as surely as in the other instances we have discussed.''

''Yet there may be a course around this obstacle, if you wish the aid of a friend, even though you do not know until the moment it shows itself what it is.''

''Indeed such aid could be of the greatest value,'' Hanna said.

''That is all I wished to know. Let us speak of it no more, lest you see what I contemplate without even desiring to see it, as I know sometimes occurs. Instead we will talk of leavetaking, which I know must be soon; yet I, too, shall have many answers to produce both for the populace and its leaders, who do not expect this departure.''

As soon as they returned to the city, the objects brought from the *Golden Girl* began to march back to the ship in a steady stream. Theo and Lise and Shen would follow Michael anywhere, but it became necessary to deal with Henrik Gaaf, who might have some useful knowledge of Gadrah. Gaaf had been wandering somewhere when Hanna and Michael returned, and he came into the house to find all the common rooms turned upside down as the others ferreted for personal possessions that seemed, now that they had to be collected, to be everywhere.

Hanna had asked Michael, ''How are you going to get Henrik onto *GeeGee*?''

"Any way I have to," he had said. And she was present when Gaaf joined them in the room just off the veranda. This room, spacious and tiled, had remained cool even on the hottest days, and it had been a favorite place for all of them. Now the tiles were dirty with the water they tracked in and out, the baggy lounges looked deflated, and scraps of their summer lives lay everywhere.

Henrik blinked at them and licked his lips. He said, "What are you doing?"

"Leaving," Michael said. He juggled a pair of music cubes and looked at Gaaf dispassionately.

Henrik focused sharply on Michael. He had given up all pretense of vacuity since Hanna's dissection of his brain. "Where to?" he said.

"Where do you think?" Michael said, not unkindly.

Hanna was near the door with Theo; she had been helping him guide a pallet loaded with foodstuffs toward the veranda. She stopped to watch. She did not see the necessity for abducting Gaaf and strongly disapproved.

Gaaf's eyes flickered in her direction. Whatever confidence he had once placed in her was gone, but still he thought of her vaguely as more sympathetic than Michael. He thought about what Michael had said. He knew the answer, but what he said next was what he wanted to hear.

"You're going back to the Polity?"

"No." Michael drifted nearer, relaxed, unthreatening. Gaaf backed away anyway. Theo moved silently into position behind him, something in his hand; now Hanna knew what would happen.

Michael said, "Will you come with us? I need to know what you know. Everything about the man you call Castillo, everything about the men with him. They'll be there. We might have to do something about them."

"No." Gaaf backed up some more, just beginning to grasp it, and torn. The prospect of remaining on Uskos, alone among the aliens, was dreadful. But Gadrah was no better, and Castillo was there.

Michael nodded to Theo, and Theo put one hand on Gaaf's shoulder and jabbed at his back with the other.

Gaaf jerked, started to protest, and went down, Theo breaking his fall.

Hanna said quietly, "You didn't try very hard to persuade him."

"Would it have worked?"

She shrugged, chilled. She wondered how safe it would be to defy Michael now—how safe it would be even for her.

They took Henrik to *GeeGee* on a pallet already loaded with bedding, and put him away in the mirrored room Hanna had once occupied. She sat with him for a time. Just before *GeeGee* took off, Shen looked in, saw Hanna's gloomy face, and said, "You expected something else?"

"What?"

"Just like a man. Thought you'd know."

"*What?*"

"How they are. Not practical," Shen said, and walked out with no consciousness of having said anything surprising at all.

VI.

When the journey had barely begun, Hanna said to Michael, "What is your plan?"

"How can there be a plan," he said, "when we don't know what's waiting?"

He waited for her answer, laughing at her, expecting a diatribe.

She said frigidly, "We could improve the odds."

He stopped laughing. "I wouldn't object to that."

"Tell us what we're going to. How much do Shen and Theo know? I don't know anything. Teach us geography. Tell us about the culture. You know what to expect. I don't. Teach us the language."

"I don't know it," he said. He was ice. He had gotten there from mirth in half a minute.

She said, "How much do you remember?"

"Not much. I think you know already everything, everything I remember." It was becoming difficult for him to talk. "The end is the only thing that's clear. Before that, I lost nearly everything before that. I don't know why. There were things I remembered later, little things, that I saw like pictures. But I don't know how they fit together. What came in between is gone. I—don't—have—"

Hanna passed her hands over her hair, self-soothing. Life in a broken mirror, shattered and refracted—

"—it clear," he was saying. "Nothing logical, nothing to teach—not any of what you'd call facts. Half of what I think I know, I think I made up. I was Lise's age when they took me away. Maybe younger. It was thirty years ago. The language—nothing. Not a word."

Her hands settled on her chest, to ease the constriction round her heart. So they were not only going to Gadrah in defiance of sane judgment, they were going without anyone who knew anything about the place, not even Michael, unless Henrik did.

She said, "It's all there."

"I don't know what you mean . . ." He had turned away.

"Everything gets stored," she said. "No memory is completely lost. D'neeran mindhealers are trained to retrieve what seems forgotten. I myself, when it was necessary to find what I knew about the People of Zeig-Daru that I did not remember, was linked with a healer. It didn't work—but that's because the People are—different. And had done certain things no human had heard of, to ensure it wouldn't work. Otherwise I have never known it to fail."

"There are no healers here."

"I'm not a healer. But I'm an Adept, as a healer must be."

"Meaning?"

"It's the trance that makes it possible."

She had told him about the satya trance, how she had used it on the *Avalon*. Slowly he looked around. "A useful thing, that trance . . ."

His voice was low and rough. He was shaken with hope.

"I could take you into it with me. Do you want to do it?"

He was silent for some time. Hanna did not press him. She knew that between the moment of decision and the moment of action, it was sometimes necessary to stand for a little on the brink, to possess for a minute longer the freedom to retreat.

He said, "When can we start?"

* * *

They lay on Michael's bed, side by side and relaxed. The room was almost dark.

They had not said anything since taking this position. From that point onward Michael had been more vividly aware of Hanna's personality than at any time before. There had been telepathic contacts like this every day, but they had been fleeting, like a word or a touch or a smile. Now it was as though she uncovered a hidden light. He had thought it would feel like a current flowing between them, but it did not. It was not even like Hanna's hallucinations. Those had been full of movement, rapid changes, a kaleidoscope of memories; this was very still. The only word he could think of to describe it was *there-ness*, and what was there was Hanna.

He knew she had begun to enter the trance, though in an odd way, as if it were not a goal to be reached but already in existence, needing only to be acknowledged; as if getting to it were not a matter of trying, but the relinquishing of effort.

It did not seem very potent. It did not seem strong enough to draw him back through the years, past the barrier of darkness. But suggestions flowed from Hanna, instructions to let go, to float, to drift back and back . . .

We will begin at the ending . . .

Even in trance, he revolted.

Let go. Let go. The beginning, then. Back. Back. And look. What do you see?

The meadow was misty with the distance of years. But flowers grew in it.

Focus.

White flowers. The stamens brushed with velvety gold, petals defined by lines finer than a hair in pink shading to lavender.

And focus.

The soft colors filled his vision. The shapes were new as each heartbeat, older than his life. The plants were tall, their slender stems bending gently in the wind. Long slim serrated leaves, bumpy and a little sticky. *The sap is toxic. I remember.*

Good. Good.

He looked up and the mist was gone. The sky was cloudless, the sun high. Mountains rose to his left, toward the east; westward the land sloped more gently to the valley with its cluster of barns and cottages set on a great stretch of cultivated fields. The vision was clear as the crystalline air. It was real, and surrounded him; the taste of herbal wine filled his mouth. The smell, the dazzling sunlight of a summer day that would never end as long as Michael lived, thrust at him and wounded him; even before the scene was fully formed he sank to his knees on the turf, clutching his belly with a crazy conviction that he had been opened and his insides would fall out. Hanna's soft hands held him together until the transition was over. The feeling passed. He sighed and lifted his eyes to the summer.

"A long summer," Hanna said at his side.

"All the summers everyplace else—summer's always seemed short. I know why, now. They were longer here."

"I see," said her thought: impersonal. Remote.

The air was pure, untainted by a few lazy columns of smoke that rose from the valley floor. Down there a broad river meandered across the basin, folding in on itself in convoluted curves, but the meadow was so high that the forest stretched out on every side looked, from this altitude, more like thick bumpy fabric on the cushions of the mountains, or like thick moss, than what it was.

He said, remembering, "I used to think, if you could jump off the mountain, you'd bounce." And he looked at his shadow and it shrank, because for a moment he was a boy.

Hanna turned for the valley. He followed, not walking so much as floating. At the top of the first steep slope, he paused. The desire to stay in the radiant meadow, where it was safe, was almost unconquerable.

Hanna waited for him at the edge of the meadow. She did not speak or even make a gesture of encouragement. He waited in suspense to find out what he would decide. Then he slipped over the edge.

The end of the meadow turned precipitously into an

acute drop, and they slid and scrambled down and down into the forest. The world changed. The trees which had looked to be all of a piece were individuals now. He had not seen trees like them anywhere else. The stems did not grow to great girth, and the branches were sinuous arms that reached for the sky and, through each day, stretched toward the sun in its path, so that in the morning all the forest seemed to lean one way, and in the evening another

Down and down he went, Hanna following easily. What difficulties could there be in this journey they made only in thought? Yet the descent was a strange blend of past and present. There were drops that had been heart-stopping thrills for a boy, and he felt the ghost of that old challenge when he took them, but now they scarcely stretched his long legs. At steppingstone rocks across a chattering stream he stopped to gauge the leap—and then walked over, crossing the gap easily, accepting adulthood and the passage of years, even though nothing had changed. Invisible bird-things called in the quiet of the day. That was the only sound; there was not even wind to stir the trees, and nothing made by man crossed the sky. He took Hanna along trails made by wild things near the little stream, and the trails were just as they had been thirty years before. The peace of the place sank into him. It might have been the morning of creation here, before any strife or evil was made.

Soon they were close to the foot of the mountain. They could not possibly have come so far so rapidly. But trancetime was not realtime.

From a rock ledge they looked down on a pool in the stream, the first pool of any size they had seen. Michael dropped cross-legged on the ledge and smiled at the water. He said, "It's good to swim in. But cold!"

They stayed by the water for a long time. The sun did not move. *A useful thing, that trance.* The music of the invisible birds blended with the song of the water, and never altered. Hanna noticed; she said, "It doesn't change because it's not real. None of this is real."

"It's real somewhere."

"In you."

''It's always been there,'' he said smiling. He was back where all smiles had begun.

Hanna said, ''We must move on to the village.''

There was a burst of cold wind. He said quickly, ''No. We can't. It's a long way. I'm tired.''

She said objectively, ''That is a lie. You half-know yourself that you lie. You are not tired.''

He said after a pause, ''I'm afraid.''

''That is the truth.''

Without warning it was twilight. The shadows under the trees were impenetrable; the bird-things stopped singing, and there were ominous rustles deep in the wood. He looked downstream, steeling himself to go on.

Hanna said, ''Not today.''

''Are you sure?'' he said, although he was relieved.

''I'm sure. Hold my hand. We're coming out of it.''

* * *

Now the star of Uskos was indistinguishable from others in its field. The *Golden Girl's* journey of some one hundred days was begun. Hanna had taken a longer voyage, she had spent a full year on the exploration ship *Endeavor*; but the *Endeavor* had not covered nearly so great a distance. There was nothing slow and patient about this. *GeeGee's* course would be essentially parabolic: straight to Omega, where she would veer up and in not toward the heart of human space but toward Heartworld, and not even directly for that world itself but for the equivalent of Omega in that sector, another endpoint. Only it was not an end, not for the *Avalon* or for the *Golden Girl* either. Like Omega, the end had become a starting place.

They had come from summer, but all *GeeGee's* chronometers said bewilderingly that it was midwinter. Midwinter in Standard time, midwinter at Polity Admin—

Hanna stood in Control and looked at the chronometers. She had left Admin more or less at the season she now left Ell, escaping winter once more. Where was

Gadrah in its orbit? What would the season be where *GeeGee* landed? Where would she land?

When she asked him, Michael said, "I don't know."

"Do you think there's a landing program included with the course?"

"There isn't. There's orbital compensation based on Standard chronology, though. The usual thing."

"*GeeGee* could work out the year length from that, anyway."

"She did." He smiled up at Hanna's surprised face. "Shen and I did it last night while you were asleep. Jumped the data through every ring we could think of. It's a singleton—"

"What?" The rarity surprised her.

"—and the star's hotter than Sol, but Gadrah's not as far out as you'd expect. The year's only about twice Standard length."

It would make for well defined seasons. Hanna said so.

"They're long, all right. But there's not much axial tilt, and the orbit's more regular than most," he said.

"That would modify the extremes, then. What an odd place, Mike. A singleton? A clear shot in, no gas giants, no big gravity wells, nothing to worry about?"

"But a lot of junk," he said. "A lot of junk! Rocks. Ice. Comets. Lots of comets. There's a warning in the program: most orbits unknown."

"Then how—we can't Jump through it, can we?"

"No. Realspace and radar."

"The best natural defenses I've ever heard of." She was baffled. "Why did they go in in the first place? The original expedition, I mean. Why did they choose that direction, anyhow, when space was open everywhere?"

He leaned back in his place. His brown hands, very dark from the Uskosian sun, rested quietly on the console. He said, "I did a lot of research at one time. I think I know where that expedition originated. I think I know who led it. I know the colonists' names on the manifest—my ancestors' names—but I don't know why they went where they went. The records don't say that."

"You never told me that. Wait."

She was suddenly on overload. She took the seat next to him and put her head down on the console just as he had done a few nights before when Gadrah looked back at him from *GeeGee's* displays.

"What is it?" he said; a comforting hand touched her back.

She said without lifting her head, "Was this what you were going to try to find on your own? After you left the rest of us on D'neera?"

"Yes. It would have been a disaster. This is one of the regions where I thought it could be, but it wasn't the one I'd picked. I guessed wrong."

"Oh, God."

She kept her face on her folded arms. It would have been a flight with no end, certain death because of the wrong guess. Hanna shivered, and he rubbed her back.

He said, "Maybe I'll find out more there."

"Surely. Yes." She straightened. There was another question. It was enormous; she did not see how she could have overlooked it even for a few days.

She said, "Starr said to me once that if you got to Alta from a Lost World, it couldn't be considered lost. It's not lost. That man knows about it, that B. How?"

"I don't know. I mean to find out."

* * *

Stone. Twilight.

The figure at Hanna's side wavered; took courage from her detachment, and stood firm. The scene became lighter. A dusty, unpaved track wound away among a cluster of structures. All were black in the scanty light, but hardly darker than the sky. Water sounded faintly nearby, a river near at hand, but otherwise the night was silent, with no sound of wind or insect or night-hunting beast. Hanna squinted at the shadowy buildings. They were well made, and did not look as primitive as she had expected them to be. Stone kept them cool in summer, kept the fires' warmth inside in winter. Wells tapped the abundant groundwater. The building stones fit together well, without gaps.

"Craftsmen here," she murmured.

"It was all here before I was born."

He didn't know how he had known that. He sweated with the effort to remember, though there was no heat in the dim light.

"We need light . . . a fire?" she said. "On a hearth?"

"Oh, not fire!"

"All right. All right—"

For an instant it seemed that he vanished. It was not good to let go of trance too quickly, but Hanna did it, falling into the intense, brief confusion that accompanied the wrench. When she came out of that, too, she was leaning over him. She kissed him and lay touching him for a long time. He was calm again. But there was an aching loneliness on the other side of the dark.

She said, "I think remembering is even more important than I thought."

"Why?"

"If you don't do it now, how will it be if you get there and it happens all at once?"

"Oh, but—" He turned his face away from her. It was a gesture she was beginning to know. But he would always turn back again. *Cut out your heart and show it to me*, she would say with each step toward the past. And each time she said it he would wince and turn away. And then turn back, and do it as well as he could. But it was going to take longer than she had thought.

* * *

Everything took longer. Hanna had expected Henrik to appear within a day or two, driven by the need for human contact. He did not seem to need it or want it. He slipped out of his room in the middle of *GeeGee's* nights and raided the galley, usually when Shen was in Control and everyone else was asleep. Hanna ran into him once or twice and he glared at her with hatred. Her liking for him did not increase. In the face of the unexpected difficulty in prying information from Michael, she thought of starting in on Henrik. That would be

much simpler than recovering the deeply buried dead.
Michael slept poorly, there were bad dreams, he was
tired—and they had hardly begun, the trip was only a
week old, what would happen to him before the end?
Maybe they would have to stop the travels in Michael's
mind, maybe the dark years would have to stay dark. If
so there would be plenty of time to work on Henrik, to
take the practical approach (as Hanna thought of it) to
foreknowledge of Gadrah—for she had started to doubt
the practicality of what she so cruelly attempted to do
with Michael.

* * *

*Try flowers again. Show me flowers. In the dark, if
necessary.*

And it was very dark. Twilight here always? Couldn't
have been.

It wasn't—

Then he remembered: *Light in the dark like a moon
I'd never heard of, never seen—*

Something glimmered at the edge of sight. It waxed
brighter and brighter, and exuberant radiance, clumps
of light climbing fences, stones, stone walls, exuding a
sweet perfume. Flowers. Flowers that shone in the dark.

The wraith beside him asked questions. He didn't
know the answers. But his heart trembled with the
beauty of the flowers.

"It only happened a few days out of the year. I
couldn't have seen it more than a few times."

"Evidently it made an impression."

He felt a great gratitude for her objectivity. It was
like having a sound wall at your back. The light of the
flowers was cold, and objects near the largest clusters
cast shadows.

"Are they cultivated?" said Hanna's wraith.

"In a way. Casually."

*Not cut till they go to seed. So they'll grow again.
Sometimes we barter the seeds—*

"For what?"

"Cloth. Metal. Things we didn't make ourselves—"

A burst of light crawled up the side of the nearest cottage. He looked at it. Hanna took his arm and said, "Home. I know."

He tried to repeat the word, but it died on his tongue. Nonetheless he moved inexorably toward the structure, not walking but effortlessly gliding, as in a dream.

"Where are the people?" she said, but he couldn't think about that.

He tried to stop at the door but slid through it. They were inside. It was very dark.

"Did it happen in the summer?" she asked. "What you said once? When they noticed you?"

"No. It was at the end, the end of—"

Everything: the bronze ceiling of the *Golden Girl* met his eyes, but he plunged back into the dark. There was a shelf . . . Here . . . He reached upward from habit—habit!—then remembered he was tall. His shadow-hands fell on familiar shapes. An old, old ritual asserted itself. He did not have to think about it.

There was light. Hanna blinked at the small metal lamp in his hands.

"Was that made here?"

"No. No metalworking here. Other places."

"What does it burn?"

"Animal fats."

"How did you light it?"

"Flint."

She was an uncomprehending savage. How did she think you started a fire, anyway?

"Laser matches," she said.

Outside the radius of lamplight the dark was thick. Michael walked into the shadow, hands spilling light. The familiar outlines around him settled into some pattern they had worn into his soul long before, a poignant fit that overpowered for a while the prospect of pain. Hanna wanted information, he could give her some now, while he remembered: "The Post is a twelve-day journey on foot. But at the Post they have machines. They can come here in a day, in the atoes they use."

"Atoes . . ."

A picture formed: wheeled vehicles, self-propelled

and nearly silent. He had never known how they were powered. Now he guessed, from the vantage of the present. Or the future: "Electric, I think." *Willow manufacture. At Newtown, the Spectator works—*

The prick of astonishment at what his present self knew threatened to balloon. Hanna said, "Don't think about it. Do they have aircraft?"

"I never saw one. No, only one. But it was a space-craft—"

The light wavered. Something started to grow, snow and fire; he would run. Hanna said, calming him, "The atoes. How many did they have?"

He was silent. She felt the effort he made, and then he answered: "I saw maybe a dozen altogether."

"And the population? And the size of the Post?" she said, because now, she knew, they talked of the Post.

"I don't know—"

"Here, then?" She let him retreat; the village was safer. "Do you know how many people were here?"

"Ninety? Eighty-five?" *Births. A death—*

Instinctively she steered away from the death. "You must have been related to all of them."

"No. I wasn't. Mirrah and Pavah, they used to live somewhere else. They came here to get away—"

The circle of light expanded. They had been pacing through the dark without being able to see anything; now some things were visible. The stone walls had an air of friendliness and safety, the austerity of the interior a grace counterpointing the lush summer outside. The stone was very clean. It had been polished to a warm glow with sand. There were furnishings well made from the region's light wood, each component made of strips bound together for strength. He saw a simple chair with double vision. One: an old friend. Two: a folk artifact, a collector's piece. Rugs braided by dark slender hands. A spray of dried flowers bright in black hair. And here in the deep well of a window cut through stone, a doll, his mother's treasure, the head of crudely glazed ceramic, the body stuffed with rag. And here: the picture she had sewn from colored scraps—

* * *

—borrowed a steel needle from Padma, she'd lost her own. A crowd of tiny figures. "They don't look much like people," I said, teasing her; she was different that spring, soft and round, and bigger day by day. There weren't many children born there, they'd thought I was all they'd have. Now here was another coming. They were happy, and I was, too.

The work pinned in the heavy frame Pavah had made was so bright the colors jumped out. "Look, Mikki, look at the gown this one wears, just like the color of the sky. Oh, if I could make it shiny, like the gown was! If I could show you how it was! And the stones the great lady wore round her neck!"

"Where, Mirrah?"

"At the Post, before you were born."

"I didn't know you'd been to the Post."

Her fingers moved quick and nervous; they were worn, but they looked just like mine. "I don't like to talk about it, Mikki."

"Why?"

She laughed at all my "why's," she always laughed, but she answered when she could. That time she didn't laugh. Her eyes weren't like mine, I had Pavah's eyes, hers were dark, she hid things in them—

* * *

It was full night again, this was Hanna at his side, her hand on his arm in reality and in dream. She said softly, "Was Mirrah her name?"

"No. No. It just means, Mother—"

He longed deeply for the *Golden Girl*.

There were voices outside. The people of the place were coming back. But he could not face them yet.

* * *

The flute was silent and neglected. Michael slept during much of the day to make up for the sleep he did not get at night. He rarely remembered the dreams that woke him each night, once with a scream. Hanna talked of ending the experiment. It was going too slowly, she said. For every day when she saw a mountainside or a stone house clearly, there were two or three when he could not or would not go farther into the dark, when he stood on the edge of it and the light would not come and there were no words in the sounds of the voices there, though he came closer and closer to giving them names, closer to knowing what they said. In the nights, after the dreams woke him and left him unable to sleep, he roamed *GeeGee*. Sometimes he met Henrik. He told Henrik what he knew about their destination, what he could remember, hoping to jar Henrik into speech. But Henrik only grunted. There was no doubt that he was sane. Nor did he seem to be afraid any more. Hanna, when Michael told her about those one-sided conversations, said Henrik was angry.

"You can tell from what I say?"

"I can tell without that. I feel him sometimes."

"I guess that's better than the way he was. Sometimes when I talk to him he seems, oh—I don't know. Satisfied."

"Satisfied? Do you tell him how much it hurts to do what you're doing?"

"I think it shows, when I talk about it."

"So he's satisfied. Because you're suffering?"

"That would be my guess."

"Ugh. Let's stop it. For a while, anyway."

"We're not going fast enough as it is. We could get there before I remember anything useful."

"Oh, crazy man—!" Hanna did not know she echoed Shen.

"Not as crazy as I'm likely to get."

"I know. I know. I know."

Hanna did not walk through Michael's memories any more, she only stood at the edge of them and watched—

* * *

—Pavah didn't talk much more than Mirrah did. He had a smile—I see it in mirrors sometimes. He talked some about space. Told me the sun was a star, showed me other stars, what you could see. Said we were on a planet, told me there were more, with people on them, he said . . .

The night Carmina came, he talked then. Anittas the midwife shooed us out when the pains got close together. We both kissed Mirrah before we went and I was scared. The animals, I'd seen animals get born, this wasn't the same. And Mirrah who always knew what to do was helpless, there was no way to stop this, no way to hurry or change it. But she wasn't scared; just busy, working hard.

We went to sit in Firmin's house. Other men kept the vigil, too, while the women stayed with Mirrah. They drank ale, Pavah let me have some, and he and all the others, they treated me different that night, more like a man. Pavah I could tell was listening, I did, too, but you couldn't hear anything through the stone. I didn't listen much to the talk of crops and herds, but after a while they started in on Otto, Otto who slipped away whenever he could to Sutherland where Marlie lived. "Your turn next," they said.

"I remember," Ugo said, "when Otto couldn't see it; couldn't see bringing children into the world. I told him then a girl would change his mind."

"I still don't know it's a good idea," Otto said.

"Maybe not in the east," Firmin said. "Here it's different."

"Only as long as they let us be," Otto said.

"What could they want with us? Some grain sometimes; they're better off letting us alone."

"So far," Pavah said, trying to hear through stone. "No reason to think it'll change. But I didn't like what I saw, when I went east two years ago."

Pavah was what they called the outside man. When there was business with another town, he did it; all the towns had somebody like that. So he usually was the first to get news.

"What did you see?" Abram said. The others all knew, Abram must have known, too, but he was old, sometimes he forgot things, though his fingers never forgot a tune the old fiddle had known. It was there that night between his feet, ready to celebrate.

"Orchards dying, for one thing," Pavah said. "And at Sutherland last summer, Joan, you know, went east to negotiate a new harvest machine. She got it without much need to bargain—because, she said, the blight's spread to the grain, they don't need all the machines they have, there's nothing for them to do."

"It's nothing to do with us," Ugo said. "That's far away."

"They're finally converting," Pavah said. "The native varieties are resistant, that's true. But when the conversion's complete, then what? Native strains follow the seasons, like you'd expect. One crop a year. With the imports they get three. Now they've gone over there's a third as much food. Stockpiles don't last forever. They'll run short. Then what?"

I never heard the answer; there was a stirring at the door and Abram's daughter Padma came in smiling.

"A girl," she said to Pavah. "Pretty as her mother, healthy, too. They're both well."

Pavah's face lit up. "Let's go see your sister, Mikki," he said. We went out, the other men trailed out, too, Abram with his fiddle, and the music followed us to where Mirrah suckled Carmina. She didn't look pretty to me, all purple and squashed! But it was a good night all the same. After a while I went out where the music was and danced, we all danced half the night. We lit a fire for dancing, but later it died, there was light enough from the flowers and the sky was alive, the arc of the Ring looked close enough to touch and the fires Pavah said were burning stones flew from end to end of the sky, even the moons looked solid not just points of light running, running, and Abram made me recite all their names. And before I went to sleep I saw Carmina again, she and Mirrah and Pavah were all asleep together and I thought: when I was born it was like this, too. And now it's all of us together and this funny-looking babe is part of us. I'm somebody's brother. She's their daughter. My sister. Ours.

* * *

Remembering was hard work, draining. When something came out of him it stayed out, and not by itself, but surrounded by a net of related memories to be examined one by one. Sometimes they triggered other things, details like electrical shocks. He could begin to sketch an outline for Hanna. The villages like a string of jewels at the base of the mountains—

* * *

"—Croft to Dunhill to Sutherland and then south," the peddler said. "Not last year, though. Not last year."

Mirrah hefted a skillet, testing its weight with her fragile wrist. Carmina on her shoulder babbled and peered around with bright bright eyes.

"Where were you last year?"

"East of here. A long way east."

Mirrah laid the skillet in the midsummer dust. She'd heard the new sound in his voice. So had I. Mirrah wasn't going to say any more and I didn't know what to ask. The other women, they were bolder. They got him to say it: Fairfield. He didn't try to hold out, didn't want to—he said: "Fairfield. I was at Fairfield."

It was quieter. The women still handled the cloth and the pots. There was a ring they handed round, it had red stones, Otto came later and bought it for Marlie, for when they married. The women kept looking at the ring. Their minds weren't on it, though. They started to use the kind of talk grown-ups used, not like they didn't want children to understand, it was just that there was so much they didn't have to say, things they knew and kids didn't. They looked grim. Most everybody that day was in the fields, just a few old women were there when the peddler came over the dusty road, not really a road, a dirt track. And Mirrah and me; I'd been sick.

"Fairfield's still there," he said. "But it's not what it was. Half the able-bodied men gone."

"Dead," someone said.

"Who knows? They took them away in the night, the ones they didn't kill on the square the first day—"

"Mikki," Mirrah said, "go look in the cart. Look for the knives."

I didn't want to go, he'd be there a couple of days, there was no hurry.

But Mirrah pushed me away, toward the cart. "You'll be trapping with Pavah, come winter. You'll need a good knife. Go look. Go look!"

* * *

Another night, this one arbitrary, a night in space. They all ran together, all the nights, the lamps of the flowers, warm summer nights in Ell, the storm with the lighting flaring, Ree with rain lashing the window-panes, night after night on the *Golden Girl*—

Michael's head lay in Hanna's lap. Her hands were soft on his face and scarcely moved.

"Tell me the beginning," said her soft voice.

The beginning was in *GeeGee's* memory, but he did not need to refer to it. He said, "The Hobbes Settlement Corporation was founded in the year 2398 by Richard Hobbes and Thomas Shadhili. Hobbes lived in the former nation of United States, in Namerica. I couldn't trace Shadhili. There was a list of nineteen hundred and four investors. Counting whole families, they represented maybe eight thousand people. The philosophical basis of the venture was isolationist. You know what Earth was like then."

Hanna said guiltily, "Refresh my memory."

"Taxes were high everywhere, higher than any time anywhere on Earth, to support the new colonies. These people had money. They hated the taxes. And the idea of the Polity was in the air. This was before the Plague Years, which was when the idea of a central authority— what turned into the Polity—really took hold. But it was coming, and it wasn't a popular idea. The people who signed up with Hobbes and Shadhili, they didn't want to be around when it happened. They didn't want their descendants to be around. That was one of the reasons for the whole Explosion. One of the many reasons.''

"Yes. I knew that," she said with some complacency. ''And then?''

''They thought it out well. They equipped the expedition well. But they needed a labor force, so they took twenty thousand other people with them, people who couldn't afford to invest, who were indigent, as far as I could tell. Desperate people. They called it, the investors called it, benevolence. I never ran across any criticism of it. Maybe there wasn't any. There was too much going on then, too much to criticize, too much even to keep up with. What were twenty thousand people, with the millions pouring out? But I've seen the manifests. If you read between the lines, look at the names, look at the places of origin, you can see where the labor force came from. The places that developed last, mostly. The people with dark skin. In Croft—''

It was the first time he had used the name of the village, and it stopped him. After a minute he said, ''In Croft, almost everybody was darker than Pavah and me—''

He stopped again, suddenly. Then he said in a different voice, ''Why?''

Her hands moved on his face. ''There must have been mingling, over the years. On D'neera we're all more or less brown.''

He stored the question, let it drop.

''There isn't much more. They left. Nobody ever heard of them again. As far as I know.''

''Somebody did.''

Hanna tried to match it up with his memories in the dark. The pieces did not quite fit. Time had nibbled away the edges on both sides. But it was possible to make a first approximation of what had happened.

''There was a distinct class system from the start,'' she said. ''Did they know where they were going?''

''Only in the most general way, I think. Remember: there was a wave of optimism all through the Explosion. The universe was full of Earths, they thought. It is, I guess. They're just harder to find than it seemed at first.

The prospectus just said, they'd establish a settlement
on a planet where a high quality of life could reasonably
be expected to be maintained. It said which direction
they'd take, but it didn't spot any candidates, and anybody who read it, I think, would assume they never
meant to go as far as they did. But maybe they meant
to all along, meant to disappear, meant to sever the
connection from the start. Or maybe they didn't. Maybe
it happened later, for some other reason.''

They were silent. She bent to kiss his forehead. He
was drifting away again. Remembering—

* * *

—Otto was distracted that harvest time, but happy all
the time. Otto had a harvest of his own on the way.

''They'd best hurry up and marry,'' Mirrah said, but
nobody could take time for a wedding during harvest,
not in Croft or Sutherland either. It didn't much matter;
the ribald teasing was just the same as it would be if
they'd married before starting the baby, the only difference was that Marlie hadn't left her mother's house yet,
still lived in Sutherland instead of in Croft with Otto.
Even at harvest the men found time to work on building
Otto's house. The women through the summer, when
the peddlers came around, had bought household goods
for Marlie as well as for themselves; now they sorted
through outgrown infants' gear, sewed soft blankets.
Mirrah had a special reason to be pleased; Carmina
would have a playmate almost her own age.

Marlie held out till after harvest, but only just. The
day before the wedding half of Croft packed up and
went to Sutherland, oxen pulling the carts. It was a fine
day, we left early in the morning when the nip of fall
was sharp in the air and frost made the grasses by the
roadside sparkle, and the stubble in the fields was bright
as broken glass. Later it got warm; we sang all the way.
Otto wanted to walk, but they made him ride in the cart.
''You need to rest up,'' they said. I didn't ride either; I
ran ahead with Pehr, we had contests throwing stones.
He was older than me and he always won, but I thought

I would be bigger than him someday, Pavah was a big man. In Sutherland there was a feast that started as soon as we got there. Marlie was as big around as the oxen, she was a little thing and now she looked just like a ball. Otto shouted when he saw her and picked her up, grunting, though even carrying the baby she couldn't have been heavy; she beat at his shoulders to make him put her down, big rough Otto who'd had this silly grin on his face ever since he started courting Marlie.

"I'll never act that dumb," Pehr whispered in my ear, but then I caught him looking at Ader, Joan's girl; I hadn't seen her for half a year, and she wasn't the same little kid any more.

It went on all night and half the next day. There was plenty of food and plenty of ale and drink made from the sweet berries that grew along the river. Abram had come riding in a cart with his fiddle. Sutherland had a piper, Kimon his name was; he played with Abram and I fell in love with the pipe. He let me use it a little, and when he saw how much I wanted it, he said he'd make me one. People came in and out all night, they'd sleep for a while in someone's house and then come back to eat and drink and dance and talk some more. Toward morning it got quiet; more people had gone out to sleep for good. Mirrah and Carmina went to Joan's and went to bed, but Pavah and I stayed up. I was sleepy, but I didn't want to miss anything. The talk was softer, Abram dozed off in a corner with the fiddle on his knees, and I sat by Pavah and tried to keep awake while he talked with Ugo and Joan and Elot. Joan did for Sutherland what Pavah did for Croft, carried on outside business. Elot her husband did what Ugo did, organized work in the fields, settled disagreements; it was Elot who'd marry Otto and Marlie next day. In the middle of the night it was cold outside. Inside the moothall— bigger than Croft's, Sutherland had more people—it was warm, there were three big hearths and fires burned in all of them. The ale went around, but Joan talked about a man who'd come to Sutherland from the Post in one of the metal wagons that ran by themselves. Nobody laughed any more. She didn't like what he'd come for, didn't like what he'd said.

"As if we'd want to move to the flats!" she said.

"Why did he bring it up?" Ugo said.

"He said more farmland has to be cleared, they've got to get more under cultivation than they've had."

"There's not enough of us to make a difference," Ugo said.

But Joan said, "They've more machines there. You can cover six times as much ground, ten times, maybe more."

"We called a moot," Elot said. "Even in the middle of harvest we met on it. Nobody wants to go."

Ugo asked, "Did he say anything about Croft?"

"He said he'd been other places, had more to go to," Joan said. "Told me plenty of people were going. I said, then what do you need us for? He didn't answer, he looked angry, I think he'd lied. I don't think people in other towns wanted to go either."

Pavah hadn't said anything. Joan said, "You're quiet, Alek."

"Too much ale," he said, though that was a lie; his hands were steady as they always were.

We split up and went off to sleep then. Next day after the wedding, after more eating and drinking and dancing, we carried Otto and Marlie home, Marlie with her bulk in a cart and Otto walking alongside, proud as one of his own bullocks. A few days after that Ugo called us to the moothall, he talked about what he'd heard from Joan and Elot. Everybody had already heard about it and their minds were made up, they didn't want to go anywhere. If the man came to Croft from the Post, Pavah would tell him that. Pavah was quiet then, too. We walked home in a light snowfall, the first of the autumn, Pavah and Mirrah and me. I carried Carmina; she couldn't walk yet, though she pulled herself up on anything handy, fences, furniture, legs; she didn't really talk yet either, but she knew how to say "Mirrah" and "Pavah" and got "Mikki" almost right.

Mirrah said to Pavah, "I thought you'd speak the thoughts you've been thinking."

"Why frighten them? Nobody likes to think of the worst. Why frighten friends and neighbors, when nothing's happened yet, and may not happen? The Post has sent no one here, nor back to Sutherland either; Joan said she'll send a message if that happens."

I was getting older, they talked to me sometimes like I was grown up, so I said, "What are you talking about?"

Pavah said, "If they need more people in the fields near the Post, what's to stop them from using force? How much good would it do to say we won't go?"

"They wouldn't have anyplace to put us," I said.

"There aren't many of us," he said.

"Everybody in Croft? And Sutherland, too?"

"That's not many people," he said, smiling. "There's more people at the Post than you can imagine, and room for all of them."

"Barracks," Mirrah said softly.

"What's that?" I said.

"Big, big buildings where everybody lives all together."

She and Pavah looked at each other over my head. She said strongly, "I don't want to go back to that, Alek."

They'd been walking with me between them, but Pavah moved around so that he was in the middle, one arm around Mirrah, the other on my shoulder; only he lifted his hand to muss Carmina's hair. The snow floated down; the long winter was almost here. But the barns were heavy with grain, the smokehouses with meat, the cellars and stone barrels with the gardens' and orchards' yield. We wouldn't be hungry, there was nothing to fear, there had never been anything to fear so I didn't know how to be afraid of a guess, a dim threat, something that was just in my father's mind—

* * *

Night in the middle of the day. Light enough elsewhere on *GeeGee*, but dark in Michael's room. Head on Hanna's lap again. She stroked his face and worried, she would make herself sick with worry. It seemed to her that Michael was dissolving, breaking up into pieces and floating away.

He was unaware of her anxiety. All he felt was the softness under his head; he might have taken root. Those soft soft hands on his cheeks: part of his own flesh.

"Not as primitive as all that," the soft voice said.

"How do you get that?"

"They speak of machines with accuracy and without fear. They distinguish between native crops and imports. Your father told you of other planets, other people; do they know that's where they came from? And the imports? And the machines?"

He struggled to remember. "It's all so far away," he said.

"Well, did they think the machines were made at the Post?"

"Some were. But—no. They thought others had always been there. A finite number. That the Post was a great treasure house, and the masters released from it what they would, gave us what they wanted to give."

"How do you know this, Mikhail? Is it something you were told?"

"Maybe." He was certain that he had spoken truth, and it was the first thing he had been sure of that did not come from the relived past of the trance, but from some store of general knowledge.

"The beasts that pulled the carts—you called them oxen, but they weren't. Were they native?"

"I guess so. I think so. Yes. They must have been. Sometimes they were hard to manage. We were careful about breeding. It must have gone back years, breeding to make them docile."

"So isolated," she murmured. "So terribly isolated."

"But it was good." His eyes stung. "Is it bad to be isolated? When life is so good? The peace."

"It made you too vulnerable. The community, I mean. Tell me about the relocation," she said.

After a minute he turned his head to press his cheek

against Hanna's flesh. "I can't," he said. He was dizzy with the effort of remembering—or the fear of it.

"We must know."

"Why? If we only go to what used to be Croft, if I only look at it and leave—"

"Oh, Michael, Michael . . ." There were tears in her voice. "Can you be satisfied with that? Did all of them die, without exception?"

"I don't suppose so—" His hand tightened on her knee.

"Your baby sister?"

He whispered, "I don't know."

"What did she look like, Mike?"

"Dark," he said, "and round, with my eyes, Pavah's eyes. Maybe she's dead. Maybe they killed her, too."

Now his voice was high and tight, his shoulders tense with held-back tears. She said with compassion, "We can stop. Do what you just said: go look at Croft, and leave."

"Without word? I see now what you meant. Can I be there, where Carmina might be, without trying to find out? We'll have to go on," he said, and knew as he said it that there had never been a choice from the beginning. If he had thought so, he had only been deceiving himself. He moved in the dark and drew an uneven breath. He felt Hanna's warmth under his head, and the soft hands, but suddenly their touch was nervous and uncertain; she felt what he felt, the abyss trembling beneath him once more, only now it was going to crack wide open.

"Mike—?"

Not even her hands could hold him up anymore. He took hold of them and pulled her down beside him, smiling in the dark. She said his name uneasily and he kissed her to quiet her, caressed her mechanically, forgot who she was; she was rigid and doubting, but he forgot to care. On the edge of annihilation he had no room to care about anything except one primal act that had nothing to do with mind or even being human, but with living forever in the face of death. Maybe she understood, because she let him do what he wanted, did

not protest or push him away, even though at the end
he forgot himself altogether and drove into her so violently that she cried out, more startled than hurt. When
the spasm was over, he lifted his head and was full of
fear as a moment before of desire, a man lost and un-
made. He looked into Hanna's eyes and knew how
greatly he was loved; but knew also that Hanna saw a
stranger, no one she had ever known before.

On the edge of the precipice he said, "What's happening to me?"—and let go and plummeted down and
down, and did not hear her start to cry.

Theo, finding Lise in tears one morning, extracted
from her the admission that she was lonely for Michael,
decided that he would talk to Michael, and set off to
find him. But at the door to Michael's room he hesitated; probably both Michael and Hanna were asleep.
While he waited, unwilling to ring, the door opened
anyhow. Hanna had sensed his presence and his wish;
she stood blocking the door and looking at Theo with
hard weary eyes. She had not been asleep. The room
was dark, however, and Michael was an unmoving lump
on the bed up against the wall of stars.

"You can't talk to him now," Hanna said.

"When?" He was exasperated; Hanna was a usurper,
she had no right to tell him when he could or could not
see Michael.

The short, soft dialogue had waked Michael, though,
and behind Hanna he sat up and said, voice dragging,
"What is it? What's wrong?"

Theo started forward. Hanna after a moment stood
aside. It had seemed that she might not; he was desperately uneasy.

"I have to talk to you about Lise," he said.

"All right." A light came on. Michael blinked in it,
half-dazed. He looked so tired and tense that Theo was
shocked.

He hid it as best he could and explained his errand.
Michael listened, but it was not the old Michael; only
half his attention was in this room; he met Theo's eyes
only once or twice, and his gaze was bleared. At the

end there was a silence. Theo was going to ask if Michael had heard, had understood, but then Michael said, "I can't do anything about it."

It was a wounding blow, but Theo did not know that at once because he could not believe that what it sounded like was what Michael really meant. He said, "You don't have to *do* anything. Just spend a little time with her."

"I can't," Michael said, not looking at Theo. "I don't have anything left."

Theo turned without another word and started out. Hanna still waited by the door. He said tightly, "Now I want to talk to you."

She said indifferently, "All right."

"Not here."

"All right."

She followed him out and shut the door. There was no further sound from inside the room. Theo said, shaking with anger, "What are you doing to him?"

"He's doing it to himself. And to me."

"What is it? What is it, then?"

"Memory." An odd expression flickered across her face. If this had been anybody but Hanna, he would have thought it was helplessness.

"Why don't you stop it? Does he want to go on?"

"Sometimes he does. Sometimes he doesn't. Sometimes I want to stop. Sometimes I don't. What I want doesn't matter anyway. He doesn't need the trance any more, he doesn't need me. He's half in it all the time. What do you want me to do? I can't do anything."

Theo began to pound the wall with his fist, slowly and not very hard, though he wanted to strike hard enough to put his hand through it. Hanna must know how angry he was, but she watched him impassively, indifferently.

"You have to stop him," Theo said. "Can't you see what it's doing to him?"

She said, "I see it. But he believes he is being made whole. It cannot happen without great pain. But he is grateful. Even in his pain he is grateful."

"Gratitude for pain—there are words for that. Sick

words. Why can't you let him be what he was?'' Theo spoke with anguish. "You loved what he was."

"What he was?'' she said. "It was an artificial construct. Not wholly. He could not have made himself what he was without a foundation. But he did not remember the foundation. Now he does. Having remembered so much he will remember the ending: all the grief. It will get worse before it gets better.''

"You're both crazy,'' Theo said, convinced of it. "I don't know who got crazy first, but you spend all your time in each other's heads and you've both got it. You make Henrik look good. I'm not going to let you keep doing it.''

"I would stop him. If I could. If he would."

There was that look again; now he was sure it was helplessness, that Hanna had lost control of the situation.

He cursed her for starting it. "I'll stop him, then,'' he said.

"How?'' said Hanna. Her eyes and voice were empty of feeling.

He did not know. Possibilities of violence and treachery went through his mind. But he knew that Hanna saw them, and his own thoughts sickened him.

Hanna turned her back on him and went into Michael's room without speaking. Theo, with nothing else left to do, returned to Lise and consoled her as well as he could.

* * *

—the man who came from the Post at the end of fall, he had the lightest skin I'd ever seen—

(Michael had begun to tremble, his face was slick with sweat, his whole body soaked.

"No,'' Hanna said. "No. Come out of it.''

He wouldn't. He had learned more from Hanna than either of them had thought he could at the start. He could stay in this state without her, and he would not come out.

—came to our house, it was Pavah he had to talk to.

Greeted him as if they knew each other, "Alex" he called Pavah, Pavah must have dealt with him before. There were two other men in the wagon outside. They got out and walked around, stamping their feet to keep warm. But there wasn't anything for them to see, it was a cold day and most everybody was inside, those who hadn't been had gone in when they saw the wagon come. It was long as our house, much too big for three men, but most of it was made to carry goods. The man who came in, I never heard what he was called. They met in the room at the front of the house, and Mirrah took Carmina to another room and they stayed there, Mirrah not saying anything; but Pavah didn't send me to join them.

The man didn't talk very long. It was the same thing Joan had said. They needed to open up more land, they needed farmers to work it. It didn't sound so bad. There was money to be made, the man said; there would be gold. Croft never had much of that, only from grain we sold outside the village, passing through so many hands that not much gold filtered back.

"Who would own the land?" Pavah said.

"Who owns it here? No one. Everyone. What's the difference?"

"It's a good life here," Pavah said.

"No difference," the man said. "Maybe better for you, as middleman. You've got the blood. That could make it profitable for you."

"It never did me much good before. It doesn't matter; it's Croft I speak for. And Croft's decided. We have no wish to go. We will not go."

"Winter's hard here," the man said. "You spend it cutting wood just to keep warm. In the east there are easier ways."

"I know," Pavah said. "I smell it sometimes. But only in bad dreams. Give me woodsmoke. Keep the gas."

In the other room Carmina began to cry. She hardly ever did that, and not for long; she'd wanted to come to Pavah, most likely, and Mirrah had held her back. I heard Mirrah talking to her, getting her interested in

something else, and the crying stopped. The man said,
"You've another, then? Felicitations, Alex. Another fine
son? Will this one take your place when you're gone?
Who'll speak for Croft when you're gone?"

There was something in his face I didn't understand,
but Pavah did. Something else came into Pavah's eyes,
it took a minute to see what it was, I'd seen him angry
so seldom.

"You're a fool if you think it matters who you deal
with," he said. "I tell you I speak for Croft. Not only
for myself, though my neighbors' wishes are mine, too.
We knew you'd been to Sutherland. We decided what to
say if you came here. Now you've heard what we say.
Be on your way."

"I would see Lillin first, with your permission," said
the man; he meant Mirrah.

"I do not tell her who she may see. If she wanted to
see you, she would come out. You've outstayed your
welcome. This is my house. I'm master here. I bid you
go."

The man left then, saying nothing. I thought Pavah
had driven him out, and I was proud. But when the
wagon had gone and Mirrah came out, Pavah said, "He
went too quietly," and Mirrah whispered, "Yes.
Why?"

"I must go to Sutherland," Pavah said.

"Now, Alek?"

"As soon as we've met. To carry the news to Joan
and Elot, to see if he's been there and what he said."

And so we all went to the moothall, and there was
worry enough but no one knew what to do, except wait.
Pavah went to Sutherland, and—

                         * * *

In the silence at the end of thought, Hanna struggled
from the past in a daze. The memories had never been
so powerful before; coming back was like a great Jump
between worlds with no sense of transition. Michael had
done what Hanna had not been able to do to him: draw

her forcibly from that place of the mind. She had to
fight to sit up and speak.

"What happened?" she said, meaning what had happened there and then, not now and here.

His gaze was still fixed in that great distance. He
scarcely saw *GeeGee*, scarcely saw Hanna even though
she was directly before his eyes. She twisted her hands
together, all she could think of was the end, there must
be an end, it must come sometime. "What happened?"
she repeated, unheard; she said it over and over again.
What happened? What happened?

He heard the question finally. He was lost in the dark
and did not look at her. "I think I went with my father
to Sutherland," he said.

He was looking into a cloud. It would be easier to die
than go into it; it would be preferable; she saw how thin
he had gotten, as if looking on disaster in the first hours
after it occurs, when the mind refuses to believe that
everything has changed and things will never be as they
were.

"Went to Sutherland," she said. "What happened
there? What happened?"

"I think I never saw Croft again," he said.

For once Hanna had taken her turn in Control. At
least that was what Michael thought when he woke
alone, looked at a chronometer, and saw the time.

He sat up slowly, shaky and hungry. It had been some
time since he ate, a day or longer. He only ate when
Hanna insisted and sometimes refused food then. He
did not know what day it was; only he knew that they
had been in space a long time. He tried to remember
his last meal. And met only mist.

He sat on his bed in the dark for a long time. His
mind was not clear, but seemed more clear than it had
been; clear enough to know that it was clouded. He
remembered—a true, new memory, this—reaching for
Hanna—an hour ago? Days ago? She had pulled away.
"What's wrong?" he had said.

"Last time you hurt me—"

She had been afraid of him, in her eyes there were

recollections of the *Avalon*. He said he could not have hurt her. She insisted until he thought she had imagined it, had lost her mind, and then it seemed to him that the only firm thing in the world had collapsed and gone away from him. But then she had convinced him that it was true, that he had betrayed her trust, given her pain not pleasure, retained no slightest memory of the incident—and then he knew that he was the one who was mad, and with it a monster.

But even that was better than the other thing, than Hanna's clear sanity being lost to him, even if she could not love him any more. And certainly after that she could not. She was gone because he had hurt her (he forgot about Control); she was gone because he was a monster.

Another memory crept into his despair: Theo seeking help for Lise. He had turned Theo away, abandoned Lise. He got up quickly at the thought, and staggered at a surge of dizziness. When it cleared he was bending over cold water, splashing it on his face. He lifted his head and saw a monster in the mirror, a tragic mask, a face that had forgotten how to smile.

He got out of the room somehow and went to look for Lise. He found her in her cabin, seated at a desk with a reader before her. She looked up calmly, not at all as if she were surprised to see him.

He said, "Puss, are you all right?" His voice did not come out the way he wanted it to.

She nodded. He found a place to sit and then could not think of anything else to say. He tried to talk anyway, stammering out some apology for his neglect, but she did not let him finish.

"I know," she said. "Theo told me what you're trying to do. I know it's hard. You don't have to worry about me."

Tears of weakness blurred his eyes. It was the saddest thing he had ever heard. He was used to worrying about Lise, he was used to taking care of people, that was what he did, that was what he was. Now Lise said he should not do it. He would have to be a monster.

Lise said critically, "Have you been eating?"

He shook his head.

"I thought Hanna was taking care of you," she said. She was surprised at Hanna, she disapproved; he heard that in her voice.

He managed to say, "I can still feed myself."

"I don't think you can," Lise said. "Wait."

She slipped out. He did not have the strength to follow.

She came back with bread and butter and cheese and strong, hot tea. He ate and drank automatically. It was hard work getting the bread to his mouth at first, but he was stronger even before he finished, and the mists cleared a little more. He really had been very hungry. He could talk more easily, ask Lise about her studies. She answered with that same calmness, but came to sit beside him and drink tea from his cup, more like herself; still he thought she was subtly older, edging toward maturity.

A picture of a baby named Carmina rose up before his eyes, and he choked on a mouthful of bread. Lise pounded his back, though it wasn't necessary. He wanted to grip her in a tight embrace to keep her safe, forever safe. But he was afraid of what he might do to her. He swung toward tears again. "Where's Hanna?" he said, though she was afraid of him and did not love him any more.

"Control," Lise said.

"Yes, it's her watch."

Lise said doubtfully, "They're all Theo's now, I think, except he makes Shen stay up and do more. But he went to get Hanna. He said he needed her."

There must be something wrong. But not too badly wrong or they would have come to get him. Or would they? Why would they?

He got up and went out, followed by Lise; made it up the spiral stairs and into Control. Hanna and Theo were there, their backs to him. It was blindingly bright. There was a high, regular sound in the room, it was familiar, he ought to know what it was.

He did. It was an audible accompaniment to some contact *GeeGee* had made, carrying no information but providing certain psychological benefits for the novice in space—or for a wanderer long out of reach of human sounds.

"A relay," he said to the pair of backs, so weakly he thought they wouldn't hear him.

They did, though. Hanna said, "It's Omega. We've crossed over." She glanced around and went very still. She had not seen him in full light for two or three days. She said in an ordinary voice—but her eyes studied him sharply—"It's a complicated course from here. There's no prime route between here and where we need to go. We'll change course several times. The interpolations are complex; it will take nearly four weeks."

Four weeks were nothing to Michael who blundered through forty years. Theo also turned around; he looked at Michael narrowly and said, "We can get news now."

Michael looked at him stupidly. Theo said, "We can find out if the situation's changed. Maybe they've made new offers, public offers. At least we can find out about the mission to Uskos."

It was too much; he swayed and they came to him, Theo alerted by his face, Hanna by something more. He clutched Hanna, trying to talk. He said, or thought he said, "I'm sorry I hurt you. I'm sorry. I'm so sorry!"

"Satisfied?" Theo said to Hanna savagely, when they had got him back to bed.

"Shut up," she said.

He heard Theo say he was not diseased and talk about what had been done for Henrik. He put out a hand and got hold of Theo's wrist. He was weak, for a man not diseased, but it was not that his body had failed him; rather, the air here, in the present, was a thick liquid hard to push through.

But he did not have to talk. Hanna translated to Theo what he thought.

"He doesn't want to be drugged like Henrik was."

"Am I supposed to just stand here and watch this happen?"

"It has a natural course."

Somehow, through Hanna, he felt Theo's incredulity.

Hanna's voice. "I don't say that. He says it. He says: let him finish."

They argued. In the end Theo won; won something. Michael knew that because he felt Theo inject something into his arm. Maybe it was supposed to connect him with some kind of reality.

He felt it begin to work. And saw reality, all right, only not the one Theo had wanted him to have.

The sense of Theo's presence faded. But Hanna's was strong.

Stop it, she said to him, *stop!*

He wouldn't; he couldn't. Hanna could not know the favor she had done him, opening the past; nor Theo just now with the stuff he had forced into Michael's veins. He saw like an open door the gate of trance Hanna had shown him long before.

Don't do it. Stop—

* * *

—walking in the dark morning, the days were shorter, we left before dawn to reach Sutherland by dark. Bitter cold but we were warm enough with movement and furs. We'd eaten before we left, hot cakes Mirrah baked on the hearth; we had more packed away for mid-day, and meat, fresh-cooked for a journey of only a day and that in the cold; but I always pitied the little caged animals killed for meat, I couldn't do it, couldn't slash the small furred throats, though Pavah said it had to be done, I'd have to learn to do it, praying maybe in apology as many did acknowledging kinship; but he'd never made me do it. *Time enough* he said— Cheese Mirrah had sent, fruit from the winter store, water and strong wine, till Pavah laughed and groaned: "You'll kill us of surfeit, woman! It's only lunch we want!"

"It's hard walking on an empty stomach," she had said. "To be warm you need to eat."

For a long time we talked little, warming with the walking and the rising sun. We did not speak of the

Post till almost midday. And Pavah would have said nothing had I not asked, and when I did it was no great question; only, "What do we do at Sutherland, Pavah?"

"Tell them what happened," he said. "Find if they've thoughts on it."

"How much thinking can there be?" I said.

"Thoughts of resistance, perhaps. There might be some. But it would be folly."

"Why?" I said. "Would it be like Fairfield?" But Fairfield wasn't real to me, it was only a name.

"You heard of that? Of course you did," he said, answering himself. "Croft's small, we all hear each what the others hear."

"I don't know what they did at Fairfield," I said. "I heard of killing, but how? There are strong men in Croft and Sutherland; Fairfield must have had strong men, too."

"With no weapons but hunters' knives," he said, "or woodsmen's axes."

"Hunters have bows, too, and spears."

"That's not what I speak of." We walked on in silence. I did not break it; I knew he would speak again. He said, "It's time you knew of such things. I thought to wait till you were older, but you grow fast. And maybe you'll age faster still, if—"

He didn't go on from "if"; he started over. "They've weapons that shoot projectiles that pierce to the heart, fired by a burning powder. They've weapons that pour out a light that burns. Those I've seen, in the hunts in the forests beyond the Post. And I've heard of a weapon that seemingly does nothing at all, except when it's pointed at a man, he dies. That I've not seen. Nor have I seen another thing they talk of, a weapon that stops and crumples man in a step, though later he wakes unharmed. It might be true. It might not."

"The hunts you saw, was it when you went to the Post for Croft?" I said, but I knew it was not.

"They were before you even were, before your Mirrah and I married; when we lived there."

"What did you do there? How did you come away?"

"We were servants of the masters, Lillin and I. It

was a hard life, though not as hard as some. When I came to know Lillin, I asked permission to leave, to go away west of the mountains, and it was granted.''

"That doesn't sound so bad," I said.

"Well, you ought to know this; maybe you'll need to know it one day. That's not something that happens often, a servant permitted to leave. To leave without permission is against the law. A man can be punished for it, or a woman; they can even be killed. But they let me go because I was an embarrassment.''

He grinned, his teeth white as cloud in the winter sky.

"Why an embarrassment?" I said.

"These eyes. Yours and mine and Carmina's. My mirrah, your grandmother you never knew, was a servant, too, and a pretty thing. A son of a master's house took a liking to her. I was the result. These are known eyes, one family's eyes, though they've spread through intermarriage. When you see them, you know whose blood runs in the veins. And you see them in the fields and factories, too; but they were willing enough to get them out of the house. And so we were allowed to leave. We had to leave behind all we had, though; came to Croft with the clothes on our backs.''

I understood about the eyes, all right, having worked with breeding stock since I could walk, but I didn't know what it all meant. He wouldn't talk about it any more; after a while I stopped asking questions.

Then in the afternoon we came to Sutherland. It lay behind a hill, else we'd have seen the trouble before it was too late; but men stepped out of a grove at the side of the road. They wore clothes like the men who'd been to Croft, and they carried things in their hands they pointed at us.

Pavah stopped and pushed me behind him, all in a moment. I didn't want to hide behind his back, but he wanted me there, it was hard to know what I should do. He said a few words to them, and they to him; he told them we weren't of Sutherland; they told us to go on, we were Sutherlanders now. And we went on; because I knew without asking what the things were the men carried, they were weapons like Pavah had told me about, and the men watched us.

When we came around the hill, I saw the streets of Sutherland were full of more of the metal wagons than I'd ever seen before, ever imagined there could be. People were carrying things into the wagons, furniture, clothes, household goods: the houses were being emptied. "So it's come," Pavah said.

The Postmen went away but there were others everywhere, all with weapons, they watched us with the others. Then Joan saw us and came to us. She'd been crying, and by the time she got to us she was crying again. "Alek, you shouldn't have come," she said.

Between sobs she told him how they'd come in the wagons in the morning, made the people come together, told them what to do. While she talked, I looked around and saw many people weeping, but they kept on anyway, carrying things to the wagons.

Pavah said, "Has there been resistance?"

"In the first hours, and two men dead." She named them; one was Kimon. "Since then, no one. We think of Fairfield. But I was nearly the third. I was nearly the third."

"How was that?" Pavah said.

She stopped crying, still too angry for tears. "One of them put his hands on Ader. He put his hands on her. And I screamed at him and went to kill him, but an officer stopped him, stopped me. 'There'll be none of that,' he said, and the animal went away. Alek, there'll be nothing left. They said they'll come back for the stores and the herds."

"Have they said anything about Croft?" he asked.

"It's next, they said."

Elot came up then; Joan cried and he held her and patted her shoulders, though he was heavy with grief. Pavah started helping the people load their goods, and I did what he did. It was late, the dark began to come; he looked around to make sure none of the Postmen were near and said, "I have to get back to Croft. I must tell them what's coming, tell them not to resist."

I said hotly, "We're to go like oxen where we're driven?"

"Where's there to run to, in winter? They'd be on us in a day. You haven't seen the guns fired yet, Mikhail, but you heard Joan: two men dead. Otto'd be the first to go in Croft, I think."

"When will we go?" I said.

"Soon, in the dusk. Listen. There's a risk. If I don't get clean away at once, they'll shoot. I have to carry back word, I have to be with Mirrah, but you don't. We'll all be taken to the same place. Stay with Joan, and we'll find each other when we get where they take us."

"I don't want to stay," I said.

"But I want you to," he said, and dropped what he was carrying and hugged me hard for a long time. I wanted to cry, but I was too old for that.

"I love you," he said. And he didn't have to go back to Croft at all; only he couldn't bear Mirrah's being without him.

When it was dark, he edged to the edge of the light and then took off, fleet of foot. He underestimated the range of the guns, I think. While a little light still caught him they fired, one, two, three—I think all three bullets found him. He was dead when he hit the ground, he was dead when I got to him, and one of them fired at me, too, but he missed and the others stopped him, knowing I wouldn't run far, only to him. I threw myself on him and cried and cried until Joan came and made me leave him—

* * *

Michael cried for an hour together, without shame or restraint. Hanna held him in the dark and cried, too. He said, "I could have run the other way, gone first, distracted them, they might not have seen him in time, they might have missed."

"Michael, Mikhail, don't say that, no. He did what you would have done in his place."

"If I had, if I had—"

"There was nothing you could do. There was nothing you could do! It would not have changed anything."

"But he—"

"—did what he had to do. Hush, my love. Hush."

As if he had crossed some dreadful threshold and, having crossed it, was stronger, Michael surprised Hanna by making a partial recovery. Sometimes he was much like himself; was himself. Turned up in Control at his scheduled hours, turned questions aside, took over the running of his ship with relief at its prosaic demands as if he visited another country and was glad for the escape. He was much quieter than before. And whenever he slipped away into the half-trance half-dream, Hanna always knew at once, even if she were as far away from him as it was possible to get on the *Golden Girl*. She went with him each time, flying to his side—

* * *

—two days in the damn metal wagons, crowded among the weeping women, a shrieking baby or two. There was hardly air for breath. An old man died and was taken away—for burial the Postmen said but I think not, I think his bones lie scattered still beside the road. His old wife cried all the second day, rocked back and forth in misery. Joan tried to take care of me, stayed at my side until then, but the old woman was her aunt, her dead mother's sister, and needed her, no, needed more than Joan could ever give; but she left me with Ader. We wriggled to a corner and kept it. In the dark Ader gave me what comfort she could; did Joan know? And look the other way? Thinking, the boy's our own kind, a good boy, Alek's son? I was too young but near old enough; did Joan think Ader a mother at, what, fourteen?—would be safer that way? And then we came to the forests flatter than the river valley, old seabed it must have been, the sea not far they said, and under the topsoil, sand. The wind blew all the time. Sea level: summers were longer there, I heard. All the same in winter it was dusted with snow, but mud squelched underfoot after morning frosts. Flocks of waterfowl darkened the sky and the sky was big with no mountains to close it in. Only forest.

Joan found Mirrah right away. Wouldn't let me see her at first; told her about Pavah so I needn't. I don't know how she told her, what words she used. Then Mirrah had to see me, was frantic to see me, as if I were dead, too, until she did. I'd never seen her cry before. Shaking with despair in the night, and Carmina cried, too, not knowing why. And I wanted to protect them to save them, but it was too late, was already done.

They made me stay in one of the men's buildings, there were six of them, nor was everyone in them from Sutherland or Croft. Altogether in ten great barracks there were fifteen hundred men and boys; in twelve more, somewhat a greater number of women and girls, and the smallest children regardless of sex. Families met in the cold evenings but only outdoors when the day's quota of trees was felled and the smoke of their burning made a reek round the camp. The land was more barren each day, each day they marched us farther away. There was great unhappiness, but not much fear. There would be towns, they promised; when the land was cleared, before the spring working of the soil began, families would be reunited, a town would be built, everything would be as it had been before only in a different place, there would be machines so the land could be farmed. They took from each barracks a few men or women and took them to the Post, showed them our herds, our goods stored away, waiting for us; they gave us back our own food to eat. We believed them. Why not? What else was there to believe?

Face sooty from the smoke, arms aching from the ax, I worked. If all Croft had been in my work party and barracks, or Croft and Sutherland together, we might have pretended to be a town. But they separated us, I was with few I knew and many I didn't, and we were all part of broken things, split and dazed. I heard that Otto and Marlie with their baby boy, they met secretly and walked away one night, out in the cold; were followed, caught, brought back; that was all. Just brought back. "So they mean us no harm," the men said. But Otto had a strong back, was valuable—

* * *

Morning, Michael's watch, but Hanna went to Control instead. She had left Michael sleeping after a night in a winter of exile. He was tired as if all night he had really wielded an ax. When she went into Control, she found Henrik. He did not hear her come in.

"Good morning," she said.

He jumped, a violent movement; turned an animal's face to her. His guilt rolled over her like an ocean wave. She gaped. "What the hell are you doing?"

"Nothing," he lied.

He gathered himself for some effort, and she braced herself, amazed and half-afraid. But he only rushed past her, out of the chamber, and she heard him skidding down the spiral stair.

She went to the seat he had left and tried to see what he had been doing. He had wiped the display with a single touch, probably the instant he heard her voice, but he had forgotten to cancel command mode, and there were indicators she could read. He had been preparing to transmit a call from the *Golden Girl*; to whom it was directed she could not tell. He had not made it, though. She had come in time to prevent it.

Not wanting to leave Control unattended, she used internal communications to call Theo. He was not in his quarters, but she found him with Lise. "Come up here," she said.

He came at once, worried.

"Henrik was trying to call out," she said.

"Who to?"

"I don't know. Who could he call? He doesn't have anybody out there. But he doesn't want to be here, he wants us to stop; he must have been trying to reach the Polity."

"We have to make sure he can't. I don't want to lock him up. Can you fix it so *GeeGee* won't transmit without out a code we all know but him?"

"Easily."

"Something easy to remember, but something he won't guess."

She used her birth-name, Bassanio, as the code. Theo said when she was done, "Why did you call me and not Mike?"

She blinked at him. "Mike's no good for anything," she said.

He did not say anything, he only looked at her, stunned. The implication was that he, Theo, *was* good for something. He hadn't thought that anyone but Mike would ever think that.

* * *

—noise all the time, the axes' thud, the crackle of the fires. A man stumbled and cut off part of his foot; they took him away. He didn't come back. Weeks later we heard he'd bled to death. It wasn't bad, not too bad. Except. A man from Honiton which I'd never heard of till that winter, he'd been there longer building barracks through the fall, one day he put down the ax. "I'm a free man. I won't do this any more," he said. Firmin said, "Think you'd better." Firmin, thank God, was in my barracks, he tried to stay close to me. The other man said, "What's going to happen? We'll see."

After a while the Postmen came, they were never far away, some always in sight. Tried persuasion. Moved to threats. Consulted with each other. Called reinforcements. And beat him. At first there was a move to help him, but they stood in a ring with their guns pointing out, fired once all at once into the air and we stood there. Trying not to watch. I saw tears on Firmin's face. They left the man bleeding in the sharp hard mud, left him to lie there all day, in the middle of the circle of guns. They didn't care if he froze to death, but he didn't. At night they let us carry him back and he groaned all night, breathing hard. In the morning they took him away. He came back in a week or two, but his face didn't look the same, that was why they sent him back,

I think, so we'd see him every day and remember. He worked, he never tried to stop again. None of us did—

* * *

Hanna started to have dreams of water. The lake at D'vornan shrouded in autumn fogs, the slow river that rolled through City Koroth; most often the sea at Serewind, where she had grown up. Maybe it was just because she was in space, where every gram of moist vapor was reclaimed and recycled. But sometimes it seemed to her that the sounds of water came to her from Michael's dreams. Sometimes behind his words, behind, even, those memories that had come fully into the light, there was the gray light of a distant sea. And meanwhile he lived half on Gadrah and half here; saw Hanna sometimes clearly, sometimes dimly as a ghost.

One day—they were more than halfway to Heartworld sector, measured in time and not by the twists of their convoluted course—she tried again to help him, to use distance and cool logic to interpret that other world he saw:

"A policy of deliberate terror." Her hands moved on his face. "They fed you well enough, with your own confiscated stores, yes? Housed you warmly. Keeping the labor force healthy. But they split families up, communities. Retaliated harshly at the first sign of rebellion."

"But you can't call it terror, not really. If you did what you were supposed to do nothing happened."

"They weren't capricious, then."

"Not that."

She leaned over him, her hands light and nervous. *Gray water meets gray sky somewhere out there.* He reached up; the graceful fingers touched her face, traced her features as if he were blind and sought to see her.

"I hurt you," he said.

She shrugged. "I could have stopped you. With force, if I'd wanted. But it wouldn't have taken that. Talking would have done it."

"Why did you let me do it?"

She shrugged again. He realized that she had never said it, not once in all the months had she said the most dangerous word her heart could conceive. But she sank down beside him, found his mouth: a cool drink of fresh water. *Salt air on a salt cold wind.*

"I love you," he said. "I want to marry you. I want to have children with you. I want to live with you all our lives."

Hanna said when she got her voice back, "That covers a lot of territory."

"All right. I know it's scary."

"I can't answer. I can't decide."

"My timing might be a little off, I admit—"

So the laughter was coming back and he was becoming himself again. Even if it was not quite the same self—

* * *

—and Georg came one day round the middle of the day while we ate, not in the big building where we took it in shifts morning and night, a hundred men at a time and less talk than you'd think because their minds were on the little time there'd be later to seek out those they loved before the lights were extinguished in the cold and the cold dark closed in; no, it was daytime, he came to the dead forest supposed to turn into fields by spring, where the midday meal was carried round by trucks. Women and old men from the barracks served the food—not Mirrah—she'd gotten herself assigned with the women who looked after the young children all day, so she could be with Carmina. There was nothing she could do to be more with me; we met in the courtyards at night.

Ate the bread made from Croft's own good grain but there wasn't much, there was less as the days went by— they said the stores ran short but they lied, there'd been enough and to spare when we left. The Postmen stood off by the unfelled trees with their share, no greater than ours—but what did they eat at night at the Post, when the nightshift came where we were and the others went back? They got no thinner that I could see. I saw the wagon come growling and humming across the waste and paid it no heed, they came and went all the time. Saw the man who went to the Postmen and later they looked toward where I was, but I didn't know they looked at me, till one came and said, "Boy, come with me."

Cold that day, I could see my breath, I followed it to the other men, thinking they'd give me an errand, send me through the wood to another worksite where it wasn't worth driving; they'd done that before. But the Postman took me to Georg with his face like polished stone, like the flint that looked smooth even oily, but with sharp edges where it was split.

"There's room at the Post for young men like you," he said in that voice that was smooth like his face, then he said what he meant—could I dance, could I sing, play music, do magic tricks? Could I learn? Could I be taught? Had I gifts?—"It's not enough to look good," he said, and almost gave up, as he told me later. I looked so stupid, knowing nothing of what he meant.

"I'll give you a trial," he said. When I understood he meant me to go to the Post, to live there, I balked. The desert wood wasn't Croft, but I'd been there a time, Mirrah was there, Carmina, everyone I'd ever known. I had no interest in leaving, none. Not even curiosity. I only wanted to be left alone.

Still he talked, dull though he thought me. He was bored, getting cold, but thorough. He said there'd be good living at the Post, I could have gold if I did well. He asked about my mirrah and said if I were apt I could help her—and had me. I didn't know that, but maybe he did.

Firmin came to us then, and the Postmen did nothing and let him come.

"What do you say to the boy?" he said.

"I've told him of opportunities," Georg said. "He's a handsome child. If he has any gifts for pleasing, it could be well for him at the Post."

"He has none," Firmin said. "An ill-tempered, inept child," so that I looked at him in surprise, though a moment's thought told me his aim.

"Are you his father?" Georg said.

"His father's dead. But I've an interest."

"Then you shouldn't wish to keep him here. I offer a chance not many have. I heard of him in passing, through the friend of a friend. A lovely boy, they said, heard singing one night, a lullaby for a little girl. Was it your sister, boy? We'll see if anything can be made of him. If not, he'll return."

Firmin wanted to argue, but I saw the Postmen moving in. Their weapons on that gray day looked not shiny but dead. "It's all right, I want to go," I said, afraid for him—

* * *

Hanna kept her watches now, and part of Michael's, too, as he kept part of hers; her presence in Control overlapped his by a considerable margin, so that it was impossible to tell, by merely looking into Control and seeing who was there, whose watch it formally was. They talked casually and unnecessarily about *GeeGee's* workings, her faithful pursuit of the course Hanna had laid in at Omega. The worlds and stars of human space rose up on monitors, were glittering beacons for a day or two, and vanished and fell behind. Michael looked nearly himself again, stronger, more active. But that was a shell and a concealment. His body lived on *GeeGee*, and some of his mind, but only enough to make the proper motions. In front of his eyes, with the substance of reality, memory played itself out. When he lay down, he would pass not into sleep but into the trance-state Hanna had taught him, and more of the veil would be withdrawn. He no longer plunged toward it, but neither did he avoid it; it was inevitable, and he was content to let it unfold at its own pace. In these hours in Control and elsewhere on *GeeGee* when he was nominally normal and awake, what he had seen in the last hours of trance gained solidity, and took its place in the context of the whole. His mother's face had the clarity

of a fine portrait now: the liquid eyes, the black ringlets
framing the high forehead furrowed with grief. The
comforts of the *Golden Girl* faded to nothing. Cross-
legged on frozen ground swept roughly clear of snow,
in the harsh glare of light that let no one escape or be
private, he held Carmina on his lap and sang to her in
a boy's soprano, strong and clear, however, and true:

> *Baby, sleep: thy pavah watches,*
> *thy pavah with infinite care. Baby, dream:*
> *sweet dreams of pretty toys thy pavah gives thee.*
> *Baby, sleep: safe in thy pavah's hands, the night holds*
>   *only comfort for thee!*

Only sometimes his tears fell on her curly head.

And meanwhile he said quite ordinary things to
Hanna, touched her sometimes, turned his head to smile
when she touched him, gave *GeeGee* the right orders (prompted by *GeeGee* herself); at some imperceptible point the watch would cease to be officially his
and become officially Hanna's, freeing him to leave;
and finally he would go, to drift about *GeeGee* aim-
lessly as a ghost until it was time to return to his room
(as alien now as Uskos) and relive another event, another day.

Hanna left behind in Control tried to think of other
things. It was not good for her or Michael (common
sense told her, and Theo told her repeatedly) for Hanna
to permit herself to sink altogether into Michael's obsession. Theo always came early, long before it was
time for him to relieve Hanna. He planted himself solidly beside her and talked of what he had lately seen on
the 'beams, talked of Lise's studies, encouraged Lise to
wander in and out, encouraged Hanna to start the lessons promised the girl in *GeeGee's* operation; he talked
of Henrik, speculating on the traits of character or the
history that had made Henrik what he was, and on what
they might expect of him; when Hanna was more than
usually silent he talked of her work in exopsychology
(which was in *GeeGee's* library and which he had read),
misinterpreting it so outrageously that Hanna in a fury

must correct him, was forced to think of something besides Michael, which was what Theo had intended in the first place.

"You think you're keeping me sane," she said. "If you think I don't see through it, you're the one who's crazy."

"On this ship, who isn't?" Theo said. "Mike's forgotten what year he's supposed to be living in. Henrik's plotting something—I swear that's what he thinks he's doing. Shen, do you ever see Shen? No? I don't either, except when she shows up at the end of my watch. I haven't heard her talk for a week. Sometimes she grunts. You're crazy because you're crazy about Mike. And Lise and me, we've adjusted. Adjusted to all that! So we must be crazy, too."

They were silent for a time—Theo could not talk continuously for hours, he had to stop sometimes—until Hanna said, "Theo, do you ever think of scanning for messages for us? When you're here alone at night?"

Theo said, not answering the question directly—but it was an answer all the same—"We used to scan all the time. When Mike first got *GeeGee*, when we used to cruise around, trying her out, playing with her, we were always in recept mode. We kept Shoreground time so Mike and Kareem could talk a couple times a day. For a while all the calls that went to the house, we had 'em sent to *GeeGee*. My God, was it expensive. We were playing . . . In the middle of the night a couple of times, this woman who was after Mike, she'd call up half-spaced and get him out of bed and tell him what she'd like to be doing with him that very minute. He didn't know whether to laugh or cry."

Hanna's nose wrinkled with distaste. "Did she get him?"

"No, but she came close. It was a long dry spell before you came along, you know. That's why I said, sometimes he was ready to cry."

"I didn't know that. He never told me. It couldn't have been because—because there weren't candidates."

"There was never a lack of candidates. But he was funny the last year or two," Theo said thoughtfully.

"Like nobody he saw was right, not even just for fun. The last year or so before we headed out for Revenge, I don't think there was anybody. I hated it."

"*You* hated it? Why?"

"Look, pretty women have pretty friends. I was doing all right with the fallout."

He was so wistful that Hanna laughed. The lighter mood stayed with her until her watch was over, but later, when she was settled in the small lounge with a reader in her hand, the words it displayed unseen, her thoughts returned to the question she had asked Theo—the question he had not wanted to answer, as was apparent now.

A simple instruction to *GeeGee* would be enough— and she wrestled more and more with the compulsion to give it. If she did, what might she hear? What message? The Lady of Koroth, perhaps: "I beg you to come home. I will make all pathways smooth. Though you have abandoned your birthright, I have not abandoned you." Or Starr: "Do you think me too small to confess to error? I'll see to it your homecoming will be safe— yes, his, too, even his . . ."

But that is not what he wishes, she said to the imaginary voices. *He would go on, on and on to the end which was his beginning, without reference to your forgiveness or your power. Perhaps my purpose should be his. Perhaps it should remain his.*

And so she would fight her compulsion, see space go by in silence, come always closer to a place where once again the voices would be out of reach. She would listen only to the voices Michael heard—

* * *

—was so amazed by what I saw around me, that I had no more homesickness than before. I dreamed of Croft and Pavah each night, but it had been so since that day anyway. I did not know what to call the place, it was bigger than a village like Sutherland or Croft, it was only the Post, and it spread over many hectares of land there by the sea, first on the landward side a great ring of cultivated land, then a circle of factories and warehouses, then one of barracks after barracks, and then the tall white wall with the towers behind. They were not really rings, as I came to see, but half-rings, and the ends of each ended at the sea. Later, too, I came to know there was more to it than my eyes first saw. Not all the barracks were what they seemed, but some were divided into rooms where families might live together; and between those and the wall, there were houses like those I had known in Croft, and in them lived certain people who had earned the right—trusted servants of those who lived behind the wall, who performed their duties at the proper hours and afterward were permitted to leave, passing in and out unquestioned; the soldiers who watched the wall and their families; and also those like Georg, and like Alban and Kia, who took me in. But though there might be a blurring in the purposes of what I saw outside the wall, the meaning of the thing itself was clear, nor was there ever any doubt of its reason: it was to keep the multitude of those outside it, out.

Georg told me nothing more than he had already said on the first day when he carried me to Alban's house. But Kia took pity on my ignorance. She fed me, rations she said, but more than I was used to getting of late, and asked as Georg had asked if I could dance, sing, juggle, entertain? I said I didn't know, I'd never tried.

"Yet you've been heard to sing; so Georg said."

"The songs we sang in Croft," I answered.

"Well, they won't do here! Here they want songs of love, child."

"Like this?—

Pretty Rosie, bouncing Rosie,
Why do you fly so fast?
Stay a while and play a while
With me while summer lasts,
Bouncing Rosie come to play
Upon the summer grass—"

"No, no," said Kia laughing. "Listen!" And she sang in a low voice, so beautifully that I was enthralled, but slowly:

No music sounds sweet as my lover's song.
Song the sea sings to me, alas!
The sea winds have blown away his adoration,
The sea waves have washed me from his heart.
Only in the wind do I hear him sing my name.

She laughed again at my expression; I had never heard so sweet a voice.

"You're too young for that," she said. "Though your voice seems good, and if it survives changing, and your face lives up to its promise as you grow, the young ladies beyond the wall will be sighing for you in a few years' time!"

"What young ladies?" I said. "What's beyond the wall?"

"The masters," Kia said. "You've heard of the masters surely, even west of the mountains."

"I've heard of them, but I don't know what they are."

Kia looked as if she thought I might be playing a joke on her, either that or my ignorance had no limit. Finally she saw the second thing was true and explained, but either she didn't make a very good job of it or I couldn't get my thought around what she said, because still it had no sense, It was a jumble of people who were different, who were rich, who ate without working for it, who had things I'd never heard of before, who did what they liked all the time. But maybe she explained it well enough after all, because even when I learned more about it, I never learned anything to contradict what I thought she'd said.

Then Alban came home, and late though it was, when he found I'd never seen the sea he took me to it. We walked with the wind stirring round our ears through cold cobbled streets, the first I'd ever seen, always curving and curving toward the north with the wall and the soldiers' houses at our right. And there were gates in the wall, with broad roads smoothly paved with stone leading straight to them; but they were closed, and over each one was a kind of little house with windows, and Alban said there were soldiers in them. Then far off I began to hear a sound, which was sometimes like thunder and sometimes like a hiss, and at last we came around a final bulge in the wall—which was not a perfect half-circle, but in places bulged out or withdrew—and the wind struck me with a force to take my breath away, and there was a glimmer of pale sand and beyond that the sea. The foam that rolled up on the sand was luminous, and the wind took it and blew it stinging onto my face. But out past where the waves broke, out to sea, there was nothing but blackness. It was so cold I shook, though I had still the warm cloak Mirrah had made for me just before leaving Croft, laughing and exclaiming on my growth, *Soon I'll have no time for anything but making clothes for Mikki*— The salt wind brought wetness to my eyes. Alban said the sea went on forever. I had to turn my head to see light, and even the lights of the walled city were set well back from the sea, and they wavered with the wind and the blurring of my eyes. It was a bigger world than I had thought, this planet as Pavah had called it, it did not seem like a place where I might have been born.

I think Alban talked a little, but I heard nothing of what he said; not that night. When he was done talking and thought I should be done looking, he said we must go home (though it was not my home), and we walked away in the dark.

I was used to working with my hands, stockherding, stone cutting, the dirt hot on my arms with the summer sun. The tricks Georg put me up to didn't seem like work, and each day it was something different. The dancing-master made me twist, sway, wanted me to fly through the air, it seemed, and Kia made me sing; somebody they called the master of hands came once, tried to teach me an illusion or two but went away disgusted; still he told Georg there was hope for me later, when I was over the worst of my growth and the parts of my body didn't run away from each other any more. Yet the dancing-master said it was too late, while Kia said soon it would be the wrong time for my voice, though it wasn't yet. I couldn't see what they wanted with me, didn't see why they kept me there. But Kia one night while they drank wine, she and Alban and Georg and some others of the performers whose services were not needed behind the wall that night, she took my chin in her hand and turned my face to the light: ''What a waste it'd be!'' she said. Saw the question in my eyes, I think, and talked about faces and fortunes. At first it made a nonsense in my head. But I understood something before she was done: ''Such a pretty flower to bloom for the countryfolk!'' she said, and like a light breaking I knew how I looked through her eyes. It explained much, the exclaimings over me by Mirrah's friends in Sutherland each time we went there as I grew, which went back as far as I could remember; it explained a man weeping with loneliness who had approached me in the barracks one night when the lights were turned out, though my sleepiness and ignorance had turned him away; and Georg, of course, what he had heard. I pondered it while they drank, seeing that in Croft they had been used to me from birth and so no one had ever commented on how I looked, or maybe didn't really see me. I was Pavah's son, Mirrah's son, a hard worker, of easy temper and, I had been told, sweet nature, and those who knew me had not cared about my face.

Then Kia, filled with wine, began to cry. They had taken me from my mirrah, she said, and from that passed into lamenting that she had no child. Alban was silent and grim, having heard it all before. And it was then by accident that they learned what I was good for, because one of the men, Norn by name, had brought with him an instrument, and it leaned in a corner; and as Kia wept, and Alban grew sullen, and it was plain that he felt himself accused and a quarrel was brewing, I crept to the corner to get away and began to play with the instrument. Norn also wishing to escape followed me and showed me its principles. Yet it seemed that I knew them and had only to be reminded how to turn my breath into music. Norn became silent, speaking only now and then in a whisper to correct my fingering or give me some other word of advice, and I played a song Kia had taught me, and then the one she had sung on that first night, and then a song I knew from Croft. I paid no attention to the others, only to Norn's whispers, which I heard eagerly and which my breath and fingers translated without further thought. I was happy for the first time since the day of the walk to Sutherland, and more than happy, there was a wholeness I had not imagined before, nor could I name it in any way. And I was not conscious of doing or being anything remarkable, and when I looked up and saw that all of them stared at me, their eyes shining in the dim lamplight, my first thought was that I had done something wrong.

But that was not why they gaped at me, as I learned soon enough.

"Still you must learn other things," Georg said. So once a day the dancing-master came to teach me pliés, pirouettes, and other moves with outlandish names; also Kia kept teaching me songs to sing and telling me where to breathe. Norn also came a day or two to teach the flute, but then desisted. "I am afraid of doing more harm than good," he said. His place was taken by a woman named Portia, who on the first day of her coming crashed into Kia's kitchen crying, "Where is it? Where is this prodigy? I must see it!" And she was not awed as Norn had been, which was good, since I was getting a swelled head; but she listened to me play and said, "You have much to learn, boy!" And proceeded to teach, thereby earning my affection without ever doing anything else to get it. She did not need to do anything else.

So the music was consolation and I needed consoling, yes, needed it. Otherwise when the novelty of being there had worn off, when it ceased to be a visit to a new place and became each day's life, I would not have been able to bear it. Pavah since his death had visited me in dreams each night; now Mirrah came also, carrying Carmina. They smiled at me and told me what a good boy I was, a fine son whom they approved and were glad to have, which in truth was what they had always done; Mirrah was the one to say the words, but I had always known that she spoke for Pavah, too. And so now they were gone, Pavah into the gray country that has no end, and Mirrah might as well have been there, too, for all I saw of her. Yet I did hear a little from time to time, for Kia knew a captain whose men went each day to the camp, the same who had first brought me to the notice of Georg, and she got him to bring news of Mirrah, and carry news back. So I heard that she was well, and that Carmina talked now, really talked, and remembered Mikki. This helped, too; I do not know if music alone would have been enough. I think not. But together, they were enough.

Thus the end of autumn passed away and the winter came in on great storms of wind that filled the air with flying snow. There were fogs that hid even the top of the white wall if I stood at its foot and looked up; and rains that lasted three or four days and consisted of a salty soup that did not so much fall as hover, creeping into houses and garments and covering everything with damp. But there were also days when the sky leapt high and blue over my head, and the Ring was a dagger-stroke across it for the sharp-eyed to see. In fair weather or foul I went about the town as I could, though with an easier heart when the day had been light, as if the sun illuminated my soul. I was not filled with any great curiosity, no, I was incurious as I had been on the day Georg first came to the camp, a truth which was not much like me, who had explored every stone, game trail, streamlet and grove within a boy's reach around Croft; but I was drawn all the same, as if one stride led to another, though I thought I had no wish to walk on. There was little enough time for exploring, for between dancing and Kia and Portia and the lessons Portia set me I was busy all the day; but an hour or two of the dancing-master was not enough to satisfy my body, used as it was to climbing and running and rough play. The dark came early, and Kia had some notion I should not be out in the night, and I sought to obey, my own notion being that she stood in Mirrah's place, and wanted for me what Mirrah would want; but the upshot was that I found it hard to fall asleep, and my legs of their own accord would kick and twitch, seeking all on their own to run. And after some days when my eyes were half-closed with lack of rest, Portia said that she would speak to Kia; and afterward Kia said I might go out at night, providing I were home an hour before the curfew, which came about two hours before the middle of the night.

It was in the dark, then, that I roamed, learning by chance the names of the streets and alleys, and what kinds of people lived in them. In the Street of Wheelwrights an old lady took a fancy to my face and then to what I had to tell her, for she had never been away from the town and loved to hear about the mountains, here where she had only ever seen flat sand, fields, marshes: "And you have to look up to see the tops!" she said often, marveling. I found the docks from which the fishermen set forth each day, but hardly ever saw a fisherman, for their work began before dawn and was done by dusk. Still I saw one of the fishers once or twice, working by lamplight to mend a plank or a net, and he talked of the storms that might come without warning and take men, boats, and all to the bottom of the sea. And afterward I never had a bite from the sea without thinking of the brave boats going light over the ocean waves.

So through the nights of that winter, while the wind blew cold and sharp, I went around the town. There were few children, which had also been true in Croft and Sutherland, and though those of the part of the town where I lived were friendly enough, it was different among the great buildings where the greater part of the people lived. None there wanted to join my rambles, or invite me into their games, or even talk to me, once they learned where I lived and what I was to be. "We want none of the masters' garbage," one said to me, a boy of about my own age, and another called names and spat at me, and a third heaved a stone at my head. I was no fighter, and was not angry but bewildered; and Kia told me there was jealousy among the mass of people for those who were attached to the masters, and worked for them or guarded or entertained them. But the boy who had thrown the stone, he had not even heard me speak, I had not opened my mouth, and Kia looked at me considering as if about to speak; but then she turned my question away and talked of something else. But she had been looking at my eyes, and I remembered what Pavah had said on the day of his death.

"Whose eyes are these?" I said.

She considered again a longer time, so that I thought still she would not answer. But at last she said, "Saddhi."

"What does that mean?" I said.

"They are one of the great families." She waited again, but this time I saw she had more to say, so I waited, too. "We've talked of your eyes," she said. "Georg did not know when he went for you that you had them. But perhaps they'll be less conspicuous with age. Sometimes they fade."

"My pavah had them," I said. I had never spoken of Pavah there before.

"You'd best hope they're not a pass back to the fields," she said. "We've talked of hiding them."

"Hiding them? How?"

"By way of small things that are put in the eyes, smaller than this." Here she showed me the nail of her little finger. "It doesn't hurt and does no harm."

"But why must they be hidden?"

"It's this way," she said, and set out on a long and unclear explanation which she strung out so long and so confusingly, to suit her delicacy and my age, that I would have been none the wiser, except that when it was rendered out it amounted to the same thing Pavah had said—somebody might be embarrassed by the bastard in the house, or in this case the bastard's son.

Yet no one else in the barracks ever looked twice at my eyes, and though I saw none like them, I remembered what Pavah had said about their being in the factories and fields. And while I did not stop going to that other part of the town, I no longer tried to make friends, and only stood on the edges of groups of men or women and listened to their talk. Much of it was not good to hear. On one night, one night alone, I heard men talking of how rations had been cut again, and wondering what there'd be to eat by winter's end, and women talking of an illness that had swept through a building which had been sealed and remained sealed, trapping those inside. They talked also of a baby which had died, though, they said with bitterness, those behind the wall had medicines which would have saved it. And at another gathering of men I heard that the fishers were being driven to sea even in dangerous weather, and told to bring back greater and greater catches.

I learned nearly all that I learned from these walks in the night, slipping from one knot of men or women to another and seeking not to stand out; for Kia and Alban spoke of the people seldom, and slightingly, and I did not know that their feelings did not match their words, and the words were said as a concealment. But had they spoken to me freely, they could have told me only what I saw with my eyes: that the hunger was growing out there where the favored of the masters did not live, and with it sickness; and the people were not yet starving and so not in despair, but angry.

Finally there came a night of bitter cold when I was taken behind the wall. There was to be an event there, one of the gatherings that went on all year long, though more in the winter when life was confined—for the masters did not stay altogether behind the wall, I was told, and in the warm evenings of summer especially were to be seen walking in the town. And even in the winter they might go abroad, but I had never seen any of them. For this occasion Portia rehearsed me with the flute in earnest, three songs only, and simple ones, one as an accompaniment to Kia's singing. Though they were simple they were no less beautiful—only I was heartily sick of them in the end! For Portia made me play them so often that I would wake in the night with fingers moving and mouth puckered, still rehearsing. I was also required to wear a new suit of clothes of fabric so fine that the touch of a finger left a mark on it, so sensitive was the pile; and if I drew my hand across it, I shivered

at the touch. There was a great bloused tunic over a
singlet that fit close, and breeches which came only to
the knee and white stockings under that, and soft crimson boots to the ankle, hard to walk in, for there was a
stilt at each heel, which made me taller and tilted me
forward; and Kia watched me learn to walk in those
boots and laughed.

"This is harder than the music," I said, but practiced
dutifully, until I could move in the things without stumbling; because it seemed important to Kia who stood in
my mirrah's place. And nothing was the same as it had
been before, and already, first in the barracks at the
woodland camp where the wind howled and Pavah
smiled behind my closed eyes, and then in the dark
streets of the town about the Post, I had concluded,
though not without tears and struggle, that it was not
the part of a man to pine for yesterday, which seemed
senseless as wishing in autumn for spring. If winter had
come to me, then so it must be.

So dressed in my crimson boots and dressed in gold
and swathed in a cloak much less fine, for the protection
of the richer garments, I passed through the wall at last,
through one of the gates which I had never seen open,
and inside the gate there was a cobbled court where
there burned enough lights to turn the winter night into
day. But snow fell and had been falling since daylight,
and the snow stopped and dimmed the light; and the
little fires that burned in their coverings of glass melted
the snow that fell on them, and the snowmelt blurred
and ran down the glass like yellow tears, to fall on the
stones, where it froze. But I forgot the cold soon
enough; for everywhere I looked, behind that bright
wall, were so many new things that it seemed I had
been transported altogether to a new place, which had
never even heard of Croft, could not even be a part of
the Post I was coming to know.

The plain size of it astonished me at the beginning,
for the structures whose towers I had seen from the
other side of the wall were lofty indeed, and stood not
separate but connected by walkways, archways, passages and tunnels, so that it was all a single thing, yet

so large that an hour's walk might be required to go from one end of it to another, and the stones of which it was made everywhere had been carved and tormented into ornament. I glimpsed many courtyards, too, and each had its fountain (though now they held strange shapes of ice, not flowing water).

And when we had passed inside there were countless hallways, and such twists and turns and changes of direction that I was bewildered; and a kitchen that had in it a dozen cooks, who gave us mugs of a hot drink that went to my head and made me dizzy; and large rooms so full of wonders that I could hardly take anything in. There were pictures that moved and made me stare, for I thought them real at first, and then was shamed by my stupidity; there was music that came from nowhere, played on instruments I had never heard, or sung by voices like none I had heard before, and rendered in words the sense of which I could not make out, not one. There were shapes and colors like a festival wilder than any dream I had ever had (but they filled my dreams for a long time after); yet in all that riot of strange new things, one stood out, a simple thing in itself: a small table of a wood I had never seen or heard of. It seemed heavier than the woods I had known in Croft or even at the camp, and it was so dark that my eyes took it to be black; only when I looked closer, under the darkness there was light trying to get out, shifting as my eyes moved, and drawing me in with the promise of gold. And its shape was simple, a matter of curves it seemed any child could think up; but the lines together moved my heart, so that I stood and looked at it as if no other table had ever been made before, and there was no other proper shape for such a thing.

Now with looking at this thing I had fallen behind, so that Kia turning in impatience came to fetch me, and she looked at me and laughed, for tears had come to my eyes.

"It is like the music," I said, because music sometimes touched me as this object did, and Kia did not laugh when it was music that moved me.

"Be glad you have music," she answered. "It is all

you will ever have. I can show you the man who made
this, I can show you his house, and you can look all
over it without finding any such thing. He cannot keep
his own work, it is too precious; the masters send him
wood, it comes from far away, and all that he makes
with it, comes here. How else can he eat? Be glad your
gift is for music, Mikhail. It does not take as long to
make as a piece like this, and it cannot be taken away
as this can. No matter how much you make there is
music left, there is more than when you began.''

And Kia laughed again, but as if the light that rested
within the wood had put a different face on all I saw, it
was plain that her laughter was a covering for some pain
that lay within.

''If your eyes did not name your fathers, your tastes
would,'' she said.

And who might my fathers be?—the question lay on
my tongue, but I did not speak it, I knew the answer:
my fathers were also the fathers of those who held this
inner city, and it might be that a cousin of mine, of my
age, with these same eyes, lived behind the wall always
in the presence of beauty.

This thought took all my attention, so that Kia was
able to take me on through the endless halls without my
protesting, for I hardly saw where we went, and at last
we came to rest in a small room behind a figured curtain.

Here the instruments were given their final tuning,
and the singers hummed, their voices running up and
down the scales which in this place did not seem familiar but mysterious, as if we prepared for some great
event. Here also Kia told me to open my eyes, and she
held them open one by one, and put into them the objects she had told me about, which I had tried already
on the day before and so knew would not hurt me, would
only feel strange going in and then be forgotten. But I
knew, because I had looked in a mirror on the first trial,
that they made my eyes appear as black as Mirrah's.

After which, a little later, one put his head through
the curtain and nodded at Kia, and we filed through the
opening and the music began.

* * *

It was good that I had little to play; I was full of
looking that night, though what I saw did not live up to
my expectations, those having become so great, and the
greater for having no clear notion of what I was to see.
Did I think the masters would have two heads apiece?
That all their garments would be made of gold? When
they entered they were different indeed, magnificent to
my eyes. They seated themselves at a long table some
distance from the dais where the musicians were stationed, and there were jewels and fine fabrics all new
to me, and gold, yes, more gold than I had imagined
being in the whole world. And I told myself that under
all this splendor there were men and women neither
larger nor more fair than any others I had seen, and
maybe no more wise—yet they were different all the
same, and it seemed to me that the difference was this:
they had no eyes. Oh, eyes they had, and in the proper
places, but their use was reserved for each other, for
their jewels and gowns and the delicacies before them.
They did not see the musicians, no, we were invisible,
and even when those eyes strayed in our direction they
looked through us as if to the wall, and it was the same
with the men and women who served at table. And there
were more who served than who ate, so that if the musicians also were counted, and the cooks in the great
kitchen, and the Postmen who guarded the entrance
through which we had come, there might be three or
four persons who lived, on this night, only to make an
hour or two pleasant for each of these folk; and I looked
at them with attention, trying to understand why this
was.

There was one at the end of the table who would be
the host, for those who served at table deferred to him,
and to the woman at its other end; and both of these
were old, the man with white hair and a great white
beard, the woman with hair gray as the winter's cloud,
and wrinkled skin beneath the collar of jewels at her
throat. There were also several others, among them a
man who drew my eyes because of his coloring like
none I had ever seen: pale, with eyes so light I won-

dered (at that distance) if they had any color or were transparent as clear ice, and on his head a stiff brush of hair that shifted color in the candlelight and sometimes showed the hue of flame. And this man was different from the others, because he saw us; or at least he saw me, when the time for my part in the music came. Though I played well, first the two songs I had learned for unaccompanied flute, and the other with Kia's voice, there was nothing to set off this part of the music or make it special; but at the end I looked up to see that this man looked at me closely. And Kia beside me set her hand on my back, and I knew that she also had seen that he looked at me; but why that should move her to touch me, I did not know.

I was done and my reason for being there fulfilled, and I continued to listen to the players, but more to the talk at table, and especially, now, to the man who had looked at me. He spoke softly, so that it was hard to hear what he said; but soon it was evident that he was a traveler, would leave this place at some time and go on, though I did not know where there was to go.

"And how many years will pass before you come again?" asked the wife of the host, and he answered, "I cannot say. It's not that I would not come more often, as you know."

"I know," she answered, sighing. "We know what you bring is not given you as gift. But what can we do, how pay?—the mines are empty, all the workers have had to turn to the fields. A nostrum for the blight—that's what you should bring!"

"And maybe I will next time," he said. "But the difficulty lies in obtaining it without stirring the curiosity you must avoid. I'll take the samples with me, the grain, the seeds and leaves, the spoiled fruit; those are all imports, and at first look no one will see anything to surprise. And if the blight should also be imported, something lain dormant these many years, then the remedy might be easy to find. But more likely it is not. More likely it is native, something never seen there before, and the business will be harder. All you've paid me may not be enough for the bribes and the mouths to be closed.''

"Yet all we have may depend on you," said another man.

"A heavy responsibility," the traveler said. "But there is another thing I might do for you: carry word."

There was silence, but I saw them shake their heads; and the youngest of the women said, "Then we would lose all we have."

"A hard choice," the traveler said. "You know what Oversight's meddling would do; but it may be that only hunger lies at the end of the path you walk now."

All this puzzled me, and I thought I would ask Kia later what it meant, and that the time would come soon because the meal was ending—and I had wondered for some time it it ever would—there were such processions of platters, changes of plate, so many flagons of drink! And I was hungry from watching all those others eat, and also tired of sitting still, so that Kia already had whispered to me that I must not fidget. But finally it did end, and those at the table rose to go out; only the traveler did not go out right away, but turned aside to the dais where we were.

And Kia stiffened at my side when she saw that his attention was for me, though I did not know why, for there was nothing out of the way in what he said to me. He wanted to know my name and age, and how long I had been among the players, and why he had not seen me before; and also, when he learned that I had only this season come to the town, he asked whether I liked it there. Then he gave me a coin and went out (so it was true what Georg had said, I could get gold here); but when I looked at Kia she was breathing hard and quick, and I saw that she was angry.

Now the servants of the house began to clear away the remains of the feast, and I understood from some words that passed that we were to return to the kitchens, and find a place in our bellies for whatever good things might be left. But Kia's anger burst forth, so that as we walked to the kitchens I saw nothing, but only listened to Kia; and she talked of the traveler, warning me against him.

"I will speak to the Mistress Ehr," she said. "I will not have it happen, what might happen!"

But one of the players said, "They all have their toys, Kia. You said nothing to Coro when the Saddhi lad attached her to his house, nor to Yav when the Mistress Conneril's husband lost his powers and she looked about and Yav took her eyes."

"Coro was not a child, and Yav was a full-grown man," Kia answered. "Such things happen; how would they not, when we live by favor of men like the Saddhi lad, and women like the Mistress Conneril? But this man Tistou is another thing. Well, maybe he will bring a remedy for the blight and maybe not—and maybe when he comes again, he will not find what he expects."

Then she said she would not bring me behind the wall again until the traveler Tistou was gone, so that he should not see me and be reminded of me. But it came upon me that I had understood nothing that night, nothing but the music which my very bones understood; and my ignorance made me sad and weary, and it took all the good tidbits the cooks could give me to cheer me again.

Now I ceased to go to the greater town, for the nights were even colder than before, and it was more pleasant to do my roaming in the streets by the wall, where I knew many and had only to rap on a door at the need to get warm. In this way, too, I met Kia's neighbors, and soon I saw that these neighbors were of two sorts, and divided by the way in which Kia talked with them, or before them. With most all her talk was small gossip of the neighborhood, of the scarcity of food in the marketplace, and other matters such as these. But with some she talked with passion of the greater town, and there were conferences from which I was excluded, and sent to stand outside the door shivering and warn Kia if anyone approached; and when this happened, then like masks the faces of those inside would change, and when the newcomer entered the talk again would be unimportant. I begged Kia to tell me the reason for these strange proceedings, but she would not tell me. So I was left to guess, and my guesses brought me no comfort; and often at night after one of these conferences, I would dream of Pavah again, and not as if he visited me with smiles; no, I would see him run, hear the guns, see him fall, and wake with a cold fist clutching the heart in my chest.

Now, what Kia would not tell me, I thought to find out in another way, and for this purpose attached myself to one of those who shared her secrets, a man called Leren who lived some distance away, but still in the closer ring. But there was more than purpose in the companionship that sprang up between us, for Leren took to me and I to him, and all the more because he reminded me of Otto in his plain blunt ways, though in stature and face they were nothing like.

This Leren was a single man, black-bearded and young, and was a handyman for the upkeep of that beyond the wall, all parts of which he knew well, though to me it was a mystery. He had a tale to tell of a summer's day when he pointed the stones of that city's highest tower, where only a scarce skyfowl might come once a year, it was so high above the waters where the seabirds found their meals; and on that day he looked out to the edge of the sea where it curved to the world's other side, the wind tearing his beard, dizzy with the sun and alone above the Post, and saw it spread small at his feet. He had a tale also of a maiden who did not acknowledge his presence at her window, where he had come to mend a casement, and whom he watched as she removed her garments, supple as a fish and white as the silver band of the Ring on a cloudless night in spring—this tale he told with humor, swearing that he had seen her eyes shift at the start toward where he stood, and wondering how she would have greeted him, had he come in. He had many stories like these and I listened to them all, and listened also to the men who came to drink ale by his fire, for the speech here was less guarded. They said that each day there were more deaths in the town, and the masters heeded them not and were sleek and fat and did no rationing for themselves, but only ordered it for others. There was anger among these men, who talked of the guardhouses over the gates like men who had studied them well. And though they said no word of plans before me, still it was plain there was a plan; for they spoke of the traveler as well, and there was something they wished to do, but would not do until he was gone, and it worried them that he tarried.

"If the sickness takes us first, there will be no hope," they said.

"It is the old for the most part so far," Leren said, and though he was a noisy man full of loud laughter, his voice was soft and sad.

"And babes," said another man, "and those already sick from some other cause: the weak. But the strong will begin dying soon."

"The masters will sicken of it, too," said still another, a man named Willem.

"They will not," said a fourth man. "He brings them medicines, the man Tistou."

"The undying," Willem said, and spat into the fire.

"No one is undying," Leren said.

"He came in my grandfather's time," Willem said. "And I have grown from child to man, and seen him at the start and end of that time, and he has not changed one jot. Where he comes from, things are different. Who knows what is possible there?"

The others said, "We have heard that he comes from the other side of the world. It might be worth seeking that side."

Leren laughed and said, "So you believe that story? They want us to believe it; they do not want us to think far. Other places! The one that spawned him is farther away than you can imagine. The sons of the masters admit it, when the time is right. There are things they will say in secret to one of their own age, swearing him to silence, which they are not supposed to tell. But some say also that this is not the man who came when our grandfathers were young. This Tistou had a grandfather, too.''

''I would not care what he had,'' Willem said, ''if he would take the flying machine and go away. We cannot fight that. But when he comes again, I will see him dead.''

''Some father will kill him someday,'' Leren said, ''or a mother holding onto her child with one hand and a knife with the other.''

Here Willem looked at me with thoughtful eyes and said, ''Animals can be trapped. Maybe we have the bait to trap that one, if we are willing to use it.''

But Leren laughed out loud and said, ''Only if you wish to die, too, by Kia's hand!'' And they spoke of it no more.

Now for a time I ceased to go to Leren's house, because something happened that drove everything else from my mind. Kia, and the captain of the Postmen who went to the camp, did a great kindness for me; and one day when a light snow fell, a wagon of the Postmen stopped at our door, and from it came Mirrah, Carmina clinging to her. I did not know how Kia had done it, what promises or payments she had made, or what might have passed between her and the captain then or another time. She would not say, she would not tell me when the excess of my joy was spent and I could ask questions. But I did not spend a long time asking them. How this thing had come about was nothing next to Mirrah's presence, though she was not the Mirrah of all my years before, but a woman who did not smile, not even at my teasing. Yet I saw in her tears at our meeting that being with me lifted a great care from her soul, and in her way of looking at me, that in me she had all of Pavah she would ever have again. She did not speak of him, though a time had come when I wanted to talk of him, but I saw that I must wait. And so I let words go, and instead made music for her, sitting at her feet for hours at a time with no sound to be heard except the crackle of the fire, and the wind moaning outside, and the melodies I made with my flute.

Yet this peace did not last long. The rumors of sickness grew more and more loud, until it seemed like the ocean tide rising over the town, and one day the Postmen came from door to door, shouting and giving orders, and saying that beginning on the next day, no man would be allowed to leave his house, not even to take his needs and his money to the marketplace, but rations of fish and grain would be taken from house to house; and also the servants of the masters would be locked behind the wall, so they might not carry contagion with passing back and forth. And when Kia heard this she said she must go to the market at once, and Mirrah went with her; and when they had gone, and I thought of confinement ahead, I ran out the door to have freedom while I could.

I went to Leren's without thought, my feet slipping over the cobbles in that direction from habit. And when I came to his house he was leaving it, brooding behind his beard as he closed the door. He was bound for the greater town, and at first he did not want my company. His hard hands were nervous, his eyes kept straying toward the town; I thought he had a burden on his back, but looked again, and saw that if he bore a weight it must be of the mind. "This is no stroll for pleasure!" he said, but my eagerness to follow him was great, and in the end he gave in to stop my begging.

So we set out at a quick pace, and soon left behind all the streets of small houses, and came to the first rows of giant barracks, where families lived crammed together in single rooms, and ate and bathed together in a crowd. These were a larger and permanent version of the forest camp I had come from, and I told Leren that had been worse, for here those who loved one another lived together. But Leren said I was wrong, he said it roughly; his mood that day was grim.

"It's maybe no better there," he said, "but no worse either, as you'd find soon enough if you tried living in one of those—" He pointed at a structure we passed: a heap of dirty brick with a few scant windows like clouded eyes. "There's no love in there," he said. "It dies with the crowding. Take a man and a maid young enough for the juices to flow in spite of the work: they find a way to get out of the reach of eyes, and he gets her with child. Then they get a room; it's the only way to get one, to get out of the men's barracks, or the women's. So far it's a change for the better. The child comes, and maybe it lives and maybe not, and maybe the mother lives and maybe not. There's little enough care beforehand, and she works right up to her time, unless she's sick near death. Now there's three of them there. The child gets bigger and the room gets smaller. They're tired with work and maybe the mother's mother gets too old to work, or too sick—well, the old one comes to that room, too, and the care of her is visited on the family's head. There's no quiet, no room or time for thought, and any love there might have been gets trodden underfoot until it dies. A man raises his hand 'gainst his wife, both raise their hands 'gainst the child, and maybe the poor old grandmother is beaten, too. You know nothing about it. What could you know, coming from the freedom of the fields?''

My heart shrank, and now there was no talking as we walked on, and I tried to imagine how it would have been, Pavah and Mirrah and Carmina and me all together in one tiny room, but I could not, nor could I think of Pavah striking me, I could not imagine it at all. And while I thought, we passed through the ring of barracks, not in a straight line but zigzagging toward the north, passing those places one by one and passing between pairs of them—they rose up more sheer than the mountains and were dark against the sky, which was gray with snow, and I tried not to look at them, for it seemed they might fall on me. And when at last we broke out of them, I was glad—only where we went then, was worse, for we plunged into the ring of factories and warehouses. I had never been there before, for that part of the town was silent and deserted at night, when I did my wandering; but sometimes in the days I had seen clouds of black smoke rising over it, to be blown away inland by the wind from the sea. I followed Leren in silence, my eyes being busy enough without making work for my mouth. The structures here did not all look alike; most were made of brick, but here and there was metal, and there were turrets, troughs, wires, and pipes in great variety and abundance. After its fashion it was not even ugly, but looked as if a giant had gone mad and thrown his toys about—and then set them afire, for some of these places spouted smoke. It was not beautiful, no, not that, unless there be a kind of beauty in desolation, for desolate it was: the ground was covered with grit, and nothing grew there, nor did it seem that anything could grow there again. But also it seemed that words like ''beauty'' and ''ugliness'' did not apply here, that this place was a thing in itself and like nothing else, and so could not be compared with anything.

Now Leren turned into one of these places, still moving swiftly, and we plunged into a maze of hallways and chambers, all dirty and dark; but there was no one inside, and it was silent, though I had expected the place to be filled with noise and machines and men working.

''Where is everybody?'' I asked, and Leren answered: ''Many of the factories are idle. They have little to work with; the mines were at half-strength all autumn long, and spring and summer, too. But this one has had work, until now. It was working yesterday, and there was no plan to close it.''

''What do they make here?'' I said.

''Plate,'' he said with loathing. ''Plate for the masters' tables, finer than my bread will ever see! Well, they'd best take care not to break any more; there's none new being made.''

He stood in one place and shouted a name, but no one answered his call, and the sounds of his voice echoed in the dark. ''Gordon!'' he cried out. ''Gordon! Are you here? Is anybody here?'' And at length he gave over shouting and stood silent in that dim place where I could hardly see his eyes, and I wished to ask who Gordon was, but I did not. I thought Leren had forgotten I was there. And he turned and plunged through the dark to where we had come in without a word to me, though he mumbled to himself, and once more in a frozen lane with that tangle of pipes in the sky he walked on ever faster, and I went beside him, half-running to keep up. ''The infirmary,'' he said, ''they must have taken him to the infirmary.'' And back we went into the ring of barracks, but through a part I had never seen before, until we turned down another street, at the end of which there was a structure much smaller than most, and all on one level not climbing toward the sky. I saw nothing of the place save the outer door; for a woman came out to greet us, and said the man Leren sought · was not there.

''He must be there,'' Leren said, ''he was taken ill yesterday, word came to me last night, and I would have come then, but curfew was too near.''

''There are other infirmaries,'' the woman said. Her skin was dark, but there were blacker pouches under her eyes.

''There are no others near Millside.''

''Millside?'' said the woman. ''Yes, there are men here from Millside. But none of that name, and none who came as late as yesterday.''

Leren fell silent and stared. And at length the woman made as if to turn away, but he put out his hand and said entreating her, ''What is wrong at Millside?''

She answered, ''What is wrong everywhere? They have the fever. That is all we do here now: nurse those who have it to recovery or death, and keep them isolated from all others. All the infirmaries are full. Soon the sick must go elsewhere; to the forest, I think.'' And she said that all the infirmaries, on the day before, had been ordered to turn out all who were not sick of the new fever; and they were by no means empty, but over-flowed.

''But how can they go to the forest?'' Leren said. ''Will they lie on the ground in the snow?''

''I do not know,'' the woman said, the words were slurred and indistinct, and I saw that she was desperately tired. ''There is a place, not far, where land is being cleared, and so there are places for the workers to live. It's said they may be sent there.''

''But there are people there already!'' I said, for I knew the place she meant.

The woman gave me hardly a glance. "There are people here, too," she said. "If it must burn itself out, better there than here, where there are so many more to die. As for me, I do not care where I go. All the nurses have run away, and only I and two others are left. I will die of this fever, I think. I do not care whether I die there or here."

Now Leren had wildness in his eyes. He said, "Is that where they of Millside have gone?"

"They have not," the woman said. She looked at Leren, and I saw that she would have had pity for him, had there been any pity left, but it was all burned and worn out of her. "There were too many," she said. "They brought us a sick man from Millside, then five, then fifteen. Then there was no room. We have babes here, children, mothers. I will not turn out a child so a man full of life may take its place."

But Leren had another question, only he could not ask it. I saw it tremble on his lips, but he could not get it out. And the woman looked at him with the last shard of her pity, which had come up from some unknown place, and answered it: "They have sealed Millside up. Those who live will come out."

But that was the last thing I heard her say, for Leren gave a great cry and turned and ran toward the north, I following and soon out of breath, remembering what I had heard before when a place had been sealed. On either hand the rows of brick stood up and were silent and full of pain, and what could it be like closed into those walls in the deadly air without escape?

Leren could not run forever, he had to slow, so I could, too; I walked with him panting as he panted. And when my breath returned I longed to ask who Gordon was, but I looked at Leren's face and did not; for it looked like Mirrah's on the night she learned of Pavah's death, only Leren did not cry as Mirrah had, but the pain inside was the same, the clawing and eating alive.

At last at noon (but the clouds were thickening and there were no shadows in the gray light), we came to Millside, which stood by itself at a low place in the

ground and near a frozen stream; also it was close to
the sea. And already when we first saw it, Leren slowed,
and slowed and slowed again as we came nearer, for at
each of the small mingy doors stood a man in the uniform of the guards of the Post, and they had guns like
the one which had killed Pavah. And Leren slowed still
more, like a man in a bad dream where the earth turns
to water and he cannot make his way through it; for he
knew it was no use to approach that place, but was
driven all the same. And there seemed no threat in the
Postmen who watched us come, they stood at first with
their weapons on their backs—and when, as we came
close, they took them from their backs, even then they
held them loosely in their arms. Only when we came to
a certain distance of one of them, then he gripped the
weapon more firmly, and so did those on either side of
him; then Leren stopped.

He did not speak immediately, as if he were trying
to think of what to say. He only looked at the Postman,
and the Postman looked at him. But finally he said—it
was a voice I had not heard from him before, a low
yearning voice without hope—"My brother is inside."

Now the Postmen were of many sorts, as I had found
at the camp, some being cold and others more or less
kind, within the limits of their duties, and this one
maybe was less unkind than unnerved by Leren's aspect, which was that of a man in despair—"Go," he
said, bringing up his weapon. "No one can go in. No
one can come out."

And Leren looked up at the Postman some more, and
then he lifted his eyes up the side of the building, to the
very top, as if he would see Gordon there; but no one
was there. He stood there long, looking up at the bricks
and then at the Postman and up at the bricks again,
seeking as I thought for a face at a window, but in his
misery he was dumb. And at last the Postman pointed
his gun at Leren's breast, and the memory of what I had
seen happen to Pavah took me, and I pulled at Leren's
arm and called his name, near weeping; at which he
looked at the gun for so long that I thought he contemplated taking it away. And he had made no move that

might be taken as threat, nor had any but those few words been exchanged, yet the day stretched out like a thread taut and ready to break, and others of the Postmen began to come toward us.

Then Leren walked away. He turned often to look over his shoulder until the place was out of sight and hidden by other barracks that came between, and he was silent; but after a time, as we came near his house, the tears began to run down his face and into his beard, and his shoulders shook with them. I could not comfort him, there was no comfort to give, but when finally he talked I could listen; still what he said had little to do with Gordon.

"It cannot last forever. There must be an end. There are stores enough of guns, and men to fire them, yes, willing men enough, and only a matter of getting the guns. It's talked of, did you know that? It has been talked of, there is more talk each day, even in Millside, especially there, and close to the wall and even behind it, too. It started at Millside. It started there. But if Millside dies, it will start again somewhere else. Do you hear?" Here he stopped in the street and seized my arm, and stared into my face with the tears still in his eyes and said, "It will start somewhere else!"

"Yes," I whispered, but he went on without hearing me: "Remember this, remember what you saw, if you live through what comes on us all. Don't let them buy you. Remember!"

"I will remember," I said.

He let go of me and gave me a push: "Go home," he said. "Go home and wait for the fever." And I looked about and saw that the street was empty.

"I will go," I said, "but I will come to see you again. And maybe your brother will live."

"Yes, and maybe the Ring will fall. Go!"

With that he turned for home, and so did I, our ways parting; and I saw no one else until I came to Kia's door.

Now the days drew near to the shortest of the year and the hardest of the cold came on us early. There was no more dancing-master, nor did Portia come, and the players ceased their trade. The snow fell, and the world stopped. We did not go anywhere and what we needed was brought to us, though scanty enough, and brought in half-empty carts; but the seeming end of time had more to do with lack of news, which we could not get any more, except sometimes when a neighbor ducked through our door looking over her shoulder to make sure she was not seen. So we heard, but as if at a great distance, of death swelling in the town; how the newly sick might disappear, no one knowing where they were taken; we heard of the sealing of more of the great barracks, and how the inhabitants of one set it afire but were shot as they ran from the flames or forced back to burn alive; and we heard of empty factories, and how fuel might soon be short, as food already was. But these whispers were like tales of events that had happened far away. The Postmen who came with food and fuel would say nothing, and we heard nothing of how things were behind the wall. There might have been no one there, all might have fled from the sickness—yet clearly someone remained to give the orders that kept us in isolation, and other orders that reduced the food the Postmen brought day by day—and our neighbors said the numbers of the fishers, too, had shrunk, so that there were fewer to bring food from the sea. And we weakened, and were often hungry, except Carmina who got shares of all our portions; and I began to think of how it might end.

But one night when I had only begun to think of the end, there came a rattle at the door, and a man put his face into it, and I saw that it was Willem. He spoke a few quick words to Kia which I could not hear, and then was gone without acknowledging my presence. Alban hurried to Kia's side and she whispered to him, and he said so that I could hear, seeming astounded, "He is running away? Where can he go? Can it be so bad?"

"His head is light with hunger," Kia said, but she twisted her hands in her skirt, and her brow twisted, too.

She looked at Alban and he said, "In the morning we will try to find out more."

"Morning will be too late," she said.

And they began to argue the wisdom of going that same night for news of some kind—of the sickness, I thought, for what else could it be?—and then they spoke of Leren and of streets and passages that led out of sight, with luck, to his house; and I said I knew all the ways there were to get there.

So they sent me out into the cold with a question: I was to ask Leren what had happened (though I still did not know what they thought that was). I made the journey safely, treading ice in the dark, for the streets were not lighted, and came safely to Leren's house and asked my question—I did not even go in, he was in no way glad to see me, his mind was on other things, and he stood in the door looking into the dark with fear in his face.

He said, "One of those at Millside wanted to get out. To get out he betrayed us all. He was not satisfied with giving the names of Millside men already doomed with fever; no, he has given them every name he ever heard. I have it from a guard who was one of those named and now runs for his life. I cannot make up my mind to run. It is winter, there is nothing but snow. It will be dying all the same; only the means will be different."

Then he turned into the room and took a scrap of paper, and wrote some lines and gave them to me for Kia.

"What does it say?" I said.

"It says get out. Get out. Get out."

"What does this mean?" I said.

"Do you know what they had at Millside?" he said. "There was a map of the wall that showed each place where weapons are stored. The locks are strange things, they are worked with numbers that are pushed with the hand. For some of them we had the numbers."

I began to understand, and not all the ice in my back came from the winter.

"If we go, where can we go?" I said. But he did not answer, and shut the door in my face.

I did not know what it all meant, but I knew enough
to be afraid as I ran back through the dark, though it
was only the beginning of fear, born less of understanding than of what I had seen in Kia's face and heard in
Leren's voice. So I hurried, scarcely heeding the ice
underfoot; only as I came close to Kia's street, I saw
light shining over the roofs; I saw, as I came closer still,
light filtering between houses and other small buildings
that lay between; and I heard voices on the wind, men's
voices, some shouting to others. I did not feel any fear,
I did not feel anything, except an urgency to get to Mirrah and to Kia's house, and this carried me over the ice.
But I ran without looking at the ground. My eyes were
all for the sky. For when I had gone only a little distance, not far from Leren's house, I had seen a thing
that hung in the sky not much higher than rooftop level,
a thing big as many houses put together. I could not
make out what it was, I saw only one piece of it at a
time, as the roofs between cut one part or another from
my sight, but it was long and slender like a needle in
the sky, and shafts of light shown downward from its
belly. *They are not directed at Kia's house,* I said to
myself. *They will not touch me.* And I continued to say
this until I came around the last corner and saw all of
it at once: the air and the street filled with light from
the thing in the sky, the street filled with Postmen, too,
all carrying weapons and looking about and shouting to
each other, and Kia's door wide open, and then, tearing
from that door greater than the noise of the crowd, a
woman's screams.

I did not know if it were Mirrah or Kia I heard, I did
not know or feel anything, I only ran on blind to the
Postmen and the thing in the sky. I was seized and
hurled to the ground, though I fought, knowing for the
first time what it was to wish to hurt men with my hands;
for they stood between me and Mirrah. And a time
passed which I could not measure. I felt no cold, though
I lay bound on the ice and bound also to one of the
Postmen's wagons; for I had continued to struggle and
seek to drag myself toward the house after my hands
and feet were tied, until they attached me to something

that would not move. I wept and bit at the ropes and when anyone came near me, screamed curses, and the men well-armed as they were, and helpless as I was, stood away from me with amazement in their eyes, as if I were a wild beast. And the sounds came from Kia's house in broken fragments, there would be a silence and then another scream, at each of which I thought my whole body would shatter; until there came the sound of guns, and after that, from that house, a silence that did not end.

At that the strength went out of me, to fight or do anything else. The street remained bright, but I saw all else that happened in colors of black. Men came from the house, the first of them being the traveler Tistou. And he waved the Postmen back, and as they removed to the farther side of the street they released me from the wagon and took me with them, dragging me across the ice; and the traveler spoke into something he carried, and a greater shaft of light came from the thing over my head, and Kia's house was not there any more. There was only fire where it had been.

Now none of Kia's neighbors had shown themselves, but the Postmen went from house to house ordering them into the street until it was filled with bodies and moving limbs edging away from the fire, and one shouted at them, a man dressed in clothes so fine that I knew he came from behind the wall; and he told them to look on what had been done and learn from it. After that for a further lesson he broke my hands. And I knew nothing for a little time after, but the cold woke me, and in my pain I saw that the traveler knelt over me. He took my chin in his large cold hand just as Kia had once done; only when he looked into my eyes, which he had not seen before in their natural state, he laughed and spoke to the man who stood by in his rich garments.

"They will not soon forget this night," the traveler said. "I am glad to have been of help. No reward is necessary. But if you insist, then I will take this—"

And his mouth smiled at me. But his eyes were transparent, as I had suspected, and there was nothing behind them but a great emptiness. And how could anything else have been there? Because where Mirrah and Carmina had been, and Kia and Alban, and no doubt Leren, too, and their homes and their lives, now there was nothing, what marked his path was emptiness and absence and lack, where there had been life. And I knew in some way what he would do to me, how it would be done, what living would be like, such living as I had left, and I knew that when he was done he would kill me; but I knew also that if he did not I would never know fear again. There would not be anything worse that could happen to me than what had happened in this season, along with what this traveler would cause to happen in the waste he prepared for me. But not all of it had happened yet, and the agony of my hands filled all my body and mind, and I could still be afraid, because I was.

"Take him," said the man from behind the wall. And the traveler took me away.

* * *

During the days it took for the last memories to come forward into light, Hanna did not leave Michael in body or in thought. She was a silent spectator (as he wished), and at the end of it he evicted her. Not forcibly, but by way of something that was half request and half order; in either case, she could not refuse it.

She told the others, "He is very sick." But she was not sure how true that was, though he did not talk to her. He lay on his bed and it was difficult to tell whether he was awake or asleep, even when his eyes were open. But he ate, when Hanna brought food to the room. And as before, in the middle of the night he left it and wandered around the *Golden Girl* with an uncanny knack for avoiding anyone else who might be abroad in the night.

GeeGee came to Heartworld, then left it far behind. They were nearly at the point of decision. Soon they must turn back, or entrust themselves to a course known, in all the universe, only to the man who had as many names as there were stars.

Hanna always knew precisely where the *Golden Girl* was. She spent a third of her time in Control, dividing up each twenty-four hours into pieces with Theo and Shen. She did the slight work automatically and otherwise listened anxiously for Michael's voice, footsteps, even a thought. She did not hear any of those things. And once or twice she whispered her birthname to *GeeGee*, the code that would permit her to reach across space and establish a connection with her own past life— but she never went any farther than saying the word. If Theo did it, too, in his own hours on watch, she did not know about it.

This half-a-life continued without change until they were a few hours from the relay which they had begun to call Theta, to mark its distance from Omega on the other side of space. In the early morning hours, not long after midnight, Shen watched *GeeGee* measure the distance to that endpoint. Theo could not sleep; he came to watch, too, not saying anything. Lise woke from a nightmare and joined them, seeking what comfort she could get from their presence. And Henrik, wide awake, got the notion that the walls of mirrors were looking at him with some purpose, and went out to escape. He did not mean to go to the others in Control, he wanted to keep away from them, but he couldn't shake the thought of the mirrors, the mirrors might follow him; so he went to Control, just in case.

Hanna woke up, too. Michael was gone. She went out shivering (she had been dreaming of winter) to look for him. *GeeGee* was waiting and silent. Hanna went into Control, into the middle of the waiting, and Theo looked around and said, "What next?"

How the hell do I know?

She was standing in the door, and she did not know the answer even when the footsteps finally came up behind her. Hands fell on her shoulders. She waited to find out whose they were.

"It's time to start feeding the course to *GeeGee*," Michael said. So if she turned around, it would not be a twelve-year-old boy she saw, a poor fit in the man's body. But maybe it would not be Michael either.

Shen asked no questions; she began talking to *GeeGee*, preparing the ship for the new course. Michael said, "The language won't be hard. It's got a lot in common with Standard. If you could learn Ellsian, you can learn this."

He turned Hanna around and spoke to her. The others didn't know enough to understand his next words; not yet. "I don't think what we're going to find is what I left. When I left, there was the blight, the epidemic, the start of a revolution. We don't know how they turned out. But I don't think anything's gotten better."

Hanna said, "You mean to do something about it."

"Something."

"You would. But what?"

He shrugged. He looked just as he had always looked, except that he was very thin. He said, "B made a lot of difference. We could make a difference, too. You can let things happen, or you can make them happen."

"What kinds of things?" she said.

"We won't know till we get there." he said.

VII.

With a kind of jolt, a thump Hanna later swore she heard, the small world of the *Golden Girl* returned to normal. Lise began to smile again. Shen told Michael daily that he had gotten too soft to be a revolutionary. Even Henrik came out of his hole, drawn by the general atmosphere of well-being, and some of his furtiveness dissipated. He said he would tell them everything he could, but except for what he knew about the men of the *Avalon*, he had no useful information. "So all that was for nothing," Michael said, meaning Henrik's abduction, but he forgot to apologize for it.

There was nothing to do but spend the remaining weeks teaching the others how to get along in his native tongue. He taught them everything else he remembered, too, warning them that information thirty years out of date might be more dangerous than none. Instead of the caution he meant them to learn, they developed a lively curiosity about what they would find. The holiday atmosphere of Uskos returned, the journey became an excursion, and at times they left *GeeGee* to run herself and played games in the lounge, shouting with laughter.

Hanna should have known better. She knew it, too, but her fear for Michael had gone on too long and gone too deep. It was enough to see him whole, enough to be loved again. He was back. It was enough.

A thread of black ahead of them got bigger, turned into a cloud, grew until it covered everything before them. When they passed into its tenuous fringe, it looked as if nothing was there, as if they plunged into black emptiness. Not even that troubled them. They sailed through the dust in a capsule of light, and the only acknowledgment they gave the dark was to agree that it was boring. They came to the stellar system of Gadrah, took a week to get through its shoals, hunted down the place itself, and finally saw it: blue and rich with water, dappled with cloud, magnificently ringed.

Hanna had taken care to time the arrival for the middle of the night, and lied about when it would happen. She did not want anyone but Michael in Control when the time came. When it did, he stood without moving, not taking his eyes off the sight. Even if the others had been there, he would not have noticed them. Hanna stayed out of his head, out of his way, for a full hour. But finally she went to him and touched him, and he smiled at her. She had never seen so much peace in his eyes.

"I'm all right," he said.

"I'll get some sleep, then."

"Do."

She was nearly at the door when he said, "Thank you."

Hanna added up everything that had happened since her last sight of Earth.

"Don't mention it," she said, and went to bed.

Cruising coastlines: at high magnification each coast was the track of a demented snake. They stayed high, out of reach of the naked eye. It was amazing how many shores were backed by mountains close enough and tall enough to suggest that the Post might be there.

It would have been faster to look for heat, but *GeeGee* was not seeing so well in infrared. She was considerably overdue for maintenance.

It took longer to explore a coastline than Hanna had ever dreamed. They limited the search to the eastern edges of continental bodies, and to temperate latitudes. Even with those restrictions there was a lot of coastline, and it was deserted, not counting the profusion of animal life. Hanna looked at the animals and shuddered. Not because these animals were especially frightening—they were not, they came in an ordinary range of shapes and habits—but because there were no humans, nothing had been tamed. *There weren't many children born here,* he had said. There had never been many children. Something on Gadrah wouldn't let humans breed.

After three days they had narrowed the search to a coast which had been masked by cloud for all of those days. The clouds were not local, but part of an immense funnel that spread over half a continent, and the funnel was not moving. "It would be a long hurricane season," Hanna said, thinking of the length of all seasons here, and Michael looked at her blankly. Hurricanes had not come to the mountains. "Radio," she said suddenly (it had nothing to do with hurricanes), and his face was more blank still.

But Lise—who sometimes still nestled against the wall, but today, prim and upright, had taken a seat—said, "They would want radio. To keep in touch with the people who ran the mines. And the soldiers, when they went places."

"I never heard of one or saw one," Michael said. And when Hanna set *GeeGee* to scanning, they heard nothing.

This part of the world was turning away from the sun, and *GeeGee* with it. It was getting dark under the clouds down there. Aboard *GeeGee*, however, it was morning.

"We'll have to wait for the clouds to clear," Hanna said.

"It's fall there," Michael said.

"Hurricane season."

"All right, but I mean, in the fall there were weeks of cloud. If we want to see anything we'll have to get under them."

"They're *low* clouds. If we get under them, anybody down there can see us, too."

"Not at night."

"*GeeGee* is not soundless in atmosphere," Hanna pointed out. "Do want him to hear us and look up? Castillo? 'B'? Why do you call him B anyway? When here they called him Tistou?"

"They called him that, B, on the ship."

There was a warning in his tone. Michael did not need to be in trance to remember what had happened on the proto-*Avalon*. But he did not talk about it.

Hanna took the warning and retreated. "Wait till it clears."

A lifetime of patience told Michael to listen. He thought about it. He said finally, "We'll wait another day or two. But not weeks."

The morning went on; under *GeeGee*, in geosynchronous orbit, evening progressed. The night would be very dark on the ground. Michael disappeared, leaving Hanna in Control; he roamed the ship, a big cat prowling a cage. Hanna tracked him without effort from her place in Control. She hardly needed to be a telepath to know what he was doing at each moment.

When she heard a voice she said automatically, "What?" and looked around, thinking someone had come in and spoken. But Lise pointed silently at a communications panel, and another voice said incomprehensible words.

Lise said softly, "*GeeGee's* got something on radio. They said: It's a false alarm. Nobody sick here."

"They? Oh!"

"It was something like that."

Mike! Hanna called, and strained to hear more. It was tantalizing, the words had a familiar sound, and at each syllable she felt herself on the point of understanding. Lise was quicker; she translated the next phrases aloud while Hanna still fumbled for their meaning.

"They say there's no use leaving tonight. They don't want to ride back in the rain."

"From where? Have they said from where? Or where to?"

"Not yet . . ."

"*Morning,*" somebody said, she knew that word. Michael came in and stood still. "*But it will be wet, all the same.*"

"*If it is, it is.*"

"*Well, it has rained for a week. Why should tomorrow be different?*"

Two men laughed together.

"We'll swim back soon as we can."

"Luck!"

The radio burped, went on with a quiet hiss; there were no more voices.

"So it's down there," Hanna said. "Under the clouds. Somewhere."

Time to go. Michael would not wait any longer. "We'll fly over sooner or later," he said, "at night, too. Why not in the rain?" And they fell through the clouds into darkness and wet. "No one's going to spot us," Michael said. "The Post won't have radar; what for? The *Avalon's* shut down. Guaranteed. Conserving power. When what she's got is gone, there won't be any more."

More coastline. It was dark, but *GeeGee* built up pictures from contrast, mimicking the human eye. Sand dunes made into islands by stands of patchy grass. Bays and inlets and slow-moving creeks like the one by Millside. Marshlands turned to lakes by the rain. Finally— there was silence when they saw this—the regular outlines of cultivated fields. All of it was in tones of gray and black.

Then buildings. There was a sound at Hanna's side, it was Michael; she heard him before she saw the heaps of stone just barely in view.

GeeGee moved on slowly, recording. The humans were silent. Hanna recognized what she saw from the air, as if all along, while she read Michael's memories, she had known how it would look from above. It was all there, the irregular half-circles, the pale wall, inside it the enclave up against the sea.

Michael murmured, "There's no light."

"Some." *GeeGee's* rendering showed bright spots that had to be lights.

"Not enough."

"It was a dark town."

"Not this dark. And not inside the wall."

He was going to tell *GeeGee* to stop, but Hanna put

a hand on his arm. "We're defenseless," she said, and Shen looked around and nodded.

"We keep moving, then," he said.

There wasn't much of it. There were fields again, and the whole thing faded behind them. Hanna had expected something bigger—but what they had seen would look big to a child. They flew on toward the north, still slowly. Hanna said, "What now?"

She did not mention Croft. There was a road that went to Croft. But first they would have to find it.

"I want to find out what's wrong," he said.

"You're sure something's wrong?"

"There weren't any lights on the walls."

"No." The dark winter and the sickness and the blight came to her mind. But that had been thirty years ago.

"It was all right a few years ago," she said. "That's what they told Henrik."

He took a deep breath and seemed to shake himself. "We won't find out any more from up here."

"Who goes? You and me and Shen," she added, asnwering herself. "You don't go alone!"

"Then find some hills to hide *GeeGee* in," he said. "And get ready to get wet."

There were no appreciable hills within three days' walk from the town. And *GeeGee* would stand out like a nova to anything looking down from the air.

After they had thought about it for some time, Michael said, "There won't be anything in the air."

The others were not of his opinion. None of them had ever lived in a place where nothing but birds flew.

"What about *Avalon*?" Shen said.

"Flying where? Looking for what? We'll chance it," he said, he smiled at them, he liked taking risks, risk had made him. Hanna was worried, Shen glum.

They would take stunners with them. Hanna thought: *At the first opportunity we must steal something better. Something fatal.* And heard Shen's identical thought. They put the stunners in the pockets of warmcoats unused since Revenge. The coats were waterproof and would be useful if the weather turned really cold. Hanna thought the coats inadequate, too. She would have liked body armor better.

They spent some hours selecting a landing site. It had to be open land but not marsh, solid ground but not forest, near a road but too far away to be seen from it. They settled on a patch that had been cultivated once—the remains of a fence still edged it—but now was overgrown with grasses and slim seedlings of native trees. There was nothing like it nearby; it was an island in virgin woodland, and Hanna puzzled over the anomaly. But it suited their purpose.

She and Michael and Shen stepped out of *GeeGee* into a wet dawn. They walked through woods at first, and it was hard to know when the rain stopped, if it ever stopped, because every step brought down water from the trees. Hanna thought nostalgically of the Red Forest of Ree, where travelers could command umbrellas. There were no umbrellas here; only water.

In an hour, however, they reached the road. Rain fell from the open sky, and when they came from under the trees it was full light. The road was lightly paved, but in poor condition; there were holes and scattered blocks of paving matter.

"Kept up until lately," Shen said.

"I wonder," Michael said. He looked at Hanna. "Think something did happen, since B was last here?"

"That field where we landed, that hasn't been fallow very long, either."

He looked up the road, not in the direction they meant to take, toward the sea, but landward. "The road from Sutherland was paved," he said, remembering how it had felt in the stifling truck. "We didn't spot many paved roads from the air." But he turned and started walking the right way.

They planned to walk all day. They carried no weight, except for communicators and the stunners; by evening they would be at the town, would look for a place to sleep but go without if necessary. They did not hurry. They did not want to come to the Post before dark. Hanna resigned herself to hunger, being wet, getting tired. But when the walking had established its own rhythm, and discomfort had come to seem the norm, she began to feel something else: the loneliness of the place. There was no sign of habitation except for the road, and they walked hour after hour without seeing anyone on it. There was no sound of machines; only wind and rain and, rarely, a rustle at the roadside when a small animal ran from their passage. They spoke seldom, and when they did their voices were loud. Soon even the slight noise of their footsteps was like thunder. And when they rounded a curve in the road and saw a structure built by hands, Hanna stood and stared, might have stared all day—except that Michael, diving for cover, turned back to pull her after him into the bush.

Shen was already there. She looked at Hanna with disapproval.

Here the soil had encroached on the road, and a tangle of grasses and scraggly shrubs rose up at the edge of the trees nearest the road. To the right and ahead there was a clearing, and the building nestled against the forest at the rear of this space, the setback having kept them from seeing it until they reached the clearing itself. Michael peered from behind the screen of brush. The clearing was in the same condition as *GeeGee's* landing site. The house was built of dressed stone and was structurally intact, but some of the glazed windows were broken, and no light came from any of them in the dark afternoon. A few tiles had fallen from the roof, the gutters were thick with debris; it was the picture of desertion. But it was not deserted. There were chimneys at each of the three corners in sight—and over the roof, from the place where a fourth chimney ought to be, a stream of smoke rose sadly into the drizzle.

Hanna whispered, "What is it?"

"I don't know." He racked his newfound memory. There was nothing. "It looks like one of *their* places. But we must be a long way from the Post."

"Five or six hours on foot," Shen said. "In a landcar, half an hour's ride."

She added, "Start here."

"Start what?"

"Questions."

Hanna nodded. Michael was slower. Then he saw what they did, the advantages. If there were people here there would only be a few, isolated from the city. They would not have to be entirely ignorant when they reached the Post; they could find out something about it here.

"All right," he said. "We'll knock on the front door."

"Wait," Hanna said. "Stop thinking."

A ridiculous request—but he tried; could stop thinking in words, anyway. Shen became quiet as a stone. Hanna bowed her head, eyes closed. Listening for what? The afternoon was darker. Michael felt himself slip some mooring and float, as if he might take leave of his body. The absoluteness of time slipped; he was back in trance. He was suddenly certain that there were three people in that dying building. Two males, one female. *They think of the past and what might be and what might never be. One with hope and one without and one whose hope is soured . . .*

Hanna lifted her head. "They're not on guard," she said. "I could find out more, if we waited. But I think some other people might be here before dark."

"I didn't catch that." He looked at her in wonder. "I saw some of it, though. Did you make that happen?"

"What?"

He looked at Shen. "Did you see it?

She gave him a dubious look and shook her head.

"Never mind," Hanna said. "You're not turning into a telepath. It'll only happen when we're together."

"Right. Come on," he said, shaken, and stepped out of the brush.

They crossed the dreary clearing, mounted a shallow flight of stone steps, and passed over the colonnaded porch without hearing a challenge. Shen's eyes darted everywhere, but Hanna's were distant; she watched for threat with another sense. They did not knock. The door opened with a creak, but nothing met them in the dark passage beyond. There were doors on either side of the hallway, some open and some not; they looked into all the rooms and found no one. The rooms were furnished, but in most the dust lay thick.

Hanna said to Michael's thought, with conviction: *There are ghosts here. Living or not, they are ghosts.*

He didn't like that. He walked more quickly, found a passage that seemed to lead toward the corner of the house where a fire must burn, and started into it. Near the end there was a door that promised revelations. But there was a staircase, too, and before he had taken three steps there was a flicker of light at the top of it.

He was flat on his belly with the stunner drawn before he thought about what to do. Behind him Hanna and Shen had dropped, too.

The top of the stair disappeared into shadow. A figure came out of the shadow and stopped with a gasp. A girl no more than eighteen stood shrinking in fright from the muzzles pointed in her direction. She held a lamp in both shaking hands.

Michael got up with a sigh and put the gun away. "I greet you," he said, the first words he had spoken to a native of this place in more than thirty years. But the girl only stared; perhaps he had gotten the language wrong after all.

Hanna had risen, too. She said quietly in the same tongue, "I am sorry; you surprised us. We will not hurt you. Please come down. We would like to talk to you." *If she doesn't come down, we'll go after her*, she added, but no one but Michael heard that.

But the girl started down the staircase. They did not move; their stillness calmed her. When she came near, the light showed a pale oval face, brown hair exquisitely dressed, soft blue eyes; she wore a richly figured blue gown that was a little large for her and looked as if it had been made for someone else. She looked from one to another and stopped in front of Michael and looked up—and stared, discomfiting him; started to speak, was silent, stared some more.

"Eyes," Hanna muttered in Standard.

"What—oh. My name is Mikhail," he said to the girl. "Who did you think I was?"

''You are a Saddhi, that is plain,'' she answered. ''But I have never seen you before.''

''What is your name?''

''Marin—of the Saddhis. Why do I not know you? Why have I not heard of you?''

He could not answer. The words took their time sinking in. Nowhere else in the universe would his eyes say who he was.

There was a sound beyond the door at the end of the passage. Hanna whispered to Shen and the two women, practical, flawless, slipped by Michael and Marin and took up positions of guard, Shen on the staircase, Hanna in the angle the door would make when it opened.

''What do they want?'' said Marin, voice rising. He thought she might flee and put a hand on her shoulder. She looked up again and was still.

The door opened and a man came in. He was clearly a near relative of the girl; his face declared it. He said sharply, ''Who are you? What do you do here?'' Then he saw Shen and her stunner and froze. He had not seen Hanna, who waited as if expecting someone else to come in.

Michael felt a lurch, a great compulsion to tell the truth, to reveal himself. Instead he said a half-truth, with difficulty: ''We are travelers.''

''Well, what of it? Where from? Why intrude on my home with weapons? Come here, Marin.''

She did not obey. She said, ''He is of the family, Pavah. But he is called Mikhail, and I have never heard of one so named.''

''There is no one,'' said the man; he was irritated, not afraid. He went forward to fetch his daughter and also saw Michael's eyes. He said, ''Marin, go. Get your uncle.'' And to Michael, savagely, ''What do you want? There is nothing here to steal. There is nothing here for you.''

He talked like a man who was used to being robbed, with more bitterness than fear. *Saddhi,* said the echo of Marin's voice. Shadhili? Michael could not say a word. Centuries ticked away while he looked at his kinsman with a bastard's eyes, disowned. The chill of the place got colder. He still held Marin's shoulder; that alone was warm. He let go and she moved for the first time since he had touched her. The silence had lasted too long.

Hanna came forward then. "We will not take anything," she said. "We are travelers, as Mikhail said. We need knowledge of this land. Do our weapons trouble you? We have them because we did not know what we would find. We will put them away—if you give your word that we are safe."

"Why, as to that . . ." The man half-smiled. "How can any man pledge to another that he will be safe at all times and in all ways? But I will not try to harm you. Is that enough?"

"It will suffice," Hanna said.

They made a strange picture on that wet afternoon, the three men, three women, two sets of flotsam thrown up by the sea. They talked by the fire in a high square room that appeared at first glance well-kept. But the fire scarcely touched the damp, and it flared up sometimes, and showed details of disintegration: spreading cracks in window cornices, water-stained walls, fragments of tile underfoot. The lamps shed no light; they only thickened the shadows in the room. The man Marin called father was Orne. The uncle who had not stirred from the fire was Hyde. Orne called him brother, but they did not look much alike. Instead when Michael looked into Hyde's face, he looked into a distorting mirror. It was not only that Hyde had the Saddhi eyes; there were other resemblances, too. They kept Michael silent— silent as Hyde, who acknowledged their presence with an indifferent nod and went on staring at the fire.

They sat in a semicircle before the fire, their backs to the door. But Hanna had turned her seat so that she could see most of the room, and Shen was openly on guard in a corner from which she could see all the rest. Hanna did most of the talking, too. Did she think Michael too simple to spin a convincing lie?—but he knew what she was doing before she was half done. She plucked Orne's own conjectures from his thoughts, let

him make up a tale that suited him; then she confirmed
his guesses. She said the travelers had come from a
settlement so far away that there had been no news of
the Post in some time, and they had come to get some,
guessing as they came that much was awry, finding
nearer settlements abandoned. They had gotten clothes
and weapons in one of these, Hanna said. (Had some
question crossed Orne's mind about their gear? Hanna's
eyes were not guileless. But they said: *Prove that I lie.*)

"One of the lost hamlets to the south, no doubt,"
Orne said, and his eyes were sharp, but Hanna answered, "No, far to the north. I did not know anyone
lived to the south." She must have seen a map in Orne's
head, and slipped past a trap.

"There were towns at the end of this road," the girl
Marin said. "I have heard that people live there again.
Is it true?"

"We saw no one, but we did not go to all of them.
What towns were they?" Hanna said. Michael lifted his
head, listening for a name.

"What does it matter?" Orne said. "They rot with
the rest. Leave the dead in peace!"

"How many dead?" Hanna said. "Of what cause?"

"Did it not come to your little godforsaken town?
Well, it was the sickness. You'd best hope you don't take
it home with you; it is not dead yet. Not quite."

Michael said, "There was a great sickness long ago,
when I was a child. But it passed. Was this the same?"

"It might have been. The leeches talk of cycles of
the thing. Where do you live, that you do not know this,
and your speech has come to sound strange?"

Michael stirred a little. He had worried about the accent that was heavy on Hanna's tongue, and Shen's, and
even his, though not so thick. But Hanna ignored the
question. She said, "We have heard that the great families were spared in that earlier time. I do not think you
have been spared."

"No, as you can see. Birds nest in the tower that was
my wife's chamber, and worms crawl in the cradle of
my brother's child. His wife also died, and our father
and mother, though we fled here at the first, to this

summer lodge. No great loss, you might think, the old being anyhow in sight of death; but their old age had promised to be hale. That was how it was. Few families lost less than two parts of their folk—this time."

"And the rest of the people?" Michael said. His tongue did not want to move. The words on it weighed it down. "The people who, I heard, lived crowded close outside the wall?"

"Worse," Orne said. "Hardly any are left. There is no help to be gotten anywhere, no one to farm, no one to work."

"How do you live?" Hanna said.

"Well, there are the fields we used to own, when owning them meant something. There are still the tithes, though so few folk remain that tithes do no more than fill our mouths."

Hyde spoke for the first time, rumbling: "It will not come again."

Orne would have gone on without giving any attention to his brother, but Hanna said, "What will not come again?"

Hyde said, "Life. Now we die. Only a fool denies it."

Marin leaned closer to the fire; Michael could not see her face. Orne said, "My brother's mind was turned by grief. He would have it that all who live now are doomed."

"I am not a fool," Hyde said. "I remember the old days, before sickness and want. It began to break then, yes, when we were boys. Now it is broken. I will see the end of the world."

There was silence, except for the sound of the rain, which began to form itself into a sad melody. At last Michael said, "Is there no more music, then?"

Orne looked at him curiously. "No, no more. I don't think there are any musicians left. If you find one, don't send him here, unless he can feed himself. And what musician ever could?"

They had stayed too long. The dark was rolling in, and they could not go on tonight. The servants of the house had gone to town for stores and might return to-night, tomorrow, next week. Their places were the empty ones Hanna had sensed; they were the others who belonged here and would come home. If they had been there, Michael thought, the travelers would have been relegated to their company. Since they were not, certain distinctions were blurred. Orne gave them a hot porridge he made himself, and bitter beer to go with it, and the parties ate and drank together. But later he told them to sleep on the floor before the fire and told them where to find bedding; then he and Hyde and Marin disappeared into the upper regions of the house, where there were beds.

They got through to Theo and took turns whispering to him, and afterward went to sleep. Only one thing more happened that night, in that house. Michael woke to find the fire dead; he was cold. It was very dark, and he got up to look for more blankets. He was coming back through the hall with his arms full when he saw a light at the head of the stairs, just where he had seen it in the afternoon. It was Marin again. She came down on soft bare feet and stood there and looked at him in silence.

He said something to her, a nothing-meaning courtesy. But she said after a further silence, "It is lonely here."

"Yes," he said. "I see it must be."

"I am young," she said in a low voice. "I have no one. I see no one. I see no one like you."

It was an invitation, the saddest he had ever heard. He hesitated, trying to find words, and she must have thought he had not understood, because she made it clear. "Will you come with me to my room?"

"I can't," he said. "I'm very sorry."

"My father sleeps soundly, my uncle, too. I walk in the night and they do not hear. I look out and see nothing. I hear nothing. There is nothing to hear." Her eyes filled with tears. "My father talks only of getting enough to eat, my uncle of how everything will end. Nothing changes, each day is like the day before, and always tomorrow will be like today, until I am old. I was to be married, but now he is dead, my cousin who was my betrothed. You are my cousin, too, though my father will not say it. I do not know why. The old ways are dead. Will you give me at least a memory to hold?''

She stepped closer and he repeated, "I can't."

"Is it because of the woman who is with you?" she said. "I saw how you look at her, but I am prettier than she is."

He remembered the jewels and soft gowns of the Mistresses of the Post, and beside them set Hanna with her dangerous hands. There was a hardness and strength in Hanna that Marin could not have seen in the women she had known.

"I'm sorry," he said again.

The girl turned away without another word, taking the light with her. He found his way back to Hanna with relief and spread another blanket over her.

They woke early and left before the household stirred; he did not want to see Marin again.

He had not slept well. All night he had been troubled by visions of sad broken windows, darkness where there ought to be light. The rooms behind the windows were empty. The dreams did not leave him with the dawn. The rain kept coming down, soaking his bare head, trickling down his neck. Beside him Hanna and Shen plodded on, heads down, not very fast, talking softly of how far there was to go.

"We still don't want to get there in the light," Hanna said.

"Sooner I see a fire the better," Shen said.

"We're not going in in daylight unless we know where *he* is. They didn't say anything about him. I couldn't ask. We shouldn't know anything about him, if we were what I said. They would have had to give me an opening, and they didn't."

She glanced at Michael, inviting his comment, but he didn't have one. B did not seem real—nor did the misty morning, nor the wraiths they had left behind. All the things he had finally remembered, a world of them, had vanished during the years of his forgetfulness. Nothing was the way he had thought it would be. *My father talks only of getting enough to eat, my uncle of how everything will end . . .*

They went on quietly for a while. Shen said, "Think we could get sick?"

Hanna paused a moment, lifted her head and looked at the rain as if it were an enemy. It might be; every breath they took was loaded with microbes.

"People have survived here for centuries," she said. "That suggests there's nothing here that could kill us before we could get help, no alien bug we've no defenses against. But something's been happening."

"The same thing," Michael said. "That's what Orne said. But they called it the new fever, when I heard of it before. Something the settlers brought with them might have mutated."

"So we could get sick," Shen said. "Real good news."

But Hanna said, "There's another possibility. I'd like to plot these cycles against B's visits."

Shen said, "A carrier?" but Michael said simultaneously, "No. They would have had it behind the wall. It would have spread out from there."

Hanna gave him another look, but she did not try to refute him.

Toward midday the forest gave way to open grassland which once had been farmed. Before the trees thinned too much they sat at the roadside and chewed on nutrient tablets. The road was very straight, and they could have seen to its vanishing point on a clear day; today it disappeared into rain. But they saw the darker shape that began to emerge from the mist, and slipped into the scant cover of the trees. What came out of the rain was a truck straight out of Michael's memories— and this one was so battered, so noisy, so old, that he might have seen this very one as a child. There were people in the cab, and a dozen bundles bounced around in the back.

They stayed out of sight until it was gone. Hanna said, "They're going to where we spent the night, I think. They're Orne's servants going home."

Shen looked into the rain where the truck had vanished. A last faint squeak-and-rattle sounded through the patter of the rain.

"Why do they go back?" she said.

"Habit," Hanna answered.

"Home," Michael said.

On the *Golden Girl*, Theo dozed uneasily in Control. He was trying to get adjusted to the cycle of daylight here, and it was hard going. There was a local-time chronometer keyed to Gadrah's roation, and another that kept Standard time. Theo had started to think Standard time was an aberration, there wasn't any such thing, Standard didn't mean standard at all. But his body didn't like this new kind of time, and today he could neither sleep soundly nor wake completely.

He came out of this twilight state for the second or third time in a Standard hour and straightened groggily in his seat. He thought of coffee and then, with lust, of his bed. If he could lie down in the dark, he might get some real sleep. But Michael might call again, and what if something happened, what if the three outside needed him fast?

He remembered then that he wasn't the only person with ears left on *GeeGee*.

He went to Lise's room, but she was sound asleep, the picture of peace. She wasn't worried about Michael out there in the rain; she thought nothing could hurt him, he could do anything.

Theo couldn't bring himself to wake her. He went to Henrik's room, found no Henrik, and set off on a tour of *GeeGee*, resolved that Henrik would do something for his keep for a change. What he found, instead of Henrik, was an open locker spilling out their winter gear. More was missing than Michael and Shen and Hanna had taken.

He went outdoors, stood in the rain, called Henrik's name, walked in circles around *GeeGee*, shouting. Maybe Henrik had only gone for a walk; it had been a long time since any of them touched ground. But he got no answer, and finally, because he didn't know what to make of it but was sure it meant nothing good, he called Michael.

"Now we don't know where Henrik is either," Hanna said.

Night falling again. They had dawdled through the last few kilometers, where the road was bordered by fields farmed only last summer. Rain had fallen all day, rarely hard but never stopping, and it had slipped through every crevice it could find and made layers of damp next to the skin. Only movement kept them warm. From here the road made a sudden, meaningless curve and turned slightly downhill. Against the dark sky at the limit of sight there was a blur of deeper shadow. It might have some straight edges—or might not; eyes played tricks in the waning light.

After Hanna spoke, they were quiet. Michael thought there was no sense to Henrik's leaving, nowhere for him to go, nothing for him to do. There was only the road to follow, to Orne's ruined summer lodge and then on to the Post. He could not hope to lose himself in the native population; he had been there when they told Theo there was little population left.

Shen said: "Tricks. B."

"Habit," Hanna said. "Home."

Michael said, "No. Oh, no. He hated them. He was afraid of them."

There was a little explosive sound in the dark, Shen's breath; her hand fell on Michael's and clutched it like a claw.

"What's wrong with you?" she said. "He would've sold them to the Polity, that's what he wanted to do. He tried to call out of *GeeGee*, didn't he? To sell us, just the same. Now what's he got to sell? Us again. To B this time. We could get the Polity here if we wanted, get I&S; if Henrik hasn't thought of it, B will. Wait till he finds out we're here! See how fast he kills us! So Henrik tells him we're here, where *GeeGee* is. Thinks he'll be safe from B that way."

"We have to get B," Hanna said. "Before he gets us."

Michael said, "Wait a minute," and they turned to him. The protest he wanted to make died on his lips. He looked silently at the women in the dark. He could not see their faces clearly; they were shadows, Fates, sisters out of myth. They had guarded his back at every step on this road, deadly enemies to any enemy of his.

"I only want to find Carmina," he said.

"No revolution?" Shen inquired. She sounded disappointed.

"Oh, no," Hanna said. "That's not what this world needs. Not now."

And it was darker still; when he moved, water fell from his shoulders. Which carried something heavy, though he could not look at it yet. It was not necessary, not yet, it could be delayed; there was enough to see in the gap between what he had expected and what he had found. And what they were walking toward was something else to see—that made enough dread to fill up his head and keep it from speculating *what if* . . .

The shadows on the horizon had been rooftops, all right. They were closer than they had appeared, and the travelers were among them quickly. Whatever was wrong with Michael's head got worse. It was not that he didn't see material reality. He walked on real pavement, splashing through puddles and runnels of water that added to the wet in his boots. He saw the stark piles of the factories, the nightmare shapes of the great barracks looming over his head. Superimposed on these, however, were pictures of the way it had been before. The loose stones underfoot reminded him of ice. And there was an unreality that had nothing to do with either now or then. The factories, barracks, streets, all were dark, and nothing moved anywhere, except water. This could not be a real city. Instead it was a bad dream in which the dreamer comes to a familiar town and finds it crumbling and abandoned. The dark was more than night; it was the darkness hidden in the heart that shows itself only in dreams, where no sun has ever come or ever will come. And because the desertion was real, and the city disintegrating in reality, it seemed dreadfully possible that endless darkness could be real, too.

Michael had feared nothing since the day he escaped from the creature B. He was not afraid now. But his vigilance was gone with his sense of what was real. Anything might come out of the dark and he would not know until it was upon him, just as in a dream.

But the women moved smoothly as cats, ears pricked, eyes everywhere. They were silent. He suspected that Hanna communicated with Shen, guarding him.

When he saw the first faint lights, on the lowest floor of one of the barracks, he turned in another direction. There was someone here after all—but he was reluctant to see who or what it was. What might answer the door you knocked on in a dream like this?

They saw more lights; came around a corner and saw other shapes walking in the dark, three or four of them, heads down and moving away. Michael did not hail them.

He did not know where he was headed. He kept going, not thinking, letting his feet carry him on. The cold rain had been falling forever. Together with the black sky it crushed his heart. Why had he come here?—if he had not tried, if he had never tried, he could have gone on with his life where the sun shone.

If he had done that, something whispered, he would never have saved Lise, never known Hanna.

But he would not have known what he lacked. And he would not have heard *what if. What if I had not been*—

They came to the stone houses. Somewhere behind them was the wall. But it was not lighted, and it was only a shadow against the dead black of the sky.

He looked inside the doorway of a house. The door hung from one hinge and water had blown across the threshold. The next house was the same, and the next. Shen produced a tiny light. It was no longer than her finger but gave off an intense narrow beam. The light showed a jumble of sturdy furnishings beginning to show the effects of abandonment and damp. The cupboards built into kitchen walls were open and empty.

Their doors swung crazily and crockery was smashed on the floor.

Hanna said, "Somebody was looking for food, I'd bet."

Her voice was not loud, but Michael jumped as at a shout. Until now, in this deserted town, they had heard only furtive rustles which he had identified at once. Rats had come to Gadrah with the original stores of grain, and they had flourished.

Shen said, "The ones we saw walking—nobody else left?"

Michael turned to Hanna with an appeal. He saw her face now in reflected light, and it was intent.

"It's happened," she said. "Colonies have failed. Fertility's depressed here. I'd guess there were less than a hundred thousand people here at the peak—on the whole planet, I mean, not just here."

"Can't all be dead," Shen said.

"We haven't looked everywhere. And listen. Orne's daughter said she'd heard there were people again in some of the small towns. 'Again,' she said; that means they're coming from somewhere."

Michael said, "There wasn't anyplace but here."

"I know. Who's behind the wall now? Why hasn't Orne come back?"

Michael thought of what was behind the wall. He had known too little about what was there; his memory had made it monolithic.

"There would be more comforts there," Hanna said. "Luxuries. Stores of food, at least for a while. The great families ran away, like Orne's. The soldiers would have been sick, too, died or left their posts. It all broke down. So where did the people go?"

"Behind the wall," he said. "Where they couldn't go before. Of course."

When they came closer to the wall, they saw that all the gates were open like cavernous mouths. They walked beside it for a long time, looking through the gates at intervals. There was only more of the wet dark in there. Michael blessed the rain, which kept people in who might otherwise have come out; but a scene rose up before his eyes, another possibility. That was a fragrant spring evening under clear skies—and still the street was empty, no foot trod it but his, and ghosts grinned from the gates with the faces of skulls.

"We have to go in sometime," Shen said.

Hanna said, "Not without scouting. We're lucky there's no one around."

There isn't anybody anywhere! Michael thought. But Hanna said, "Oh, yes, there are people in there. But where's B? That's what I want to know before I walk in blind. The *Avalon* didn't show up on *GeeGee's* visuals. Why not? Where'd he put it?"

"They'll be looking for us real soon," Shen said.

Hanna nodded and Michael said, "How do you get that?"

"Henrik," Shen said. "Gone how long? Theo didn't know. Gets to Orne tonight, maybe takes that truck— could be right behind us. Get in, get out before he comes." The last words sounded final. She said to Hanna, ignoring Michael, "Go in now."

Hanna said thoughtfully, "We could wait for him. Go back to the road we came in on and get him when he comes."

"And do what when we have him?" Michael said.

Shen said, "Pointblank stun to the brain."

Hanna said, "If that doesn't do it, bare hands."

He looked at the guardian shadows in disbelief. They looked back and Hanna said, "All right."

"Guess not," Shen said. "Move fast, then."

"Up there," Hanna said, pointing. "That gate."

"Then?" Shen said.

"Straight back, straight east, toward the sea. No, we're near the middle, aren't we? We haven't seen any lights. We'll try a diagonal, then, toward the southeast. We'll cover more territory that way. Does anybody remember how the lights were distributed?"

"On record," Shen said. "Call Theo."

But Michael said, "Never mind. There was a cluster in that direction. That's what we flew over first, coming in. I remember—"

He didn't finish. *Because that's the way Alban took me my first night here.*

Hanna might have heard it anyway, but she said nothing. They walked on to the gate.

Stumbling through courtyards: they did not want to show a light. The sunken gardens were ponds. Hanna walked into one, fell, rose soaked and bruised, knowing she was lucky to have no broken bones. After that they had to risk light.

The dark mansions were all connected. Michael had not forgotten that. But for the first time he knew why, saw the builders, or maybe the image came to him from Hanna. It had been strange and frightening here, a new world unconnected to anything the masters had known before, so they had huddled together, building passages and tunnels so they would never be out of reach or separated from one another—

They found an unlocked door at once. Were there any locked doors left in this place, on this whole world? What was left to guard?

Michael thought he heard a whisper as he stepped inside: *Mikhail!*—a summons. Not Hanna's voice, not her thought. A product of imagination, then.

Now they had to use the light, because the dark inside was so thick that it seemed material, could envelop and smother them, if they wandered out of the circle of light. They were in a great hall, empty except for a thick carpet running its length. Their feet stirred puffs of dust. Hanna led them, light in one hand, weapon in the other. Michael followed blindly, and Shen was at his back. The first hall led into another and another, and that into dark rooms. There was nothing in them to see, they were empty as if no one had ever lived in them. Everything was gone. Here and there an ornament remained, glass or metal or stone; nothing else. Presently Michael realized, without knowing how he reached the conclusion, that everything that could be burned had been taken away for fuel. Even walls not made of stone were gone, even floors; the light saved them from falling into black pits. There was a smell of dust, the air was thick with it, it got into their noses and made them sneeze, so that they abandoned the instinctive attempt to walk in silence. The corners were heavy with cobwebs. And there were sounds. Rats were masters of these rooms. Also the wind had risen; or did he imagine that? He heard it, anyhow: howling round rooftops and corners till the howls turned to distant screams, and the scurryings inside walls turned to chuckles.

They might have been going in circles, but Hanna never stopped, or even hesitated. He could not imagine what compass had its home in her head. Or was there no compass at all? Was it only that she trusted her zigzag course would lead them somewhere? Left then right, left, right—she went on steadily. But it was odd that they never were outside, never passed into an open courtyard. They might as well have been underground.

He kept following the steady light while the wind and the rats tore at his ears, the screams got louder, the endless chuckle swelled to laughter, an uproar of mirth. So this was what he had dreamed of, what he had had to find. The passion for freedom was wasted. There were no masters left—save one; Chaos ruled here.

The sunlit place where aliens had told him about that Master was gone. He could not remember the sun.

If I had not been self-seeking, self-protecting—

Hanna stopped suddenly, and he bumped into her. He put his arms around her from behind, holding on. She whispered, "I heard something," and turned the light off. Michael only heard screams; they were louder in the dark. But his eyes adjusted and it was not perfectly black. There was a glow ahead.

Hanna stepped out of his arms. She put away the stunner she held and gave the light to Shen. "Wait," she said, and walked toward the light.

The old gaslight fixtures still worked. Gas burned in a fireplace, too, with a steady subliminal roar, in a row of tiny jets that looked like teeth. There were cooking pots at the fire, a pile of blankets in front of it. An old man sat on the blankets and looked up from hollow eyes.

Travelers, Hanna said, and spoke her piece; told the old man about Michael, half-truths. *He lived here as a boy and seeks old friends.*

Dead, most like.

His name was Conwy, he told her. Only half her mind was on what he said. The other half was on B. She did not know how to ask this Conwy about B, not without rousing more interest than she wanted to rouse.

Three of us. May we—?

I have little to eat, but it is yours—

She walked back to Michael and Shen and saw that Michael was far away, farther away than he had ever been in trance or memory. He was in shock, she thought dispassionately. His face, which would be the pattern of beauty for her all the rest of her life, was bewildered. Shen had seen it, too. Hanna did not say anything to Shen about what the two of them must do. Shen already knew. There were two of them to think; that would have to be enough.

A dream. He remembered feeling like this before sometimes—when he was saturated with drink or drugs, and nothing that happened was connected to anything else, and faces were phantasms that came out of air and went back into it, and every phrase uttered by every voice was significant, masking a secret that in a minute, just a minute, he would understand. It was stupid, not to be able to understand.

Here was a lean old face with sunken cheeks. "I lived in the barracks in those years," Conwy said, "in Zed-Alpha-Eight. I had a wife. I had a child. Two other children were born dead. Now my wife and the child who lived, they are dead, too."

Croft, Michael heard himself say. *Sutherland*, he said.

Conwy had not heard of them. He had not known a woman called Kia.

"Dead, so many dead," he said.

"This time?" Michael was learning. The smell of the gas was strong, it must be full of impurities.

"Every time. This is the fourth, and the worst. Fin-

ished, some say. I don't know. No doubt it will come
again.''

The shadows in the room jiggled at a draft. They were
all Michael could see. He heard Hanna murmur questions, Conwy answering. Conwy knew a man, old like
himself, who had been a musician once.

''Take us there,'' Hanna said.

''He will be sleeping,'' Conwy said.

''I know.'' She knelt at Conwy's side and smiled at
him. She was not hard now. She was softened, and the
softness was real, not deceit, and when she smiled even
Marin must have thought her beautiful.

''Well, then, we will make him wake up,'' Conwy
said.

And it was not far, and the man at the end of the path
was Norn, bald now, with deep eyes under heavy brows.
Michael recognized him, and wept.

Hanna squatted side by side with Shen. Shen whispered, ''Past the middle of the night.''

''I know.''

''Where's B?''

''Maybe this one knows.''

''Wouldn't count on longer than dawn.''

''No.''

Shen inched closer. She said, ''What's wrong with
Mike?''

Hanna said calmly, ''He'll be all right.''

''Never seen this.''

''I have.''

''All right. All right. Look, he's different. Not like
anybody else. I know that. Think I don't know that?
Never seen this, though. Gotta get him out of here.''

''In a while.''

Shen did not find this satisfactory. She retreated into
sullen silence, fingering her stunner. It would not be
good enough if B caught up with them.

Norn in rags was enthroned on a magnificent chair.
''I was not there, but I heard,'' he said. ''There was
nothing left but burnt bones. There were three of them,
yes, three piles of smoked bones. I heard they were

kind to Kia, that after what they did she would not have walked again, nor sung, and killing her was kind. I heard Alban was there, and died, too, and the visitor, the woman Lillin, your mother. Did you hope she had escaped?''

''No.'' On the ship without a name Michael had heard too much about Lillin's death. He had never hoped it was a lie. The details had been too cruelly clear.

''The babe lived,'' Norn said.

''Lived . . .''

''Oh, yes. Snatched out living at the last by one of those who killed her mother. I did not know the man. But evidently there were some things he could not do, and leaving the child in that house, knowing the fire would be next, was a thing he could not stand for. He handed her to the first woman he saw in the street. Ercole; do you remember Ercole? She is dead now.''

''I do not—no, perhaps I do. What happened then to the child?''

''Why, I do not know for a certainty. Ercole kept her a time, though the winter was lean. There has not been a winter of such thinness in my lifetime, not even the last, though the one that comes now will starve us all. Ercole kept her until a man and woman came seeking you and your mother and the babe.''

''When? Who were they? Where did they go?''

''Slowly, slowly. It was a long time ago. With Kia gone I had no reason to go to that part of the town, you understand? I do not remember what else I heard. It is too long ago. Why did you wait so long to come back? They said Tistou took you away; where have you been?''

''I didn't know the way back,'' Michael said, but Norn looked at him with mistrust, so he said, ''There were people, when I was a boy, who thought Tistou came from another world. Do you remember that?''

''Yes,'' Norn said. ''There are those who think so still. They say he comes from a homeland of which this was to be an outpost. But we are forgotten; that is what they say. When I was younger, I believed the part about the homeland, because surely this world is forgotten, but not that the traveler went back and forth. Now I wonder. He comes and goes, he has the only flying machine ever seen, and he has not grown old, as I have. Did you learn the truth?''

"It is all true. When I escaped from him, I was not here any more. I have tried to find my way back ever since.''

Michael waited for Norn to take it in. Norn scowled and was silent. Hanna said gently, "It is hard to understand. But what Mikhail says is true. We will go back, and you will not be forgotten any more. People will come with food and medicines. But now Mikhail must find his sister, if she lives; and the traveler is here now, is he not? We found this place by following him, but he does not know that yet. If he finds out, he will try to kill us before we can bring help. Do you know where he is?''

"No," Norn said. He looked at Michael shrewdly. "If that is true, you must have a flying machine, too. Where is yours?''

Michael's mind was on the piles of bones, the weeping child given to a stranger in the street. Hanna answered, "It is hidden, we hope. We cannot allow Tistou to know we are here.''

"Is it warm inside, like his? Is there plenty to eat? That is what they say of his, but he does not give much away. He came in the summer, there was food then, not much but enough. Now there is hardly any. Men have gone to Tistou to beg, and he has sent them away with empty hands. Then he grew tired of beggars, it seems, for the last one who went, he killed. Do you have food?''

"We have food. We will bring it, if we can. But if we are to do that, and if we are to get away to bring help here, we must know where Tistou is. Is there anyone who knows?''

Norn said to Michael, "Do you still play?''

Michael nodded slightly. Hanna saw fire reflected in his eyes, red against the snow. She said, "He has become a master of the instrument. If there is a chance, he will play for you. But you must help him get the chance. Norn, we are in deadly danger from this Tistou.

There is a man who came here with us, who knew Tistou from before, and he has disappeared. I think he will betray us, do you understand? We must know where our enemy is. Will you not help us?"

"I have told you I do not know," Norn said, and it was the truth. But then he said, "There is one who may know. I will take you to her."

Deeper into the night, into the maze. Even Hanna was lost now. Norn could not move fast. His spine and the joints of his legs were knobby and inflamed, and every step was painful. Michael supported him. He thought of the medicines on the *Golden Girl*; he thought that where he had grown up, Norn's condition must be a footnote to the history of medicine. And then he wondered about Norn's age. He could not be more than sixty in Standard years.

Hanna murmured, "We take them for granted, the anti-senescence treatments. I've had one. And you?"

"Two."

Norn ought to be still a young man.

Norn talked as he cautiously, painfully moved.

"A bad winter, that. But this one that comes, I will not see its end."

Sometimes there were sounds in the rooms they passed, as sleepers roused at the slow footsteps. But only once did anyone look out.

"By that spring so long ago, many folk were scattered, and the guards too weak to follow."

The years flickered as Norn talked, springs rising and falling. A slow recovery; the next two waves of sickness had not been so bad. The masters had still lived behind their wall.

"All who might have risen up were dead, or fled. There were none fool enough to do what Kia did."

New seedstock appeared, blight-resistant, giving great yields. "Did he bring it?" Hanna said. "The man Tistou?"

"Perhaps," Norn said, and Shen said, "Why?"

Hanna answered, "Why did he do anything? He does

not seem to have gotten rich through coming here. How did he come here to begin with? Who is he?''

Now for the first time there was a gust of outside air. They turned into a hall where arched windows made up one side. Some were open and others broken, and a strong breeze blew through them. The sound of the sea was audible. Hanna turned to one of the windows. She had been born near an ocean, and could not resist the sound of any sea. But the night was so dark that the waves, however close, were invisible.

''This way,'' Norn said, not pointing but shifting his weight on Michael's arm to indicate the path. They went through an arched door opposite the windows and stood in the dark. ''Darya! Daryeva!'' called Norn, and Hanna's light picked out a figure on the floor.

She was Norn's granddaughter. She was perhaps sixteen, with a little pointed brown face and large eyes. She looked at all of them, even Norn, with fear, and Norn stood there and told them her history: how in the first weeks after Tistou had come, in the summer, one of his companions had seen Daryeva, and liked what he saw; how Daryeva had not stayed out of sight but sought out the man, and lived for a time now and then on the flying machine; how she had started a child, and lost it, and then seemingly lost her power to charm the big fair-haired man, because he rarely came to see her now; how her own folk, virtuous, would have nothing to do with her.

Not calculated to gain her confidence, Hanna said to Michael's head. But the girl said to Norn: ''When you thought I could get food for you, you were not so quick to cry punishment! What do you do here, old man? Will you sell me for the night for half a loaf, as before?''

Norn began to shout. Hanna said quickly, ''Get him out of here,'' and Shen did it without much trouble, marching the old man out with an arm locked behind his back. They heard him cursing in the hall, in a burst of wind that blew in.

Hanna and Michael sat down uninvited, but with a

common impulse. There was no point in scaring the child with shadows twice her size.

"You do it," Hanna said to Michael; he read the meaning in her eyes. *You can gain anyone's trust.*

But he asked his own questions, not the ones Hanna wanted him to ask. *Did you ever hear of a woman called Kia? The name Lillin? A girl, no, woman, Carmina, now twice your age?* Daryeva thought him mad; harmless, though; his eyes were so hurt, his voice so gentle. She developed a small frightened coyness, a poor residue of her liaison with the man Wales. Hanna moved at Michael's side, said impatiently in his head, *Ask her about the* Avalon! He only thought: *Poor little Darya.* "Soft," Hanna muttered in Standard, "you're too damn soft. Shen was right." She shifted languages. "Where have they gone to, girl, the man who got you with child, and the others, and the machine that flies?"

"It does not only fly," the girl said. "It is a spaceship." She said the Standard word well, with little accent.

"Well, and where has it gone? Where is it hidden?"

Defiance flared in the great eyes. Michael touched her arm and said gently, "Please answer."

She would answer for him. She said, ignoring Hanna, "It has gone away to the south where it is warm. Once before it went, and I went, too. He did not take me this time. But he will come back."

"Do you want to wait for him?" Michael said. "You could come with us instead."

The defiance melted. Her eyes became luminous; she was a child, reminding him painfully of Lise.

Hanna said, "We can't take her now. We'll come back for her if we can."

She was exasperated. There was nervousness in her voice, in every quick movement.

"He's not even in this part of the world," Michael said. "We don't have to hurry any more."

"Just how long do you think it will take us to question every old man and woman in the place?"

"Not long. When it gets light, not long."

* * *

They waited for dawn in Daryeva's little room. It was scarcely more than a closet, but she had made it her own. There were shells from a southern sea, a bracelet of Polity manufacture—part of the *Far-Flying Bird's* stolen trove, Hanna guessed. There were dried native flowers in a Polity vase, a music cube made on Willow, a head clumsily carved of highland wood. It was supposed to resemble Daryeva; Wales had made it for her.

Hanna and Shen wandered in and out. One of them was always in the hall, listening, watching. Michael stayed with Daryeva. She told him the story of her short life. She was young and resilient and she did not know how sad it was. He put his arm around her, half-blinded—sometimes she was Lise, sometimes himself. He was too torn with pity to see clearly. But it seemed to him that none of what had happened to Daryeva needed to have happened.

If I had not been so self-protecting I would have, could have—

Morning finally came. The rain had stopped. Hanna and Shen looked through the broken arches uncertainly, as if, deprived of rain, they might no longer be on the same world. Outside the arches was a broad stone esplanade set two meters above the wet sand, which stretched a considerable distance to the receding tide. Sea and sky alike were gray.

When it was full light, Michael had Daryeva take them to a courtyard she had told him about in the night. It was almost in the center of the occupied portion of the maze, and it was all the marketplace of which the Post could now boast. In the early morning people straggled in. Some brought food from outside, not much; those fortunate enough to have food grown and stored against the winter begrudged it. But there were still warm clothes and blankets to be looted from the ruined mansions, and a certain trade was carried out that way, food for warmth.

Michael moved from person to person, group to group. His questions were thrown back at him unanswered. He might as well have been on the wrong world.

I knew no one of that name. Nor that. He was an antic figure here, too well fed, too well clothed, with the dark women dogging his heels and the pariah Daryeva following. *How old do you think I am, to remember those days? Why, I was not even born!* There was no body of shared knowledge, no collective memory, it had died with the old and with displacement, or what was left was crippled and incomplete. *I have never heard of such a town. Never. Never.* "Every old man and woman in the place," Hanna had said; but the old were rare. The look of age was deceiving. The "old," like Norn, might be only of an age that elsewhere would be the beginning of life's prime. Shen thought little of it, Michael nothing. But Hanna that morning felt stifling horror for a while. It was unnatural and obscene for death to come after so few years. She told herself anti-senescence was really the unnatural thing, but it didn't help; she was horrified still. The specter of early death made ghosts even of the young.

It was in the center of the circles of the doomed, then, that Michael stood and shouted, reckless. He threw names into the gray wind and they blew back to his mouth. Shen grumbled without ceasing, watched the crowd with slitted eyes; Hanna watched the sky. Both missed at first the man—a young man—who finally came forward and tugged Michael's arm. But they saw Michael bend his head to the other's, and started forward, hands on their hidden weapons.

The man slipped away before they got to him. But Michael came to meet them. His eyes glittered.

"That was the road to Croft, the one we came in on," he said.

Hanna looked at the circles of murmuring men and women, but she could not see where the man had gone.

"It is dead," she said. "Marin said so."

"No, no. People have come back, she said."

"And what does that mean, when the people who once lived there are dead? They were all taken from the town when you were. Does it matter who lives there now?"

"It might. Do you remember what Norn said? The

man and woman who took Carmina, knew us. They must have come from Croft or Sutherland. And later, he said, the people scattered. They could have gone home.''

''All right. All right.'' She pulled the communicator from her pocket. ''We'll get *GeeGee* in. Follow the road to its end.'' She looked at the sky as she thumbed the transmittal switch. If *GeeGee* could monitor ground transmissions from the air, the *Avalon* could, too. But the gray sky was empty.

GeeGee was ready for quick flight, as she had been everywhere. A very sleepy Theo landed her at the Post thirty minutes after Hanna's call. ''I'm going to bed now,'' he said, but he didn't. He waited in Control with the others, watching the land unroll beneath the *Golden Girl*. They passed over Orne's house in minutes and flew steadily north over the deserted lands.

''It's not paved all the way,'' Michael said.

''You remember?''

''I remember—'' *The dusty track through Croft*. For all he had ever known it was dust all the way to its unknown end. He closed his eyes briefly, remembering, and constructed a map in his head. The paving stretched to Sutherland. Croft lay a little to the southwest, with the dirt track (how deep in mud today?) curving through its tiny heart. One end went to Sutherland; the other must keep up the curve, and come around to join the main road to the Post.

When he looked again, they were flashing over *GeeGee's* first landing site, that abandoned clearing in the wilderness. He might never know why it was there. Orne's summer lodge had surprised him, too. He had not known the masters ever left their walls, except to walk in the town like gods. There was so much he did not know, might have learned long ago—if he had told the truth at the start on Alta. Instead he had allowed the last, the only memories to seal his lips, had turned away all questions, until it was too late and the *Pavonis Queen* separated him for good from any power that might have tracked down B and uncovered the secrets of this place.

While here the people died in waves of sickness, their brutal unbalanced civilization toppling.

I could have stopped it. I let it happen—

But he had been rattled and shaken like a die in a cup, and the hand that had done it was here somewhere. He thought of that soft white hand with an awe so deep it was nearly terror.

Hanna said softly, "He is only a man."

Maybe.

He was weak, so sick he doubled over. When he recovered enough to straighten, he said, "How could one man get so much power?"

"Why, chance," said the dark woman, an oracle again. He looked into her eyes and thought he saw the ambiguous eyespots of Uskos. "Not much is predictable and not much is just," she said; she might have been Norsa citing a lesson of the Master.

"No," Michael said, rejecting it.

"You knew that," she said. "Every day of your life has proved it."

He felt the others watching him, and felt the burden of their lives, which all of them, even Hanna, owed to him. He felt the futility of it in the face of the desertion below.

"Yes," said Hanna. "But you'll go back for Daryeva all the same, when you can. Won't you?"

The sickness began to pass. "Of course," he said.

The land rose under *GeeGee*. There must be changes in the nature of the forest below, but they were not evident from the air. The road snaked on patiently and the horizon billowed with mountains. They were flying low, under the cloud cover, but before they reached the mountains the clouds changed, were higher and thinner, the air brighter; the great funnel was moving at last. They did not have to slow as much as he had expected to follow the road, which after a tortuous course of preliminary turns made straight for a gap in the last fold of land. Sunlight flashed off *GeeGee's* nose as she emerged from it, the flanks of the mountains fell away, the road swooped down in the sun on a broad plateau and turned north. There was silence in Control.

He saw the dirt track veering west before anybody else. When he told Theo to turn *GeeGee* and follow it, nobody said anything.

The land moved under them dun and green. The mountains threw out a feeler, and the village on its unhurried river nestled up against them. He had seen it from the air before, yes, from that mountain peak. The perspective was different, but he would have known it in spite of worse distortions. Home.

He took the helm and set *GeeGee* down slowly in a barren grain field, wondering if he would have to ask someone to finish the job; his knees and hands were weak. Croft appeared eerily unchanged. Even the field was recently harvested; people lived here, then. *Most likely nobody I knew,* he cautioned himself. And a figure walked across the field toward *GeeGee*, stopping, however, a hundred meters from the nearest structure (Annitas' house), too far from *GeeGee* to make out a face.

"Mike," said Hanna. "Look." He looked, and saw what she indicated: a second figure, this one half-hidden by the corner of the house. It held something. A weapon?

"Covering the other one," Hanna said.

He went alone to meet the man who stood in the field. The brilliant sunlight shone on his head with a trace of autumn warmth, but a strong wind was blowing, pushing the clouds away. The air had the heady wine taste he remembered, had never tasted anywhere else. He walked quickly, but it seemed to take a long time. The man who waited was powerfully built, with a grizzled head and broad familiar face. His eyes got bigger and bigger as Michael came near. Michael stopped in front of him and said, "Otto?"

"A-Alek?" said the other man, hardly getting it out.

"It's Mikhail. I've come back. Looking for my sister; is she alive?"

Otto got his mouth shut. He turned and waved a jerky arm and the other figure, armed, came into the open and came up to them. It was a woman, tall and slender, with a hard lovely face and eyes Michael knew. They were his own.

"Greetings, Carmina," he said.

"Somebody has to stay on *GeeGee*," Hanna said to Shen. Lise and Theo were already gone at Michael's beckoning, Lise tumbling out of *GeeGee* with eager haste, Theo looking stunned.

"You go," Shen said.

"All right." Hanna was nervous. She quivered with alarm; she had caught some of Michael's superstitious fear in spite of herself. *B is a real man with real guns*, she told herself, but she heard Rubee's comfortable voice telling tales all the same.

Finally she left *GeeGee*. Shen could be trusted, she told herself. Shen knew what to do.

The wind outside was sharp, the sunlight dizzying. A faint, luminous streak arced across the high sky: the Ring. The long slopes tilting up toward the mountains were deserted, but when the wind fell for a moment, she heard the tinkle of small bells where herd animals clustered in sunny hollows, gleaning the last sweet mouthfuls of summer growth. The people who had come out of the stone houses had all disappeared into one. Hanna went toward it slowly. Up close, the village did not look whole. Some houses were deserted and falling, succeeding summers and winters having shifted their stones. But everything was here, on the whole just as Michael had remembered it. She went into the house where the others were; it was Otto's, she found.

That was Marlie and I who came for you. Our son was dead, the first; later we had another, he lives, here he is. We did not find you, but we found Carmina. Brought her home.

Michael could not take his eyes off Carmina. It was strange to see Alek and Lillin in her face. There was a tranquillity in her that he recognized; he had had it, too, sometimes. But rarely, only on the very best days. She had given him up for dead as soon as she was old enough for Otto to make her understand what had happened. Her only brother had been Milo, Otto's living son.

No one here was ever troubled again. Life went on, and death; Marlie died last year. But not of that evil, that sickness brought from outside.

From outside? Are you sure?

Yes. Sure. It came only when the traveler came, he brought it like a gift. Not every time. The last time he came, though, it followed again. And the masters were not exempt as they had been before.

It was what he had feared, the guess Hanna had made, which he had not wanted to face. He looked at her quickly. He saw in her eyes the acknowledgment of his responsibility. But then she looked away, at nothing in particular. She seemed to be listening for something above the chatter. Theo had not registered what Otto said; he was busy trying to be invisible, and failing among these dark people. There were perhaps sixty, most strangers to Michael, and half, he learned, were recent refugees from the Post; they had abandoned it and made their way north at the first report of fever. Life here was lived much as it had been lived before, and the disintegration of the city in the lowlands was a rumor that hardly touched Croft.

Shen waited stolidly on *GeeGee*, ready to take off with an instant's notice or none at all. She was not restless as Hanna would have been in her place, but checked all the indicators with an occasional steady sweep of the eyes. Hanna spoke with her from time to time.

"I don't know when I'll be able to get him out of here. He won't want to go."

"So tell him to bring the sister along."

"It's a thought."

Shen said irritably, "Wouldn't matter if every last body back there didn't know where we are."

"Yes."

And somewhere there was a radio. And somewhere there was Henrik, creeping toward the Post, maybe already there.

"Nowhere to go anyhow," Shen muttered.

"That's not true any more," Hanna said, her voice light and thoughtful. "He'll want to go back now. Just as fast as we can."

"Whatever." Shen went back to studying what *GeeGee* had to say. Ready to run.

The shadows shifted in the clear afternoon. People left Otto's house in twos and threes, going back to their occupations. They cast curious looks at *GeeGee*, but they knew what she was; they were not ignorant.

"We know more than they do on the flats," Otto said. "That's Carmina's doing."

Carmina smiled and shook her head, disclaiming the praise, but it was true, Michael found. She had asked questions from the time she could talk, and put the answers together with remarkable accuracy. Nothing Michael said surprised her greatly; only the details fascinated her. She was prepared for days of conversation.

"There can't be days," Hanna said, close to Michael's elbow, touching it impatiently.

"No, I know, that's true."

"Come along with us," said Hanna, addressing Carmina. "We have to get in the air." It was safe in space; safer than here, on the ground and exposed.

"I'll stay. I'll wait for you to come back."

There was a heartbreaking serenity about Carmina, as if she had resigned herself to waiting many years ago with unflagging patience. She was unmarried and childless. It seemed possible that she had never been touched, had held herself always a little apart from life. Not what Michael would have done, here or anywhere; not what he could have done. She was detached even from this exotic brother. Who could be nothing more to her, after all, than a dim memory of song.

"Michael, we have to go!" Hanna said.

"I know." But he did not move. He stayed near Otto's fire, not next to Carmina but placed so that he could look at her without interruption, tracing resemblances.

Hanna jittered, dancing with nerves. "Mike, *please!*"

"It's just that I might not be able to come back

again," he said to her in Standard, not wanting to alarm Carmina. "There'll be help from the Polity; I'll make sure of that. But when I turn myself in, it might be the end for me."

"Nonsense," Hanna said. "All you have to do is trade. Information for freedom. I thought you saw that, I thought you knew it. That this was the way out."

"I can't trade with this, I can't take a chance. Enough's happened because I was thinking of myself."

She was unconvinced. Well, she would have all the weeks it took to get back to Theta to try and change his mind. But he did not mean to let it be changed. His survival was not important any more. Gadrah's was.

"Come along, come along, Mike. We have to go."

"In a minute. A few more minutes."

Hanna chewed her fingernails.

The mountains swooped into the great valley and then started up again on the other side, not as high there, but high enough to cut off the sun at a rather early hour. The western shadows crept across the valley and made a final leap; suddenly it was dusk. The gleam of the river faded. Shen got food from the galley and carried it back to Control. There was nothing to see out *GeeGee's* nose with the naked eye any more, so she adjusted the monitors for night vision and watched them instead. But the radar was more important, the radar searching the sky. Though that, she knew, was terrifyingly limited. The *Avalon* could wind through the mountains low and slow, come up behind that last tall peak, and never be spotted or suspected till she came around the mountain accelerating and spitting fire.

Shen began to think about lifting *GeeGee* into the air, getting above the mountains and scanning exhaustively for an intruder. The only recourse of an unarmed ship facing one with arms was flight. With people on the ground to be picked up, seconds would count.

"Come on," she growled. "Get him out of there. Come on!"

She took the remains of her meal back to the galley and put them away. When she returned to Control, she had made up her mind. She would take *GeeGee* up and look around.

She was reaching for the communications switch to tell Hanna that when the Avalon rose up from behind the mountain peak, and radar picked it up and set off a shrill alarm.

The communicator on Hanna's wrist went off frantically. The noises outside were unmistakable, the scream of *GeeGee* taking off in a single max-power burst, the thunder of other engines, then a roar that split the night. Hanna flung open the door just in time to see a gout of flame erupt where *GeeGee* had been—but no longer was; she was a flurry of light streaking up the valley and up into the air, headed for space. "She's gone!" Theo said in despair, but Hanna said, "*GeeGee's* our only chance. Shen's got to keep her safe. And she's drawn them off. We've got some time."

There was another burst of fire, high this time, and far away. Hanna held her breath, but there was no explosion, no fireball. *GeeGee* was still intact, still running hard.

She looked around and saw Michael with relief—the old Michael, to whom danger was a practical problem with concrete solutions.

"They'll come back," he said. "Theo and Lise could stay here. B doesn't know them."

"Henrik does."

"Henrik. Damn him. All right; we've all got to go." He asked Otto, "Have you got anything that would help us get out?"

"Carts," Otto said. "Beasts."

"We'll go on foot, then."

"Where to?" Hanna said.

"Sutherland," Michael said. "Come on."

He had lied, though. As soon as the night hid them from Croft he turned away from the road and led them down the riverbank. "There were too many people back there," he said. "Otto won't tell them what I saw, Carmina won't—maybe. What are they going to say when their neighbors are threatened? And there were people there I don't know. Who don't understand what it means, why we have to get away. There used to be a ford here.'' It was still there. They had to use the light, worrying Michael, but a hillock on the edge of the stream largely hid the ford from Croft. The rocks were slippery underfoot.

''Where's there to go?'' Theo said.

''The mountain. Caves there. We've still got food tabs, there's plenty of water; if we're careful we can even use fire. We could hold out for a while.''

''They won't stop hunting till they find us,'' Hanna said.

''If they're looking around Sutherland, though, it'll give Shen a chance to come back and get us.''

They ran up the long bare slope of the mountain's foot until Lise lagged behind, her breath coming in painful gasps she had tried to suppress. Michael carried her for a time, and they walked, but they did not stop. It was imperative to get under cover. Even the line of the first trees above was no guarantee of safety; there was no reason to suppose anything was wrong with the *Avalon's* infrared sensors. They had to get under the earth, into the caves Michael remembered. There was still a long way to go.

Lise said finally, ''I can walk.'' It was the first thing she had said since the crisis began. He put her down and trudged upward. The wind had died with the day, and walking kept them warm. Hanna's face was turned to the sky; she tripped once or twice. But she was no longer looking for the *Avalon*, at least not entirely. She was looking because the sky, clear now, was alive. A tiny moon that cast little light moved across it so quickly the motion was visible; before it disappeared another came, describing a different arc. The Ring was a high distant arch, unchanging; only now that she could see it well, she saw it was really a plurality of rings, a series of delicate-looking bands separated by strips of night. Now and again a meteor flared. It was not the season for any of the great showers. But in one quadrant of the sky a comet shone like a stylized picture of all the comets that had ever existed. All these phenomena stood out prominently in a sky that otherwise was scantily starred. No sky anywhere else was like it.

They came up under the trees, which quickly thickened and cut off the sky. Michael cast the light about, hesitating. His hearing seemed unnaturally sensitive; now he, too, listened for the sounds Hanna strained to hear, the noise of a spacecraft moving across the sky. But there was icy silence on the mountainside. There was only a small cold wind which they had come high enough to feel, a wind that did not touch the valley below. The dying leaves on their malleable trees rattled in the wind; they would not fall until spring.

"This way," he said with more hope than certainty, but when they had wound through a grove where the trees stood close together, he saw he had been right. The game trail he remembered had scarcely shifted. They followed it up.

The *Avalon* was as Henrik had remembered it, only worse in some ways. It was still dark, and it smelled worse than ever, as if no one ever bothered to clean any part of it up, and remnants of food had lain carelessly in corners for months. A bin of foodstuffs had gone bad—as Henrik discovered when he opened it, looking for something to eat, and the stench nearly knocked him over. He closed it quickly, but not before he got a glimpse of what was inside—a writhing heap of something white and wet.

He tried not to think of the *Golden Girl*—the light and the music. But the music would not stay out of his head. *Tambours and sackbuts*. "It's not my fault the bastard got born a thousand years too late," Henrik said, but he only said it to himself. He couldn't say it to anyone here. It was strange to think he could have said that to Theo, or Hanna, or even to Michael Kristofik; Kristofik would only have laughed.

Since there was no one to talk to, he went back to his old cabin and crouched in a corner with his head in his hands, in the dark. Maybe he had done the wrong thing. But it did not seem to him that he had done anything at

all. He had watched Michael leave the *Golden Girl* and
plunge into the sea of trees and rain, tall and confident,
with Hanna and Shen—leaving Henrik behind, like Lise,
with Theo to babysit for both of them. There was nothing to do but wait, nothing but stay where he was put.
He had resented it, and the resentment had grown
through a day and a night until it filled him and burst
out. He had been carried here against his will, and was
he now to be left behind while the others were out in
the rain and fresh air? Was he less of a man than the
women? At the end of the second day Theo was dozing,
Lise invisible. It took only minutes to get what he
needed and get outside. He made his way to the road
and started down it; maybe he would meet the others
coming back. He did not, and the night came, and he
meant to turn back, and then realized that he would
never see, in the dark, the place where he must leave
the road to get back to the ship. And the ship might
take off before he reached it; what if it took off? He did
not think Theo would wait for him.

The rain came down drearily. The night was colder
than he had expected. There was nothing to do but keep
following Michael. There was shelter on this road, at
least; he had heard the others tell Theo about it the
night before. He had to find it. He kept walking.

He did find it; found Orne, his suspicions now fully
aroused; woke at dawn with Orne grumbling in his ear,
was urged into the ramshackle truck. "I want to find
the others, I just want to find them," he said. Orne
said, "Well, and this is the way they went." And the
town in the cold morning, the curiosity, the talk that
went so fast he could not keep up with it. And the pretty
brown girl, the radio hidden among her scant belong-
ings, preset for the issuing of warnings. She had not
wanted to use it, but her grandfather pushed her aside
and took it, plain fear in his eyes. And then the *Avalon*
came in across the sky, and it was too late for Henrik
to run, too late for him to do anything even if he had
been able to think of anything to do.

So now he crouched in the dark, ignored, unimportant, trying to think. B would never go back to the Pol-

ity, and Henrik's only chance was to get back to Michael and get away when the others did. Unless they had already gone on the ship B had failed to shoot down.

But B did not think they were all on that ship.

He had asked Henrik: "If some were on the ground, would the others go?"

"No," Henrik had said. He knew them well enough to be sure of that. He had lived with them long enough to know.

He huddled in the dark and waited. No one came near him. No one had spoken to him except B. Ta had not said, "Where you been?" Bakti had not said, "Good to see you." They had not looked the same. There was strained desperation in their faces—and it must have predated the *Golden Girl's* coming here, it was etched too deep to have sprung up all at once. They looked like men who did not want to be where they were.

The *Avalon* was moving, but no one had told him where. The door opened, the light came on, and he looked up. Maybe someone would tell him something. B stood there, the old empty smile on his lips.

"I think I've got it straight what you did," he said. "Think of anything else I ought to know?"

His voice was toneless. Henrik was reassured. He had told B only what he had to, more than he wanted to, he had not dared to refuse. But he would not offer any more information. He could give Michael that, he could give Hanna that.

"I don't know any more," he said gratefully. "There's nothing more that would help."

"Sure?"

"Sure."

B's hand came around from behind his back. There was something in it, laser pistol or disruptor, Henrik never decided which and there was no time to think about the mistakes he had made; there was an instant of shock, and he was dead.

If the caverns had been too high on the mountain, they could not have made it. Michael was sure of that; sure the *Avalon* would be back in the night, whether it

caught up with *GeeGee* or not. If it caught up with
GeeGee—his first thought was of Shen, but he forced it
down. Shen wouldn't like that. She would call him soft.
Well, then, even with Shen and *GeeGee* gone there
would be a way out, though it would mean getting control of the *Avalon*.

But all they could do now was hide. He urged the
others up the mountainside, climbing, climbing. Old
landmarks rose up in the dark and fell behind, it was a
shorter climb than he remembered; no, his legs were
longer, twice as long, an eerie echo of trance. Theo and
Hanna went on steadily, breathing hard till the second
wind came; then they seemed, as Michael felt, tireless.
But it was hard on Lise. She leaned on his arm; he half-
carried her.

They came around the edge of a high bluff, and he
turned and plunged into the brush at its base.

The opening was still there, and hidden even better
than in his childhood; a tree had grown up in front of
it. He probed at the undergrowth, using the light openly
now, and carefully. Not all the beasts in these mountains were harmless, and some visited caves. He heard
Hanna behind him, listening. For bestial near-thought
from the cave? For something in the sky? If the latter,
there was nothing to hear but Lise gasping and wheez-
ing, desperate for rest.

Hanna said nothing about an animal presence, and
there was no sign of a path through the dried grasses
underfoot. He got on his knees—the opening was low—
and crept in, flashing the light now ahead, now back
for the others. His hands and knees sank into mud and
scraped on pebbles. Lise objected to the mud, fretful,
and he heard Hanna speak to her softly, encouraging,
promising sleep.

The mud dried up and faded into rock. A dislodged
stone rolled ahead on a gentle downward slope; the ceiling lifted overhead. He got up and walked, crouching,
then straightened fully. "Mind your head," Hanna said
to Theo or Lise; then they stood beside him in a clutter
of loose rocks. The stone underfoot was cool and damp.

There was the sound of water nearby, a slow-moving stream; he knew just where it was.

He said, "This is far enough. Somebody's got to be posted at the opening all the time. If Shen calls, we might not pick it up in here."

Theo said, "We can't call *her*. They'd hear."

"Yes. We can only listen, till we know she's close. I'll take the first watch."

Theo looked relieved. He had had even less sleep than the others. He kicked stones away and sat down on the rock without further discussion, leaning against the cave wall. "This feels soft enough," he said. Lise nearly fell next to him. She put her head on his shoulder and he put his arm around her.

Michael turned the light to a dim glow and left it with them. It would shine for months, maybe years; at least they did not have to fear the dark. "The water's just down there," he said, pointing downhill, and made sure they saw where he pointed. "If you need some, for God's sake don't get lost!"

"I'm not that crazy," Theo muttered, and closed his eyes.

Michael crawled back to the mouth of the cave, Hanna following. They laid one of the communicators on a rock in the open and retreated just inside the cave, where they could hear it call but sit upright in some comfort. They swallowed nutrient tablets and took turns going to the stream for water, tiptoeing past Theo and Lise, already sound asleep. When Hanna came back, she had no coat; she had spread it over the other two for warmth. Michael took off his coat, too, and they huddled together under it.

Hanna said, "Oh, God, how I want a bath!"

"There's the stream," he said.

She shivered. "It might come to that."

She leaned against him, still shivering, but not with cold. "Somebody's dead," she said.

"What do you mean? Shen?" he said anxiously.

"I don't think it's Shen. But somebody's died. I felt it on the way up. I would have known if it was Shen. But somebody I know is gone."

Michael held her in silence. He was so accustomed to living with a telepath that she had ceased to seem strange, but sometimes he was reminded that her humanity was of a different order from most, from his.

"It couldn't have been anybody in Croft," he said. "The *Avalon* hasn't come back yet. Somebody at the Post? Somebody on the *Avalon*?"

"I don't think so. I don't know any of those people well enough to feel it if they died. It might not even have been here, it might have been somebody at home. But I think it was here." She paused. "I hope it wasn't Henrik."

He moved involuntarily. He didn't want it to be Henrik. He said as lightly as he could, "What the hell are we going to do about Henrik, anyway?"

"Leave him," she said. "He made his choice. If we get away and get the Polity here, he can go home. To prison, probably."

"I wouldn't like to see that happen."

"No. I guess I wouldn't either. He doesn't really try to be the way he is. He just never knows what he's doing," she said, and Michael laughed.

"I don't either. Do you?"

"Not till it's over," she admitted.

"I stayed too long," he said as if it were the logical sequel. "I couldn't tear myself away."

"I know," she said, forgiving him. She added, "Carmina gave me her gun."

"Is that what you were carrying? Do you know how to use it?"

"I think so." She dug in a pocket and pulled out a bulging pouch; something rattled inside it. "Ammunition," she said.

"That's good. And we've got two stunners. But either way we'll have to be at close range."

"We'll arrange that if we have to," she said.

They sat in silence, waiting. *At the end of the universe*, he thought. Because of the stone overhead and the brush outside, he could not see the sky, not a single star to say there were other places. *Run to ground*—he knew what that meant, now. All the running he had ever done had been only a prelude to this.

But he could not feel despair. Not with Shen out there, faithful; not with Hanna at his side.

He got his hand under her chin, turned her head and kissed her. This night ought to belong to the painful, necessitous nights he had spent dragging himself through memories. But there were all the others, too. Luxury was where you found it, where you made it.

He felt the tension begin to run out of Hanna, melting out like tallow. "I don't want to take too many clothes off," she said.

"We'll see what we can do," he said, and they lay down together on the stony bed, cushioning each other as best they could.

The lights went out one by one in Croft, until the only one left was in the house where Carmina lived with Otto. They had talked for a time, but Carmina was not inclined for conversation, and Otto at length had left her alone. Now as the night wore on, they were silent. Carmina's face was calm but watchful; her eyes moved at every sound. Anyone who knew Michael would have recognized that look.

Her mind was not as quiet as her face and hands. Strangely (but it would not have been strange to anyone who knew Michael) she had no difficulty in accepting what had happened—and might happen. Her brother had come home. That was a fact. He carried the seeds of a revolution; if he got away he would make it happen, and Carmina's life and the lives of everyone she knew would change. That was a fact. Carmina had always dealt in facts, some of them hard. These were better than most.

But the bones of a hard fact, and the richness of the flesh that clothed it, were different things.

Her mind wandered among riches. The man who shared her blood, looking no older than she in spite of the difference in their ages—how little she had learned about him! But much about Gadrah, and much about the worlds outside it. He had seen her thirst for knowledge and ministered to it; she was ashamed, thinking of it; she had not asked what she could give in return. But all he had seemed to want was to look at her.

The candle burned low. The town was silent. There were many who slept, and Otto's gray head drooped and his eyes were half-closed. But no doubt others sat awake in the dark, waiting for a return.

Carmina dreamed, though awake. She dreamed of the worlds of which Mikhail had told her, the busy home-world, the colonies unlike Gadrah where human life had thrived. She dreamed of governments, too, and law, and what they might do here, where there had never been any law but custom—or the caprices of power.

She had been dreaming this last dream a long time when the sound began. She knew it at once, she had known it when she heard it in the afternoon, and it had brought a stark memory of danger, of screaming and terror and fire.

In the afternoon it had only brought her brother home. But now it was night.

She stood in the open door with the candle behind her, inviting danger. Her view of the landing was clear. One spacecraft looked much like another to inexperienced eyes, but she had studied the *Golden Girl* hungrily while she waited in the day at Otto's back, and even in the dark she was certain this was not the same one. The hunters, then.

She stood unmoving while lights came toward her, drawn by light. Two men came to the door and at last she gave way, backing into the room; there were weapons in their hands, and she knew, by description, what they did. She knew one of the men by description as well. The undying. Tistou.

"Where are they?" he said. He looked at her strangely when the light flashed on her face. Otto had gotten up behind her. Tistou said, "Where are they, old man?"

"Gone," Otto said. "The gold ship came and got them."

The traveler said smiling, "The ship has not come

back. It did not turn back soon enough, to have come
back. They are here."

"Well, search, then," Otto said.

They did search; they looked in every house and byre,
the spaceship hovering overhead and flooding the town
with light. The searchers took Carmina with them, and
at each cottage, when the householder was roused, they
put the end of a weapon to the base of her skull, to
show what would happen if there were protests. At each
house she smiled, calm and unafraid, and endured it.
She even endured (though she did not smile) a clumsy
caress from the man with the gun at her head; but Tistou
said, "There's no time. Keep your eyes open." After
that there was only the gun, better than the heavy hand.

One thing frightened her, though she did not show it.
The ship at the rooftops, the light pouring down—she
had seen that a long time before, her earliest memory.

When they were satisfied Croft hid no fugitives, they
took her back to Otto. They put her against the wall and
pointed the guns at her breast. "Where are they?" Tistou said.

"I will not tell you," she said, dreaming of law.

"Well, old man?"

"Sutherland," Otto said. "They took the road—" he
pointed—"that way. At least, they said they would go
that way."

"Do you agree?" Tistou asked her, but she would
not move or speak. He looked at her closely again, as
if some memory or moment of knowledge were near.

He stepped back and put the gun in his belt and went
out, followed by the other man, who was very big and
fair. Carmina moved to the door and watched them go.
Otto said, "I had to tell them, child. They would have
killed you."

"Yes," she said. "But maybe Mikhail thought of
that."

"He was a clever boy," Otto said.

Theo had not looked at the time since nightfall, and
he did not know how long he had slept when Michael
woke him. His chronometer showed Standard time, and

it could not tell him how long it was to dawn. When his eyes were fully open he saw that Michael was exhausted. Hanna stood there, too, heavy with sleep.

"Your turn. Wake me in a couple hours," Michael said.

Theo went for water first. On the way back to the mouth of the cave, passing the others, he saw that Michael and Hanna were already asleep. Hanna had taken his place and slept with her arms around Lise, who had hardly stirred, and Michael held Hanna. The three were very close, very beautiful—and vulnerable. There was a mountain over their heads and it could fall and crush them in a moment.

The chill of the cavern reached into Theo's bones. The only help he could give was to watch, so he did it.

He did not wait inside the cave but just at the opening, ready to duck inside at the first sign or sound of anything in the air. He was cold and alone, and even when his eyes adjusted to the dark, even here looking into the open, he felt smothered; the bluff was a mass of black hung over his head and he faced a tree. On either side of the tree, and at either hand, brush shut out everything except a few patches of starless sky. He longed for a clear line of sight to the valley, for *any* sight of it. Michael had said B would return to the village, but if he did, it would be hard for anyone on the mountainside to know it. The wind rustled gently, and whenever it rose Theo started as if he heard hunters creeping through the wood. Once in a windless moment he thought he heard a spacecraft lift off, and jumped to his feet, ready to run. But as he stood in the dark the sound faded and was gone. He strained his ears and heard only the night, until he was not sure he had heard anything at all.

He sat down and waited again. He was still very tired. But he was on guard, fighting sleep, when the communicator set up a sweet steady signal and an unmistakable voice said, "Mike?"

He had never been so glad to hear anything. He said shakily, "Mike's asleep, I'll get him," and scrambled to wake the others.

They came out to a filament of dawn, It wasn't much, because the mountain blotted out the east. Shen said, "Coming in, where are you?" and they stood in the open and looked up at the lightening sky.

Michael got his communicator back and talked into it, thinking *This is too easy.* "Meet us just under the tree line," he said. "About forty-five degrees south from a straight line up the mountain from Croft. See it?"

"Not yet," she said. There was no sound to indicate *GeeGee* was near, and Shen would not tell them where she was, not when someone else might be listening.

They started downhill in a hurry, running and skidding on the steep decline. "What if the other one comes back?" Lise said nervously.

"They'll go after *GeeGee*," Michael answered to reassure her, and saw Hanna nod.

The light strengthened as they went on. Going down was easier than climbing had been, and there was no stopping to peer around in the dark for old, changed landmarks. They were close to the open when they heard *GeeGee*, and a few seconds later saw her gliding in at an altitude not much greater than theirs.

"That's fine," Michael said. "Set her down."

"Hell of a grade," Shen complained. But *GeeGee* stopped in midair and slowly lowered herself toward the ground.

Made it, he thought, and saw Hanna freeze, staring across the valley through the lacy tops of the last trees.

"Tell her to get out!" she cried, there must have been a burst of thought, too, or Shen had seen what Hanna saw, because there was a roar from *GeeGee* and she was gone, leaping into the air as from a catapult. "Back," Michael said, "everybody back!" They did not need to be urged, they all saw the other shape now, a dark blot racing across the valley, and they turned and climbed for their lives. Michael ran behind the others, looking over his shoulder, waiting for an explosion in the air or among them, but there was none. Then the valley was empty and the sound of engines was gone.

They kept running until they tumbled through the

mouth of the cave. The dark past the opening was a wall. *I thought I had stopped running,* Michael thought. He had shoved the light into his pocket as the day grew, and now he got it out and turned it on and they wormed their way back to their first resting place. They sat in a circle round the light, panting and sweating in the chill air.

Michael wondered for the first time what would become of them. He looked at Hanna and saw her hunched, head bowed to her knees. He had never seen her like that before.

After a while Theo stretched out on his back on the stone. He said, "They had us. If they'd fired, it would've been over."

"They went for the ship," Michael said. He looked at the stone because otherwise he would look at Hanna, and he did not want to. For once he did not want her reading his thoughts.

She did not have to read them. She had been a soldier and a killer, and she could make out the strategies of violence for herself.

She said without lifting her head, so that her voice was muffled and expressionless, "*GeeGee's* a lot more important than we are. If he killed us first, there'd be nothing to keep Shen here. So we're bait to keep bringing her back till he shoots her down. Then he can just pick us off . . . He'll come back sooner next time. He was over there waiting. I wonder how long . . . Could you persuade Shen to leave us and carry word home?" She was talking to Michael now, but she still did not raise her head. If Shen did that, a ship of the Fleet would come in a few months' time—but the four left behind would be dead long before then.

She's a realist. Maybe she'd go.

He could not say it. Lise had lain down with her head on Theo's chest, hiding her eyes. How could he tell Shen to go and leave Lise?

"We're tired," he said. "We're not thinking straight. Get some tabs down and get some rest, all of you."

Hanna looked up finally. Her eyes were veiled and she said nothing, only made a one-minute meal of food tabs with the others and afterward said, "Shall I watch?"

"I will. I'll wake you later."

He kissed her quickly and took off for the entrance to the cavern, as if being out of sight meant she could not read his mind.

He waited in the dark and thought about taking a chance.

The first notion had come into his head as he crawled back into the cave, leaving the day behind. He had put it aside as fast as he could, afraid Hanna would see it. He did not think she would like the idea if she knew about it.

The situation was hopeless. The four people on the ground were much less dangerous for B than the *Golden Girl*, which had the course to Gadrah in her data banks. B could not allow her to get away and take that knowledge back to the Polity. But she had to get away—with Hanna and Theo and Lise on board with Shen. He had thought of a way to change things—maybe.

The day had turned bright, and when he looked out from the dark it dazzled him. Time passed, but Hanna did not come out to him, to his relief; she must be asleep; he wanted her to stay asleep. He turned to go where she was—but it was Lise he wanted. And heard someone slither over stone and a moment later saw, to his further relief, that Lise had come out seeking him.

She hunkered down with him between day and night and said, "I couldn't sleep."

"Want to take over on watch?"

"Yes," she said, pleased with his trust.

"Good for you. Wait here a minute."

He crept through the passage of stone for the last time, to the light at the end of it. He meant to steal Hanna's communicator. He was afraid he could not do it without waking her, but she had put it down on the stone beside Carmina's tooled blue-black gun, and he picked it up without disturbing her or making a sound. The disc of light metal was no larger than his palm, and he remembered, incongruously, why he had bought the things in the first place—so he could talk from the great house on Valentine to Theo or Shen on the sand far below at the foot of the cliff, or they could talk to him. Not that anyone going to the beach had ever remembered to take one along. It hadn't mattered; nothing had ever been too urgent to wait.

Then he picked Theo's pocket. Theo muttered and groaned at the light touch, and turned his head back and forth, but he did not wake.

Hanna did not move. He looked at her with longing, but he could not risk a kiss.

He took his booty silently back to Lise. She was in the light now, using the shiny surface of his own communicator as a mirror while she wiped grime from her face with her sleeve.

"Here," he said. "This is Hanna's. I'm taking mine with me. I'm going for a walk and I need it. This is Theo's clock. You keep it. Now, listen. In exactly an hour, if nothing happens sooner, go wake Hanna and Theo up. Tell them I'm going to create a diversion. Do you know what a diversion is?"

"To make those men look the other way?" she said shyly.

"*Very* good. Tell Hanna and Theo that the three of you should go down to the place we were making for this morning. When you get there—this is very important—Hanna's got to get in touch with Shen. Not by voice; telepathically. She has to make Shen understand three things. First, if Shen's not close she's got to come in as close as she dares without being detected. Second, when she's at that point, she's got to let me know. There was a code we used on Revenge, she'll remember it; Hanna should tell her to use it again. And third, when the diversion starts, she's got to pick the three of you up."

He made her repeat it back to him twice. She had it right, but he had also taken the precaution of recording what he said; Hanna would see the blinking light on her communicator and play it back. He gave it to Lise, and with it the packet of food tabs he carried. Win or lose, he would not need them; the others might.

He got up finally, smiling down at Lise. She had listened to him carefully, too caught up in detail to see any flaw in what he proposed, but a trace of doubt came into her eyes at the last.

"What about you?" she said.

He said readily, "You just wait and see. I haven't come this far to get stopped now. All right?"

"All right . . ."

"Remember, let them sleep for another hour."

Which would give him time to get well away before Hanna woke up and wondered exactly what he meant to do. Maybe it would be all right if she did. She might say grimly: *Yes someone's got to do something it might as well be you.* But maybe not. It was better to leave her no choice.

He had come up the mountain once or twice at this time of year to say farewell to summer. The puffball bird-things with their faceted eyes were gone. The forest still tilted in the sunlight, leaning toward morning then evening as the day progressed; all the trees were nearly vertical now. The tenacious leaves made a warm brown roof, and sunlight danced through the spaces between them. The wind had stopped blowing and the silence was so deep as to be a tangible thing. A silence like this was compelling. It warned you to be still and wait and listen, as if the universe had stopped and any sound, however slight, would carry the monumental meaning of its starting up again. His own footsteps made a little noise, but all that did was give him an eerie feeling that he was the only thing in this stasis for which time counted, the only thing that went forward in it, while everything else was frozen in a moment that was, for him, past.

He did not make for the goal he had set the others, the place they had tried to reach at dawn. Instead he crossed the face of the mountain in as straight a line as he could contrive until Croft was directly below him. Then he turned and started down.

He judged that something more than an hour had passed when the trees began to thin and he could see

where he was going. He sat down under one of them.
Hanna would be awake now, and they should have
started for the point that would, he hoped, mark a rendezvous with Shen. They would be moving more slowly
than they had in the morning's futile dash for safety;
give them half an hour. Then Hanna would have to touch
Shen's mind; how long would that take? And then there
would be a little more time, or a lot of time, while Shen
got into position.

Nothing would happen quickly in any case. No matter
how close Shen was now, she would not come in openly.
She would creep in behind the mountains, hugging the
ground and squeezing *GeeGee* through passages cut by
mountain streams. And B would know something was
getting ready to happen. He was over there somewhere,
watching; maybe he would see the spots of heat on the
mountainside, wonder why one had split off, guess it
was Michael. He would not do anything about it yet.
He would wait for the *Golden Girl.*

Michael settled down under his tree and waited, like
B, for the universe to start up again.

Hanna spent the whole way downhill trying to get
herself into a condition where entering trance would be
possible. She could not even breathe deeply, could not
take that first step. *Why, I am afraid,* she thought. She
did not know what Michael was going to do. But, *It's
too dangerous!* she cried to the indifferent trees. Theo
talked gently to Lise, even cheerfully. He did it well; if
Hanna had not been a telepath, she would not have
guessed that he was afraid, too. But he would not let
Lise see it.

The sun had started an imperceptible slide into afternoon when they got to the edge of the trees. The valley
was a bowl of light. Croft, to the right and far below,
looked as if nothing but peace had ever touched it—
except for the charred gouge the *Avalon* had left with a
single shot. Smoke rose gently from chimneys and vanished in the transparent air. A few tiny figures moved
in and around the village. Harvest was over, the great
work of the year was done. They would be mending and

repairing, looking after stock, maybe hunting—but no hunters would go abroad today.

Theo warned Lise, "We have to be quiet now. Hanna has to concentrate." Hanna gave him a bitter look. Concentration seemed impossible. All her mind was busy wondering where Michael was; she couldn't think of anything else.

It was necessary, however. She reached for every bit of discipline she had ever learned in her life, and began what she had to do.

This was another mode of being, and the world was a different place. For eyes there were mountain, valley, sky; for Hanna in trance those things, though perceptible, were unimportant and remote. Much closer were the not-voices in her head.

"Think of stones," she had said to Lise and Theo. They had gathered a handful of pebbles and dutifully fixed their eyes, and their thoughts as well as they could, on that object. They had no training in meditation and it was hard. Other things kept breaking in. *Where is Shen, where is Mike? What does Hanna do so silent and still? What's going to happen? Stones. Stones. Stones.* She identified and detached herself from them. There was something like a soft murmur she identified as Croft. There was apprehension there, but no threat. She set that aside, too.

And touched Michael: *Oh, Michael!* she cried; he had been relaxed, but she felt him come to his feet, startled. She was so close to him that his body might have been at her side.

Love, what do you mean to do?

She got a dim picture in answer, dim because he didn't want her to see it. It had something to do with the *Avalon.*

Only the detachment of trance kept her from objecting. In trance it seemed reasonable enough.

He thought with concentration of Shen. The air seemed a little colder when she did.

There were other presences. She measured them. She had met them before, on the *Avalon.* They had changed, were less confident, and there were not as many as there had been before, but she knew them.

When she had placed all those minds, the men of the *Avalon*, the people of Croft, her own friends, she marked a barrier around them, and reached out for Shen.

Found her at once; saw through her eyes. The warm light in Control, panels blinking as *GeeGee* talked to herself. Shadows of mountains outside the port. Shen was very close, *GeeGee* hidden somehow in a narrow gorge. *Fancy flying to get in!* Shen thought when she was over the first surprise of Hanna's touch.

Excellent indeed, Hanna thought. *Listen now to what comes next—*

Michael sat under the tree, cross-legged, hands folded. The shadows on the mountainside moved slowly, deepening in the hollows that followed the great slopes, trickling into depressions in the valley. The scene took on a texture deep-piled as velvet, and the afternoon light bathed it a rich tinge of gold. He watched it in deep contentment. He looked at the village and put names to the houses. He had not gone to the house where he and Carmina had been born, and he contemplated the unlikelihood that he would ever enter it again. He was calm; he wondered where the old rage had gone. If ever it should appear, surely it should be now, in this trap. But it was gone. Having lost all he had owned, on the point of leaving behind his friends and the love of his life, he was rich—and not alone. He was swimming in gold, the abundant golden light of the valley. The light was the work of a moment. But all moments were filled with gold.

He had lost track of time when the sound came. *Ready*, it had meant on Revenge, and it meant the same thing now. There had been no sight or sound of the *Golden Girl*, and he did not know where she was—but with luck B did not know either.

He did not get up at once. When he did, the universe would start moving again, and he held it back for a minute.

He moved finally; stood up and walked out from the

shelter of the trees. The long fall of land before him was smooth, close-cropped by a summer's grazing. He walked down it without haste, his shadow trailing behind. It was silent here, too, as if the land itself was watching.

He reached the valley's edge and veered a little north to pass Croft by without entering it. All the tiny figures had disappeared. He wondered if Carmina watched, and wondered what she thought.

He meant to walk all the way across the valley if he was allowed to get that far. He might not make it—but he went on and on through field and pasture without challenge. He glanced back sometimes and saw pure peace, and Croft was farther away each time. The silence continued undisturbed. Doubt crept into his mind—was he going the wrong way, was B even there?

He is there, said a whisper like a thread of ice, and he faltered for the first time, knowing Hanna on the hillside not only watched him but accompanied him. He had not meant for her to do that.

Go on, she said, *he is waiting for you,* and he recognized the cold voice of trance. She did not ask what he meant to do. Perhaps she knew he had no clear idea. It depended on B.

He came finally to the hills opposite Croft. They were neither as high nor as heavily forested as those on the eastern edge of the valley, but there was plenty of room to hide in them, and to hide the *Avalon.* He stopped and looked ahead and to either side without seeing a sign of the ship. There was no whisper in his mind to guide him. Hanna could not know precisely where it was either.

He took the communicator from his pocket and held it in the open. Anyone listening would hear what he said.

He said, "B . . ."

He made a long sound of it, almost a caress. Most likely the creature had not been called by that sound for thirty years.

"B," he said, "let's talk."

* * *

The silence was so long that he thought it might not work, even come near working, even make a start. He had nothing to offer and no threat to make. *If I were B, I would kill me now and go right on waiting for* GeeGee. Picking off a leader made good sense. But B might think Hanna the greater threat that way.

Nothing happened. The lovely country spread around him in the same silence as before, until he thought there would be no answer and he must stand here disregarded until he gave up and went back, impotent.

The cold voice split the quiet when he was almost ready to turn. It said: "What's there to talk about?"

"There's questions," Michael said, playing his empty hand. "Questions nobody's asked you before. And there's staying alive. I can't go back either. One minute under probe and I'm a candidate for Adjustment. How about a truce? It could be comfortable here if we get together."

He stood waiting as calmly as if B had a reason to keep him alive. There could not be one. The only question was whether what he said would spark a little curiosity. To come to B like this was an admission of defeat. B would know it, and maybe that would work on him. Maybe confidence would lead him to indulge in some play before he ended it.

The voice said finally: "Talk, then."

Michael said, "Face to face."

He took out the stunner he had, held it out for watching eyes to see, and threw it away from him.

"That's all I've got," he said. "You'll search me anyway. I'm alone and there's four of you. I'll never catch you sleeping like I did the other time."

He waited again. The reminder of what he had done to B one night as a boy was deliberate. It might get him shot down where he stood, but he didn't think so. For this *thing,* he thought (not "man"), that last headache wouldn't matter. Instead B would remember the child and the months of power.

He was right enough for the voice to start up again. It directed him to an opening in the hills to the north, a short walk. When he entered it, long shadows fell over him; it was late. He walked up a grassy cleft, turned into another, followed a winding stream to another. Shadow passed into dusk. A small wind rustled the grasses through which he passed and there were sounds of water. The sky on its way to night was the deep blue of Hanna's eyes. The toneless voice spoke from time to time and told him where to go. In spite of it he was at peace. He was filled with a deep, calm expectation. It was necessary to see the face again, to look into the empty eyes; it had always been necessary. He hardly thought at all. Only he thought, *They are listening over there, Hanna and the rest. They will know where he is. It will help.*

He had not brought the light the others needed, had not expected to have to use it, but his eyes adjusted to the falling night. The sky was clear and the Ring cast some light, maybe as much as Earth's moon, which he had seen once at the full and treasured in memory. He did not stumble.

He crossed, as he was told, a tiny streamlet the width of a stride, and crossed a flat wooded space with a hill rising sharply to the left. That brought him to the bank of a larger stream into which the small one flowed. He turned to the left, downstream, as instructed, and worked his way through the brush. The stream was a barrier to his right, a sheer cliff three times his height to the left. The cliff suddenly cut back, the stream meandered away, and he came round the outcrop of the cliff and saw an open space. It was not large, but it was large enough for the *Avalon*.

The *Avalon* was shut down, or so it looked from here; at least it showed no lights. He wondered how it had tracked him from its place in this creek bottom, how *GeeGee* had been spotted in the morning. He hesitated for a moment, awaiting challenge, but none came, and he went on toward the ship, picking his way among stones cast up by the creek in times of flood.

When he had come nearly to the side of the ship a hatch opened near the ground, falling silently to make a ramp. That was where he had first seen Hanna. There was an oblong of dim light and he walked up the ramp

and into the light, and men hidden on either side stepped
forward at once and the muzzles of weapons dug into
his sides. He held his hands up and open. He did not
even look from side to side to see who the men were
until they had searched him, which they did thoroughly
and not gently. He got by with the communicator,
though. It was made to fasten to nearly anything and he
had attached it to his coat right over his heart, in plain
view, and they did not take it away. He had hoped for
that. It might make things easier, if Shen and Hanna
heard what was said.

When the men flanking him were done, he looked at
them. One was even taller than Michael, and fair; that
would be Wales. The other was a smaller brown-eyed
man. Michael recognized him from Henrik's description: Bakti.

The weapons shifted away. One moved around, settled in the small of his back, and urged him onward.
He kept his hands up and started forward. Wales talked
softly, telling him where to go. "Left, all right, now
right." They came to a ladder and he stood still while
Bakti climbed it; Bakti crouched with a laser pistol while
Michael went up. Wales followed. After that they took
him through two short corridors at right angles and
showed him through a door.

The door took him to the *Avalon's* equivalent of Control. It did not have *GeeGee's* plush light and he had
not expected it. He had been on other private spacecraft, though, and his flesh tightened fastidiously at this.
There might have been a visible movement, because the
pistol rammed hard into his spine. There was hardly
any illumination besides the *Avalon's* displays. What
there was, was probably Sol-normal, but it was ashen.
He looked at a light source and saw the transparent cover
deep in dust. Running was taking a toll on the *Avalon*,
too.

B waited for him with folded arms. There were lines
on his face that had not been there thirty years before,
or even twenty, in the glimpse Michael had gotten of
him in Shoreground. On Gadrah he was called Undy-

ing; but Michael thought: *He is old. Without the treatments he will die soon. Even with them.*

Bakti and Wales still stood behind Michael with weapons at the ready. B took a laser pistol from his own belt and armed it; then he nodded at the other two and they went away. There had been no sign of the fullblood Oriental, Ta, or the one Hanna had called Suarez.

"Back up," B said. "A couple more steps. You can put your hands down now."

Michael let his hands fall. The sense of peace was still with him, and it deepened. In all important respects his objective was accomplished. There was only a moment of distraction to create, and he could pick it. There was no hurry. He had all the time he would ever have, and the last mystery stood in front of him and looked into his eyes.

He said with genuine curiosity, "Why'd you decide to talk to me?"

B answered, "Thought I'd see how you turned out."

"A lot of people have been doing that lately . . . Tell me this," Michael said. "What are you?"

"A traveler," the man said, but the eyes had some expression for once; they were a wolf's. "A merchant," he said.

"I've known a lot of travelers, a lot of merchants. They didn't come here. How did you find out about this place?"

"Luck," B said.

"You weren't just cruising around out here."

"Oh, no," the man said. "There was a record. There was a course. The ship that came here in the Explosion, the first one, went back. One man took it back. He was supposed to sell it, use the money to buy smaller craft. So they could keep the connection, go back and forth. Instead he kept the money and stayed on earth. Kept the course, too. It floated around . . . Never got to a Polity data bank. Not while he was alive, because if anybody came back here they'd find out he was a thief. Not after he died because nobody knew what it was. It was during the Explosion. It was just another course. It got passed down with souvenirs. It was a rich family, thanks to

him; they kept their property together. Then they had
some hard times. I was trading in curiosities and heard
they had some to sell. Looked them over and bought
the lot. They didn't know about spacegoing, didn't know
what they had, threw it in with the rest for junk. Wasn't
anything like it in Polity records. I came to see.''

The wolf-look was still there, but there was a new
attention in it. Michael knew himself, knew what his
transparent face must show: a child's wonder at the tale.

''Then they never meant to stay cut off,'' he said, as
if B ought to have personal knowledge of that time hundreds of years ago, as if he had been alive then.

He is only a man, Hanna whispered in his mind; and
as if to confirm it B answered, ''Guess not.''

''But when you came—didn't they want to make contact then?''

''No,'' said the man, faint amusement on his face.

''Because they'd have lost what they had. Because
Oversight would have come, and they couldn't have kept
running things like they did. You told them that. You
told them whatever you wanted them to think. But the
sickness?'' Michael said, not pausing to consider what
it meant that the answers came so easily, that this information would not be given to a man who might live.

''It was nothing much,'' B said. ''Dawkins fever. I
couldn't get the vaccine, last trip.''

''But when you had it, the other trips, you only gave
it to the—''

He stopped because he couldn't say the word. *Masters* had never come easily from his tongue. Now he
could not say it at all.

B said, ''You haven't changed much,'' and there was
a threat in it. He looked at Michael just as he had thirty
years ago. Michael knew why. His face and body had
grown into mature beauty, but the child who had never
been quite lost had returned. All the time in between
slipped away, and a child looked at B with clear eyes.
This time he was not afraid. There had been wounds
inflicted in that earlier captivity, but they were healed.
There had been too much kindness given and received
since then, too much love. Even the sharp edges of Lil-

lin's death were smoothed since he had seen Carmina, gone with the old rage. There were monsters, all right, real ones, and B was one of them. His monstrosity was his indifference. There were no people where he lived, only objects. He was a sport of nature; there was nothing of him in Michael; he was something that had happened to Michael, and that was all. The monster faced him and held Michael's death in his hands, but he was wrapped in peace, even joy. *I am,* Michael thought, joy rising, *I am Hanna and Theo, Lise and Shen; nothing can change that.* He smiled, and B moved the pistol suddenly, tightening a slackened aim.

"What did you want with Gadrah?" Michael said. "What could they have here you'd possibly need?"

B did not speak. But it was the last question Michael wanted an answer to, and he persisted. "They haven't got much to sell here, they can't buy much. Not enough to make coming out here worth it. Why'd you do it?"

B said with a shrug, "Thought I might need the place. Nobody knows about it, nobody finds me."

"If they started hunting you back there? Because of the children? Or were there other ships like the *Far-Flying Bird*?"

He saw the answer in B's eyes. Private spacecraft disappeared from time to time, luxury craft like *GeeGee*, without a trace. They used common routes and there would be ways to hail them, ways to get aboard with an innocent tale. You would take what you could, jewels, cash, leave no survivors, plunge the dead craft into a sun.

They hadn't done that last thing with the *Bird*. The alien controls would have been beyond them.

He waited a little longer, looking around without being obvious about it. He was looking for the monitors that had to be here somewhere watching the valley.

"Want to talk truce?" he said, not meaning it, not listening for an answer; only buying time.

The thin smile crossed B's face. "Why not?" he said. He shifted position and Michael saw the screen behind him, hidden by his body until now. There was only one and it was not scanning in infrared, though the picture was enhanced to compensate for the dark. It was coming from the air; there was a mobile spyeye out there, of course. But B had his back to what it showed.

B had seen his eyes move, and looked at him narrowly. Michael thought carefully and deliberately, in words so clear Hanna, if she were with him, could not mistake them: *Get out of my head. The others need you.* He said aloud, "Now, Shen!"

B was not a fool. He guessed. He did not turn to look at the monitor; he moved away from it instead, waving Michael toward it, so he could see monitor and man at the same time. Michael walked in front of it, blocking B's line of sight, counting seconds. He turned his back on the screen and said casually, "What kind of truce would you have in mind?"

B knew what it was about now. He lifted the pistol. There would be no more talk; his eyes were empty as they had always been. Killing was not a pleasure, it was only a task, a permanent, efficient means to an end.

Seconds: Michael charged head down. The last step was a leap. A tremendous shock hit him, a planet fell on him oceans and all; half conscious, he didn't know where he had been hit till pain started in his shoulder and arm, tentatively at first. It was going to get big and not give him much time. He had bowled B over and the pistol had spun away somewhere and he would never get to it; he tried to use his weight to hold B down and was flung away, strength gone, vision blurring. B yelled for Wales and the smell of burned flesh filled the room. B scrambled for the pistol. *Seconds, more seconds!* B had the pistol and turned, and Michael tried to move his head to look at the monitor but could not do it; the full weight of the pain came down, there wasn't room for anything else, and he blacked out not expecting to wake up again.

Just before *GeeGee* came, Hanna fainted. She had gone suddenly shaky and vague, and Theo, when he saw it, questioned her sharply. "Broke trance too fast," she had said, and then, while Theo watched for the *Golden Girl*, collapsed.

Shen set *GeeGee* down too hard, thinking of nothing but speed. A hatch yawned open on the side and Theo and Lise between them dragged Hanna through it. "We're in!" Theo yelled at an intercom and *GeeGee* lifted. A buzzer went off at the open hatch and Theo could not hear anything else till Shen triggered the closure from Control. The cover lifted into place and sealed itself, and there was quiet again.

Hanna sat up and shook off Theo's hands. Her face was bloodless and her eyes looked bruised. "Oh, God, he's hurt," she said.

"Who? Mike?"

"Yes." She ran trembling hands over her hair. She looked as if she might cry. "How are we ever going to get him out?" she said.

"What did he do?"

"Kept them busy," she said, remembering the weapon in B's hand, and buried her face in her hands.

"Kept them *busy?*" Theo said incredulously.

She did not answer. She got up holding on to Theo, still shaky, but she got steadier on the way to Control. They were skimming over mountains, down low, to Theo's surprise; he had expected Shen to take them into space, dodging the *Avalon*. But there was nothing after them.

"He wanted to keep their attention off the monitor," Hanna said, and repeated, "How do we get him out?"

Theo said, "Look, you're not going to like this. But he must have meant to look after himself. I think he wants us to go."

She was furious—but cut it off; that was more than fear talking. Whatever Michael wanted was what Theo wanted, and he was thinking of Lise. *Get out*, Michael had told her, and she had obeyed blindly; she could not be angry at Theo for doing the same thing.

Theo said persistently, "If he can get off the ship, he'll be all right. He knows the language, the territory—there's Carmina. Maybe he means to go to ground till the Polity comes."

"But he's *hurt*." She realized then that she did not know how badly. She had broken the thin trance-link before it happened, had been pulling herself together from that, and whatever had happened to Michael had come up behind her and knocked her out. She thought for an instant, *Oh God is he dead?* and Lise saw her face and went white.

But if he were dead, she would know it beyond doubt. The best part of her would be dead, too.

Lise said in a trembling voice, ''Couldn't you make him stop?''

''I didn't know what was going to happen. It was like he, he knew just what he was doing— Oh,'' she said in anguish, ''God damn him for not being afraid!''

Shen had not said anything. Hanna leaned against the back of Shen's seat. Theo was trying to comfort Lise and *GeeGee's* normal sounds went on steadily, but there was a great silence, an absent voice. Hanna was weak and could not think.

Shen said, ''Theo, you think you could get *GeeGee* home?''

He looked around, his arm around Lise. He was silent for a minute, working it out. ''Sure,'' he said.

''Post.'' She was talking to Hanna now. ''You and me, we steal a truck, see what they've got for guns. Get back there and come in behind, on foot. All right?''

''Wait a minute.'' Hanna's head started to work again. ''They were only at Croft because we were. They'll go back to the Post.''

''Yeah. We go, too, then. Get off *GeeGee* farther away. Send Theo back to Theta. Walk in like before, us two. They think nobody's left here, think we went with Theo.''

''But if they think that—'' There were flaws everywhere Hanna looked. If the *Golden Girl* escaped, B would give up on Gadrah; he would have to make a desperate flight to human space, try to disappear there; nothing else would be left.

Shen said practically, ''Find out what he's thinking.''

''What? Who''

''B,'' Shen said, making a curse of it.

''Oh, but—'' She wanted to say she couldn't. Every time she had touched B's thoughts it had been like a breath of the cold of deep space. And she knew, thinking of doing it now, that she was not as competent as she had been before. Because something had happened to Michael, and it was as if it had happened to Hanna herself. Hanna had been wounded, too. Nothing like this had happened to her before; she did not know whether she was diminished or augmented by Michael, but there was no separating one from the other, and the shock of knowing it made her tremble.

Shen looked at her with slanting eyes. "Communicator?" she said, distracting Hanna; what had happened to the communicator Michael carried? It had been broadcasting right up to the end. Shen on *GeeGee*, and the others on the ground, had heard every word of the last dialogue. If it had been destroyed— She turned suddenly so no one could see her face. She had a clear memory of Michael being searched, hoping they would leave the communicator *over his heart*—

If he were dead, she would know it. She clung to the thought.

As if it had been waiting for her to think about it, the communicator she had taken from Lise began to speak.

"Who's in charge?" said the voice like a snake, like a slug; a spider would talk that way. Hanna had the thing in her pocket; she pulled it out as if it were hot. "Where's the D'neeran?" B said.

She kept the shaking out of her voice. "What do you want?" she said without illusions, remembering the *Far-Flying Bird* more clearly than she had in months.

"Want him back?" said the voice.

"I want him back."

"Give me your ship," B said. "Fair trade."

She looked around at the tense faces. But Theo only looked at Lise.

"We have to think about it," she said, the hardest thing she had ever said, and shut off the transmission before B could speak again. Had he been listening to what was said on the *Golden Girl*? No, there had been no sound at all from the other end; the instrument must be shut off.

GeeGee slowed and hovered over forest. Shen said,

eyes gleaming, "If we could get back there fast enough. Surprise 'em."

"*GeeGee's* the fastest thing on the planet," Hanna said. "If we take her back, we give her up or get shot down. Or just get shot down. What's he need *GeeGee* for?"

Shen shook her head. "Nothing. Trick," she said.

Not even Michael would recommend this risk, because it was a certainty, not a risk. B would use Michael to entice them to return, and kill them at once; then he would kill Michael, too. And *GeeGee* would never carry news to the Polity, and nothing would change on Gadrah, ever.

It all pointed to one end, the logical thing. If Michael could talk to them now, he would make it clear what he wanted them to do.

But Hanna said, "I can't leave him. Whatever the rest of you do, I can't."

Shen said patiently, "Told you. Find out what they think."

Hanna said without hope, "I'll try."

It took a long time. She retreated to Michael's room, and when she lay down on the bed and tried to clear her mind she was so tired and afraid she did not think she could get up again. She had not known that fear like this would be worse than fearing her own death. Her hand crept out to the empty space at her side, as if she could bring Michael back to it with her yearning. She did not want to touch B's mind. She had touched it before she knew who he was, when he had called the *Far-Flying Bird*. Then she had not even been revolted; her senses had cried *Caution!* but given no more specific warning; there had been no rage or hatred or even madness to trigger recognition. *Evil is cold,* she thought, fumbling. And she thought of what the creature had done, feeling nothing, on Gadrah—bringing death and bringing it finally to his allies, too, indifferent—and of the boy locked in B's quarters, uncomprehending, no mercy given to his sweetness. *He liked, liked ruining things, I think—*

She forgot what she was supposed to do and searched for Michael. She found him, and horror nearly drove her from the dream she had fallen into. He was in shock and in great pain. Nothing had been done for him. The burning light that had made his wound had cauterized it, and there was little bleeding, but every movement started agony up again. He breathed so shallowly that he hardly breathed at all. But then he would have to take a deep breath, and when he did, sometimes it came back out as a cry.

He did not know Hanna was with him. He thought he had made her up, along with her grief. It did not seem to Hanna that anything could drive her from his side. But the traces of Shen in Michael's thought, Shen's purposefulness, did it.

I will come back, Hanna said. He thought he made that up, too. Pain took his attention again; he did not notice when she left him.

Too weary for discipline, made small by grief, she wandered. It was only luck that took her to B. Like Michael, he did not know she was there, only thought he was thinking about her. He might not like D'neerans (she thought later), but he disliked them without knowing much about what they could do.

Something was missing from his mind; it lacked a part. She wrenched herself away and thought: *He is not a human being.*

Yet by all criteria, he was. He was certainly not an alien, he was not even the Master of Chaos, he was master of nothing.

She opened her eyes and looked at the worked bronze Michael had set overhead. It looked back with the warmth of his eyes. She was so tired that exhaustion itself had shielded her from B, as if, without it, she might have been spattered with filth. She thought back reluctantly. She had learned something, she realized; she had no hope, but she could not say she had come to the end. Not yet.

She got up and went wearily back to Control. *GeeGee* was over ocean now, moving steadily but not fast, just

to keep moving. The other three watched the ocean,
where reflections of the Ring made a glittering path.

Hanna said without preamble, "He doesn't know we
came without telling anybody."

Shen made an impatient movement; Hanna was talking gibberish.

"He's not sure nobody else knows how to get here,"
Hanna said.

Shen said comprehensively, "Henrik."

"He didn't think about Henrik, maybe he hasn't seen
him, maybe Henrik didn't tell him, I don't know. Henrik's dead," she added, sure now. In all the exploration
she had done since the morning, there had been no trace
of him. Theo started to say something, but Hanna went
on talking. "That means he won't kill us right away.
Look, there's more of them and they're armed. I don't
know what we can do."

"Find out," Shen said, very pleased.

"Theo?"

"If we put Lise down somewhere safe first."

"No!" Lise said, full of indignation, and Shen said,
"Nowhere safe."

After a minute Theo nodded. Hanna said, "Then we
all go back."

Michael was left where he had fallen, out of the way
and harmless. The chamber was a blur. There were
meaningless sounds and he could not move, did not
want to. After a long time of pain he could think again.
The pain had not gone away, but he was not stupefied
any more. But his thoughts followed random paths, and
he had no direction to give them. He had not thought
of this eventuality, of injury, immobility, captivity. He
had expected swift death or a chance to escape, and had
gotten neither.

He thought that since he was still alive, he must try
to stay that way.

He thought that there were five men in front of him
now, all armed; that only if he kept very still was the
pain even tolerable; that he could not move without

groaning, try to stand without falling, walk without staggering.

There was not much hope of escape. He gave up thinking about it.

Sounds began to fall into words. The blurred edges of the flight deck came into focus. The men stood between Michael and the consoles that housed the controls. Their backs were toward him, but from time to time one or another looked around. To the left was an open locker. He could see some kind of weapon in it; there might be others.

It would do no harm to get closer.

When the five were all turned away from him, he hauled himself up so that he sat with his back to the wall. The cost was blinding pain. They must have turned to look, but he was half unconscious again, gasping like a dying fish and too weak to move. When the mist cleared, they were looking away.

He started to inch along the wall, using legs and his one good arm, pushing the useless left one ahead. He had looked down once at the black crater the laser had left and absorbed what it meant. If he were trapped on Gadrah he would lose the arm, at the least; without sophisticated medical attention, he would most likely die.

The hand at the end of it, dangling, got in his way. It was turning blue.

The world contracted, all his life contracted, to a simple sequence he would repeat and repeat forever. Hitch and move and brace against the pain and the fog it brought along. Wait for it to ease. He felt no diminution when it did, but his vision would clear, and he would know it must have gotten better.

Watch for another chance. Do it all again.

When he had been doing this for a long time he had moved a meter. The locker was still twice that far away. What was left of his strength was ebbing.

In one of the pauses he thought he heard Hanna's voice. He had imagined it once before, and he thought he must be losing consciousness again. But this time she was not talking to him, and he realized, slowly, that he heard a real voice, and real words, and what they meant.

"You will board, one of you, and we will give you our arms. I understand. If we make any resistance, Michael will be killed. Yes, we all understand."

After all his costly silence, after choking back a scream at every furtive move, he cried out then: "No! No!" He meant it to be a command and a plea for Hanna to hear, but it was a whisper. B heard it, though, and looked at him. He looked at the place Michael had started from, at the locker with the weapon in plain view, and he went to it and picked it up: another laser pistol. He swung it toward Michael and smiled with the faintest amusement, as he had smiled sometimes years ago when he did some unspeakable thing and watched the contorted, tear-stained face like a scientist observing the outcome of an experiment. "You won't need that any more," he said, and aimed for Michael's groin. Michael twisted away and the light burned another crater in his thigh. He made one wretched sound and sank on his face without tears or hope, and the *Avalon* and everything else went away.

The *Golden Girl* skimmed over seaboard, moving quickly but doing nothing like top speed. Shen looked ready to fight; she was the only one who did. A bleak feeling that death was near had come to Hanna. She tried to look back at the path that had led her to it, but she could not see one. *Courses.* Silver necklace of Earth, golden alien treasure, a piece of plain utilitarian metal: exactly what had B found all those years ago? A sheaf of paper? A microchip? She looked for some meaning in the objects, and found none. They had fallen into her life and she had had to make choices about them and that was that. *You choose what you can and the rest is just there.* He had said that to her once. She could not remember when.

Without warning her left leg gave way and she fell on the floor. There was an instant of nothing—she knew that because Theo had been at the other side of Control, and now he was bending over her. Her leg did not hurt;

instead she held both hands over her heart. Theo took her pulse, examined her skin, he thought her heart was failing. It was not, but it was breaking. He wanted to know what was wrong with her and she would not tell him. Why hurt him by telling him Michael had been hurt again? But he must know by the tears that ran out of her eyes and down her cheeks. Her will was paralyzed; she could not stop them.

When *GeeGee* got back to Croft's valley, the *Avalon* had moved. It was not hidden but brooding in the open upriver from croft. Shen brought *GeeGee* in slowly and landed a few meters away from the *Avalon*. She had been told to make the distance between as small as she could. She opened *GeeGee* up and they waited in Control, and Shen looked at Hanna and saw no help. Hanna was broken.

The thing that was supposed to be a man, looked like a man, was biologically a man, crossed the space between the ships. He came quickly. He would not make himself a target any longer that he had to; he thought he might be attacked; he thought they might hurt him though it meant Michael's death. That was how little he knew about them. It was how he thought.

They did nothing. They let him come. He walked into the golden light of Control like a bloated white spider and they only stood there, except Hanna who could not move and did not look up. Close to the door where he stood was a pile of weapons. There were three stunners, all they had left and Carmina's well-made, old-fashioned gun. He looked at them as if he did not believe they had gone where they had gone, done what they had done, with a handful of stunners.

He squatted and picked up the stunners one by one and snapped out the power pack from the butt of each. He put the packs and his laser pistol in a pocket, got up holding Carmina's gun, and cocked a finger at Lise. No one had uttered a word. Lise stood still. She was very pale.

"I want to look around," the soft voice said. "You show me."

Theo said to her quietly, "He won't hurt you yet. He wants another hostage."

"That's right," B said, "Listen to your daddy."

Lise took a step forward, shaking. The next step was stronger; she made it the rest of the way a step at a time, haltingly. B put his free hand on her shoulder and pushed her to the door. He said to the others, but mostly to Theo, "You know what happens if you do anything."

Theo said, "You don't need her for that. Unless Mike's already dead."

"Not quite," B said.

Lise looked up, the first time she had dared lift her eyes to his face. "You can kill me," she said. "I don't care. But don't hurt Mike!"

The transparent eyes were impersonal. He watched a performing animal.

"Why do you hate him?" Lise said. Her voice shook. "He never hurt you. He never hurt anybody."

B was not interested. He pushed her again. But Hanna said from the floor, "Earthquake." They looked at her again, even B, but her eyes were empty. She spoke again, with great effort. It was evident that she hardly knew she was speaking, and that she was talking to Lise—for her education. For some reason B listened, too. She said: "Wind. Volcano. Flood." Her eyes met Lise's. They were still empty, but after a moment Lise nodded as if she understood something new. Her face was sad. She was calmer, and she did not look like a little girl.

"People can be like that, too," she said. "Sometimes you don't live through it."

B shoved her then and she went out ahead of him, the gun at her back.

She did just as she was told, though she was slow about it. She had almost stopped thinking. *I used to be afraid like this sometimes before,* she thought, when she did think. But for a year she had forgotten this kind of fear.

B followed her through the galley and the lounges. *Cooking and luscious food, games and conversation.* She wanted those familiar places to mean what they had meant before—she wanted it so badly that she was disoriented, which was why she was slow.

The medlab. "Ever use it?" he said. Theo was a physician, she said with difficulty. The old staff quarters with their alphanumeric locks; they had modified one to lock from outside for the I&S operative, and B looked at it carefully. The cargo hold, and down to the engine rooms, living quarters, Mike's room, Lise's own. *Theo patiently repeating a lesson.* And back to Control.

She wanted to run to Theo, but B held her by the arm. He held her in front of him and poked Carmina's gun into her back. He talked into the air, his voice traveling to the *Avalon*. Who would be killed, who would not be?—it remained an open question, that was the meaning of what he said. There was Polity medical technology here and a Polity-trained doctor. Maybe Theo would be spared. And Lise, as hostage for his good behavior. She got that much out of what B said. But that meant—she shuddered, and the hand was harder on her arm—that Mike wouldn't make it, or Hanna or Shen. There was no use for them.

Hanna's body had forgotten who it belonged to. When she got up it was weak, and twitched. It rose in obedience to some command from outside and let itself be herded out of Control and through *GeeGee* toward the craft's rear, into the room they had made into a cell. The door closed and they were locked in. Lise could finally cling to Theo. Shen stood by the narrow bunk, her face dark with thought, but Hanna sank to the floor again. Her body was numb, especially on the left side, shoulder and thigh. She had never felt anything like it before, she had not know this was possible, this connection of flesh through the spirit. Her efforts at thought did not get anywhere; they spiraled into the pit of Michael's unconsciousness.

Shen came and squatted in front of her. When Hanna did not look up, Shen took her shoulders and shook her. "Wake up! Pay attention!"

It was too much effort to speak aloud. *I can't,* Hanna said in thought.

Shen shook her again. "What are they all doing?"

I don't know.

"Find out!"

She tried halfheartedly. When she reached out there was only one place she wanted to go, one mind she wanted to see. If she tried hard enough, she could wake him. But only to pain and despair—so she would not do it; but the struggle not to do it, to let go and give him up so his end would be easier, took all the little she had left. She put no name to what she felt, the vast misery. She only knew that Michael's coming death was the most important, the worst thing that had ever happened, and she could not spare thought for her own fate, or Shen's.

Shen felt enough of it to know what was happening in Hanna. Real pain, sharp and stinging, forced its way through Hanna's fog; Shen slapped her methodically, cursing. "Gonna lay down and die? Say where they are. Say it now! Now!"

B's in Control. Doing something.

"Doing what?"

I don't know. The navigational systems. Crippling GeeGee. *So we can't go back—*

"What about the rest? They coming over here?"

No. Later. Not yet. She saw through someone's eyes for half a second. The man was on the *Avalon.* There was tension and some kind of suspicion there: dissent inside the wolf pack, directed at B. She couldn't concentrate on it, she couldn't concentrate on the import of what B was doing, exiling them here; she was drawn too hard to the dark shape on the floor at the edge of someone's vision.

Shen got up and roamed the tiny room, furious, thinking.

"How bad's Mike hurt?" she said, got no answer, turned to see tears streaming from Hanna's eyes again; went back to her, and went back to slapping her. The wet cheeks were starting to bruise. "Can he walk? *Can he walk!*"

"I don't know, I don't know! I don't think so."

"Gonna have to try. Soon's they leave."

Hanna got a glimpse of what Shen was thinking.

"He can't, it would kill him—"

"You remember before? Broken ribs, fever, you remember what you did?"

"I remember. But—"

"So?"

They stared at each other. Shen shook Hanna again, gently this time. "Gonna die anyway, him, you, everybody. All we got left's one surprise. You're it. You and Mike."

He was conscious of being cold. His body was shutting down. The pain had removed to some distance, was with him and would be there until the end, but hung back for a time like a live thing, a scavenger waiting for an opening. In the half-world of relative peace, images played at random in his head, the mind shutting down, too. He saw the house on Valentine, much too big, ridiculously big, but it had given him the seclusion he wanted. A dark blue-eyed woman lived there, completing his peace. He was not capable of questioning the image. It seemed as if it had been so. It was what he had wanted, and here at nightfall he believed he had had it.

Hanna sat beside him on the beach below the house, dressed in white. The wind gusted hard from the sea and she put up a hand to her frivolous floppy hat, to hold it on. Wisps of hair escaped and stirred softly in the wind. She was smiling, and her eyes were as blue as the sunlit water.

"It won't hurt to get up now," she said. "I'll keep it from hurting."

"Can you?" He did not really doubt her. It was Hanna, he realized now, who kept the pain at bay, so that it made a circle around him but did not quite touch him.

"It's your useful trance," he said, pleased. "All right, then."

The bright white sand dazzled his eyes. If he squinted, he could see other things through the sand. He was somewhere else as well as on the beach, simultaneously. It was too dark to see much of the other place, but he was alone there. There had been other men; they were gone. He had to learn to stand. "Try locking the knee," Hanna said, and it worked. He would never walk normally again, too much muscle was damaged or gone, but if he kept the leg straight and balanced carefully, he could use it as a prop to heave himself along.

The beach was gone, but Hanna walked ahead of him, still in white. One side of the skirt was slit nearly to the hip, and when the wind blew it away, he thought he had never seen anything more lovely than her shapely brown leg. There had been other women, and he remembered them with love and gratitude. They had helped educate him for loving Hanna.

"I didn't tell you often enough how beautiful you are," he said.

"That's all right," she said. "Be careful here. There's a ladder you have to get down."

It helped a lot that he was weightless; or maybe he felt that way because there was, in his undamaged limbs, a strength he had never dreamed he had. Sometimes he hung by his good hand from a rung, supporting his weight one-handed without effort, feeling for a foothold for the usable leg; sometimes, weight on one foot, he leaned precariously inward while he shifted the hand. It was not a long ladder, but it took time all the same. "Don't hurry," Hanna said.

"It would've been good," he said. "Wouldn't it? Nothing else like it for either of us. Once in a lifetime. You couldn't do this with just anybody, could you?"

"I could not." She stood on air beside the ladder. It had gotten very dark, but she was illuminated, and the sea breezes from nowhere stirred her hair and the long white skirt. He looked at her with love.

"I heard of it long ago," she said with the cool objectivity of trance. "It's called a true match, I think. You don't see it often on D'neera or anywhere else—people who go on together for years and years and it only gets stronger. I think that's what we might have been. But there has to be time to find out."

"Why us?" he said. "You and me. We're so different."

"But you have what I need. And I have it for you. Why shouldn't we be different, otherwise?"

"I almost had the rest of what I wanted, once," he said.

"Plain peace. I wish I could have found it and given it to you. But we've got more than most people get."

"I know that. I didn't see it at first. Not until this happened, not really. But I know now."

Negotiating the ramp was hard. The ground between the *Avalon* and *GeeGee* was uneven enough to be a worse trial, and it was dark. There must be an end to the body's resources even in trance, which only permitted them to be drained far beyond ordinary limits, beyond safety. Michael's pace, which had not been fast, slowed even more. *GeeGee* had not come any nearer for some time. Michael wondered it he had been moving at all, or had only thought so. He paid close attention to the next awkward step. "I was standing still," he said. "It's not going matter anyway, is it?"

"Probably not," Hanna said, and he looked up and could not see her any more; only *GeeGee* looming ahead of him in the night.

They had not bothered to close *GeeGee* up. There was a ramp here, too, and he dragged himself up it and through the air lock and into the belly of his ship, which hummed and showered him with golden light. His own bed was close at hand, but he turned the other way and saw Hanna at the top of the spiral stair, her face serene and, now, transparent. A fragment of lyric came to him, part of the old music he most loved: *God grant every gentleman such hawks, such hounds, and such leman!*

"Where are they?" he said. "Do you see anything?"

"I see nothing except what you see. I'm not really there, Mike."

"Oh, that's right. How am I going to get up the stairs?"

"Pull," she said. And waited without moving, a dimming figure of light, while he humped awkwardly up the endless stair, pulling with the good right arm, pushing with right knee and foot, up one step at a time. Toward the end he had less strength. He was nearly finished, and when he finally reached the top, he had to try several times before he could stand up. *GeeGee's* light was fading, and to breathe he had to will his chest to move in and out. He stood wondering why he had not yet been discovered and stopped, and then his ears told him why. They had been (he realized) attuned to a different level of reality altogether. But now when he paid attention, he heard voices from the direction of Control, angry voices, an argument building. The men were too busy quarreling about B's erasure of the way home to think they might have left a threat behind.

He turned and hitched his weary way past the galley, through the main lounge and the small one, past the medlab. The corridor bent to the left and he took the turn awkwardly. In a minute he would turn right again and would face the door behind which Hanna was shut up. He could not see her any more. She waited for him where she had been all the time.

He kept listening to the real world, straining to hear the voices that had dropped away behind him, and that saved him, because he heard the sound in the corridor through which he passed. Just before the second turn there was a setback, something to do with the mechanical systems, to his left; he staggered into it and pressed his back flat against the wall. Someone made the turn he had just made and came level with him, looking ahead and to the next turn, to his right therefore, so that Michael had an instant of grace. It was B, with something in his hand.

Michael saw what it was, Carmina's gun, a deadly thing, B was going to kill. For an instant, a second in which time stopped, everything was clear. The riddle of B was simple after all. Something that might have been a man had said *No!* to life some time a long time ago.

Yes! said Michael, and fell on B's back. They went down together and the gun went off with a great noise. He had no strength of his own but there was a great inrushing, Hanna's strength, more. Knee in back, arm around the throat, he heaved, pulled, felt the straining spine—and heard a crack. The last air rattled out of B's mouth and he was limp.

It was not Michael but used-up flesh that jerked through the last few paces, punched the simple sequence that opened the lock, and held out the gun to Hanna. She took it, but she never did anything conscious with it. Wales had come, drawn by the noise, and he fired straight at Michael's back. The blast took his heart, Hanna felt the heat on her breast as Michael fell on her, and it was by reflex that she fired and killed Wales as she fell down with Michael into his death.

After that Shen went after them, Lise said, *I heard her, she had that thing that makes the noise and one of them came and I heard it go off. The others—they're dead, too. She got them, too. I didn't see that, I was busy. Helping with Mike, till Shen came, then Theo said go help you, I thought you were dead, too, you were so still—*

There was something in the medlab which Hanna could not believe had ever been Michael. It was cold in the medlab, icy. Theo had partitioned off the space where Michael's body lay. He and Hanna argued bitterly. They had been arguing for a long time.

You shouldn't be here, he said, *I shouldn't be here, Mike shouldn't. You have to know when to let the dead go, that's what they told me a long time ago. If this was Earth, Willow, maybe Co-op, there'd be a chance, if I'd got him wired in in time, if his brain wasn't dead, but it is—*

Hanna sat in the cold wrapped in blankets Lise had brought. Once, early, she had gone away. Theo left to himself had sat down on the floor and held his head in his hands as if the weight of his own living skull would give him strength to do what he had to do, the last thing he could ever do for Michael. But before he could do it, Hanna had returned. She had found one of the laser pistols and gotten it powered and armed. *You will not let him die*, she had said.

B wiped the course while we were locked up, Shen said, *while the rest were still over there. Been wiped from the* Avalon, *too. They didn't want to stay, he fixed it so they had to. Did that to their ship then did it to* Gee *in secret so we're trapped, too. They come and find out, that keeps 'em busy, I guess, while Mike's coming here—*

Theo looked at Hanna's eyes black with madness or grief, he looked at the laser pistol, he grieved, he looked and grieved for hours, hardly comprehending what Shen had said, that they had been robbed of the way home.

He looked also at the lines and lights that told him where
Michael was and they never changed. Machines kept
blood pumping steadily through a cadaver but the brain
would never think again, and the sun was gone for good.
Between fits of weeping he screamed at Hanna and she
screamed back or was silent. *Let me let him go.* He
begged abjectly. *Please let me let him go!*

Shen could have taken Hanna from behind with a
stunner, and she would have done it if Theo had given
her a sign, but he didn't. He thought obscurely that he
was doing what Michael would have wanted.

After twenty-four hours of this Hanna collapsed without warning in a silent heap. Theo made sure she was
all right and then, weeping, turned off the machines.

Michael was buried in a mountain meadow with
Croft's valley spread out below. Hanna spent her days
and some of the cold nights in the mountains. She went
back to *GeeGee* when hunger drove her, and at those
times spoke to no one. In the mountains, though, she
talked. She talked to the hills, the streams, and the
slanting brown trees, but her words were for ears that
were not there, chiefly Rubee's.

"I don't want any more of your stories," she said to
Rubee, her hands full of shreds of leaves; she plucked
them off the low branches from which they would not
fall, still glossy though richly brown, and tore them
slowly one by one to bits. She did this all day long. She
resented the leaves; they behaved as if they would not
give summer up. "What's the use of doing anything? I
wish I had never heard of you," she said to dead Rubee.

She got things mixed up. She knew about the deities of
a wild mix of human and other cultures, but the only god
she clearly remembered was the Master of Chaos, to whom
she insisted, at times, that she was not Uskosian, so his
rules should not have applied to her. It would have been
good to think the Master had a single face—a pale one with
transparent eyes—because if that were so, he would be dead.
She had felt him die and be killed by joy, she had felt the
victory of laughter. But she had also seen the light go out
afterward, which proved that horror might take any face,

and the twitch of a finger could sweep love and courage away, and it was best to count on the worst and go on free from the illusion of hope.

Crouched by the grave in the early snow like Michael's monument, she "heard" people come up the mountain.

Theo and Lise. And a man and woman not of Croft. Of the Polity.

Her mind took the longest Jump it had ever made.

"There could be help," Norsa had said, "though you will not know until it shows itself what form it will take."

Norsa called them and had them record the course, she thought. *They got onto GeeGee while we were in Ree and recorded the course.*

She felt Theo and Lise halt at the meadow's edge. Theo thought approaching Hanna wasn't safe, and he would hold Lise back until it was.

The others came on until they stood beside Hanna, and she looked up at them. They were healthy and fit in their green Fleet uniforms. They looked back at Hanna cautiously. She heard them think that she was not as bad as Theo had said.

"You didn't get him," she said, "he got away," and they changed their minds.

That was all she had to say to the Polity. Two ships had come to Gadrah; one soon went home, and Hanna was on it. In the first weeks of the trip she spoke only once. That was immediately after departure, when she submitted with unexpected docility to medical examination. At the end of it the examining physician said, "Did you know you're pregnant?"

"Yes," Hanna said.

"How long have you known?"

She shrugged.

"Do you want me to end it for you?"

"Try it and I'll kill you," she said.

VIII.

So she had decided to live, as was evident from what she had said. She did not feel like living, but she did not feel like dying either; she did not feel much. She was mute at her parting with the others who had been her companions for so many months, and Michael's companions much longer. They would survive. Theo would look after Lise, Lise would give Theo a reason to live, and Shen would tell them both what to do. Someday Hanna would have to finish it with them, they would have to see the child, and Carmina ought to see it too, when Hanna was alive again. But for now she waited for something to bring her to life. Her child was not real yet; it was flesh busily making the structure to be human, but there was no mind that could even sense the echo of her thought. She was still alone, and only on another journey.

And that was your last, she thought to Michael who was not present either, *that was the end of the journey of your life. Why did you take me, if it was the last? And if you took me, why did you let it be the end?*

The physician came back to see her loaded with charts and readouts. He said she would have a boy and talked about genetic analysis. The child would be much like Michael, he said.

When the physician was gone she said to the child who was not present yet, *You'll be a handful, then.*

The Polity's ship came to Theta and crossed into the relay system of human space, and Hanna spoke for the second and last time on that voyage. She asked for and got permission to contact her House, and, not meeting much resistance, resigned what remained of her tenuous position there. Her son would not be a telepath, and D'neera was no place for a true-human.

After that, there was nothing to do but wait for the journey to be done.

It was summer when Hanna got to Earth. The year had come round and started again since she rested under a tree with Rubee and Awnlee. She was put into a medical center and continued to be silent until she was left alone in a room of her own. There were no windows and it was impossible to see the summer. She had acknowledged to herself that she would have to start talking sooner or later; when she tried the door, determined to walk out of the place, and found it locked, she thought she might have waited too long. But it opened suddenly from outside. She stared up in horror; it was too much like what had happened at the end on *GeeGee*. her mind slipped and she thought Michael would be there, his eyes a blaze of gold and sick to death. The vision passed; Starr Jameson stood in front of her. She leaned against him in relief. "Oh, you came," she said.

"Your people at Koroth asked me to. Come on, then," he said.

So she finally came back to his house, the new weight in her belly making her steps nervous, though the swelling was scarcely visible yet. It was not a homecoming, but at least she could talk to Jameson, because it seemed that she had known him all her life, and he was not new as Michael had been, but a constant. All the same, she was slow to find her voice. She had been at Jameson's house for a week before it returned. One evening just at dusk he came to her and suggested they sit in the garden. She went outdoors for the first time since coming here, and was overwhelmed. On spaceships the air had all the life filtered out of it, and no wind ever moved. The garden on this summer evening was fragrant; there were grasses and leaves and flowers to smell. A breeze pressed against her skin, and moonlight made everything silver and black. She was dizzy with the night. Questions crowded to the end of her tongue.

She tried to hold them back; to ask them to be answered, to hear new things, would be to start living again. She had thought herself unready to do it. But she had promised. The child growing under her heart was proof of that.

And then she could not hold it back any longer. "What happened?" she said. "I don't know anything. What happened to Theo? To Lise? To Shen?"

"It's too early for anything to happen. Nothing's happened," Jameson said. "You nearly cost me Contact; don't you want to hear about that?"

"No. I don't care," Hanna said, feeling an enormous relief. Jameson would not change. Some things remained predictable. "What's going to happen to them, then?"

"Probably nothing," he said. "They're not very important any more, in the view of I&S. They'll soon be free to do whatever they like."

But they'll have to learn to live without Mike, she wanted to say, but instead, as still sometimes happened, a fit of sobbing overtook her, and now that she wanted to talk she could not do it. They were sitting at a table and she put her head down and felt the cool wood against her cheek. Jameson came closer and began to rub her back, and she turned and pressed her face against him. When she could talk, she said, "We could have gotten away. He stayed in Croft and stayed and stayed and I tried to get him to leave. I tried so hard."

"I know," he said.

"You can't know. I didn't tell anybody."

"Jadinow was there. Unlike you, he was willing to tell the story. I heard about it from the reports that came back with you."

"You know everything, then . . ." Because the others had seen everything—except for that last night on the mountainside. She had not been able to think about it consciously, though she had dreamed about it, as if the erotic bond that held her to Michael had reached its flowering then. She supposed her son would be a permanent reminder of that night; she supposed that was when it had happened.

Jameson dropped to the ground by Hanna's chair, an unaccustomed pose. He looked out into the night as if he were waiting to fend off whatever came out of it. There were thoughts she had not let herself think because it had not seemed safe to have them. They came on irresistably as speech, as the smell of the grass.

"I *told* him so," she said. "I told him it was dangerous to go there the way we did. I told him so!"

"I expect he knew," Jameson said. "He was not a stupid man."

"But it was stupid to stay so long in Croft. Stupid!"

Jameson still looked into the dark, though the moonlight must blind him to whatever waited there. "I was not surprised to learn you had gone to Uskos," he said. "I rather thought you would, after the failure at D'neera."

He was starting for some point. Hanna waited.

"You had the necklace," he said. "I worried about it. I mentioned it once or twice. Eventually I&S thought of it themselves, and finally approved the mission to Uskos. By the time it got there, you were gone."

She repeated, "You mentioned the necklace once or twice. That we might go there."

"Yes. Once, I think."

"It's on record, of course. That you did warn them."

"Of course. But they paid no attention. I knew they would not, if they were not reminded often. Daily, perhaps."

"I wondered why no mission came . . ."

They were quiet, watching the moon climb. The silence went on until Hanna said very quietly, the words pushing themselves off her tongue, "Did Mike stay too long in Croft on purpose?"

"I've wondered," Jameson said. "But why would he? His chances were good, after Uskos."

"He never believed that," she said. "He did kill that man so many years ago. In cold blood."

"Did he?" Jameson said. He looked up, but it was hard to make out his expression in the ambiguous light.

"Was he right, then, not to believe?"

"He was probably right," Jameson said. He added,

"To wait was understandable, in that case. To seek a final confrontation. I suppose the decision was unconscious, or you would have known. But he risked your life, too. I cannot forgive him for that."

She had no answer. Instead she said, "I dreamed you told me he had no center. It was before I even knew I loved him."

"Well," he said, "you do learn. Slowly, but you learn."

He took her hand and held it, still watching the night, an unshakable guard. "What will you do next?" he asked.

"I don't know. I am truly homeless now."

"You've seen too many deaths," he said.

"I don't want to see any more!" It was awkward to lean against him, crouched at her side as he was, but she managed it, bending to press her head to his shoulder. He reached around to touch her hair. He said, "I could give you only, some time too soon, another death."

"I know," she said. "That's no reason to withhold all the rest you could give." But her hand rested on her belly, waiting for the quickening.

"You can stay here, you know," he said. "Until you're ready to go."

"I will. For a while."

She had no worries about the means to live; Koroth would take care of its own. But where she should go after the child was born, and what else she should do with living, were different questions.

"I could go to Willow," she said. "Or live on Uskos for a while; I've never met an Uskosian I didn't like. Or I could just travel, or . . ."

Her voice trailed away. It did not matter what she said. Something would come up. Something always came up.

Jameson said, "Your plans seem very uncertain."

"What other kind is there?" she said.